CONSPIRACY OF SILENCE

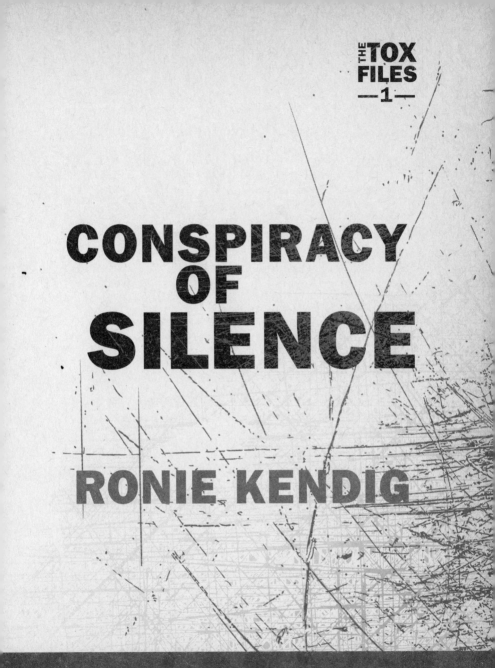

THE TOX
FILES
—1—

CONSPIRACY
OF
SILENCE

RONIE KENDIG

BETHANYHOUSE

a division of Baker Publishing Group
Minneapolis, Minnesota

Published by Bethany House Publishers
11400 Hampshire Avenue South
Bloomington, Minnesota 55438
www.bethanyhouse.com

Bethany House Publishers is a division of
Baker Publishing Group, Grand Rapids, Michigan

Printed in the United States of America

ISBN 978-0-7642-1765-4

Library of Congress Control Number: 2016942749

Scripture quotations are from The Holy Bible, English Standard Version® (ESV®), copyright © 2001 by Crossway, a publishing ministry of Good News Publishers. Used by permission. All rights reserved. ESV Text Edition: 2011

Scripture quotations are from the Holy Bible, New International Version®. NIV®. Copyright © 1973, 1978, 1984, 2011 by Biblica, Inc.™ Used by permission of Zondervan. All rights reserved worldwide. www.zondervan.com

Scripture quotations are from the *Holy Bible*, New Living Translation, copyright © 1996, 2004, 2015 by Tyndale House Foundation. Used by permission of Tyndale House Publishers, Inc., Carol Stream, Illinois 60188. All rights reserved.

This is a work of fiction. Names, characters, incidents, and dialogues are products of the author's imagination and are not to be construed as real. Any resemblance to actual events or persons, living or dead, is entirely coincidental.

Cover design by Kirk DouPonce, DogEared Design

Author is represented by the Steve Laube Agency

16 17 18 19 20 21 22   7 6 5 4 3 2 11

To the Special Forces veteran on the cover of this novel:

Thank you for your tireless pursuit
of justice and freedom, for the sacrifices you
(and your family) have made.

Sacrifices that separated you from each other
and put you in harm's way. Forever grateful . . .

Study the past to define the future.

—Confucius

PROLOGUE

— KADESH BARNEA, ISRAEL —
CIRCA 1440 BC

"Separate yourselves from this assembly, so I can put an end to them at once!"

The voice of the Lord froze Yehoshua. His legs quaked. He cast a look at Korah, Dathan, and Abiram, who stood with the two hundred fifty stirred up in rebellion. Moshe had warned them Yahweh would answer, that He would show them who were His chosen.

The answer had come.

With a shout, Moshe lay facedown with his brother, Aaron, beseeching the Most High. "O Lord, will you be angry with the entire assembly when only one man sins?"

Yehoshua watched Korah and his band of rogues vanish around the corner, seeking refuge in their tents. They should be on their knees begging El Elyon's mercy. Instead, they cowered like dogs. In that sacred moment, Yehoshua realized how easily Yahweh could have annihilated His people, just as he had the Amalekites at Yehoshua's hand.

Finally, Moshe rose to his knees, struggling to stand. Yehoshua rushed to assist and saw the determination etched in Moshe's face. Aaron bore the same grim determination. Resolute in unwavering devotion to Adonai, Moshe pushed forward.

The others gathered, and as one, they trailed Moshe to Korah's camp. Korah waited, hand on the flap of his tent as he shouted something about Moshe's skills with drama. Nearby, a tiny arm clamped around Dathan's leg as he lingered with his family, his tent set up by his brother Abiram's.

Arms withered with age rose into the strangely dark dawn. "'Move back from the tents of these wicked men,'" Moshe shouted, quoting Yahweh. With the warning came instruction not to touch anything belonging to them. "'Or you will be swept away because of their sins.'"

Swept away? Awe speared Yehoshua as the crowd parted, receding from the wicked just as the waters had split apart at the Red Sea. Perhaps the Great I Am would send a coursing flood through this rugged terrain. That would be a miracle. Or maybe the Messenger of Death would return. At the thought, Yehoshua shuddered.

A shadow slunk along the earth, spindly black tendrils reaching for Korah.

"See? He still resorts to magic and signs as he did with Pharaoh's magicians," Korah shouted. "Moshe, will you kill me as you did the Egyptian?"

Breath stolen by the cruel words, Yehoshua could not keep his gaze from the creeping blackness that stretched forth. It coalesced and took form as an undulating shadow. No, as an undulating *figure*. A finger of the shadow draped across the children.

A cry went out from Dathan's tent. His little girl slumped to the ground, a bulbous shape now protruding from her neck. She lay still in death, Dathan's wife cradling the child as the shadow receded.

Shock riddled Yehoshua.

"*Resheph*," a man breathed, terror coating his tone.

Recoiling at the name of the demon-god who spread disease through the use of his bow and arrow, Yehoshua's insides quivered.

A shriek rent the day.

"*This* is how you will know," Moshe promised in a loud voice. "'If these men die a natural death and suffer the fate of all mankind, then the Lord has not sent me. But if the Lord brings about something totally new, and the earth opens its mouth and swallows them, with everything that belongs to them, and they go down alive into the realm of the dead, then you will know that these men have treated the Lord with contempt.'"

Go down *alive?* Into Sheol? It seemed absurd. Impossible. But Yehoshua had come to learn that with Yahweh nothing was impossible.

As if a horn had been sounded, the shadows snapped back, trickling into the earth like water down greedy desert cracks.

The ground shook so violently that Yehoshua stumbled. A woman beside him screamed, clutching her child. Elders stood more bravely, but the confusion and shock shone plainly on their bearded faces. When the earth canted left, then right, Yehoshua stretched out a hand to steady himself.

The ground opened as if it were a garment torn in two.

Screaming, Korah dropped out of sight. Bodies vanished into the darkness of the void. *Whoosh!* His tent collapsed in withered defeat. Down it rushed into the yawning chasm of Sheol, dragging with it Korah's family.

As Yehoshua's mind registered the same fate devouring Dathan and Abiram with their families and tents, he stood speechless, uncertain whether to flee or lie prostrate.

"It's going to swallow us, too!" an elder shouted, pushing past the others to distance himself from the judged.

Just as fast as it opened, the earth closed over the claimed lives, the dirt garment stitched back together. The way the Red Sea had taken the Egyptian warriors, a sight seared upon Yehoshua's young eyes.

Three massive gaps in the camp left echoes of what had once been. Space no longer marked with people and life, but with emptiness.

Without warning, a raging wall of fire burst from the Glory of Yahweh. Scalding and devastating, the flames spiraled over the camp. Shielding himself, Yehoshua bent away.

When quiet fell over the camp, Yehoshua looked to Moshe, whose face bore the expression of grief. Heavy, terrible grief.

Levites, Reubenites, Gershonites—all manner of tribe and people— fell to the ground, fearing the wrath of the Lord. The fire had shot through the camp with intent. The two hundred fifty who had burned censers with Korah, Dathan, and Abiram the night before now lay as ash, seared forever in their rebellion.

Weeping women and shrieking children were the only music to be heard this grim day. Moshe stalked to Eleazar, son of Aaron and gripped his arm. "Remove the censers from the charred remains."

Stricken, Eleazar looked to the still-smoking, blackened field.

"The censers of the men who sinned at the cost of their lives . . ." Moshe seemed to have aged years in that moment. His weary eyes finally found Yehoshua, and together, they both considered the cost of rebellion, the full weight of Yahweh's answering justice. "Scatter the coals some distance away, for the censers are holy."

"Wh-what am I do with the censers?" Eleazar asked, his voice quiet, desperate.

"Hammer them into sheets to overlay the altar, for they were presented before the Lord and have become holy." Determination glinted hard in the Lord's chosen. "Let them be a sign to the Israelites."

Somber, Yehoshua sat and stared at the field. The clinking of hammer against bronze sounded as heartbeats through the night. Banging reminders of rebellion, of justice, of Yahweh's answer. That none save a descendent of Aaron should burn incense before the Lord or he would become like Korah and his followers.

Yehoshua knew, even with the deaths at his hand as God's warrior, this day would ring in his mind for the rest of his years. Even as morning dawned, he remained sitting, watching, listening.

A murmur caught his ear. He turned, noticing two men who'd emerged from their tents. "They've killed the Lord's people," one said.

Yehoshua came up with a start, ready to defend Moshe's honor.

A touch on his shoulder. He jerked around and faced his bent master. "Have you not yet learned? Yahweh will answer. He will defend His."

But as the sun rose, so did the complaints, the murmuring. Yehoshua could not believe his ears. The people would rebel? Again? Had they learned nothing with the burning of their own?

An assembly gathered, shouting at Moshe and Aaron, and moved toward the tent of meeting. Suddenly, a massive cloud covered the tent. Hot and white, the glory of the Lord appeared.

"Quickly." Waving his brother over with wrinkled hands gnarled but strong, Moshe dragged Yehoshua to the front of the tent. A strange wail went up somewhere outside. The sound of intense grief, so great that it sent a chill down Yehoshua's spine.

"Get away from this assembly, so I can put an end to them at once."

Moshe and Aaron threw themselves to the ground, faces to the dirt. Moshe motioned to his brother. "Take your censer and put incense in it, along with burning coals from the altar, and hurry to the assembly to make atonement for them. Wrath has come out from the Lord; the plague has started."

Aaron scrambled to his feet, grabbed his censer, and rushed to carry out Moshe's command.

Screaming poured through the air as they rose and followed him to the assembly. Yehoshua was taken aback at what greeted them. Half among them already showed signs of the plague. A man tumbled to the ground, dead. Another.

And another.

Aaron offered the incense and made atonement for them, standing between the living and the dead. That day the dead numbered nearly fifteen thousand, save three hundred. Had Aaron not made atonement, the plague would have ravaged the entire camp. So many paid the price for rebellion, for questioning Yahweh's chosen. For making themselves gods.

Future generations must be warned. Protected.

Vindication tasted like sweat. Backbreaking, limb-aching sweat. Tzivia Khalon pushed onto her knees and used the back of her gloved hand to wipe away the perspiration plastering her hair to her face and neck. She needed a break. In the logbook, she recorded her progress, sketched what the B23 grid site resembled, then stood and started for the sorting tent.

Noel Garelli, her assistant, looked up from B20. "Giving up?"

Tzivia snorted. "In your dreams." Though they'd all thought about it. Two weeks onsite, and they'd uncovered nothing of significance, nothing directly connected to the Bronze Age or the Israelites. But there was no way she'd walk away so soon. Dig sites could go from mundane to extraordinary in the space of an inch.

Just an inch. *I just need an inch.* Just 25.4 millimeters to clear her résumé of the Kafr al-Ayn disaster three years ago, when a toxin from an artifact stolen from her mentor, Dr. Joseph Cathey, nearly wiped out a village. The president of the United States had been killed in the aftermath. Despite being cleared of negligence and wrongdoing, Tzivia bore the dent in her reputation from that incident. It had endangered grants. Stalled donations.

Jebel al-Lawz was her chance to expunge that humiliating experience from her life. One amazing find, and she would be sought after. Respected. She wouldn't let anything or anyone ruin this chance. Not even her nosy brother in the States. Or his brooding, handsome friend, Tox Russell.

Tzivia huffed. Tox had died three years ago. It still stung. Not to mention the way he'd shut her out when they arrested him. Told her to move on. *"It's for your own good."*

She *had* moved on—she was now *Doctor* Tzivia Khalon. Had it not been for the weight Dr. Cathey's name carried, Kafr al-Ayn could've destroyed her career and life. But being an authority on Ancient Near Eastern studies, he pulled a few strings and had them cleared of misconduct. When she compared her résumé against his, she might as well be in kindergarten. Her focus had strictly been Ancient Near East, but Dr. Cathey had degrees in Hebrew Bible and semitic epigraphy as well as Ancient Near Eastern Studies. With two doctorates, he now served as an adjunct professor with Oxford's Oriel College.

She scanned the archaeological dig site. Her site. With the help of Dr. Cathey, they'd won the grant to search for answers about Jebel al-Lawz, the land purportedly where the Israelites had encamped. Gaining the permission of the Saudi Commission for Tourism and National Heritage to work this site hadn't been easy, but the promise of cooperation and sharing all artifacts got her team onsite. Having Dr. Cathey backing the dig gave her clearance to even be here, gave the dig credibility, and provided her with an authority who could review any recovered artifacts.

Years ago, the Saudis had erected a fence with a guard hut around this area to keep out looters and vandals. They believed something significant happened here, and she shared that belief, though she wouldn't fall prey again to Dr. Cathey's religious ideals—that was his one detraction. Or should she call it "distraction"? He believed the Bible to be more than a piece of literature. He believed Moses had been here. That the blackened mountain in the distance was where the Hebrew patriarch received the Ten Commandments.

Many scholars refuted the site. Some had outright called her desperate for coming here. Supernaturally carved tablets or not, she and

14

her team would attempt to answer whether this site truly was the biblical Mount Sinai.

"Just one inch," Tzivia whispered as she pivoted.

Earth gave way beneath her feet. Rocks scraped and clawed her legs, yanking her downward. With a scream, she shielded her face. Terror grabbed her by the throat. Dirt and rocks smothered her face.

Then didn't. She felt the world fall away. Coldness wrapped her tight in the split second before she thudded to a stop.

Pain slammed into her back. She landed, staring up at the hole. It seemed impossibly small for her to have fallen through. Dirt dribbled into her eyes. She jerked away, peeling off the ground. Her hand suctioned against mud. Mud? This arid region wasn't exactly fertile terrain. She squinted around. To the left, a short, two-foot-high stone circle. Worn, broken boards straddled the stones.

Plop! Plunk!

Water rippled. Water! The stones encircled the lip of a well.

Wiping muddy hands on her tactical pants, she climbed to her feet. Before her—she froze. Mud bricks laid out in a consistent pattern. A wall? She bent, her fingers tracing the mortar that had formed through the years between the bricks. No, not years—*centuries*!

"Tzivia!"

"Here," she called, waving a hand behind her but unable to take her eyes off the wall. Something protruded from the ground at the base. Gloves back on, she gently brushed aside the silt. "Noel, c'mere!"

"Sending a rope down."

Tzivia followed the lower edge of the wall with her gloved finger. How far back did it go? Bricks crumbled at her touch. Her heart climbed into her throat as years of history were reduced to rubble and dust. "No no no." She drew back her hand, afraid to create any more damage before it could be logged. Afraid she'd undo the miracle just discovered.

The wall stood about six feet tall. What was this place? A dwelling? It didn't look right for Bronze Age. Her hope dimmed. She shifted and checked right and left. It stretched the entire length of the underground cave.

But there was a well here. So . . . Tzivia stepped back a few paces.

Took in the wall. *What's behind you?* She went to her knees. Shoulder to the wet ground, she peered into the new hole. Darkness. She yanked the torch from her hip holster and flashed it into the darkness.

Light stabbed the ebony blanket beyond. Dust particles danced in the beam. A room!

Whoosh!

As another section of wall gave way, Tzivia shoved back and turned away. Coughing, she blinked quickly to clear her eyes.

"Tzi!"

"I'm okay," she said around another cough. "We need to stabilize this. It's all damp and collapsing. My cave-in must've weakened the supports or something." A sweet, pungent odor filled the tunnel, nauseating her. "Ugh."

"Look out below," Noel called.

With a hefty thump, a rope ladder dangled behind Tzivia. Noel's frame filled the hole topside. Once down, he screwed up his face. "What is that smell? It reeks!" He steadied the ladder as Basil, one of the interns, clambered down, too.

Flashlight in hand, Tzivia wiped her face. Something caught her eye in the darkened room. She froze. Something had moved. A dark shape. Shadow? Tilting her head, she bent over the partially destroyed wall and sucked in a breath at what she saw. Dust caught in her throat and made her cough. Basil started coughing, too.

"Should we go back up?" Noel asked, his lanky frame towering over her.

"The air's stale, but we'll be okay for a few more minutes." Tzivia pointed. "Look." Shoved up against the far side of the earthen room sat a chest, maybe two feet by two feet. Frayed rope handles didn't look like they'd hold its weight. "Come on." They climbed over the crumbled wall, causing more of it to collapse. She cringed at the damage but allowed the lure of discovery to lead her on.

"I'm not feeling so great," Basil muttered as they squatted.

"There's something stamped in the lid." She wasn't ready to admit it looked like a Templar cross. "Let's get it to the sorting tent."

Noel nodded, grabbing the sides of the chest. He lifted it.

Crack! Pop!

"No!" Tzivia cried as the bottom fell away.

Three objects hit the ground.

Sucking in a disbelieving breath, she lifted one of the items in her gloved hand. "Noel!" Exhilaration spiraled through her veins as Basil aimed his flashlight at it. "I think . . . this is a Hebrew *miktereth*." Though most censers were made of pottery, these were bronze and roughly six inches in length, with a handle supporting a small cup-like space for the burning incense. She traced the markings. A giddy laugh surged as she looked at the other two censers on the ground. "I can't be sure of the date down here—it's too dark and we need to test scrapings—but they look Bronze Age."

"But . . . bronze?" Noel asked, pointing to the metal censer.

"True." Most miktereths of this age were made of pottery. "Except. . . ."

"Did we find it?" Noel's voice was but a whisper. "Please, tell me we found it—this is where the Israelites camped, isn't it?"

She laughed, looking up at him with history in her hand. "I believe we did."

* * * *

— TWO DAYS AGO —
OKOMU FOREST RESERVE, EDO STATE, NIGERIA

"If you do this thing, do not think I will come save you."

Slinking through the humid jungle, Cole "Tox" Russell almost grinned at the words of his "conscience" vibrating in his comms piece. "If you're right," he subvocalized, leaning against a tree and scanning the dense vegetation through his thermal binoculars, "there won't be anything to save."

"It is a bad idea." His own personal Jiminy Cricket came in the form of a six-foot-five Nigerian named Chijioke Okorie.

"It'd be boring if it wasn't. Remember, three minutes." Their self-imposed assurance that no tangos came out of there alive.

Ambush. They'd agreed the probability was high. As in more likely than not. Enough to tell anyone with half a brain not to engage. But Tox was missing that half. This half had him stalking through the jungle because of a twelve-year-old girl. No way could he sit back on the savannah, watching cheetahs outrun gazelle, knowing his niece, Evie Russell, was in the hands of sadistic guerillas.

Not after the promise he'd made in a pool of blood.

So here he was, shirt soaked to his chest and boots rubbing blisters into his ankles and toes, working his way north to the camp. Wiping away the sweat, he scanned the forest, alert. Nerves thrumming.

"It is not safe, *Ndidi*," Chiji huffed.

Tox nodded to no one but himself. His friend had it right—this wasn't safe. In fact, it could end his life. But securing the objective would fulfill that promise.

He glanced up at the canopy, where fading sunlight poked through defiantly. Sweat slipped down his temple, traced his jaw, and raced along his neck. This had to be done. And even with the calloused warning of no help from his friend, Tox knew Chiji would come. Tox had made the mistake once of thinking Chiji only warred with Bible verses. He could still feel the *thwack* of the stick across his back, unprepared for the skilled kali strike that face-planted him in the West African desert.

Skulking, Tox made his way around the tree trunks. The guerillas had made it too easy and too obvious. Yep, a trap. Within a few hours of the hovel he called home—where he'd managed to stay hidden for the last three years—and Evie just happens to end up held hostage by some rogue outfit with connections to DC?

Right.

Despite the infinitesimal possibility that Evie was actually here, Tox couldn't ignore it. Could not risk the potential threat against her life.

"Two targets, twenty yards north of your position," Chiji said from his nest in one of the tree houses overlooking this narrow swath of forest. Tox bet the national park hadn't imagined their perches for bird watching and appreciating the unique environment would come in handy as the vantage point for a mission.

Tox moved east to flank the targets. This was stupid. Really stupid. Anyone setting him up would also know it was stupid to try. He wanted to believe nobody was asinine enough to play chicken with the life of a child. Especially not with him involved. He'd more than earned his "Toxic" moniker.

Snap!

The sound of breaking branches sent Tox into the buttresses of a nearby kapok, its gnarled roots looking like the foot of a monstrous dog, nails digging into the soil. Shoulder pressed to the trunk, he peered around, keeping his movements slow and fluid as the palmate branches swaying above. Nothing sudden to draw attention. Using his legs, he pushed up.

A shadow moved.

He dropped, locked onto the target. Was there only one? Prostrate, he keyed his mic. "Count?"

"One."

Only one? Tox stared through the heavy forestation at the shape. Why weren't there more? He could take out this tango and nobody would know. He was almost insulted.

Regardless—no need to waste a life. Tox slid south around the kapok buttresses. Swiftly darted westward, directly into the path of the perimeter guards.

The ten-meter base of the trees and their root system made navigating the area tricky. But also assisted him. Trip alarms would be more visible. The placement more obvious. Tox hiked up on the thick buttress of another kapok. From the larger limbs hung bulbous seedpods surrounded by a fluffy, yellowish fiber much like cotton. Resistant to water but highly flammable. He skirted from one buttress to another, using the roots to protect himself from trip sensors, and watched the thick trunks for higher-placed sensors.

Crack!

Bark spat at him.

Tox dropped to the ground, unholstering his Glock 22.

"You've been spotted."

Understatement of the year. Since the enemy knew he was here, no need for skulking. Tox hunch-ran along the perimeter. After several switchbacks, he was hopeful he'd lost the guard who'd spotted him.

A dozen yards ahead, the outer rim of the camp they'd reconned with the long-range scope Chiji now used finally came into view. Beyond it, a hastily assembled, thatched-roof squat sat beneath a massive kapok, ripe with fruit. Good protection and cover. But within the building—cement. At least two feet thick. Too formidable to get thermals and heat signatures. Security had been tight. He'd have preferred bribing a local to get eyes on the target, but time didn't allow that. Their timeline had been way too short.

"Moving in," he subvocalized, switching his gun for his KA-BAR Kraton-handled Mark I with a serrated edge. He rushed up behind the first sentry, who was armed with an M16 and a handgun, hooked an arm around his neck, and severed his carotid. Tox lowered the guard. A boot knife glinted.

Tox slung the assault rifle and pistol into the dense foliage. He tucked the knife in his boot. The crunching of twigs pushed him into a low crouch. The thick stench of cigarettes polluted the air. Didn't these two know smoking got them executed by Boko Haram? By Tox Russell, too.

He slipped behind a tree and took aim, aware that even silenced shots could be heard. No choice. He eased back the trigger. Fired two shots at the first man, taking him down. He acquired the second and neutralized him before the guy could figure out what was happening and call for help.

"Two more en route," Chiji warned.

Tox scurried forward, ready to silence them. When their forest camo came into view, he launched himself at the first soldier. Slammed a hard right into his nose. Heard the bone crack, ramming into gray matter. He spun to the second—

A weapon muzzle stared back. Tox stilled for a half second, then hooked the man's leg and swept him off his feet.

Crack!

The bullet went wide as the man's head hit a buttress with a sickening thud. His neck lay at an awkward angle. Tangos neutralized, Tox sprinted toward the structure. Inside, he'd be on his own. Chiji couldn't guide him.

He stared at the door that hung awkwardly to the side. *It's a trap.* But if it wasn't . . .

"Going in." Tox slid his M4A1 around to his front and took in a quick, measuring breath. Blew it out. Shimmied around the wall. Then lifted a flashbang from his belt, pulled the pin, and tossed it through the space where the flimsy door gaped.

He jerked back. Waited.

Shouts preceded the concussive *boom* by two seconds.

Tox rushed in. Went right. Scanned the scene as he moved to the corner for protection. The interior served one function—to conceal the cement shelter. A small table with knocked-over tin cups was the only barrier between him and two disoriented guards. Hands over their ears, they writhed. Tox put them out of their misery.

"Two tangos down," he muttered, swinging around so his back wasn't to anyone entering the hut. His gaze hit a steel door. Moment of truth. Who was behind Door #1? He slid along the wall and palmed the handle.

Locked.

Tox pivoted. Drove the heel of his boot against the door. It bucked but held. He kicked again. This time the lock surrendered. He shouldered the door open.

Tox stepped across the threshold. Darkness devoured him. He flicked on his night vision goggles and pushed to the corner. When the wash of green draped the area, Tox bit back a curse. Empty. "Trap!"

As a shadow moved, he snapped to the right.

White light exploded across his vision.

Grunting, he ripped off the NVGs, knowing the attacker was coming at him. Temporarily blinded, he silenced himself. His pain. His panic. And listened.

To his right a subtle shift of air. Tox hesitated. Pain exploded across his temple. He flipped backward. His head cracked against the cement wall.

Singular focus was all that would keep him alive right now. He rolled and slid the boot knife free. He came up, his vision clearing, his ears ringing, and sighted the attacker. On his right. A flurry of kicks.

With lightning-fast reflexes, he drove the knife into the man's leg.

"Augh!" The man twitched but came unyielding, determination gouged into his Caucasian face. And he hadn't shot Tox. Which proved this was a trap meant to capture him. Just like they'd suspected.

The idea lit fire down Tox's spine. He again drew out his KA-BAR.

His attacker produced one of his own. Matched determination and weapons. But Tox had been fighting for his life for the last three years.

21

The man lunged with a stab.

Tox deflected. Grabbed the man's wrist. Pulled him forward and rammed his elbow into the guy's face. At the same time, the attacker jammed a knife-hand into Tox's back—his kidney. Tox howled.

They both stumbled. Tox twisted around just in time to deflect a knife from his throat. He leapt backward, his abdomen exposed. The blade sliced his stomach. With a strike, the man nailed Tox's wrist, sending the knife clattering. Searing pain from the cut nearly disabled his thinking. He thrust the fleshy part of his hand against the man's carotid.

The man dropped, gasping for air.

Pain vied for Tox's attention. He flung around, searching for his knife. Found it—in the hand of the man grinning around bloody teeth.

"Shouldn't have come," he growled, sounding one hundred percent American.

"Yeah," Tox gritted, lifting a stick. "You shouldn't have."

The man lunged with the KA-BAR. Tox slapped his arm away, cracked the stick against his wrist. Then drew back and snapped it at the right side of his neck. At the last minute, Tox diverted. Struck his head.

As a massive *whoosh* ignited the air, the man tumbled forward. Chiji had held up his promise to send an RPG into the shelter if Tox hadn't emerged in three minutes. If it hadn't been for the cement and steel, they'd be toast.

Tox cringed as superheated air burst through the shelter. Oxygen sucked out. With the kapok around them, the forest would quickly become an inferno.

He considered his attacker. No doubt a brother in arms. Doing his job. Like a loyal dog returning to his vomit. *No man left behind.*

Tox grabbed his attacker's ankles and dragged him out of the hut. Dropped him at the entrance then limped into the forest with only one thought: They'd pay for this.

President Galen Russell strode to the dais in the White House briefing room. He gripped the lectern and peered out at the bay of reporters and journalists. "It is with the deepest regret that I confirm the death of former vice president and current ambassador to the United Kingdom, Howard Lammers. He died tonight from wounds sustained in an attack three days ago as he and his wife, Lorraine, attended the National Theatre in London. My condolences and prayers, as well as those of all Americans, are with the family and loved ones devastated by this horrific act."

The president stared into the cameras, clearly affected by the incident. "At this hour, we have few details, but we are working closely with the British authorities to locate those responsible and deliver justice. Thank you."

As the press secretary took the podium to field questions, Barry Attaway fell into step beside the president, who headed out of the congested room. The entourage trailing him, which included the DoD, CIA, and other three-letters, made its way down the hall to the Oval Office.

Out of sight of the reporters, Galen looked to Barry. "Anything new?"

Barry shook his head.

"Keep on it. I want to know who did this, and I want them to face the fullest measure of our justice."

As he'd said a dozen times in earlier meetings. "Of course, sir."

Galen turned to his administrative assistant. "I'd like to talk to Lorraine Lammers."

The fifty-something woman nodded, lifting a phone. "I'll try again."

"You said you were going to handle this," a voice hissed near Barry's ear. He tensed and turned, staring into the gray eyes of Rick Hamer, director of the CIA's Special Activities Division.

After a quick glance at the president making his way back to the Oval Office, Barry whispered, "Relax."

Hamer stopped, his eyebrows rising to his hairline. "Relax?" He'd been a Force Recon Marine and wasn't used to being rebuffed. "We have another dead American. How many people do they have to hit before—"

"First," Barry said, making sure the president didn't hear, "it's still fresh. We don't have proof—"

"Seriously?" Hamer growled. "You're going there? And where is this guy you said could handle it?"

Barry tried to shake off the nerves tightening his gut. "En route."

The fire in Hamer's eyes warned he didn't believe Barry. He pursed his lips and gave a terse nod. "He'd better be. We need this stopped. The president—"

"*Cannot* be implicated." Barry felt the thunder in his chest louder than the bombs in Iraq. "He and the United States must be kept clean—"

"Which is why we gave you a week. You promised it'd be taken care of. It's not."

"Two days. My man is bringing him in."

"Wait—does this guy even know what he's after?" When there wasn't an answer, Hamer muttered something under his breath. "You should've left this to the big dogs, Attaway."

"Why? So more can end up like Lammers?" Attaway saw he'd overstepped, saw the anger that pushed past the director's tough persona. He needed to soothe him. "We'll get this assassin."

"We need results, not talk." Hamer's gaze raked Barry over live coals. "Where are you getting this guy anyway? How does a chief of staff have connections big enough for an op like this?"

"Don't worry about that."

"I am worried." Hamer cuffed Barry's arm, angling in. "I let you have this. My men were ready, but you said you had a way to keep the president clean. You may want him for a second term, but with screw-ups like this—"

"Barry." The president stood at the end of the hall, his dark brow knotted as he glanced between the two of them. "Ready?"

Saved by the bell. "Sir." Barry unhooked his arm and moved to the president without another word to the SAD director.

They rounded the corner and Galen glanced at him. "Hamer looked ticked."

"He always looks ticked, sir." At his own office, Barry slowed. "I have to get some things taken care of before the next briefing."

"Keep me posted."

Barry nodded.

"You will, won't you?"

He stopped short this time. "Sir?"

With a sigh, Galen turned to him. "That conversation back there . . . it feels like you're not telling me something." He patted Barry on the chest with the back of his hand. "Always trying to protect me, eh?"

"Of course, sir." With that, Barry headed into his office. He slid behind his desk and eased into the chair. The engraved crystal clock on his desk showed 1300. What was taking MacIver so long?

Muddled in conspiracies and threats by every three-letter agency that existed, as well as committees and subcommittees of the House and Congress, Barry was exhausted by the alphabet soup and the pressure. He was standing on a catwalk suspended over two very large, boiling cauldrons. One wrong step, one more failure . . .

The U.S. needed this assassin dealt with, yet they couldn't touch this. Everyone on the Hill wanted answers about who had killed the kindly former vice president. So Barry had taken a risk. One he felt certain would pay for itself a hundred times over.

His phone rang. Spotting the caller ID, Barry snatched it from the cradle. "Where have you been? They're breathing fire down my neck! And you're a day late."

"And one rogue short."

Barry fell against the desk. So Vaughn MacIver hadn't secured the target. The former SEAL commander had a pristine record, a fierce one. He succeeded where few did. That was why Barry handpicked him. That was why Barry moved forward with this desperate mission. "What went wrong?"

"He smelled us coming."

"How did you let that happen?"

"He's good, sir. And I expected that, but . . ."

"But what?"

"It's just that I know this guy—not personally, but this type of soldier. Their instincts are razor-sharp. They get the job done no matter the cost or length of time it takes to complete the mission."

"Yes, I thought you were that type of man, MacIver. That's why I tapped you!"

"Tox Russell is in a league all his own. I can't explain how he knew we were there. Most of the villagers didn't know. He walked into the trap and shouldn't have walked out, but the instant he entered, things changed."

Barry cursed under his breath. When he had to come clean with all this, Hamer would eat him for lunch—and Galen would have the leftovers for dinner.

"I knew coming down here . . . that if he beat me," MacI continued, "I'd come home in a box. Probably in pieces."

Barry closed his eyes, willed the torrent of anger churning in his chest to stay behind the dam. He had to think. Had to plan.

"But I'm alive."

"I'm not seeing this as a benefit."

"It's not," MacI said. "It's a warning."

Hackles raised, Barry tilted his head. "Come again?"

"It's a warning, sir. From him."

Barry stilled, his mind racing.

"Next time, it'll be on his terms. His game."

Barry peered out his window overlooking the Mall.

"Tox Russell is coming, sir. He's coming for you."

— DAY 2 —

WASHINGTON, DC

The view from the Truman balcony inspired Galen Russell, who sat facing the Washington Monument. Splendor and power were his. But they felt empty without his wife, Brooke. She'd been at his side from his first run for Congress and his swift rise on the political tide that swept him right into the Oval Office. But then she'd died—murdered the month before the inauguration.

Voices pushed aside his solitude and thrust him into another busy working day. He glanced at his watch. "Ever punctual, Barry." He lifted his coffee cup. "You can be late, you know. I won't fire you."

Hands in his pockets, Barry nodded and stood at the rail. "Sir, we need to talk." The forty-three-year-old had grayed early, even though Barry had weathered the DC storm like a pro. In fact if it hadn't been for his chief of staff, Galen probably wouldn't have survived the insanity. Yet here he was—shaken.

"Barry." Galen joined his chief of staff at the rail, bracing himself. "What's wrong?"

Barry hung his head. "I've tried a million ways in my head to come at this, but I"—he huffed and tightened his lips—"I'm just going to come clean and tell you the truth."

Galen tried to laugh, but it came out more air than laugh. "Good. I'd hope you're always honest with me."

"He's alive."

"Who's alive?" He reached mentally for a name, a face. "Lammers?"

"Tox."

As if struck with a baseball bat, Galen jerked back. Images of a face, one not unlike his own but younger, more intense—raw and edged in fury—crowded his vision. "*Cole*? Wh–what do you mean?" Legs rubbery, he dropped into the chair. "How can he be alive?"

"What I need you to understand," Barry began, his tone placating, "is that things were complicated. Messy."

"Things were—" Another revelation whacked Galen over the head. "Wait a minute. You *knew* he was alive?"

Frustration or guilt, maybe both, pushed Barry's hazel eyes down. "You were running for president. What happened, you had to be protected. You were told what you needed to know."

Galen stiffened. "What I *needed* to know? I'm the *president*! I need to know everything."

"No." Chin tucked, Barry held his gaze resolutely through terse brows. "Not everything. Plausible denia—"

"Don't. Don't handle me." Galen's thoughts jammed with a million different scenarios, with the unbelievable, jarring truth that his brother hadn't died in prison. He couldn't think past it. Couldn't process information. He wandered back inside, through the Yellow Oval Room to his private sitting room, seeking shelter. From what, he didn't know. But he felt naked. Exposed. Everything he knew to be true suddenly became fluid and false. The man he'd trusted as his closest ally had kept a major truth from him. "Tell me. Everything."

Hesitation thickened the air.

"My anger's rising fast."

With a sigh, Barry nodded. "Tox had an agreement. Do a job, leave the country, and nobody would bother him again."

"An agreement with whom?"

"Department of Defense."

Galen couldn't shake the shock. "You told me he was dead." The funeral. The memorial with—"My parents . . ." He'd never forget

28

his mother's raw, palpable grief that had infected the family for the last three years.

"That's what everyone needed to believe. He did a mission, and—"

"What mission?" Galen turned to Barry. "What did they have him do?"

Long silences had become Barry's trademark in the recent days.

"Barry," he said in warning.

"Al-Homsi."

Galen leaned forward. "Amir al-Homsi?" He recalled the news footage of the massacre . . . the roar that disturbed an American-Syrian summit. His gut churned, imagining his brother— "*Tox* killed him?"

Why was he so surprised? His brother was an elite operator. Nausea roiled through Galen. If someone found out his own brother had killed al-Homsi . . . The DC machine had pegged al-Homsi as the rising star, catapulting him into the senate and priming him for a vicious run against Galen in the next election. "You realize what they'll say when this gets out?"

"Nobody will find out."

"They will!"

"They won't because Tox is dead as far as they know. And we're keeping it that way."

"They always find out, Barry. Look at my life!" He lifted a signed baseball from a credenza and fingered it. "They always do. Somehow."

"He was a U.S. soldier neutralizing a terrorist."

"On U.S. soil!" Galen threw the ball at the wall. His wicked curve made it narrowly miss Barry's ear. "My brother killed a senator on American soil." It didn't matter that the citizenship of that particular American citizen was invalid, that his father was the head of a massive extremist cell in the Middle East. Al-Homsi had been a plant, groomed to take power and cripple America. That didn't matter either.

"Intel made it irrefutable that al-Homsi was a danger to our country." Barry sighed. "It wasn't an easy decision."

"Which one? The one to kill an American citizen—"

"A *phony* American citizen."

"To the people, he's American. That's how they'll see it." Galen bit back a curse and retrieved the ball from the hole it'd created in the wall. "What a disaster." He wiped his face, suddenly exhausted. All this time Barry had known. Had kept that secret. Had . . . "Did you put him on that mission?"

"I was your campaign—"

"No." Galen flung around, pointed the ball straddled between two fingers at Barry. "No more lies. You knew about that mission, knew what Tox would do and that he'd disappear."

Barry, a slick negotiator and skilled politician, held his gaze firmly. "Sir, I think we have more important things to worry about."

So Barry *had* put Tox on the mission. Galen scoffed. "Like *what*? My re-election campaign—which is flagging—will collapse when this comes out." He threw his arms wide, his pulse pounding against his temples. "What could be more important than me going down as a thug who murders potential opponents?"

"Killing al-Homsi wasn't about you. It was about this country. Al-Homsi had plans—"

"*I* represent this country," Galen snapped. "It was my—"

"Would you shut up and listen?" Eyes that normally remained placid stared back with a startling wildness.

Galen jerked straight. A hyper-focused beam suddenly seemed to shine on the man before him, slicing open weaknesses and flaws Galen had overlooked for too long. Alarms clanged against his already stoked panic. Why was he telling Galen this now? "Wait. What's wrong?"

"I stirred a nest."

"What nest? What do you mean?"

"We set a trap." Barry pinched his mouth tight. "Laid fodder for Tox to believe Evie was kidnapped."

"Evie?" The only light left in Galen's world after Brooke's death. Disbelief choked him. "You used *my daughter*?"

"It was the only way. We both know his triggers are family—"

"*How*? How did you use her?" Rage surged.

"We made him believe she was in danger." He quickly shot up a staying hand. "She never was."

"I would kill you myself if any harm came to her." A thousand thoughts swirled in Galen's mind, trying to slog through the quagmire his chief of staff had dumped on him. But it was a smart way to get to Tox. He didn't give a rat's behind about Galen or their father, but dangle Evie out there . . .

Mom. She would be beside herself to know her hot-headed son was alive. "So . . . you have him?" Temptation to look around the room, straining for voices in the hall, tugged at him.

"No."

"I don't understand."

"We set the trap." Barry shrugged. "He came. Just like we knew he would."

"But he got away." The possibilities of what happened in that engagement with his brother seemed infinite.

Nodding, Barry scowled, his knotted brow hovering protectively over a dark secret. "I think we ticked him off."

"You've ticked *me* off." But there was something . . . something his chief of staff wasn't saying. "I can't believe my brother agreed to kill al-Homsi, leave the country." Galen shook his head. "That violates every code of conduct and moral—" He stopped. Locked gazes with Barry. "What did you promise him?"

"Freedom."

Galen snorted. "For Cole? No way. He had his head so far up his backside with that stupid military code of honor of his, he wouldn't care what happened to himself."

Barry shifted. "It was for his team."

That Galen could believe.

"We wiped the slates clean for the men with him at Kafr al-Ayn, declared Tox dead, never to be heard from again."

Galen felt sick. "He was a legend, Barry. You knew that."

"He's been out of commission for the last three years."

"No." Galen snickered. "That would be true if he had really been dead. But he's been hiding, and I'd wager honing those skills." He returned the signed baseball to the credenza and stood behind his desk. "You can take the dog out of the fight, but you'll never take combat out of Tox's veins." Rubbing his jaw, he slumped into his leather chair. "Your trap blew up in your face. That's what this is about, isn't it?"

Barry again broke eye contact.

"You idiot." Galen huffed, shaking his head. "Tox has that name for a reason—he's toxic. To everyone around him."

"As you said, a legend. And we need that legend."

Galen considered him. "What is it this time? The news conference—"

"To respond to Ambassador Lammers's murder."

Revelation coursed through Galen. He eyed his friend for a long time, still angry that he'd kept such a colossal secret. He'd read the intel report on the ambassador. "Tox is the man you were bringing in for the black bag."

Barry nodded. "Word came down that the U.S. could not be implicated—as you know—so in an effort to protect you and this administration, it seemed best to use someone already dead, someone familiar with the terrain of assassins. Lammers was a warning. A warning to anyone thinking about working with you, sir. Against our allies." Barry's chest heaved and he let out a long breath. "We needed Tox's skills to stop this. We needed him."

"And you tried to trap a wild animal, and that animal outfoxed you." Thoughts swirled and coalesced into one sharp dagger. "You used Evie and now you think he's coming here."

Barry nodded.

Galen turned away, trying to put distance between himself and Barry. Between himself and this nightmare. Tox. Alive. Why couldn't it be Brooke who was really alive? Evie would—

"Evie." A crazed panic stabbed him. He lifted his phone and dialed. The call went to voicemail. His gaze sprang to Barry's as he hit redial. Same thing. "She's not answering." What if something had happened to her? "If my daughter is in danger because of this—"

"He wouldn't. Tox may be deadly, but his core values won't allow him to hurt you—"

"You just admitted he acted as your assassin once already. Obviously his core values can be compromised when the triggers are right."

Down the hall, a door clicked open.

Galen rushed into the long, narrow corridor of the second-floor residence. Evie trouped toward him with two Secret Service agents. Relief and anger collided. "Why didn't you answer my call?"

Evie scowled. "Because I was two minutes from seeing your face?"

"When I call, you answer." *Calm down. Calm down.*

She grunted. "I will be *so* glad when I'm on that plane headed to London in five days and"—she checked her phone app—"four hours, thirty-three—two minutes." Her device chirruped. She frowned as she looked at the screen. Then frowned deeper. "What the . . . ?"

"Language," Galen warned.

But her face had gone pale. Her eyes confused, tormented. "I got a text."

"You get hundreds every day."

She looked at him, her lips parting, quivering. "But not from a dead uncle."

Galen snatched the phone. Bile shot up his throat at the words: SEE YOU SOON.—UNCLE COLE

Monotony had claimed her life. Reviewing interview recordings and testimony transcripts hardly proved to be the exciting life of an FBI special agent. But Kasey Cortes hadn't been looking for excitement when she took the job. She'd been looking for truth.

Being an expert in deception gave her job security. But it also made her ache, listening to brutal killers talk about their crimes, whether denying involvement, confessing, or giving themselves away in interviews. She grunted. Though she'd found truth—so much it made her eyes and heart bleed—she hadn't found *the* truth she'd been looking for. A way to clear a man sentenced to life in a federal prison.

She bent over the statement she was analyzing.

> *I saw the woman come in but I wasn't there for no woman.*
> *I got my soda then headed to the counter. Then the woman*
> *went down the snack aisle. I paid for my food. Then that witch*
> *jumped in her car and sped off.*

She marked the word *woman* and *witch* with a blue highlighter, then drew a line between them.

"Gotcha," Kasey whispered, lifting her phone. She dialed Agent Lewis's extension.

"Lewis," the special agent barked.

"Hey, this is Kasey Cortes."

"Oh hey, Cortes," he said, his voice suddenly friendly. "How's it going?"

She smiled at the demeanor change. "Good. Listen, I just finished the Barillo statement."

"Yeah?"

"He left something out."

"I been saying that, but what'd you find?"

"He went from referring to the victim as 'the woman' to calling her 'the witch' while relaying the events." She tugged her notebook closer and glanced at her notes. "When language changes, it means Barillo had a change in his thinking, circumstances, or situation. We know the circumstances and situation didn't alter in the store, which leaves his thinking. But the statement doesn't tell us why his thinking changed. So that means something happened between the snack aisle and him leaving the store. Ask him about it."

"Will do. Thanks, Cortes!"

She smiled as she hung up. Lewis could hopefully put another thug behind bars. Kasey leaned back in her chair, kneading her nape where her thick bun rested. She glanced at her watch. Maybe she could take that lunch break. Make a latte run.

"Yo, Cortes."

Kasey groaned without looking up. "What do you want, D'Angelo?"

"I met this girl last night—"

"No."

"Wait, wait. I just want you to tell me—"

"No." She pushed to her feet. "I'm not here to vet your girlfriends."

"But she's not my girlfriend. *Yet*."

Kasey sighed. Men. They never got it. "Not my problem."

"Kase."

A strong, deep voice drew her around. Special Agent Levi Wallace stood in all his six-foot-four glory. Dark hair. Broad-shouldered. Clark

Kent's long-lost cousin. When they'd first met, he'd given her butterflies and sweaty palms. She still found him crazy-attractive, but . . .

She smiled. "Hey." Attraction or not, Levi was one of her closest friends.

A lone, dark look from Levi sent D'Angelo scurrying away. "He bugging you about girls again?"

"Yeah," she said as a leggy blonde sauntered down the aisle to the cubicle where D'Angelo pretended to be busy. "Anyway, what's up? You have lunch yet? Want to grab a latte?"

"You should eat real food and drink real coffee."

She shrugged. "I should also get a *real* life, but since that's not happening . . ." Again she glanced at D'Angelo and friend. There was maybe some physical attraction there.

"I'm supposed to escort you to the White House."

The words jolted Kasey back to Levi. "What?" She scowled. "Why would you need to escort me? Galen's my brother-in-law." Even if her sister had died, making the president a widower, Kasey still had a niece behind the fence and white columns.

With a one-shouldered shrug, he cocked his head. "Got the order a few minutes ago. You're due there in twenty."

"Twenty!" She grabbed her purse. "Did they forget about DC traffic?"

He grinned as they headed to the elevator. "I'm Mario Andretti, remember?"

"Ha." She checked to make sure she'd brought her phone. "I remember saying you were a kamikaze with a car. Not someone as notoriously revered as Mario Andretti."

"Same difference." In his field car, Levi hit the lights.

"Cheater," she mumbled.

"You were summoned by the president. I'd call that an emergency." He grinned, sailing around vehicles and through a red light.

Summoned by the president. Why would Galen send for her? They'd had an agreement to keep their lives separate. She wanted her own life. Which made it nice being married to a Navy SEAL and taking his last name, getting that much farther from the spotlight. At least for twelve months, until Duarte died on a mission, ripping apart her life and heart.

36

Of course, for celebrations with her twelve-year-old niece, Evie, she and the president spent time with his parents and hers. And holidays. But that was it. She didn't need more of Galen Russell in her life. He served to remind her of too many painful memories.

"Hey." Levi shot those blue-green eyes at her. "Maybe after this meeting we could grab an early dinner, then make it to Community for service."

She smiled. "Sounds perfect." Attending church helped cleanse the heaviness that soaked her after the daily immersion of cases dealing with death and darkness.

He returned her smile. "Good."

The White House had two checkpoints—one outside before they parked that had an explosives-detection dog walk the car, and then one to enter the White House. As they cleared the latter, a Secret Service agent emerged from a side door. His face brightened. "Levi." He extended a hand. "Good to see you. How's the family?"

She'd almost forgotten both she and Levi had connections to the white-pillared house on Pennsylvania Avenue. Levi's brother had been with President Montrose's security detail in Nigeria three years ago and was kidnapped along with the former president's wife. The First Lady had survived, but President Montrose had been taken to Syria by the terrorists. He hadn't come home.

"Doing good. Thank you, Paul."

"Agent Cortes." The agent bobbed his head to the side. "They're waiting."

Not only waiting, but *they*. Who? And what was going on? Escorted to the Yellow Oval Room, Kasey tried not to squirm in her navy skirt and blazer. She was visiting her niece and brother-in-law, that was all. Nothing odd.

Except the heavy security detail.

And the summons.

As the door to the main living area opened, Levi extended a hand toward the office and gave her an affirming nod. That he'd noticed things were off, too, gave her little comfort as she entered.

At a window, Galen stood rubbing his jaw. He turned and buttoned his jacket. "Haven."

She crossed the room and hugged him. He'd never been willing to call her Kasey. Though her full name was Katherine Haven Cortes, she'd always gone by Haven, since she and her mother shared first names. Duarte had dubbed her "KC" after they married, which easily morphed into Kasey. After he died, she'd clung even more tightly to the nickname. "How are you?"

"Stressed. Tired." His smile was feeble, his words even more so. He shook Levi's hand. "Agent Wallace."

"Mr. President."

Galen motioned to the sitting arrangement. "Please. Have a seat."

"This is all very formal," Kasey said, noting he took the lone chair. She lowered herself to the thick sofa cushions, glancing at last year's photo of her niece. "How's Evie? Ready for London?"

His expression was strained. "More than. She's got a thing on her phone that tells her exactly how many seconds are interfering with her escape."

She managed a smile. "I bet." Okay. She couldn't do this. Couldn't do fake. "So why did you ask Levi to bring me here?"

The door opened, then closed. Footsteps crossed the padded carpet, ushering Barry Attaway into the discussion. At his arrival, Kasey had to work to keep her irritation concealed.

Galen scooted forward in his seat. "I won't beat around the bush . . ." Doing exactly that, he hesitated. "What I am going to tell you must stay in this room."

Ignoring Barry's nod, Kasey focused on her brother-in-law. "Understood." It was weird to have Levi here, but since he was a special agent in charge and had a higher security clearance than she did, she shrugged off his inclusion in this mysterious meeting.

Galen looked at the floor. "There's no easy way to say it, Haven." He met her gaze with eyes so similar to a pair she'd adored years ago. "I was informed two days ago that my brother is alive."

She started. Sucked in a breath as her mind caught up with his words. Shook her head as if she'd been struck. "Cole? He—wh— how—" She sounded like an idiot, so she clamped her mouth shut. "How? I don't understand." Tears stung her eyes. "We buried him."

Levi moved closer, his arm draping her shoulders.

She shrugged it off and slipped to the edge of the sofa, staring at Galen. "How is he alive?"

"Most of this is classified, Agent Cortes," Barry said, inserting himself. "Just suffice it to say that Cole Russell, legally, does not exist. *Cannot* exist. Not in any public record. His pardon will be sealed."

"What pardon? Wait—never mind." She held up a hand. "Where is he? How—*what* happened?"

Galen sighed, darting a look to his chief of staff. "We don't know where he is."

She saw it in their glances. Heard it in what they didn't say. "What *do* you know?"

"Haven," he said, again using her middle name, a ploy no doubt to corral her anger. "There are things I can't tell you about Cole—"

"What *can* you tell me?"

"Kase," Levi whispered in warning at her tone.

Galen hunched forward. "I know you always had a soft spot for Cole."

Barry snorted. "Soft spot? She constructed her whole career to prove he wasn't guilty."

"No. No, you two don't get to turn this back on me, Galen." Angry tears burned the back of her eyes, defeated only by a cloud of confusion and frustration. "Why are you telling me this? To yank my chain? To warn me?" Because he'd always acted like Cole was the bad guy. The troublemaker. "Why were we told he was dead? If he didn't die in prison, where has he been? How did he get out?" She couldn't erase the mental image of his flag-draped coffin at the very small, very private burial she'd attended, hugging herself tight on that wintry afternoon.

"He wasn't supposed to return to the U.S., but—"

"He's coming back." There was too much hope in her words, she knew, but she couldn't help it.

"For revenge," Barry said, his tone seething.

Kasey sniffed. "Cole is a better man than that."

"When was the last time you saw Tox Russell?" Barry challenged. "He's not exactly the hero you believe him to be."

Heat infused her cheeks, her embarrassment betraying her. But that sparked her irritation. "Really? Then why are you willing to grant him a pardon if he's guilty?"

Another exchanged glance between Galen and his lackey. "Because a pardon is what it's going to take to get my brother to work with us."

"Work with you on what?" Kasey asked. "Where is he?"

"Unknown." Galen rubbed his knuckles. "But we expect him. Soon."

She narrowed her eyes, sorting his words. "So he's not coming willingly."

Galen snickered. "Oh, I guarantee he's coming willingly."

Why would he return if they told him not to? It'd been three years . . . Revenge. Barry said he was coming for revenge.

"You ticked him off," Levi said.

The words drew Kasey's attention. Yes, that made sense. But if Cole was coming after them . . . "What did you do?"

Galen's gaze was so much like Cole's, yet nothing like it. "He's coming after me because he thinks I set him up."

"But you didn't?"

Galen shook his head and looked away. "They baited him."

So Barry Attaway was the true culprit. That, too, made sense, because Galen would never do anything to bring Cole back into his life.

"Can I speak to you privately, Mr. President?" Kasey asked.

Barry let out a huff and headed to the door. "I'll wait outside." Levi looked at her warily and moved to stand behind the couch.

In terse silence they waited for the subtle click of the locks. Galen sighed, his shoulders heaving. "Please, Haven, I need—"

"You once blamed Cole for Brooke's death." She stared into his eyes. "Do you still believe that?"

He dipped his head, rubbing his knuckles hard. His jaw muscle popped. Lips went taut. "I recently learned where he was the night . . . the night she died." He shook his head. "He couldn't have been in two places at once."

"I don't understand." Her sister had been brutally beaten to death in their Arlington, Virginia, home by an intruder. Kasey had never understood why Galen thought Cole had killed her.

"Brooke shouldn't have been home that night. She had a fund-raising gala—"

Kasey sniffed a laugh. "She always had a gala." Her sister lived for luxury and high society. It'd been bred into her.

"True. But she was at home. And . . ." His face screwed tight in consternation. "Cole knew a detail he shouldn't have known—at least, I thought so. He justified it with some mention of tactics. But he also apologized to me."

"Apologized? For what?"

Galen shook his head. "I don't know. Guards said our time was up and took him away. I didn't get to ask him again, and it never left me." He let out a sigh. "But with the information that has come to light, I know he wasn't at the house with her that night."

"So you know he was somewhere else?"

Hesitating, Galen considered her. Then nodded.

"Where?" Brazen move but she couldn't *not* ask.

A soft smile pushed aside his momentary lapse into grief. "Sorry, I can't tell you."

"Had to try." She hugged herself. "Look, I know you two didn't speak, even after Evie's birth, but . . . Cole never would have hurt Brooke. Especially not in such a brutal way. He loved her." As much as it pained her to admit.

Galen looked forlorn. "But she wasn't his to love."

"But he did—does. And he has a code."

"You weren't there the day fists and curses flew." Galen straightened. "Haven, whatever you felt for him—all these years you've worked with the Bureau to prove Cole wasn't guilty . . ."

Embarrassed, Kasey dropped her gaze.

"He's not that man anymore, Haven. He's a trained killer."

"*Operator.* A trained Special Forces operator." It still angered her the way he talked about Cole. "And I have a hint of what that type of man is like. I married one." She tried to calm herself, but this . . . "Galen, he was—*is*—your *brother.*"

"Who has been hiding for the last three years. I don't know who he is, where he's been. And with the training he has, with the way he took down a man—" Galen bit down, obviously not intending to mention that. "We can't trust who he's become."

"And yet you're offering him a pardon, despite his having been charged with disobeying lawful orders, Dereliction of Duty under Article 134, and then there's the involuntary manslaughter under Article 199 for his negligent actions leading to the death of the president."

Galen's eyebrow winged up.

Embarrassment rubbed at her cheeks. "He was facing the death penalty—"

"Which they virulently fought."

She sighed and flicked a wrist at him, wanting to move away from her intimate knowledge of Cole's case. "What happens when he returns?"

Galen studied the tip of his polished shoe before looking up at her. "Why do you want to know?" he finally asked.

"You're sending him on a mission." As soon as the words escaped, Kasey felt the tendrils of an idea coiling around her mind.

"What you need to know," Galen said, "is that in light of the ambassador's murder, there is now a credible, deadly threat against America and her allies that must be stopped. It's a mission perfect for Tox."

"You mean, it's a mission where you need someone who's already dead, so you can wash your hands if something goes wrong." Anger churned wild and hot through her veins. Kasey could hardly remain in place. Her calves twitched, demanding she stand and walk out. But she had a better idea. "You'll want an expert trained in deception."

"Haven—"

"Put me on the team."

"No way."

She had never been a particularly forward person. Until it came to something she really believed in. Like Cole. "Put me on the team, or I go to the media with this."

"A threat like that," Levi muttered from behind, "could land you in custody."

Kasey didn't dare pull her gaze from Galen. "You said you don't know where he's been or who he is. My skills can help figure that out. This mission is important or Attaway wouldn't be dragging Cole back from the dead, right?"

Galen's eyes widened a fraction. "You've never cared for Barry."

"Mm," she said with a lift of her shoulder. "You should wonder

42

about that, considering my expertise." She brushed away a strand of hair. "Attaway drew Cole out. Which was dangerous—you both admitted that. So whatever this is, it's big. Important."

Galen sighed.

"Cole might have skills for combat, but I have skills for life. I can be an asset to the team." Maybe even to Cole.

"Levi? You agree still?"

Kasey flinched. "Still?" She frowned at Levi. Then it hit her. "You *knew* about this?" Suddenly, everything roiled into the perfect storm. She turned back to Galen. "Wait. You . . . you wanted me in on this." It was too incredible to believe. "You're using me. That's why I'm here. You knew with my fondness for Cole I'd want to be a part of this."

"Don't give me that much credit."

"Barry." The one person willing to put everyone at risk but himself— and Galen, since it guaranteed his job. Attaway knew her mother's younger brother had gained a new, powerful job. Pardon attorney. "You want me to recommend to my uncle to give the pardon."

"*If* you think he should be pardoned."

— DAY 4 —

JEBEL AL-LAWZ

Air. She just needed fresh air. And light. Air and sunlight.

Tzivia Khalon shifted, her boots suctioning against the mucky earth of the underground cistern. Squatting, she waddled back against a wall of stones. Perfectly placed to protect the well. The south-facing wall had collapsed and revealed the miktereths. But this one, the stones placed perfectly one atop the other was . . . different.

Tracing it, she imagined the hands that had placed the stones. Labored to protect a water source in the forbidding terrain. Someone thousands of years ago. Infused with the humbling realization, she sighed.

"Tired already?"

She glared at Noel. "I've been down here four hours."

"Got you beat by two." He swiveled around with his sieve to work another dump of silt.

"Didn't realize it was a competition."

"Of course it is. If I stay here and you go topside, you get to deal with the Ministry of Health and I don't."

She groaned. She hated being up there with health organizations breathing down their necks. "How's Basil?" The intern had developed

44

boils after joining her in the subterranean area, then couldn't get rid of a nagging cough. He was the first of several at the dig site to fall sick.

"Not good." Noel headed toward the tunnel entrance that led to the sorting tent. "Keeps slipping in and out."

"Has WHO showed up?" That morning Dr. Cathey had warned her they were inbound.

"No idea," Noel said. "You know, the more agencies that get involved, the more likely we'll get shut down."

"Don't jinx us." But that was why she was down here working, not defending her actions topside. She had too much of a temper. That was better left in Dr. Cathey's hands. She dropped back against the wall, allowing the hands of history to support her.

Beneath her weight, a stone shifted. Put her off balance.

"No!" Tzivia flung out a hand to break her fall. Mud splashed her face. Squished between her fingers. "Augh!"

Noel laughed. Too hard and too loud.

Using her calves and thighs, careful not to create more damage, she pushed upright, out of the muck. She used her shoulder to wipe the mud off her face. As she did, Tzivia noticed a rock in the wall had slid back, now sitting at least an inch farther in. She bent forward, her head lamp beam tracing it. "What . . . ?" She'd seen this before—secret hiding places. She swiped her muddied hand down her pant leg as she smoothed her left hand around the stone. It resisted.

"Did you find something?"

Tzivia dug her fingernails into a type of mortar created as years hardened the dirt. She pried. No good. She grabbed the small pick from her tactical belt. Gently picked the mortar away. With a noisy scrape, the rock gave. She drew it out. Rock in hand, she arched back to cast her head lamp into the void.

"Ah," Noel muttered over her shoulder, disappointed. "Just a loose rock."

Light caressed a color variation. She reached in. Three . . . four . . . six inches. The width of her arm blocked her view. Maybe he was right—it was nothing. Loose dirt sifted. She flicked it. Felt something firm but not rocklike. Something . . . She brushed it with her fingers, using her mind's eye to put the shape together. Finally, she found the edges. Lifted it out. As she did, she felt resistance and heard a clanking.

Tzivia frowned and stepped back, letting Noel's lamp bathe the hole. "Parchment," she whispered. Something was tied to it. Clattered out of the hole. She caught it, her heart thudding. Disbelief coiled around her as she stared at the dark piece, marred with mold. "A miktereth!" Number four. A length of red cord tied around the parchment had been secured with wax. Her heart skipped a beat at the seal—Templar! She traced the corner of the parchment, noting it'd been folded. The edges torn. As if it'd been . . . "Bound."

"Then not Bronze Age," Noel said. "But why is it with the miktereth?"

True. Books weren't bound until much later.

"No idea." Tzivia unfolded the parchment. She gaped, staring at the inked lettering. "Early Roman." Such beauty, the precision of writing in columns. Three columns. Wait. She counted the lines . . . twenty-eight. The words at the top: "*cursed be he who steals this*" and others. But mostly—"Cantillation," she breathed.

"What?" Noel asked, his tone pitched. "Are you serious?"

Different handwriting in the margins. Excitement fluttered through her chest. Tzivia whirled. "Baggie!"

Noel frowned but retrieved one from his supplies.

She tucked the miktereth in the plastic bag and sealed it. "I have to find Dr. Cathey!"

"Why?"

Exhilaration shoved her out of the tunnel. She hurried, anticipating his joy. Imagining the look in his weathered gray eyes. Little excited the old professor—he'd done much. Seen even more. *But this . . . !*

Tucking the parchment beneath her shirt, she hurried up the narrow, thinning tunnel to the cave entrance. Immediately, the heat of Saudi Arabia accosted her as she hopped down from the opening, even though the tent covered it. She sprinted past the topside excavation site, drawing looks from the workers. Ignored the white medical tents the Saudi Ministry of Health had set up.

"Dr. Cathey!" Tzivia felt like a kid who'd discovered her first fake dinosaur bone at a museum dig. She stopped short, finding him in the sorting tent. With Maloof. The colonel couldn't care less about

Dr. Cathey's credentials. Here, he had no authority when it came to this officer.

"Ah, Ms. Khalon."

Fire shot up her spine as she locked gazes with Colonel Maloof of the Saudi Commission for Tourism and National Heritage. He had been scavenging from their dig—lamps, pottery shards, wood pieces—since he'd arrived a few days ago. Tzivia froze, praying Maloof didn't notice the miktereths. "We've found nothing new—"

Dr. Cathey moved toward her. His elbow bumped the sorting shelf. A miktereth rolled out from a cubby onto the table, its unusual shape rocking to a stop between them.

Maloof lifted his brows as he retrieved the artifact. "And this?"

Tzivia cursed herself and Dr. Cathey. But she wasn't going to give in easily. Not again. She started forward.

"I wouldn't." Maloof's weapon whipped toward her. "It is our right to reclaim our cultural heritage." A primeval grin smeared across his face. "Even if you Americans do all the work."

"It is *not* right!" Dr. Cathey declared.

The weapon swung at him.

"No!" Tzivia shoved herself between the men. Held up her hands, knowing that with a well-placed knife-hand strike she could cut the breath from the impudent Saudi colonel. But he had soldiers. And more would come if she attacked. Then they'd undoubtedly shut down her dig. "I will take this up with your superior."

"Do that." With a smug, satisfied nod and the censer, Maloof ducked back into the afternoon.

"Why did you let him take it?"

Tzivia whirled. "You just had to bump that shelf!"

"It was an accident—it should have been properly secured. Besides, why did you not use your street skills to stop him?"

"Krav Maga doesn't make me equal to an entire unit!" Tzivia pushed him back to the table as she double-checked that Maloof hadn't returned. "Anyway, look!" She spread the parchment over the table, being sure it wasn't visible to anyone who entered.

Hesitating, Dr. Cathey slid on his glasses and bent over it. He pulled in a long breath. "Tzivia," he breathed. He started mumbling as his thick, hairy fingers traced the lettering but didn't touch it. "This . . ." He shook his head, as if he didn't believe it. "It's a leaf from the Keter Aram Tzova—the Aleppo Codex!"

She bit her lip, watching. Feeling as elated as he looked.

He smiled down at her. "But you already guessed that."

"You're sure?" If Dr. Cathey said it was, then that was as good as carbon dating. Sometimes better.

"Not without more tests, but I am more sure than I have been before." Gray eyes peered over silver rims. "You found this here?"

"In the tunnel where we located the censers." She wagged her hand at Noel, who entered the tent. "And look what else!"

Noel showed him the fourth miktereth.

Dr. Cathey's eyes went grave as he returned to the parchment. That it was not in English was no obstacle to the multilinguist.

A nervous bubble popped her excitement. "What?"

He read,

The Lord said to Moses, "Tell Eleazar son of Aaron, the priest, to remove the censers from the charred remains and scatter the coals some distance away, for the censers are holy—the censers of the men who sinned at the cost of their lives. Hammer the censers into sheets to overlay the altar, for they were presented before the Lord and have become holy. Let them be a sign to the Israelites."

So Eleazar the priest collected the bronze censers brought by those who had been burned to death, and he had them hammered out to overlay the altar, as the Lord directed him through Moses. This was to remind the Israelites that no one except a descendant of Aaron should come to burn incense before the Lord, or he would become like Korah and his followers.

Tzivia stared. "Why do you look like death warmed over?"

Dr. Cathey met her gaze. "It's from Korah's rebellion."

"And?"

"And there was a plague that killed some fourteen thousand Israelites."

Tzivia rolled her eyes, but she couldn't deny the squirming in her stomach. A plague then. A plague now.

"It was only checked by—"

48

"No." Tzivia held up her hand. "No, I'm not listening. I've already had a bad enough day without your proselytizing."

"We must consider this—a miktereth found tied to the leaf. And so close to the others?"

She swallowed.

Dr. Cathey drew out his tablet, tapped and swiped, then showed her the screen. "It is from Numbers 16." He read,

> Moses said to Aaron, "Take your censer and put in it fire from the altar, and lay incense on it; then bring it quickly to the congregation and make atonement for them, for wrath has gone forth from the LORD, the plague has begun!" Then Aaron took it as Moses had spoken, and ran into the midst of the assembly, for behold, the plague had begun among the people.

Tzivia took an involuntary step back, her gaze drifting to the medical tents. She thought of Basil, unconscious with some strange illness.

Without looking at the tablet, Dr. Cathey quoted, "*So he put on the incense and made atonement for the people. He took his stand between the dead and the living, so that the plague was checked. But those who died by the plague were 14,700, besides those who died on account of Korah. Then Aaron returned to Moses at the doorway of the tent of meeting, for the plague had been checked.*'" He lifted his head. Looked so defeated.

"What?"

He glanced down at the fourth censer. "This was Aaron's censer."

"You don't know that."

"But if it was, this—"

"Stopped the plague?" She snorted, hating how harsh it came out, but if he could be vocal with his belief, she could be just as vocal.

"No." He scowled, drawing together those bushy eyebrows. "No, the plague was checked because Aaron offered a sacrifice." Another scowl and he lifted the leaf, muttering to himself.

Tzivia shook her head. "I don't care two wits about some ancient tale as long as we keep the remaining censers out of Maloof's—or anyone else's—hands. At least until we can verify them."

"But now that Maloof has taken one"—he shrugged—"we cannot complete the cycle."

"What cycle?"

He pointed to the leaf. "Unearthing the censers, more specifically, removing the first three from the chest, unleashed the plague Aaron made atonement for."

Anger spat through her veins. "Stop, please. Just . . . stop."

"You have seen the sick and dying!" He motioned toward the medical tents. "Four—*four* have died this week alone. Same illness—protrusions, blackened digits. This is not a coincidence. It is—"

"Don't you dare call it a curse!"

"Then what, Tzivia?"

She tried to swallow against a mouth filled with the sands of Saudi Arabia. The censers. The sick people. "It's just a coincidence." If only her voice carried conviction. But this challenged her scientific reasoning. "We . . . we must've disturbed something when we found the censers—opened the chest," she conceded. "Or a latent bacteria . . . in the wood . . . seeped into the water." Yes, that made sense. Didn't it?

"You fail me with your doubt."

"What would you have me do, Dr. Cathey? Burn a censer from an altar with holy fire?"

"Of course not!"

She sighed in relief.

"You are not from Aaron's line—it would do no good."

"Bah!" She waved a hand dismissively. "God wouldn't listen to me anyway."

He turned, shoulders slumped. "It is painful enough for me to listen." He started toward the entrance.

"Where are you going?"

"I must talk with a colleague." He wagged the leaf at her. "And you should immediately request that fourth censer back. And stop digging."

"Stop—" Tzivia lunged for him. This site was her chance to redeem her name. "Are you crazy? This is my life's work! We have to seize every minute possible before one of those organizations finds a reason to shut me down. I'm *not* stopping now."

"Yes, I am crazy—people are dying and I actually want to make sure nobody else does."

* * * *

— DAY 5 —

WASHINGTON, DC

Exhaustion tugged at Galen as he returned to the White House. He made his way to his bedroom, unknotting his tux's bow tie and stifling a yawn. His mind was weighted. Not with the delicate serenade of Asian officials but the turbulent tango coming.

Where was he? Why hadn't Tox shown yet?

Galen warned his chief of staff to add guards and be alert. But Barry had already done that. Realistically, Tox would link Galen to what happened in Nigeria. He'd assume Galen sent the team.

"Was it good?"

Galen turned at the sweet sound of Evie. His daughter stood, holding the jamb of her door, hair braided and eyes sleepy. He wandered back to her and planted a kiss on the crown of her head. "Boring."

"Figures," she mumbled, deflating against the wood.

"You ready for your trip tomorrow?"

She almost looked alert. "Def!"

"I could tell Eleanor to cancel it. I'm sure she could—"

"Just try keeping me in this asylum." She tiptoed up and kissed his cheek, then whirled around, shutting the door as she called over her shoulder, "'Night, Daddy."

Daddy. The word lodged in his chest. She hadn't called him that in a long while—a sure sign she was excited about going to London. Smiling, he tugged his tie off and unfastened the first two buttons of his shirt. Evie was the most precious gift Brooke had left him. He made his way to his room, waving good-night to the Secret Servicemen. "'Night."

"'Night, sir," they said in unison.

Galen dressed for bed and then stopped. How could he have forgotten? He moved to the credenza at the window, poured himself a glass of bourbon, then tipped it toward heaven, stars dimmed by the lights of downtown DC. "Happy anniversary."

"Got a glass for me?"

Galen spun, the brown liquid splashing over the crystal.

Shadows, heavy and dark, concealed the owner of that voice. Though he didn't need a visual to know, Galen squinted at the form in the armchair by the other window. He gulped the adrenaline that exploded in his veins.

"Tox."

Somehow, the shocked expression on his brother's face bore the same fear Tox had seen in too many eyes before he'd neutralized the threat they posed. And Galen posed a massive risk to Tox. "Why?" he managed around the breath that seemed trapped in his throat. "Why'd you send them?"

Sleeves rolled up, his brother stood like one of the statues lining the gilded halls.

Anger coursed through Tox's veins like venom, hot and poisoning. "I did what you asked—neutralized the threat and vanished."

"I—" Galen shook his head. "It wasn't me, Tox."

Three large strides delivered him across the semi-darkened room. His fist drove straight into Galen's face. His brother went down hard, unconscious.

Tox stood over him, hand throbbing. Molars clamped did nothing to tame the storm within. Trembling, he eased himself onto the edge of a nearby chair. Elbows on his knees, he watched a stream of blood slip from his brother's lip. As Tox waited for the adrenaline to fade, for the shaking to stop, he stared at the carpet.

He hadn't lost control like that in a long time. Chiji would be disappointed.

Who was he kidding? *Tox* was disappointed. But his brother had always been able to bring out the worst in him. Turned everything into a competition. All their lives, Galen had everything—the girls, the grades, the pretty-boy looks . . .

Dad's approval.

Tox had one thing—Brooke. The best thing since the Glock 22.

Then Galen took her. Popular as royalty, Galen and Brooke had climbed the political ladder to the White House, complete with their perfect child. Tox hadn't talked to them since their wedding.

But just like he'd walked into that trap in West Africa a week ago on the off chance his niece was in trouble, he'd come here. To give his brother the opportunity to explain.

Just like his choice in love, Tox's choices in life had sent him on a bullet train to disaster. Didn't matter that he'd qualified for Special Forces school as one of the youngest in history. Didn't matter the medals he'd earned. Didn't matter the lives he'd saved. Dad had never approved. Mom only feared for his life, couldn't see the hero behind the uniform or the ultimate good he'd done. Army life fed him, clothed him, and drove him. Right into the federal pen, where shame smothered what little pride he had left.

Tox rubbed his knuckles, his gaze sliding around the room and ignoring his brother's unconscious form. The original artwork. Signed baseballs. Leather-bound books. Pictures . . .

A gold-framed photo on the nightstand snagged his attention. Even from here, he'd recognize her—slightly rounded face, dark brown hair cut to her shoulders. She'd worn it long in high school. He could still remember its silkiness in his hands. And her brown eyes. They had been "the" couple in school. But he hadn't wanted a life like his parents' nor did he have Galen's political aspirations. So he went to Basic. Then Iraq. And lonely Brooke found power-hungry Galen.

He curled his fingers into a tight fist. He needed answers, and though he'd created interference on the security feeds to protect his movements tonight, it wouldn't last long. He shouldn't have coldcocked his brother. Couldn't get answers from an unconscious man. But the anger had possessed him like a demon.

Chiji had warned Tox about coming. Said he'd end up in prison. Again. He wished for a comms piece to talk to his friend. To hear the steady voice that acted as his conscience.

His gaze slid to the door, where light peeked over the threshold. Two Secret Service agents were within shouting distance out in the hall. Well, they were *unconscious* agents right now, but that wouldn't last long either. Knocking them out was necessary, but there were other, much more conscious agents throughout this cold marble castle of Washington.

And none of them had stopped Tox from reaching his brother. He could've killed Galen. A piece of him wanted to.

Galen groaned and shifted on the floor.

"You used Evie."

His brother started, mind still swimming in apparent confusion at how he'd ended up on the floor. His blue eyes met Tox's as he used the back of his hand to wipe the blood from his mouth. "You knocked me out. You know what they'll do to you—"

"She's your daughter and you used her to get to me."

"And you texted her a threat."

He gave Galen a pointed look. "I'd never hurt her. You don't—"

"It wasn't me." Galen peeled himself off the floor and stumbled toward a chair. "Think I'd wave her *anywhere* under your nose? I didn't even know you were alive." He dropped into it heavily. "It was Barry. He baited you back here."

Tox flexed his jaw muscle. "He wanted me, so I came."

"Wait, you knew West Africa was a trap." Galen frowned. "And you knew this was a trap, too. That he—"

"What do you want from me?" On his feet, Tox tucked his hands under his armpits.

"I don't—"

Tox scowled, silencing his brother's denial. They were running out of time. "This about Lammers?"

Galen twitched, confirming Tox's theory that they'd brought him out for something connected to the ambassador. His brother finally nodded. "He was killed in London."

"Overkill."

His brother hesitated, a frown covering a face that looked more like their father's now that Galen was in his mid-forties. "What do you mean?"

"They could've killed him anywhere, quietly. But they killed him in public."

Galen grunted.

"It was a message." He met his brother's gaze evenly. "One you want me to answer. Right?"

A whisper of commotion outside gave him the necessary warning. Shadows scampered across the well-lit threshold.

"I can't believe you're alive."

Holding his brother's gaze, Tox went to his knees and threaded his hands behind his head.

"What're—"

The door burst in. Light flooded the room. "Mr. President!"

Footsteps thudded behind Tox. Weight plowed into his back, sending him face first into the thick rug. A knee planted against his neck forbade him from moving.

"Easy, easy!" Galen shouted to the agents who secured him. Two more held weapons on him.

"Tox Russell." Ah, Barry Attaway had returned. Probably ticked more than ever that Tox had gotten past the added detail. "How'd you get in here?"

Hands grabbed Tox's arms and secured him with zip cuffs. They hauled him to his feet.

Tox hated games. Hated playing the games. And hated even more the man behind the games. He balled as much of that putrid hatred as he could into his gaze as he faced the chief of staff. "Isn't that what you wanted?"

The steady thump of footsteps preceded a stream of men in tactical gear. Six . . . eight . . . ten men swarmed the hall.

Attaway glowered. "Get him out of here."

Wood dug into Kasey's knees as she knelt before the oversized antique handed down from her great-grandmother, a hope chest intended for girls looking to the future—a husband and children. Kasey had given up on that dream when Chaplain Vogt arrived with two officers, on the day that should've been their first anniversary, to inform her Duarte would not be coming home. Ever again.

She removed the preserved wedding dress and set it aside, along with the wad of grief that pushed its way from the past. She dug around the wedding album, her scrapbooks from high school and college, down past her yearbooks. Her hair broke free from its bun, sandy hair tumbling into her face. "Ugh." She dove deep, as if digging for gold. And to her, it was gold. "I know it's in here."

Her hand hit something beneath a stack of vinyl records, and the crinkle of paper reached her ears.

That's it! A jolt of excitement shot through her as she gripped the packet and freed it. With it came memories, unbidden. Warm and sweet. Clutching the brown paper bag in both hands, she shifted around and slumped against the wall, knees up. With care, she unfolded it. Drew out the bundled stack of photos. Some were almost two decades old. Some a little newer, but not by much. He'd vanished from their lives nearly fifteen years ago.

Sliding off the band that secured the photos felt like awakening the dead. As the gray acid-free band slid away, his face took shape on the first photo. She breathed a smile and relaxed against the wall. Always so handsome, in a rugged, bad-boy sort of way. That was what had drawn Brooke to him in the first place. Cole had never fit in. He'd done things his way. Never cared what others thought.

Kasey traced a finger over his attractive features—his hair shorn, his grin dangerous. She snorted at her thoughts. Her finger moved, uncovering her sister's image. And that familiar hot poker of jealousy seared Kasey. "You didn't deserve him," she whispered.

It'd been poetic, she'd thought, that Brooke died one week and Cole the next. Even though the two hadn't spoken for almost ten years by then. "What did you see in her?" She remembered screaming that into her pillow after he and Brooke had left on a date.

She went to the next photo. Prom. Behind that one, him at the pool at her parents' house. Shirtless. Though now she was fourteen years older, a widow, and knew better, Kasey blushed. He'd worked out even then. Enough that her twelve-year-old self had crushed hard and long on Cole Russell.

Her parents' only concern had been that the Russells and Linwoods be irrevocably linked. Her family's money and his family's power combined for an indomitable dynasty. It was so eighteenth century. She had hated it. Especially because it meant *she* wouldn't be Cole's wife. Her sister would. But then fickle, self-absorbed Brooke dumped the military hero with a Dear John letter and married his brother.

Her breath caught when her gaze landed on a shot taken at the wedding. The last time she'd seen him. In the photo, Haven stood off to the side, eyes on Cole, who—of course—was oblivious to her. As he always had been.

Even in his tailored suit, he had an edge to him. Simmering in anger. She was surprised he'd even attended. Though "attended" might have been an overstatement. He *brooded*. Clung to the corners and shadows. Avoided conversation. Avoided *people*. Classic Cole.

She'd said hi, but he'd muttered hello and moved off without even looking at her. Thirty minutes later he'd left the reception. Brooke hadn't noticed. Galen had, but shrugged off his brother's departure to enjoy his wedding.

Twelve-year-old Haven, furious with her sister and Galen, made a vow that night—to always love Cole Russell. It was naïve. She was only a preteen. And she never saw him again.

She grew up.

He went to prison.

She married a Navy SEAL.

He died—supposedly.

She buried her husband.

Kasey lifted the photo closer in the waning light. "Where have you been all these years?"

"Who?"

Kasey blinked and looked at her bedroom door. Her roommate and best friend, Emilie, stood there, looking smart with her glasses and dark-brown hair. Memories of Cole faded into a mist of guilt and embarrassment. Kasey tucked the photos back into the chest. "Nobody."

A buzz drew her attention to her phone on the floor nearby. She saw the screen and Levi's name. She groaned—but stopped as she read his text: HE'S HERE.

The words pushed Kasey to her feet, and she closed the hope chest, watching the brown paper bag vanish—just like Cole had so many years ago. "Sorry, Em. Gotta run."

"Say hi to Levi for me."

"Right." Minutes later, dressed in nondescript tan slacks, a white blouse, and navy blazer, Kasey rushed out of the house.

She hopped into her compact car, quadruple-checked that the text said what she thought, and pulled into traffic.

Cole. Enigma. Mystery man. Dead. Resurrected. With WGTS, the DC-metro Christian station pumping out music to steady her nerves, Kasey wove in and out of traffic, growled at red lights, and nailed her brakes at stop signs. Brooke had brought Cole home for the first time on the weekend of Kasey's tenth birthday. He was tall, dark-haired, and had blue eyes that melted her soul.

The blare of a horn startled her. She flinched, thinking she'd crossed lanes, but it wasn't her they'd honked at.

The exit raced up on her.

Kasey whipped the car across two lanes of traffic and wedged in between a semi and a tow truck. A few minutes later, she arrived at the secure entrance of the White House. When her vehicle was cleared, she hurried up to the security access point and turned over her purse and keys. She got wanded, then as she retrieved her belongings, she spotted Levi coming down the other side of the hall.

He shot her a grin. "Agent Cortes."

Purse on her arm, she nodded. "Agent Wallace." She joined him, and they headed in the opposite direction, his gaze never leaving her.

"Are you going to hate me forever for not telling you?"

She had never been one to hold a grudge, though it seemed she was in the minority among the people she knew. "Maybe a day shorter," she said.

He managed a smile, that attraction glinting in his eyes again.

Her mind, her thoughts, her ramming pulse, however, were focused elsewhere. "When'd he show up?"

"They discovered him late last night."

"Discovered?"

"In the president's bedroom."

Kasey widened her eyes. "He got past security?" Okay, maybe that wasn't the best thing to say while surrounded by those who were supposed to protect the president. And failed.

"He got past everyone. Assaulted the president."

Kasey stopped. "What?" She wanted to say Cole wouldn't do that, but he'd always been intense. And whatever he'd been through the last three years since his purported death . . .

"Busted his lip." Levi escorted her through a few more security checkpoints until they were walking down to a cement bunker. "They've got him locked up. Questioning him."

"That sounds a lot like *torturing* him."

At the end of the corridor, a cluster of suits and uniforms gathered. The thrum of excitement and conversation reverberated through the area.

"He's caused a stir."

"Kase," Levi said, catching her arm, gently stopping her. He towered over her, his unique scent of woods and spice embracing her. "Be careful."

She frowned. "What do you mean?"

"There's a reason they've got him down here." His expression waxed soft. "I don't want you to get hurt."

There was something in Levi's words, his demeanor, that made her falter.

"Also, the president doesn't want you to reveal your identity to him."

She scoffed. "You don't think he'll know?"

"He hasn't seen you in almost fifteen years. You were pretty young."

Agitation cinched her throat. She wanted to argue that Cole would know. That he would flat-out recognize her. She was sure of it. She smiled. "I'll be okay."

"Agent Cortes?"

Kasey turned toward the voice. Barry Attaway waited with a man in a dark blue suit—FBI? CIA?—and a 1-star. Her stomach squirmed, feeling suddenly and distinctly out of her league.

"Don't let them scare you," Levi whispered as he brandished his ID to the guard who separated her from the high ranks. "Remember, the Office of the Pardon Attorney will base their decision on your report. You're holding the golden ticket for him, and without that—"

"I will not taunt him with a reward. He's either worthy of the pardon"—siphoning from Levi's strength, Kasey forced out the last part—"or he's not."

"And we have to consider that very real possibility."

"Right." Golden ticket. But the bigger problem nagged at her— what would she do when Cole recognized her? She might have been invisible to his Brooke-blind self back then, but Cole Russell never missed a thing.

BLESSED IS HE WHO PRESERVES IT

"What do you want?" Benyamin Cohen struggled to push the question past his frantic heartbeat as he stared at the man standing in his living room. From somewhere came an icy breath, swirling, slowing his heart rate.

Digging his fingernails into the padded armrests of his wheelchair did little to help Ben get a grip on his sanity. He hadn't thought death so close. "Who are you?"

There should be a halo of light around the man if he were an angel. Yes, light. But there wasn't light. So he was a demon then?

"Come for my soul, have you?"

Hands clasped in front of him, the man remained in the hallway, silent.

Yet . . .

Ben could feel it. Could feel . . . whatever it was. "Why are you in my home?"

"It is time," the man spoke, his voice resonating like a shofar.

"Time? Time for what? To die?" Ben shoved away the panic. Challenge solidified in his chest.

Gratzia came to mind. Her final moments as she lay on their bed. They'd been through a lot. Escaping Damascus in their youth. Living in Israel, then coming to New York, where they'd raised their three children as he ran the shop.

Illness had been his adversary. He'd consistently lost battles in the last decade, but Ben didn't feel ready to release the reins of life. There were months, if not years, to be had and conquered. Surely.

"*Sabba?*" Alison's voice called to him from an empty hollowness. Ben dared not look away from this intruder.

Wizened eyes held his. "Truths are known to you, Benyamin Cohen."

Ice snapped through his veins. "Nobody knows that name." At least, not anyone alive. "Who are you?" he demanded louder this time, feeling the squeeze of panic in his chest.

Chest. Yes. His hand went to his chest. Smoothed his jacket. Tugged the lapels tighter. He was safe with it. "How did you get in?"

"Sabba, I let myself in, as I always do." Round-faced Alison stepped into the room, tossing a dish towel over her right shoulder. Puffs of white on her black blouse betrayed her efforts in the kitchen.

The stranger had said little and moved less. He must be a demon, for he tormented Ben with his silence. They stared at each other in the gaping void, a challenge. A duel. Ben would not yield. "Get out!"

"Sabba?" Alison came from the front door, and in the dark shadows of his mind, he thought perhaps she'd been checking the locks. But fright and old age addled a mind so.

"You can no longer protect that which cannot be protected," the man finally said.

"I don't know what you're talking about!" But he did. It burned against his chest even now, his heart writhing under it. And he could almost hear it crinkling, cracking beneath that burning. "Leave me be!"

"Sabba" came Alison's soft, pleading voice.

Ben blinked, and instead of the stranger's baleful gaze, brown eyes probed his. The fragrance of vanilla and flour clung to his grand-daughter as she bent over him. "Alison," he whispered, disbelieving. Was she in danger? He caught her shoulder and looked behind her.

They were alone. In his apartment in Brooklyn. The kitchen—it sat empty. The bathroom—dark and vacant. He strained to see down the short hall to his bedroom. Was the man lurking there? Where had he gone?

"Sabba, is something wrong?"

The quiet lull of her voice drew him back. "Alison . . ." Had she not seen the man? Why did she not react?

"Yes, Sabba. It's me." Long, soft fingers touched his cheek, their gentleness reflected in her mahogany eyes. So like Gratzia's. "I'm baking scones for you. Blueberry—your favorite."

Again, he searched the foyer. Only the umbrella stand and hat rack stood in the shadows now.

"It's warm." She reached for his jacket. "Let me help you take this off, and you'll be—"

"No!" He swatted at her hands. "Leave me!"

"But you're sweating, Sabba."

"Leave me!" When her eyes widened and she drew in a sharp breath, Ben deflated. He crumpled in on himself, disappointed. Frightened. She would think him mad. Believe he'd lost his faculties. He could not let her think that of him. "Forgive me." He patted his wrinkly, arthritic hands over her soft, supple fingers. The contrast struck him as sharp. Poignant. The past and present colliding. Just as the parchment promised. "Perhaps some water?" He dragged his palm over his forehead. "I find I'm thirsty." From fright?

She smiled. Every inch her *savta* all over again. "Of course, Sabba."

Probing the shadows once more, he mentally followed Alison into the kitchen. Who was the man who'd stolen into his home and haunted him?

His fingertips grazed the wool jacket, the rough texture comforting. Reassuring.

Yes, yes, he would be safe.

Fire bled through every cell and pore of Tox's body. The pain pulled at him, drowning him in an agony he could never have imagined. Darkness crept in, deeper and heavier than the blackest of nights. Tempting him to let go. Taunting him with the mockery of his life, his worthless life.

And yet, somehow through the thickness of pain and despair, a figure appeared. Brightened against an ebony sea above him. Took shape. Grew larger, stronger.

Dead. I'm dead!

A white tunic emblazoned with a red cross swam through Tox's vision as the man reached for him.

Heat roaring across his chest, Tox flinched at the memory. Shuddered away the haunting darkness of it. No, he hadn't really seen a man in those flames. It'd been the pain—being trapped alive in a cave-in. Terrified of dying, he lost focus. Kafr al-Ayn had ruined a lot of things, but Tox wouldn't let it ruin his mind. He'd told the story once, only once, of seeing that conjured knight. Then recanted. Shoved the memory as far from his consciousness as possible. It wasn't real. Couldn't be.

Clank. Clank. Hisssss. Clank.

With a heavy groan, the reinforced steel door receded into the wall enough for a man to enter. Dressed in Navy combat dress with no insignia. No rank or unit designation. It was as if he'd pulled the uniform off a Goodwill rack. Black-and-blue eyes and a crooked nose. He'd been in a bad fight, but he wore it with comfort and ease, like a second skin. He was here to interrogate Tox. Tox gritted his teeth and pushed his gaze back to the blank wall.

With practiced calm and precision, the sailor interrupted Tox's stare. He seemed familiar. "You came in for a reason. Knew Nigeria was a trap."

Everything's a trap.

"But I imagine with your training, you know everything's a trap." He folded his arms and tucked his hands under his armpits. "Attaway says you were free out there in Nigeria."

As free as a dog on a leash.

"But since they had your location, we both know you weren't *free*."

In the place that had been his home for the last three years, Tox had learned to sit for hours, thinking. Searching for what eluded him: peace. Talking didn't bring it. Fighting didn't bring it. Family sure didn't bring it. Now he could stand for as long as necessary in silence. A comfortable silence that would annoy the crud out of these interviewers.

"I think you came for a reason. A purpose." The sailor stood less than four feet away. Just far enough back in case Tox chose to test the durability of the chains anchoring his wrist and ankles to large hooks in the floor. "I think you're here because we ticked you off in Nigeria."

Knew he looked familiar. He was the commander of the team who'd tried to capture Tox. Tried. Failed. But wanted Tox to know it was him. Interesting.

"Your vitals are normal. You're not agitated. You're not demanding to see your brother." The sailor squared his shoulders. "So what do you want, Sergeant Russell?"

Sergeant Russell died three years ago.

"You're not leaving this room until we get answers."

Wholly untrue. Tox didn't need to look into his eyes to detect the lie so easily carried in his posture and words. They were baiting him. Again.

Shouldering in, the sailor caught the steel bar bracing Tox's hands. "How'd you get them to set you free?"

The words burned his conscience. Tox still denied his gaze to the sailor, even as the fool leaned closer.

"Because of you, the president and villagers died—and SEALs."

Few knew what really happened three years ago in Kafr al-Ayn, a village south of Damascus, Syria. Tox had been roped into the black op to rescue then-President Montrose, held hostage by a terrorist wielding a relic that gave him a god complex and a truckload of insanity. The relic emitted a toxin that resulted in the deaths of dozens of villagers. When U.S. forces dropped a couple of bombs on the terrorists, the president had been a casualty. The world wanted someone to pay. Tox and his team were the lucky fools. His team lost their careers to life in a federal pen. Tox lost his freedom. Regret was Tox's first, middle, and last name.

But then . . . then came an opportunity. One that should've made *this* impossible.

Clank. Clank. Hisssss. Clank.

The sailor gave a slight shove against Tox's restraints and stepped back. Planted himself against the wall. Tox held his gaze, noting in his periphery the soldiers entering.

"Commander MacIver," one said, "we need you to clear the room, sir."

"What's going on?"

"Taking him to another location." The guard motioned to the corridor. Four more guards entered, long poles extended between chains. So much for the freedom promised him for carrying out "one final mission." He knew better than to believe back-office deals made in the dead of night. But this . . . this was Tox's chance to settle a score with Barry Attaway.

And the chief of staff knew that.

They led him by leash and collar to another cement cage. As they entered, Tox took in the room. In the center, a raised cement dais boasted a cement block. His place to stand trial, he guessed.

A plexiglass wall separated him from the other half of the room, which sported a rectangular conference table with twelve comfy leather chairs. Eight of them occupied.

A faint buzz sounded. The chains slumped to the ground. Guards backed out. Tox stood alone, steel weight pulling against his arms and ankles. Only as he dragged his feet toward the dais did he realize the steel links were resisting. Then he noticed the subtle thrum.

"The floor and walls are magnetized." A voice reverberated throughout the tank.

Tox slid his gaze to his audience and, behind the glass, found Barry Attaway beneath the glare of a fluorescent light panel that drowned the room behind him in darkness. Try as he might, Tox could not keep the animosity and unquenchable thirst to kill that man from his eyes. "We made a deal, Attaway," he growled.

Barry removed his glasses and motioned to the cement block. "Have a seat, Russell."

Tox squinted to make out the shapes skulking in the half-darkened room. Commander MacIver entered, allowing a brief glimpse of light to stretch over the others. A couple of suits and two women. FBI—the guy looked familiar. And—

He hesitated. Attaway's spotlight struck a shoulder—he noted the uniform, the star on the shoulder, then the face eased from the darkness. "*Major General* Rodriguez." So he'd gotten a promotion since their last encounter three years ago when Rod had sent Tox's team after the relic-wielding terrorist.

"Please, Sergeant Russell," another voice said, "we should get on with this."

Tox rotated his wrists as much as he could with his restraints. "What are we getting on with? Last I was told, I had a get-out-of-jail-free card." Zeroing his gaze on Attaway didn't help his annoyance. "Why am I here?"

"You came to us."

His muscles constricted involuntarily. "I don't take kindly to my niece being used as bait. If you wanted me, you obviously knew how to contact me."

"And you would've come?" MacIver asked. "If we'd simply asked?"

Tox weighed the man's question and the challenge therein.

"Sergeant Russell," said one of the women, "quite frankly, we need your expertise."

"What expertise is that, ma'am?" He squinted, trying to make out her face in the darkness. Her voice was older, experienced. "Who am I talking to?"

"It's best we keep names out of this" came a male voice.

He'd been right. "So this isn't about my experience." He eyeballed each shape around the table. "You want me to put my butt on the line, but you won't tell me your names or let me see your faces. You trust me to do this mission, but you don't trust me to stand before you without killing you."

"Without compromising us." Light bloomed through the rest of the room. A man in a suit stood. "You're right, Sergeant Russell. I'm Rick Hamer, director of—"

"Special Activities Division." Tox knew the name because, though he might have vanished from the grid, he hadn't been a stranger to it either. They should be glad they'd cuffed him. SAD was the same organization that'd ordered the bomb for Kafr al-Ayn, killed the president, and engulfed Tox in a fireball.

The man hesitated before pointing to his right. "My colleague, Dru Iliescu."

CIA. DoD. The White House.

Hamer focused a hard stare on Tox. "We're coordinating this effort through a small branch under our purview."

"You mean, it doesn't officially exist."

"Just as you don't."

Tox gritted his teeth and slid his gaze to the slimeball in the room. "This is smelling a lot like another ambush, Attaway."

"Sergeant Russell—"

"Died three years ago," Tox growled to Hamer.

With a nod, the director acquiesced. "There is a situation that desperately needs your skill set."

"Stop lying to me."

Hamer walked around the table and stood with his toes to the bulletproof and shatterproof glass. "I get it. They screwed you over. Broke promises. It's a crappy mess they handed you."

Placating. Establishing a relationship with the target. Almost as bad as baiting. Possibly the same thing.

"Russell, we need you. We need you to do something nobody else can do."

"Bull."

Confusion flickered through Hamer's gaze. "Sorry?"

"Don't feed me some pile of manure about how I'm the only one who can do this." Tox nodded to the sailor who'd nearly taken him in Nigeria. "He has the skills. Heck, even that suit next to you might have the skills." *Easy, easy* . . . There was no question why they wanted him. "But the only qualifications you really need are expendability and deniability. That's me. Right?"

Hamer swiped a finger down his nose.

Yeah. Thought so. "Forget it. Let me go or put me back in prison." No more baiting. No more collars or leashes. "Or kill me. I don't care."

"What about a full, legitimate pardon?"

Whoever had spoken had a voice like warm honey. Or hot oil. He wasn't sure which. One was great for baiting flies. Another for boiling. Either way the flies ended up dead.

His gaze skipped around the table. A young blonde pushed to her feet. The FBI agent caught her arm, but she tugged free with a reassuring word to the suit. Athletic but thin, she had a presence all her own. Everyone in the room had locked onto her. Including Tox. Especially after those words—a pardon.

Words *too* sweet to be honey. Therefore, oil.

They were out of their minds if they thought throwing an attractive, naïve woman at his feet would coerce him into their game.

She smoothed her tan slacks as she drew in a breath. "President Russell has requested that a full pardon be granted to you upon completion of this mission. Upon my recommendation."

— DAY 6 —

WASHINGTON, DC

The way he drilled holes through every morsel of her courage made her tremble. Cole owned the room. And everyone, including Kasey, knew it. Raw intensity rolled off him, even though he was chained to a cement tank.

That was the power of Cole Russell. That was the reason she'd fallen hard for him as a teen. In fact, standing here in front of him wasn't much different than the days when he'd dated Brooke. Though he might look at her, he still looked *through* her. As if she didn't exist.

Clasping her hands in front of her, Kasey ignored the urge to cower. She moved to the glass. "Did you hear me, Mr. Russell?" It felt strange to speak to him formally, but she'd honor Galen's wishes. For now.

Though he hadn't answered, he also hadn't told her off. She'd expected that from him, not this stony silence. Icy. Chilling.

His jaw muscle flexed and popped. Blue eyes narrowed.

Her stomach flipped. Then flopped. What was he thinking? Would he reject the offer?

"Is this the golden ticket?"

Hearing him speak the same words Levi used knotted her stomach. "I'm sor—"

"Attaway, you send a hot chick to do the work you weren't man enough—"

"That's not what's going on here," Barry said from the corner. "You know that, if you think about it."

Cole turned his steely gaze back to her. "How long have you worked for the pardon attorney's office?"

Whiplashed by his change of topic, Kasey blinked. "I don't."

He snorted. "FBI." He'd always had an uncanny ability to gauge a situation and person. "How long?"

"I started a year ago."

"One year." The words came out crisp and sharp. "And these wolves bring you into the den with me?"

He still had that raw intensity she'd seen as a kid, but now it was amplified a thousand times. Levi was right. She didn't know Cole anymore. In a few words, he'd managed to destroy her Pollyanna view of him.

She wouldn't look at Barry or Levi. This was her and Cole. If she couldn't sell it, then he wouldn't have a chance at freedom. "What does it matter who comes in here as long as you get what you want, Mr. Russell?"

"It matters, Miss—"

"*Mrs.* Cortes," she said quickly, then corrected herself. "Agent Cortes."

"Mrs. Cortes, it matters because if you don't have the power to deliver the goods, we're wasting time and money."

"Is that what matters to you, time and money?"

"It matters to them."

"But not to you."

He stared. "Can you deliver, Mrs. Cortes?"

"Would I be here if I couldn't?"

"Do you have a record that supports your claim?"

She had to prove herself. How? Feeling the familiar ache of her shoulder injury, she folded her arms over her chest, knowing he'd misread it.

"Am I making you defensive, Mrs. Cortes?"

She shot him a smile. "What? Folded arms?"

"Universal sign of deception."

"Wrong," she said forcefully. "There are no universal signs of deception. Folded arms could mean the person is cold or, as in my case, has a shoulder injury."

He shifted on his cement chair, leaned slightly to the side, and scratched his chin. Good.

"Am I making you defensive, Mr. Russell?"

His cheek twitched beneath probing blue eyes. "Annoyed."

"This whole thing, you believing this is all about you, is annoying." She took a measured breath before going on. "We have a situation. You have skills. Is it hard to believe we need your help?"

"When there are hundreds of black baggers around the globe who could handle this situation, yeah. It's hard to buy." A flicker shot through his brow. "Where'd you go to college?"

Kasey tried to lasso the question that came out of nowhere. "George Mason."

"Cum laude?"

"Summa," she responded, caught in his web that easily plucked answers from her.

"Impressive." He gave a slow nod, his gaze burning through every reserve she had. And having to prove herself every day in a man's world, as an FBI agent, she'd created some hefty reserves. "Expert in deception?"

She refused to move.

"Does he know her?" someone at the table whispered.

A grunt from another. "His questions are probing."

Crows feet scratched at his eyes. Amusement. He enjoyed this. Enjoyed making them nervous. Making her sweat.

"I don't like the way he's looking at her," someone else whispered.

Cole cocked his head. "Family? Lovers?"

"We're getting off task," Levi said, his reflection sliding up into her periphery as he came to his feet behind her. The flurry of conversation blended into the thrum of the A/C system. She flashed a palm to silence the men barking orders but not reclaiming the control Cole had stolen.

Cole *was* probing. For what, she didn't know. Why was he asking so many personal questions? Had he figured out her identity already?

Levi joined her. "Back on track, Russell."

"I see you brought an attack dog, Mrs. Cortes." Cole's gaze lazily shifted between Kasey and Levi. "Most married women don't make it a habit to bring a lover into the game."

Kasey stepped back. "Lover—"

"Hey!" Levi barked at the same time.

"But then, you aren't married any longer, are you, Mrs. Cortes?" How could he possibly know that?

"In fact, you weren't married very long at all."

"Get her out of here," an officer snapped.

A presence loomed at her side—Levi, no doubt. "Kasey—"

"I'm fine." When hands clamped onto her shoulders and tugged her back, she wrested free. "I'm not a mule you need to drag around."

"Relax." Levi guided her out of the limelight. "He's agitating you—"

"He's not, actually."

"Please, Agent Cortes," Barry said, "it's best if you leave. Your presence isn't necessary at this point."

"If Mrs. Cortes leaves, I leave." The finality of Cole's words crackled through the room with chilling severity.

The team turned to him, their minds no doubt churning and tumbling over his threat. Would he truly not cooperate if she left?

"What are the terms?" Cole's voice bounced off the walls and bulletproof glass. "What's the mission?" He paused. "What do you want me to do that nobody else can do?"

10

Three men in hazardous materials suits lifted the thick black bag containing the body of Basil Hamilton. Another bag conveyed the remains of a second man, a local worker. Bulbous protrusions from his neck and groin had made it hard for Tzivia to look before they sealed the bag. Knowing his wife and six children were outside made it harder. The hazmat team rolled the bodies through a series of chambers designed to keep the contaminated separate from the uncontaminated.

Two weeks. Ten men, so far, had succumbed. And still they were no closer to figuring out how this had happened. Was the room they'd uncovered infected with something? Or perhaps something in the chest that fell apart? The cloth . . . she remembered a cloth the censers were wrapped in. If they were from the Bronze Age, plagues were as common as today's cold, coming and going almost at will.

Her dig was a disaster again. Just like Kafr. And now the Ministry of Health and the UN were rushing in with soldiers and regulations, locking the site down until whatever happened could be determined, contained, or stopped.

Tzivia shuddered a breath, looking at the dozen men still in isolation chambers, unconscious. Disfigured by disease. Dying.

"It's gone!"

Tzivia pivoted toward Noel, her stomach plummeting. "What?"

"Number two."

She sagged in defeat. The second censer they'd found. She'd sent the fourth with Dr. Cathey, thankfully. And she'd been working with number three. "You're sure?" Did a missing relic really matter when people were dying?

"Absolutely. You're sure you secured it?"

"Of course I did." She glowered.

He widened his eyes.

Tzivia regretted her sharp tone. "I'm sorry. I just . . . I can't believe this is happening." She wandered back to the main room and glanced around, gingerly touching the sorting table. "I placed it there and locked it." But she remembered seeing a worker lingering . . . "Bhavin." She cupped her forehead. "Bhavin Narang was hanging around. I couldn't figure out why."

Noel paled. "I tried to find him a few hours ago, to get some help cataloging, and one of the workers said he'd taken a Jeep and left the site. I assumed he'd had enough of being surrounded by plague."

"But this makes no sense." The censers would yield little on the black market. She pointed to the sorting table that bore jewelry and pottery shards. "All these jewels, gold. But he takes a censer?"

She rubbed her temple, depressed about the dying men and the imminent failure of yet another dig. Her heart cramped with grief. "I would give away all these treasures if it meant those men did not die."

The sickening potion of antiseptic and antibacterial solution, mingled with the rank stench of vomit, rotting flesh, and feces, wafted into the room. Nausea surged up her throat, demanding escape, but she choked it back. Dr. Ellison, the head of the UN medical team, emerged from the second decontamination chamber.

"How are they?" she asked, bracing for bad news that seemed as virulent as whatever was infecting the dig team.

He stood almost a foot taller than her five-six, and his stooped shoulders were indicative of his desire to lessen that height. Today, she knew they sagged more than usual because of the weight oppressing them. "It's not good."

She followed him from the tent into the scorching afternoon sun. With a skip to keep up with his long strides, Tzivia stayed close as they headed across the cordoned-off area to two large trailers, connected with joints and locks, that formed a massive mobile science laboratory. Dr. Ellison diverted and aimed to another trailer that served as offices and quarters for the medical team.

"Are you any closer to identifying it?" she asked, anxious for answers. For relief from this nightmare.

He shook his head, reaching the mobile office. They stepped inside, the air conditioning a shocking reprieve from the Saudi heat. Dr. Ellison strode to the back, where his small desk of clutter and crumpled coffee cups waited. He dropped into a chair and let out a heavy exhale. "I've never seen anything like it." Weariness tugged at his gray eyes, which matched his salt-and-pepper hair. "Traces of one disease, markers for another." He shrugged and held up his hands. "Bubonic is generally treatable if caught early and antibiotics administered."

"So why are they dying?"

"Because it's also septicemic, in the bloodstream. As I said—traces of one, elements of another."

"Can you stop it? Are we safe to resume digging?"

His intelligent expression furrowed. "Is that all you care about?"

"No, what I care about is the people I hire falling ill. If they can't go in those tunnels, I want to send home anyone not infected."

"Until we find out what it is and how they're being exposed, whether through the spring down there or airborne or contact, nobody's leaving."

Frustration coiled around her weary body. The medical team had been here for a week and were no closer to finding answers. "This is so insane." She was beginning to feel like the plague whisperer, drawing the diseases of the past into the present. This site had been her chance for redemption.

He eyed her, his jaw sliding to the side as he took on a speculative look. "What I want to know is how your blood is clear. Why haven't you gotten sick?"

It sounded like an accusation. Tzivia took a step back. Crossed her arms. "I stood in the same room that Basil was in. I worked the same tunnels as those men, so if you're suggesting I'm somehow to blame . . ." Her courage waned when he didn't argue. "Look, I'm not the only one—Noel hasn't come down with it."

"Actually . . ." He slid a few files across his desk and lifted one marked GARELLI, NOEL. He flipped it open. Pointed to a rectangular section near the bottom, where it read: SUBJECT INFECTED. NO VISIBLE SYMPTOMS.

Tzivia frowned. What did that mean? "So . . . he has it."

Dr. Ellison nodded. "He has it."

"But he's not—"

"Not sick." Sighing, he flapped the file closed. "He's a carrier. Happens every so often that an individual can carry a disease but doesn't succumb to it." He stabbed a finger at her. "But you."

Again, the accusation. Tzivia swallowed.

"You aren't sick or carrying." His steel eyes narrowed. "Why?"

"How should I know?" She would not be made to feel bad for something that wasn't her fault. Or that she had no explanation for. The same thing had happened in Kafr al-Ayn. Was it the same here? What made her immune? "Does it matter?"

"It does—if you have a natural antibody, we need to know, figure out what's preventing the disease from using your body as a host—it could help stall or neutralize the pathogen killing these people. We need another sample of your blood."

"You can have it." Even if she had something in her blood to stop this disease, it would take time to find what and even more to replicate it as an antigen. "So bubonic and septicemic?"

"The protrusions from the glands." He motioned to his neck, where she'd seen the bulbous growths on the workers and students. "That's indicative of the bubonic plague, also known in medieval times as the Black Death. But the discoloration of the extremities—tissue bleeding and death—that's septicemic plague."

"Meaning what?"

"Meaning a new variant, a combination of the two plagues. The New Black Death, if you will." He lifted his eyebrows and sighed. "Meaning you have a whole lot of trouble on your hands, so let's hope your blood helps us."

Tzivia lowered herself onto a cooler by the rear door. "H-how did it happen? What caused it?"

"That could take months, years, to answer—or it might never be answered. When these diseases were virulent centuries ago, they were most often transmitted via fleas and infected rodents. Sadly, both plagues had high mortality rates." Dr. Ellison ran a hand over his stubbled jaw and stifled a yawn. "You've already lost ten men. It's contained, but if someone leaves or left . . ." He shook his head. "It'd be very easy for this thing to go global."

She swallowed hard, remembering Bhavin. "We've had one worker leave already."

"Dr. Ellison?"

They both turned.

A young scientist stood a dozen feet away. "He's on his way."

Dr. Ellison nodded, then flicked his gaze back to Tzivia, his expression almost apologetic.

"Who's coming?"

"You said someone left?"

Strange twitching in her mind warned he was evading her question. Who had he called? They already had the Saudi Ministry of Health, World Health Organization, Global Health, and even soldiers to keep people out.

"If someone left, we need to know. Track him down. Quarantine him until we determine if he's infected." But Dr. Ellison looked guilty. Afraid.

She straightened, alarm spreading through her. "What did you do?"

"Do you understand what will happen if this goes global, Miss Khalon?" His frown and furrowed brow came across as condescending, as if he were talking to a child. "I had to take measures."

Who had he called? "Who is—"

"Do you realize how many people died in the bubonic plague?"

Her stomach squeezed. "Who. Is. Coming?"

"I will *not* let that happen here." He shook his head, defiant for this sixty-something man. "Not when I have the power to stop it."

"*Who?*"

He gave her a stern look that pushed her from the trailer. Tzivia rushed out, tugging her phone free as she did. The bright sunlight blinded her, making it hard to see the screen. After a few blinks, she went into her contacts. Found her brother Ram's number.

The nauseating smell of diesel fumes saturated the air, followed by a snorting rumble of a Deuce and a Half cargo truck. Tzivia stopped short at the olive drab green trucks pouring into the site. As soldiers flooded from the vehicles, Tzivia's blood went cold.

Dr. Ellison appeared behind her.

"What have you done?"

He scowled. "These men are disorganized, chaotic."

"Meaning the people you called are organized?"

"These men are here to rob you." Eyes on the men flooding across the dirt road, he spoke without looking at her. "You might want to leave."

"I'm not leaving anything."

* * * *

— WASHINGTON, DC —

Curiosity got some people in trouble. But it kept Tox alive.

Something was up with the blonde. She didn't fit. Not here, not with her affable nature. Not with her honesty. Not with the buzzing at the back of his brain. Something . . . something was . . . off. Familiar. Weird. He couldn't put his finger on it. But he would.

Arms hooked by guards with enough muscle and height to pound Tox into next year, he shuffled into the conference room, where the misfit team waited. He focused on Attaway as brute force shoved him forward.

Tox caught his balance. Straightened. Turning his hands over, he made the chains *shink*. "If you'll keep your pens and other sharp objects away from me, I think we can do away with these." He knew his joke wouldn't be appreciated, but the measures were overboard.

"Remove them," gruffed Hamer.

As the guards unlocked the cuffs, he took in the room. The items scattered on the table—a field report, file marked CONFIDENTIAL, one labeled TS-1, another hidden beneath that seemed to indicate it was

Above Top Secret, and EYES ONLY. A stack of papers rested in front of the woman, the top page showing a grainy black-and-white image. MacIver and Attaway waited, irritation scratching age lines into their faces. Especially Attaway's.

Tox nearly smirked. He wasn't here because of the pardon. They'd sold him the "one last mission" lie before, and he'd bought it, hook, idiot, and sinker. They sure weren't going to hand him freedom in a bow-wrapped box.

Free of the shackles and security band, Tox was guided by a very firm grip into a chair at the head of the table. He didn't fail to note that nobody sat within arm's reach. And the guards maintained a close proximity. "Is this trust, Hamer?"

"Tox, we're going to get to the brunt of this," Attaway said, as if taking charge would make him the man he wanted to be. "Mr. Hamer?"

A buzz cut defined the SAD director, bespoke his military experience, and dictated how he'd expect to be treated. He opened a file and lifted a page from the large stack. He slid the paper down the table, the others passing it along until it fluttered to a stop in front of Tox. "That is a consolidated report on events to date."

Tox noted the DoD header and quickly scanned information. Two killings. One the commander of the US Special Operations Command. General Kerr. Tox had heard about this. "News said he was in the wrong place at the wrong time."

"He was," Hamer snapped. "Only it was strategically wrong. They set him up."

"And Ambassador Lammers was killed—"

"Assassinated," Hamer interjected. "In London at the National Theatre."

"Two hits," Tox muttered, glancing at the intel. "Did Lammers have connections to the military?"

"Other than serving in Iraq One . . ." Hamer shook his head and pointed to the paper. "That shows our only clue about who is responsible for this."

They had a picture of the alleged assassin but not much else. He looked at those surrounding him. "All this brass and you don't know who you're sending me after?"

"He's a ghost," a skinny suit answered. He looked to be in his mid-forties, neatly trimmed hair. Hamer's colleague, Iliescu. "We've run facial recognition and can't identify him." He nodded to the page. "You'll see we managed to track him to London. Then he turned up about two hours ago in southern Jordan."

"Jordan."

"Asset on the ground confirms it's him."

"And this asset can't identify and neutralize him?"

"He can," Hamer said, "but he won't. Too many things would be at risk. And this needs to be completely black. No one can know you're ours."

As he expected—on his own.

Iliescu smirked. "We're giving you a team."

Tox snorted. Shook his head and shoved the paper back. "No thanks."

He'd gotten into impossible scenarios before. Seen horrible things. Been the cause of deaths. Deaths that put him in federal prison. And they wanted to recycle all that? Do it again? No way.

"Mr. Russell." Mrs. Cortes's voice had this quality that made his brain act like it'd flatlined. Made his mouth feel like it was made of stone and couldn't move. Her chest rose and fell deeply. She was irritated. Or . . . nervous. Her green eyes came to his. "You're a soldier."

"Was."

"Once a soldier, always a soldier."

"I believe that's Marines, ma'am—once a Marine, always a Marine."

"The sentiment is true regardless of which branch you served. Am I right, *Sergeant* Russell?"

Tox gritted his teeth.

"Did you not recite the Oath of Enlistment?"

What was she getting at?

"'*I do solemnly swear that I will support and defend the Constitution of the United States against all enemies, foreign and domestic; that I will bear true faith and allegiance to the same; and that I will obey the orders of the President of the United States and the orders of the officers appointed over me, according to regulations and the Uniform Code of Military Justice. So help me God.*'"

Silence dropped like a mortar, destroying his ability to talk or converse. The general and the suits sat in stunned silence as Tox stared down Mrs. Cortes. Worked to determine her purpose in throwing the oath at him. What was her game?

"Well, Sergeant Russell, the president—your brother—has ordered you on this mission." She licked her lips, tucking a strand of hair behind her ear. "As a thank-you, a *reward*, he has asked that I recommend you for a full pardon. Upon completion of this mission, I will make my decision whether to recommend to the pardon attorney that your freedom be returned."

She had chutzpah, he'd give her that. "Mrs. Cortes, you will pardon one life"—he locked onto her for several long seconds to let that sink in—"*my* life, if I willingly and knowingly put the lives of a team—*six to twelve* lives—at risk?"

She gave a semi-acknowledging nod as she stared at a piece of paper. "'. . . *I will teach and fight whenever and wherever my nation requires.*'"

"I don't need—"

"'*I pledge to uphold the honor and integrity of their legacy in all that I am—in all that I do.*'"

The futility of arguing as she quoted from the Special Forces Creed felt like a minefield ambush. He detested the way the others smirked. They all knew she'd cornered his honor.

Her green eyes came to his. "Are you a professional soldier?"

"I'm nobody."

A semblance of a smile tugged at her lips. "You're Cole Russell. A legend who embodied the elite operator."

"That man died."

"I think he resurrected himself," she said. "Because a dead warrior wouldn't have come back." Her voice was soft, but not in a romantic way. In a way that seemed to read from the very pages of his soul. As if she had explored those passages he'd blacked out years ago like an Above Top Secret file. "You broke into the White House but didn't kill anyone, least of all Attaway."

Tox remained still, his heart skipping a beat.

"And you're here. Listening to us. To the details of this mission."

She smiled at him. "You knew it was important, whatever had Attaway risking an attempt to draw you out. You came because your warrior ethos demanded you answer the call for help."

The thought set off tiny charges in him, demanding he sever any opportunity for her to dig in and find more deadly revelations. He pried his attention from her and checked her guard dog. The man rested his elbows on the table, as if shielding her from the poison in the room. And Barry—confusion flickered through Tox at the pale expression on the man's face. What was he worried about?

"Russell," Major General Rodriguez barked, shifting forward. "She's right. Your curiosity got the better of you, dragged your sorry butt back from wherever you were living your poor excuse for a life." He nodded to the report before him. "We need you."

Tox met the general's gaze. Then MacIver's. He trusted that guy as much as he trusted Barry. Tox slid his attention back to Cortes, who was rattling the charm on a gold necklace back and forth.

Tiny fragments of some memory scraped and shrieked through the dark halls of his mind. Tox glanced down, trying to capture the fragment. Straightening did nothing to dislodge the unease slithering through his gut. Mrs. Cortes—who was she? The memory dangled in front of him, taunting. Elusive.

"Well?" Rodriguez demanded.

Ordered back to the present, Tox knew there was only one way he'd do this. "I want my own team."

Hesitation thrummed through the room, the suits conferring with the uniforms. Dragged on for minutes. Minutes that felt like hours.

"Your team no longer has clearance," Rodriguez said. "They were discharged."

"Honorably." Because Tox had given up everything so Kafr al-Ayn didn't destroy their careers, too. It might have ripped it out of their hands, but he'd made sure they could get jobs and pick up and move on. "Reinstate them."

MacIver chuckled. "Doesn't work that way."

"If you can bring me back from the dead, you can clear five men for this mission."

"Five?" MacIver glanced at his notes. "You only have four."

"Chijioke Okorie is the fifth. He's Nigerian, served in the NA. Start with him."

"He's a foreign national. We can't clear him for a black-bag operation," Hamer said.

"But you can resurrect a dead Special Forces soldier?" Tox cocked his head. "I thought you didn't want the US connected? Having a foreign national could be a benefit."

Everyone stared. Nobody moved or responded. Because Tox had made his point.

He glanced at Barry. Then at Cortes. "Those are my terms—my men, my team."

"It is a nice car."

They'd accomplished a lot in twenty-four hours, including delivering Chijioke Okorie to the bunker as the first of Tox's team. Now, as he and Tox headed northeast on I-95, they'd hit enough construction to get under Tox's skin. "They made me take it." He'd have chosen an SUV or truck, but DoD saddled him with a sedate sedan.

"To track you."

Actually, he half-expected the car to shut off if he took an extended detour. He held up a cell phone. "Don't forget this."

Chiji's deep, resonating laugh was another thing that had a way of getting under Tox's skin. "How did you get them to let me come?"

"Wasn't up for debate." He kept his gaze on the road. "Had to have someone on hand to keep me out of trouble."

"Even I am not that good, Ndidi." Chiji's voice bore humor, as it often did.

Cole laughed and shook his head. "That's cold."

There wasn't much that annoyed the Nigerian, who had a Bible verse for every situation. That was one reason Tox kept his thoughts to himself. Spending three years with Chiji's family had injected him with a hefty dose of respect for Christianity—real Christianity. Where people lived and breathed what they believed rather than putting it on for Sunday service. Quiet settled between them as the potholes and numbing vibrations of the drive needled Tox's nerves. He hated the city.

"Ndidi, they do not trust you."

"Smartest choice they'll ever make." Because he could easily pawn off the vehicle on someone else and leave the phone in the car. But he wouldn't. Not because he wanted the pardon—he didn't believe that was going to happen.

"This mission," Chiji said, lifting a bottle of water from the cup holder in the console. "What do they hope you will do?"

"Stop an assassin."

"Why are you doing this thing?"

"Someone's killing Americans."

"No." Chiji waved his ebony hand at nothing in particular. "Why did you come back? You walk on burning embers."

The truth of that statement couldn't be ignored, but it didn't have to be answered. Because there wasn't an answer. Except that Tox had been drawn back. And . . . was it wrong that "home" still called to him? His mind pinged farther northeast, where his parents were probably working from home.

The tough-as-nails Barbie had a point. His inner warrior demanded he answer the call. Hiding in the savannah alone with his thoughts and the burning heat had melted what little confidence he had in his own system of justice.

Kasey Cortes. Knuckling his grip on the steering wheel, Tox strained his mind. Who was she? She seemed familiar. Or maybe he just wanted her to be familiar to explain how she so easily read his mail. She'd taken a backhoe to his one soft spot—honor—and turned it on him. She had it right: he was a soldier who'd vowed to do everything his nation required of him.

But chasing a nameless assassin? He didn't need that. Didn't want to put his men on the line again. Besides, they probably hated him for Kafr al-Ayn.

"You think too much," Chiji muttered as the sedan blurred past endless fields and trees.

"I'll have to convince them to join me." He wouldn't face this with strangers.

"They are your men. They will follow."

"They're not like you." Tox glanced at the man he'd come to think of as a brother. More than Galen. Way more. "I put them in some serious . . ." He gulped the swell of emotion. "They lost their careers because of me."

"No."

"You don't understand."

Chiji laughed. "This, I understand. Your men, they follow because they believe in you, Ndidi. Not because you order them to go." He shook a long finger at him. "Men are strong. American soldiers are stronger. They know who to follow. They know *why* they follow—not just because the leader says go." He flung a hand toward the right, smacking the window. "These men—they are *your* men. They go because it is you, Ndidi. And this thing, this is what I tell you: God wants you here."

If only that were true.

Three years in Nigeria had not given him peace but had allowed him the space and time to figure out how to live with himself. Tox wasn't really into the whole God scene before Kafr al-Ayn, but what happened there had a way of messing with a guy's head. He wasn't sure if he was crazy or what. That man in the flames had seemed so real.

Chiji had thoughts on it all. Thoughts that involved the supernatural and a God who orchestrates things. Maybe God had allowed Tox to return to redeem a terrible, haunting mistake he'd made to buy his way out of guilt and clear his team of his wrongdoing.

Chiji's finger stabbed forward.

Tox caught the sign for the Holland Tunnel and aimed that way. Buildings closed in on them, tightening the perimeter and making it hard to see the sky. Back in daylight after leaving the tunnel, he breathed a little easier, far too many thriller movies playing in his mind.

Driving down Wooster Street, Tox let out a low whistle as he read the signs over the shops. "Chanel, Ralph Lauren . . . How does Ram afford a shop in a place like this?" He turned left onto Spring Street. "Should be here somewhere." He slowed, coasting, as they scanned the buildings.

"There." Chiji tapped the window. A multistory structure with two blacked-out windows sat as nondescript as possible, with a low-key sign advertising RK GALLERY.

It took them a few minutes to find a place to park, but eventually they were on foot headed back to the gallery. Eyes sweeping the area, Tox struggled to understand why Ram would want a shop here. Too many people. Too many eyes. Too many scenarios for trouble. Quickening his pace did little to ease his tension, but he let out a breath as he reached for the door handle. Gave it a tug. It didn't budge.

"By invitation only." In his thick accent, Chiji read the sign to the right of the door. The one next to the bell. The one Tox ignored as he punched the button. A drill-like noise grated through the walls of the building. He waited a few seconds, then hit it again.

"Maybe we should give him a chance to answer."

"Maybe he should—"

The door opened. An impressive figure blocked the entrance. Jeans slouched around his waist, and a gray t-shirt hung over his frame. Curly, light-brown hair hauled back in a ponytail, Ram Khalon stood with an impassive expression. He looked at Tox, then at Chiji.

"Can we come in?" Tox pushed inside, anxious to be clear of prying eyes.

Ram stepped back. "Sure. Why not?" His sarcasm echoed to the high, bare ceiling.

Five paces carried Tox into an open area broken up by occasional dividers boasting artwork. Spotlights perched on top glared down at the paintings. Steel and iron sculptures hung on brick walls. Stain splotched the cement floor. Little decoration besides a wood-paneled divider at the very back that served as a desk on one side and a barrier on the other. For an office?

Ram stood with his hands tucked in his jean pockets, the outline of a phone at the end of his right hand. His expression hadn't changed. Neither had his demeanor. And he wasn't asking questions.

"This one," Chiji said, hands behind his back as he leaned into the light beneath a painting of an orange flower, examining it in careful detail. "It has great . . . heart."

Ignoring the Nigerian, Tox nodded and remained focused on the man who'd once been his right-hand man. "You knew I was coming."

Ram held his gaze.

"How?" Tox swallowed the question. "Never mind." Ram had more connections than a tech company. "It's bad."

"You wouldn't be here if it was good." Ram walked to the back and tossed his phone on the desk. "Where?"

"Jordan."

"At least it's not Syria." Leaning back against the wood paneling, Ram adjusted the beanie on his head. It sagged like a pregnant dog. "What are we chasing?"

"An assassin."

He gave a slight twitch. "When do we leave?"

Tox considered the man who'd been through more battles with him than anyone else. "Too easy."

Ram eyeballed him.

"We have to round up the others."

"Maangi and Thor might be easy to rope in, though I imagine Maangi might want to kill you, but Cell . . ." Ram shook his head, then thrust his chin toward Chiji. "Who's he?"

"My conscience." Tox glanced back to his friend, who moved from one painting to another, leaning close and studying them as if they might contain answers to the mysteries of life. "Chijioke Okorie. He saved my life." That was all he needed to say.

"Never mentioned him before."

"Didn't know him before."

Ram nodded. Lifted his phone and glanced at the screen, his thumb swiping over it. "Let me grab my things."

"Pack light."

Snick.

The subtle noise made Tox hesitate. He glanced at the phone. Realized Ram had it aimed at Chiji. Taking his photo? To check him out. "He's safe."

Ram met his gaze for a brief second, then vanished through a door.

What was that? Ram had always been rough around the edges and solitary, but he'd worked well with Tox. Then again . . . Kafr al-Ayn

92

changed them. Apparently, it had changed their relationship, too. They'd followed him before—but out of military obligation. He had no right to ask them to do this. No right to ask them to put up their safety. For what? A pardon. For him.

Thud.

Tox spun, reaching for the Glock holstered at the small of his back. Ram stood with a full ruck at his feet. He'd been in that back room less than two minutes. "You were already packed?"

"Cell lives an hour from here."

Tox frowned. "I had him at—"

"Info's wrong. On purpose." Ram nodded to the door. "Maangi and Thor are en route. They'll meet us at Cell's."

* * * *

"Why does Maangi want to kill me?"

Ram stayed eyes front in the sedan. "His fiancée left him after Kafr al-Ayn."

"I thought she was good for him."

"Being shredded by the press isn't good for anyone."

Ah. The story of the burned village and death of the president had hit national news. The US needed a scapegoat, someone to blame for the president's death. His team was it. Media ate the story and the men alive. Until Tox made it go away. "Think he'll work with us?"

Ram adjusted his slouchy hat. "He's coming to the meet."

Which meant nothing. Maangi could be coming to tear Tox's heart out. Not that he could blame him.

Chiji rode in the back seat, and Ram served as co-pilot, but it wasn't the same. Strange how Ram had been his right-hand man once, and now things were . . . jacked. "So. A gallery . . . that's what you've been doing?"

Ram eyed him.

"Making good money, apparently," Tox said. "A shop in SoHo. That's not cheap."

Stony silence met the unwritten invitation to dialogue.

"You got a girl?" It was stupid to ask, but their dynamic had changed and put Tox off-kilter. "You haven't settled down? What about your sister?"

"What is this? An interrogation?" There was almost a laugh in the clipped words.

Tox shrugged. "It's been a while."

"Yes." Ram angled toward him with a spark of anger. "It has. Doesn't mean you can demand information about my life."

The reprimand stung. Showed Tox he had a lot more than lost time to earn back. "No demand. Trying to reconnect."

"Why the sudden concern?"

"Not sudden."

"You never asked before."

"Didn't ask because I paid attention. Knew what was happening. And I left you guys to your lives. Didn't mean I didn't care." He tried to slow his rapid pulse. "I trusted you all to take care of your business. As long as it didn't interfere with the mission, I didn't intrude."

"Exactly," Ram said. "So let's do this job, and don't intrude."

"Point taken." Tox tucked his chin. Drove. In silence. *Icy* silence.

Twenty minutes later, they pulled up in front of a three-story condominium. Tox slid the gear into Park. He glanced up the fifteen steps to the stone porch, white pillars flanking a blue door. It wasn't a brownstone but was more than he'd expected from Cell. "What's he doing now?"

"Working for a large cyber-security firm." Ram exited the vehicle.

When Tox stepped out, so did Chiji. His friend stood over him, watching as Ram climbed the front stairs. "I would prefer trust over idle words," Chiji said.

Tox glanced at Ram as he knocked on the door. "They hate me, but he's willing to do this."

"They do not have to like everything about a leader to follow him."

"Maybe, but they'd be more inclined to talk to him," Tox said as a white Suburban slid down the street and eased to the curb.

Doors opened. Two men emerged—Tane Maangi and Victor "Thor" Thorsen. The latter hadn't done Syria with them because of a previous injury that sidelined him for a while, but it was good to see him. At least one member wouldn't have a grudge.

"Time to face the music." Tox moved around Chiji.

With a wary smile, Thor nodded and extended his hand. "Sarge."

Tox took it—and got pulled forward. A firm slap against his back knocked the wind from his lungs. Probably on purpose. "Thor."

"What're you? A cat with nine lives?" Thor grinned. "Glad you're not six feet under like they said."

"Me too." He shifted and angled toward the man of Maori descent. "Tane."

"I want to run a spear through your heart."

"I'd appreciate it if you didn't."

"He's not here," Ram called as he hustled down the steps of the condo. When he greeted Thor and Maangi, Tox noticed the gold band on Thor's left ring finger.

"You're married?"

Thor grinned. "Six months. My physical therapist. Had to wait until I was done with therapy to ask her out."

"I tried to stop him. Dropped the ring and everything," Maangi said.

Thor laughed. "Tane was my best man."

A numbness spreading through his body, Tox could only bob his head. *You're an outsider. Don't belong.* The men had gone on with their lives. Lives that included each other and now a wife. A strange twist, being an outsider with men he'd once led. Men who had depended on him. Operated fluidly with him. Could he do it now? Would they even listen to him?

"Hey." Thor extended a hand to Chiji. "Victor Thorsen."

Tox snapped out of his fog. "This is Chijioke Okorie." When they stared at him, Tox stiffened. "He saved my life—he's like a brother."

After the introduction, he stood back, listening as the men got acquainted, and tried to tell himself they could still handle this mission.

Barclay "Cell" Purcell . . . was he in his condo, hiding out? Tox checked the windows, looking for a blind or curtain shifting. No sign of the squirrelly guy.

"Should we wait or head somewhere to talk, then come back?" Maangi asked.

Talk. They wanted to talk. He'd never been good at that, but this also sounded more like a Come to Jesus meeting than a mission brief.

When he refocused, Tox saw a man round the corner, gray plastic shopping bags dangling from his right hand. The awkward gait. "There he is."

Ram and Maangi turned.

Cell waved. "Hey—"

Tox broke through the group.

Cell's eyes widened. He stopped. Dropped the bags. "No." He backed up. "No no no." He threw himself around and darted back the direction he'd come.

"Cell!" Tox sprinted after him for a full thirty seconds before Cell veered across an open park, heading for a wooded area. If he made it there, Tox might lose him. "Stop!"

Cell slowed, his feet thumping hard against the grass and shoulders drooping. He turned and met Tox with a weary gaze. "Dead. You're supposed to be dead." Wagged his arms. "Why are you back? What, ripping our careers apart wasn't enough? Here to finish the job?"

Cell's animosity and defeat struck Tox center mass. "We have a mission. I need your skills." He glanced back to where the others had grouped up. "The team needs you."

"No!" Cell jabbed a finger at Tox, his voice raw. "No, you don't get to do this again."

Tox held his peace.

"You destroyed my life," Cell growled, spittle forming in the corners of his mouth as he bit back tears. "I had to start over because of you."

He knew. In fact, Tox knew more than they did. He'd bought their lives, their freedom, at a price he never thought possible, doing something he never thought he'd do. Violating his own moral code to make sure Kafr al-Ayn didn't destroy them as it had him. He'd expected a lot of things out of that, but not their mistrust. The accusations. The hatred.

"All that media coverage, all the things they said about me, about the others." He waved at the team. "Do you have *any* idea what we went through? How our lives were shredded?"

Tox swallowed, hated himself, hated what'd happened. "An idea."

"And was it not enough?" Cell held out his arms like he was being crucified. "Are you here to finish it?"

Tox felt the urge to turn around, walk back to the rental, and never return. But he deserved this. And they had the right to take it out on him. So he listened. Let Cell unload the poison in his veins.

"We were hounded night and day by those vultures. 'Where is Cole Russell?' they demanded. 'Why'd he kill the president? Let those villagers die?'" His eyes went wide. "Or the best ones, 'Why didn't you stop him?' 'Aren't you his teammate?' 'Does that mean you're guilty, too?'"

Misery cradled Tox in its venomous arms. "I didn't—"

"Of course you didn't! Because you *died*!" Cell's voice pitched. "You died, and they buried you. I saw it on the news."

Empty casket. All for the benefit of the media, friends, and family.

"I saw your mom sobbing in your dad's arms beneath that canopy." Cell scooted forward a step, his shoulders squared. "I actually felt sorry for you—for *two*. *Whole*. *Seconds*!" He touched his temples. "That is, until the vultures asked if I had killed you. Or if Maangi or Ram had! Your friends, your teammates."

"Where were you?" Ram's voice was ridiculously calm in light of Cell's tirade.

Tox glanced around the woods and the backyards of the condos, uncomfortable with having this conversation in the open. Or at all. He could lose everything.

"Were you bought?"

A lightning strike to his heart would've shocked less. "*Bought*?"

Ram remained unbending. "Yes—did you do something to get off, get away?"

That strike hit very close to home. He *had* been bought. But the price had been for his men. Tox had wondered many times on the cliff overlooking the plains if it'd been for himself, too—to ease his guilty conscience.

"We are drawing attention" came Chiji's gravelly voice.

"Just answer the question," Cell said. "Did you get off scot-free because you were bought?"

"Nothing is free. And if you think anyone walks away untouched from a situation like Kafr al-Ayn, you've been brainwashed." Tox hoped it'd be enough to end this conversation permanently.

"Where have you been?" Cell demanded. "Why didn't you do something?"

"He was with me," Chiji said, moving to Tox's side. "I have no brother closer than Ndidi."

"Ndidi?"

"It's the name his mother gave me," Tox said, biting off the rest of that story.

"He was dying when I brought him home." Chiji was more loyal than a pit bull. "I brought the doctor. God brought life back to Ndidi."

"God?" Cell snorted. "I don't care, man, if you need that to get you through a day or whatever, but this . . ." He refocused on Tox. "This is whacked." He tapped Tox's chest. "You weren't there. If you were alive, why didn't you speak up? How could you leave us to the wolves? We broke orders to find you after *you* broke orders." His voice grew hoarse. "We hauled your sorry carcass out of that tunnel, flames burning us." He held up a marred hand. "And what—*what* do we get? Accused! Court-martialed—then not"—confusion knotted his brow—"for whatever reason. But we're out. On our butts. No amount of pleading allowed us to stay in."

Tox remembered. The flames, yes. The crushing collapse of the tunnel, yes. The hallucination of the man standing over him and calling to him just as the team broke through to save him from suffocation. He'd gone in to save the president. Got him out alive, only to have Montrose die trying to save *him*. "I remember."

"Good. Because that's us—we don't leave a brother behind. We learned that from you." He snorted again. "Or maybe not."

Tox ground his molars, refusing to violate the gag order they'd placed him under.

"This man . . ." Chiji motioned to Tox as he stepped closer. "You worked with him, no?"

"No—yes." Cell blinked. "Yes, we worked with him. We were a team. A unit. And he left us to hang."

"How long?" Chiji asked.

"What?"

"How long were you with him?"

"Five years," Cell growled. "Ram six."

"And in that time, did you go on missions with Ndidi leading, trusting him with your life?" Chiji's game plan was simple. But it wouldn't matter.

Tox shook his head. "Chiji—"

A large palm nearly touched Tox's nose, silencing him. "Maybe my question is too hard." Chiji's nostrils flared. "Did—"

"I know what you're doing." Cell scowled.

Chiji leaned in. "Then you also know what I am saying." He paused, meeting each man's gaze. "Ndidi is the most loyal of men I have ever met. You followed him into war, you trusted his orders . . . yet you accuse him of this thing."

"Because he left us."

Seeing the bulge in his Igbo brother's eyes, Tox stepped in. "Chiji, it's okay. I get it. And . . . they're right."

"But the mission—"

"Doesn't matter." Tox's phone rang.

"Just tell us," Cell insisted. "How'd they buy you? What'd you do?"

He considered the wiry comms specialist, the man who'd never been afraid to speak his mind. "I can't, Purcell. I can't talk about it." The phone buzzed again, seemingly feeding off the agitation infecting the air. He glanced at the screen, noted the 202 area code, and answered. "Russell."

"Did you find your team?" Attaway wouldn't know pleasantries if they bit him in the face.

He refused to look at the men. "Yeah."

"Good. We need you airborne ASAP. Sending flight info to your phone. Get moving."

12

Armed with a duffel, tac gear, and kit, Tox stalked across the hangar at Wheeler-Sack Air Field. The attempt to recruit his team had failed. He'd expected questions but not the anger. Only Chiji walked the line with him now.

Commander MacIver waited just outside the steel and aluminum structure. "Where's your team?"

"This is it." Tox tightened his grip on his ruck and nodded to a C-17 Globemaster fueling on the tarmac. "That our ride?"

"Yeah." MacIver was built like an Abrams tank. He had the height, the brawn—and the brains, if his rank was a tell. "We'll need to recruit five or six operators."

Tox stretched his jaw, annoyed it'd come to this. He needed guys he trusted. Not strangers.

"Some good candidates in SOCOM and DEVGRU." MacIver lifted a finger as he reached for his phone, the screen lit. He plugged his left ear and strolled further inside the hangar, away from the whining of engines. A call from Command, no doubt. There was a day that would've come to Tox, not his babysitter.

Chiji glided toward him, his long legs giving his stride a stealthy feel. The Nigerian knew how to do that, too. He'd come up on Tox's six many times with very little noise, sometimes none at all. A veritable ghost out of the darkness. Even in broad daylight. His friend stood at his side without a word, but there was much said in his expression. He'd always had a way with probing gazes.

Or maybe that was Tox's guilty conscience contrasted with the serenity that sat on the planes of Chiji's ebony face like a morning sunrise. He exuded a peace that drew Tox in. His antithesis. They could read each other well and often, so much that even now he saw Chiji's concern. It'd upset his Igbo brother to see how the men reacted. Tox huffed. It upset him, too.

Trying to warn off the coming lecture, he shook his head.

"'He will fight for you,'" Chiji said, quoting Scripture again.

That one Tox had heard a thousand times sitting in the blazing heat of Nigeria. "Well, this is one He *will* have to fight because there's nothing I can say."

"You did not tell them the truth, Ndidi. Not the whole truth."

"Can't." He'd told Chiji, but only because he'd never expected to set foot on American soil again. That'd been the deal with Attaway.

But he couldn't argue the disappointment coursing through him. The men really believed he'd left them high and dry. That he had so little honor, so little character, he'd willingly leave a man behind.

A stern wall of six-foot-four insistence pressed him.

If they believed that of him, then how could he ever explain the truth? Besides . . . "I spill my guts—" They both knew if he talked, he'd be in a cement cell for the rest of his life—or an oak coffin, depending on which route Uncle Sam took to silence him. "Why didn't they just leave me alone?" he muttered.

"Hey," MacI hollered above the airfield din. "Thought your boys weren't coming."

"Opted out," Tox called back.

MacI pointed behind Tox.

Across the field, a Jeep rolled to a stop beneath the stark stadium lights and disemboweled itself of four men. Thor, Maangi, Ram, and even Cell strode toward the hangar.

Reading their faces gave him no pleasure. They'd come out of obligation.

At least they were here. The only way he'd face this nightmare of a bus Attaway had thrown him under. Tox nodded, accepting their sacrifice. He extended a hand to each and clapped their shoulders, thanking them for coming.

"Load up!" MacI yelled, pointing to the jet.

"And who are you?" A dark line drew across Cell's tanned brow.

"Tour guide. Let's go, ladies." MacI didn't miss a beat before stalking out onto the tarmac with a ruck and weapons.

Cell and Maangi glanced to Ram. The Israeli-American turned to Tox, who answered by heading to the jet.

MacIver gave them orders. The team looked to Ram.

Why am I here?

* * * *

From inside the Globemaster, Kasey had watched the team reunion. It hadn't been hard to see Cole's complete disappointment when he'd showed up without his team. The tall Nigerian at his side seemed to anchor Cole, provide a means of support in a stormy life. The two only talked once, but even as they waited, Cole stayed close to him. A safety zone. Buffer. He trusted the Nigerian. Implicitly.

She envied that.

"Makes you wonder," Levi muttered—loud enough over the din to be heard, but not by everyone.

"What?" she asked to the side, not taking her gaze off the team that grouped up around Cole.

She selected one face to watch, waiting for a micro-expression, a leak of concealed emotion, to give away his thoughts. The shorter, stockier man squinted, brows pulled down, and lips thinned for a fraction of a second before clearing. He stepped forward and offered his hand to Cole, then clasped it with both of his.

One by one, each man came forward and repeated the two-handed shake.

"They don't trust him."

"No, they're angry with him," Kasey said. "They wouldn't be here if they didn't trust him."

He gave her a quizzical look.

"What? I'm the deception expert, remember? I read body language, actions . . . what's not said more than what's said."

"Sometimes I think we're watching two different versions of the same life." Levi nodded to the tarmac. "Here they come."

Jitters in her belly, Kasey made her way to a seat with its orange harness. She had no idea how Cole would respond to her presence or that the DoD had attached her and Levi to the team to expedite transmission of information. She'd bullied her way into this, but it served two purposes: more oversight and an additional set of eyes. Of course, she knew Hamer—and even Galen—wanted feedback on Cole, though it hadn't been said quite so directly. But Kasey's hope was that Cole would see her as a friend. Allow her to help.

The steel beast thrummed beneath the powerful engines, yet the additional thudding steps of the team as they climbed the ramp into the belly proved noticeable. This wasn't foreign terrain to them. It was home. She saw it in the way they hiked up the rear door.

Cole spotted her immediately, though she sat near the front and across from the modularized office installed for their trip. Wariness crowded his terse expression.

As the men took seats, they openly studied her and Levi. Curiosity ran rampant. Maybe even a little annoyance sparked as they parked themselves in the first few rows spanning the middle of the aircraft.

But then Cole came over. Stomach knotting, Kasey hated the heat that climbed into her face.

Cole glanced at Levi. "Wallace?"

"Yeah?"

"Your brother—"

"Was on that mission." Levi's gaze hardened.

Cole nodded. Then went to his seat. Not a word to her.

Disappointment held Kasey fast. But what could she expect? After all, she probably represented the evil overlords forcing him back into service. She glanced at Levi and found his eyes already closed, head against the vinyl rest mounted to the interior hull of the transport jet.

Ten minutes later they were airborne and leveling off. Commander MacIver freed himself, gave her and Levi a nod, then strode into the modularized room in front of the guys' seats. Kasey unbuckled and

followed Levi and the commander, noting in her periphery that Cole
and his team came to their feet as well.

She'd barely entered when she felt his presence behind her. He
trailed her closely. Made her insides squirm.

"MacIver," Cole boomed, "didn't know we'd have company."

The commander nodded to her and Levi. "They're sent from the top."

"So," Tox said, his elbow nearly in her face as he stared at MacIver,
"Galen."

It wasn't that he was crowding her—the modularized unit was
small. Cramped. They were like the proverbial sardines in a tin can.
The portable's door shut, cutting off a considerable amount of noise.
Kasey stretched her jaw to clear her plugged ears.

"They're assigned and that's it," MacIver said. "Let's get on with
things."

"Hold up."

Kasey eyed the wiry, intense man who stood her five-seven height
and had light brown hair. They'd called him Cell?

"*Why* are they here?"

"More babysitters," Ram muttered.

Kasey wished she couldn't hear as clearly in here. "We're here as
consultants."

"Consultants." Cell's expression was flat. "Yeah, that's not working for me."

"Agent Cortes has a specialty in deception detection," Cole said,
his gaze never meeting hers. "Could be useful."

"I'm sorry," Cell said, "but I don't think we have to worry about
these terrorists deceiving us."

"Why?" Levi asked, his defensiveness thick.

"Because they'll be shooting at us with AK-47s," Cell growled.
"Miss Consultant, just so you are up to speed on combat, if someone
aims a gun at you and says he's going to kill you, he's not lying."

Cole straightened. "Hey. Dial it back."

A trickle of warmth shot up Kasey's spine. "Lying and deception
aren't the same thing."

All eyes locked onto her. Even Cole this time. He nodded with a
near-smile.

Kasey took it as encouragement. "A lie is a deliberate, made-up untruth. Most people don't lie." She noted several shift in the group. "Most people deceive. They give half-truths."

"You know, we were a good team without you and Superman there," Cell said. "I don't see why we need anyone else." He turned to Tox. "They just mean more people to look after. This isn't a good idea, you know?"

Kasey tilted her head. "This is personal to you."

"Heck yeah, it's personal." Cell gave a curt nod. Then hesitated. "Wait. What do you mean?" He frowned. "Why's it personal?"

"You tell me."

"No." Cell shifted, hands sliding into his pockets. "I mean—why'd you say it's personal?"

Glad to showcase her skills, Kasey explained. "Your use of 'you know' twice in a short defense of why I shouldn't be on this team says it's personal." She squinted at him. "Something made you protective, *angrily* protective of it."

Skating a glance to Cole, Cell drifted aside, acting as if she had read his palm or something.

"We done?" Cole looked between them. "MacIver, what do you have?"

* * * *

MacIver spread field maps and intel across the table.

"Who's in charge of this mission?" Ram scanned the documents, files, and laptop monitors, then looked at Tox and MacI. He pulled out his smartphone, the screen glowing, but slid it back into his pocket without answering. Maybe a text message?

"Technically, the DoD." MacIver either didn't hear Ram's annoyance or chose to ignore it. Probably the latter. "In field, that'd be me. Tactically, you answer to Russell."

"Tactically?" Ram frowned, studying a document on the table. "Too many fingers in the C-4."

MacIver removed the document, glowering.

"Why do we need babysitters again?" Cell wasn't letting go of this. The conversation would run in circles for hours. Unless Tox nipped it.

"It's me." He pressed his fingertips to the table, staring at each man individually. "They're monitoring me."

"Because we aren't the only ones afraid you'll vanish again?"

Tox tried to conceal the wound Cell's dagger-sharp words left but failed. He clenched his jaw. "We need to get past this. Understand"—he tapped his fingers against the table—"I was *forced* to leave the country."

"So they could make everyone believe you were dead."

Nod, just nod. Attaway had made sure Tox knew he was six feet under as far as everyone on U.S. soil was concerned. "I can't give details on what happened. But now? I'm here. You're here. An assassin just killed a former vice president and the SOCOM commander. They need this shooter dead. They tapped us."

"Yeah, but see? That's not making a lot of sense," Cell said. "There are any number of black baggers around the globe, some much closer than we were. So why us?"

"Because I'm expendable."

"But I'm not," Cell countered, scowling. "I got family, friends."

"You got friends?" Maangi snickered.

"Then why are you here?" The feminine voice was soft but strong. Agent Cortes stepped into his team, crossing a line she didn't see or know about.

"You—"

"Hey—" Tox spoke at the same time as Cell, but then both fell silent, and Cortes filled the gap.

"Point as many fingers as you like at as many people as you want, Mr. Purcell, but you're here." Color stained her cheeks. Anger? Embarrassment? "Your choice. Nobody held a gun to your head."

Tox reached toward her, needing to quiet her. This wouldn't help. This would only make things worse, getting defended by someone who hadn't been there. Someone he hadn't hurt—yet.

"You didn't see him chase me down at my house," Cell said.

"Still no gun," Maangi muttered. When Cell shot him a wide-eyed glare, Maangi shrugged. "What? She's right."

"Yeah, but—"

"Okay, that's enough," Tox said, gently touching Cortes's arm.

"This is a dead horse. We need to quit beating it. What happened is done. I can't change it. If you want me to say I'm sorry—then I'm sorry." He took a breath. "You *know* me. If I did something, it had to be done. Not talking about certain missions is as much a part of what we do as the weapons and kit we use." He looked directly at Cell this time. "What happened three years ago . . ." He shook his head. "I want it gone. Buried."

Understanding coursed through Cortes's green eyes. "You don't *want* to talk about it."

"No." Could she see what three years ago had cost him? "I don't."

Ram nodded to MacIver. "You're in charge, right?" When the commander agreed, Ram folded his arms. "Brief us."

"Okay," MacIver slid out an image. "This is our guy—he's called Tanin."

"Dragon," muttered Ram, staring at the picture, his phone in his hand again. "It means 'dragon' in Arabic."

"What's his real name?" Tox dragged the glossy across the table and memorized the man's face. Middle Eastern. Single brow. His left ear was a melted mess, half gone. Could he hear out of that side still? The hooked nose had been broken—maybe when he lost the ear.

"Nobody knows," MacIver said. "He's a ghost. We don't have any information other than he seems fond of an Arabian prince"—he tugged out another image, this a composite aerial shot of a compound with an inset of a man in a suit—"Salih Abidaoud. In fact, last known location of Tanin was at Abidaoud's sprawling property in Jurf Al Darawish."

"Jerk where?" Cell asked.

"Jurf Al Darawish," Ram repeated, his eyes never leaving the documents and images. "Southern Jordan."

"So the assassin is working for Abidaoud?"

"We don't know."

"But he's holed up at the dude's palace?" Cell said, his voice pitched.

"He's there. Why, we don't know. Abidaoud could be a target."

"No," Ram said firmly. "No, if he's not working for him, he's working with him." He snapped his gaze to MacIver. "What committees was Ambassador Lammers heading? Why was he in London?"

"To oppose a measure being presented to the UN on mining and distribution rights."

"Yes, it makes sense." Ram nodded. "With his partying and penchant for luxury purchases, Abidaoud became a problem for his family, so they relegated him to this wasteland, overseeing the quarry that funds about one-fifth their wealth."

"A fifth?" Tox repeated. If they had this family's wealth divided up into numbers like that . . .

"They own oil fields in a couple of countries, have a sapphire mine, others, I'm sure." He nodded to MacIver. "That bill would directly affect Abidaoud's personal coffers."

"Dude, how do you even know all that?" Cell asked.

"Worked a mission involving him a few years ago."

MacIver nodded. "Back to the intel." He showed an image with what almost looked like fortified walls.

"Is that the property?" Maangi asked. "It looks more like a fortress."

"Quarry," Ram said. "He got the worst location and lowest-producing mine to oversee as punishment by his family."

"So is this where we're going to find Tanin?" Tox didn't care about the family's wealth. He wanted to hit this guy and get out of there.

MacIver showed a grid layout of the property. "One hundred acres of desert," he said as he displayed another photo, this one zoomed in.

Tox trailed a finger along dark lines framing a sprawling white structure that abutted a small mountain. "Tiered access."

"Intel shows three perimeter gates leading up to the main complex. You'll HALO in and come over the eastern side of the mountain. Bypass the electrified fence, then find and neutralize your target."

"Exfil?" Tox asked, already eyeing the best route to escape.

MacIver pointed to a small huddle of structures outside the compound. "A vehicle will be waiting here."

"That's what? Two, three klicks?"

"Two-point-six," MacIver confirmed.

"Agent Cortes isn't trained in HALO jumps," Wallace said.

"Are you?" Ram studied the guy, his eyes full of unspoken questions. Ones even Tox wanted to know. Had the guy been military prior to suiting up?

"Doesn't matter," MacIver said to the agent. "Neither of you are going in with Wraith."

Surprise shot through the noisy temporary structure within the Globemaster, but Tox savored the relief. Two less bodies to worry about.

Wallace flinched. "Excuse me, but—"

"That's just it. Your butt. We need it here." MacIver huffed as he looked at the intel. "You'll be of better use when we get tagged by Jordanian authorities for entering their airspace. When we are forced to set down in Amman, you'll be our get-out-of-jail-free card."

Cell grinned. "Hooah."

The team sat in the modular structure studying the schematics. Making notes. Logging info into devices they'd strap to their forearms. Ram stood at the grease board, going over exfil plans. His phone must've buzzed because he drew it out and glanced at it. Thumbed the buttons, then slid it back into his leg pocket. What was that about? Tox made his way down the line to Ram and shouldered in next to him.

Ram's hard gaze hit his.

"We've been together since day one," Tox said, his voice just loud enough to be heard. "You never worked a mission involving Salih Abidaoud."

Ram scanned what he'd drawn on the whiteboard, clearly not wanting to talk.

Tox angled around, staring behind Ram. "How'd you know about Abidaoud?"

"Just do."

"And the phone—who's calling?"

"Tzivia."

Tox's heart skipped a beat. For two reasons—one: his friend had answered that question, so it could be considered diversionary. Meant to distract Tox from the information hidden behind the chatter. And two: it was Tzivia.

He shifted, unable to stop the question. "How is she?"

Ram nudged him with this shoulder. "Without you, fine."

"Ouch."

"Yeah, well, you gave her a raw deal."

Tox snorted. "We had one dinner—at a picnic table at Leavenworth." He looked down, recalling with clarity the hurt that had shone in her eyes when he'd told her good-bye. "She didn't need to be shackled to that."

Ram didn't answer.

Tox had hated telling Tzivia to move on with her life. "She finish her doctorate?"

Ram nodded.

"Still working with Cathey?" It'd be good if she was, because the professor, though a bit absentminded, was wise and revered. He spoke a dozen languages, including useful ones like French and German, as well as ancient ones. And he was a believer, which Tox knew annoyed the tar out of Tzivia. Good opportunity to stretch her.

At the mention of Dr. Joseph Cathey, Ram's cheek twitched. "*With him*, but not for him. She has her own dig in Saudi. Fairly significant. Kafr nearly ruined her. This is . . . punishment, but promising, she says."

"Good that it's promising."

"Yeah, she's pretty worked up about it—historic find."

Tox nodded to the phone. "She's texting you more often than a lover would."

Ram hoisted his helmet from the rack. "They're having problems. Looters. Some of the team are sick. Not sure why." He shrugged. "She gets worked up easily when it comes to the digs. Not telling me everything either."

The door to the cube swung open and MacIver stepped in again. "Suit up!"

* * * *

"Five mikes!" came the droning announcement through the comms piece tucked in Tox's ear. He glanced at the digital readout strapped to his wrist. Thirty-four thousand feet.

The warning claxon barreled across the wind noise hammering the aircraft through the open bay door. Abidaoud and Tanin waited some eight klicks below. Tox mentally walked through the plan—scale down the mountain, fight off resistance, penetrate the compound, locate and kill the target, exfil.

Streamlined but not as simple once boots hit ground. Tox was ready, though. And glad to be back in the game. Glad to have the adrenaline surging through his veins once more.

He thought about Ram. The information he had. His friend always seemed to have access to more intel than normal. There'd been rumors around SOCOM that Ram had ties to Mossad, Israel's agency for intelligence collection, covert operations, and counterterrorism—among other things. Unofficially, they were the world's most efficient killing machines. Tox never broached the subject because Ram's stony silence told him not to. It could amount to treason and a court-martial, but his friend knew the laws.

A sharp pat to his shoulder signaled the two-minute warning. Tox disconnected from the oxygen panel and switched to his bailout bottle. The first burst of icy air shot through him, proof the bottle worked.

With his own O$_2$ bottle, MacIver served as jumpmaster and moved into position at the bay door. First to jump, Ram lowered his goggles and lumbered toward him with his gear and chute. Ram first, Tox last. Maangi, Thor, and Cell trudged past him, taking their cue from MacIver for safe jump intervals. Tox glanced back and saw the agents watching, oxygen masks keeping them alive at altitude. Chiji gave him a look steeped in both panic at the open bay door—he hated flying—and frustration at being separated from Tox. After a nod to him, Tox turned and stalked out to the lip, vibrations insane.

MacIver patted his shoulder, and Tox pitched himself into the wide-open sky. Gravity yanked him down, the frigid air tearing at his clothes. Terminal velocity of over two hundred miles an hour gave a thrill unlike any other. Pressure pushed against his ears and he forced an exaggerated swallow to clear them.

At two thousand feet, he caught the rip cord. Tugged. Below his boots, he saw the others, chutes already open. Verifying his altitude, Tox opened his. Jerked up and back, he navigated toward the eastern face of the mountain, out of sight from the compound. Ram landed, secured his chute, then quickly grabbed his weapon, and took point. Thor had removed his chute and was digging a hole where the team would bury their chutes, jump helmets, and jump gear.

As soon as his boots hit terra firma, Tox released the chute and twisted around, going to a knee. He hurriedly balled the nylon, then drew off the helmet. He shouldered out of the pack before removing his jumpsuit. The whole process took the team close to twenty minutes to land, remove the jump equipment, and bury their gear.

With his weapon up, he knelt again. Glanced at the readout, and with a gloved hand gave signals for the team to head south. Once they crested the spine, they headed down and northwest, straight up behind what intel said was a gardening shack.

Tox had to admit it was nice. Nice to be back in action. Nice to be with his team. These men. Each one had a skill vital to the mission—Cell's ability to jury-rig two sticks and create a long-range radio; Maangi's combat medic skills; Thor's brute force; Ram's connections to just about every major contact you could need running an operation; Chiji—well, didn't matter what his Nigerian friend did as long as he had Tox's six.

A shout went up. Tox crouched, staring down his scope in the direction of the noise. Like ants on a hill, people were moving quickly around the compound. Cars whipped up to the front of the structure.

"They're going ape," Cell muttered, staring through his nocs.

"What's happening?" Maangi asked.

Tox pulled out his own binoculars, going flat against a boulder. Silence cut through the cold weather. Tox watched. Sorted what he saw.

"That's Abidaoud," Thor said, "hurrying to the third vehicle."

Tox felt the success of this mission sliding through his fingers. "What about Tanin?" He scanned the scene. The people in the compound were excited. Fear? "Anyone got eyes on Tanin?" They couldn't lose this guy.

"He might not be—"

"There! Just exited the south portico."

Tox jerked left and centered on the assassin. "Maangi, he can't leave there. Cell, call it in."

"On it," Maangi said, laid out with his sniper rifle. Beside him, Thor ran calculations and gave him numbers to dial the gun. If Maangi missed, any subsequent shots would be a homing beacon for return fire, RPGs, and whatever else that place had in their arsenal.

Cell radioed in the change in the status of the mission.

Lanky, entirely too confident with that swagger, Tanin had nearly reached the awaiting armored Lexus. This was going south before they could even dip their toes in the waters of combat. Men scattered to vehicles.

Cell's voice scratched. "Repeat, Pie in the—"

Tox grabbed his radio, needing this taken care of now. "Maangi, you got joy?"

"Pie in the Sky, we receive you, Wraith Six. Go ahead."

"I have joy." Cheek to the rifle, Maangi lay very still, listening as Thor did calculations of distance and wind speed.

"Take the shot when you're ready."

"Copy that," Maangi said.

Crack!

After firing, Maangi worked the bolt, ejecting the spent shell, and chambered another round without taking his eye off the target. "Broke one-fourth mil left."

Tox had his nocs, watching the entire time.

"Negative hit," Thor called. "Target is—"

Crack! Maangi fired another shot.

Expecting return fire, Tox put his finger into the trigger well of his M4 and stretched out on the ground, waiting. He slanted a look to the others, low on the hill with him. He eased a mirror from his pocket and slid it up over the rock to get a view.

"Move out—head south."

Rocks shifted. Dirt crunched beneath boots as the men moved, staying low and starting the retreat.

Rocks spat at them, the shards of splintered stone like tiny daggers. "Taking fire, taking fire!"

As the others cleared out, Tox searched for the shooter. He found him hunkering behind a large potted plant on the back terrace by the pool. Tox eased back the trigger and neutralized the threat. The entire compound seemed to have emptied. It made no sense. Had they been tipped off?

He shifted and turned to catch up with the team.

Crunch.

He froze at the noise from behind and to his left.

Crunch-crunch. Scritch. Boots slid then caught traction, the person uttering an oath in Arabic.

Shoulder against the large boulder, Tox pressed himself out of sight. He dared not move, even as light hit his leg. Move and he'd be dead.

A short, potbellied man with a Kalashnikov slipped and stumbled past him. But then he stopped.

With all the stealth he could muster, Tox reached to his thigh holster and drew out his suppressed Glock 22. They couldn't risk this guy getting away to tell anyone else where they were, and Tox couldn't risk his shot being heard.

Potbelly whipped up his fully automatic weapon and took aim at the team.

Tox eased back the trigger. The man pitched forward, and Tox scrambled over to him, then hid his body behind the rock. He negotiated the steep hill, his weapon ready, his gaze never leaving the direction the first guard had come. Surely Abidaoud's security wasn't this bad.

It took him ten minutes to catch up with the team at the base of the mountain. They hoofed the 2.6 klicks to the village and their vehicle in silence, eyes out, adrenaline pumping hard, expecting a bullet to expose their gray matter or an IED to send them home in pieces.

With the secure phone, Tox dialed in. "Command, this is Wraith Actual."

"What happened back there?" Major General Rodriguez demanded.

"You tell us, sir. Infil went without a hitch until we were ready to breach the perimeter, then things go ape. They're running to vehicles."

"Tanin?"

"Still alive."

"Possibly clipped," Thor put in.

Tox nodded. "Might've clipped his wing. If we get satellite, we can drone this."

"Negative. We are not authorized and too many civilians. Even if we were, can you verify which vehicle he got in?"

"Last one, sir."

"Have you had eyes on them the whole time?"

Tox bit down on the frustration. "Negative."

"This isn't a total waste. Because you were there, we're able to track them. And . . . we might know where they're headed."

"Sir?"

"Get to the extraction point."

Glancing at the phone did nothing to lessen his confusion or frustration. Tox bounced it in his hand and peered out the cracked, dirty windshield of the rusted SUV. "He thinks they know where they're going."

"I might know, too." Hand hooked on the steering wheel, Ram curled his wrist and pointed down the road. "Tzivia—she says they're in trouble down there."

"Down where?"

"Saudi, Jebel al-Lawz. Not more than a forty-minute chopper trip out."

"What kind of trouble?"

AND CURSED BE HE WHO STEALS IT

She did not believe him. And it was okay with Benyamin. Understanding required context, and that she did not have. To be sure, even he did not have enough.

Alison bent over him, tucking the blanket around his shoulders. She squatted, her brown eyes so like her *savta*'s. "The beach will do you some good, eh, Sabba?"

As Alison went to the shoreline and dipped her toes in the sparkling waters, he tried to ignore the din of noise, shouts, and laughter. Squeals and wailing children. Coney Island was a nice respite from the dull monotony of their home, and Gratzia had always loved visiting when the children were young. But now, with its carnivals, sidewalk vendors, and throng-infested sandy-rocky shore, Coney Island wept of things lost.

It was not so far away nor so long ago. Not in his mind. She was close, so close that he could hear her voice. Smell her perfume . . .

Car lights swung onto the beach. Blinded and unable to see, Ben lay motionless with the others, huddled and shivering in the predawn hour. Rocks and sand beneath his fingers told him they'd made it. But the hurried footfalls of those who'd come from the vehicle warned he might have made it . . . to the end. Fear clawed at him, prickling his skin. Syrian Jews were imprisoned if caught.

But then he heard it—the beautiful sound he'd missed: the tongue of his people. It had been so long. It was good, was it not, that these strangers spoke Hebrew?

"We can trust no one," Abba warned, sliding his arms into his suit jacket. It was dry, unlike most of their other clothes, because Abba had held it above his head as they waded in from the boat. Abba caught Ben's arm and hauled him to his feet. "Shalom," he whispered to a man as they embraced.

Words darted back and forth, the conversations quick and hushed, competing with the water slapping the shore.

"Come, Benyamin," his abba said, pulling him up the embankment where two cars waited. The door creaked open with a loud groan, as if protesting their presence as Germans had done. As some Syrians had.

"Quickly," the man said, pushing Abba, Benyamin, his sisters, and Ima.

From the moment he first saw her, he vowed to never forget the angel sitting in the car. Hair the color of barley fields and eyes like a cool patch of earth, she motioned him inside with a smile of welcome and friendship.

Crowded into the small car, Benyamin sat with one of his sisters on his lap, his mother's bosom pressed against his shoulder and the beautiful girl on his left. With Rachel leaning against their mother, sniffling and crying, he found his head turned in the angel's direction. His pride knocked hard on the door of his heart that he must sit with his sister on his lap.

"You are brave," the girl whispered as their abbas chatted in the front seats, the car creaking and groaning over cobbled roads.

"Not so much," he managed. At ten years old, he was not brave.

Not at all. Especially not brave enough to look at her. But his gaze wandered there anyway. And he tripped into those eyes that seemed to reach his very soul.

"If you were caught—" She shook her head, her golden hair glowing in the darkness. Her fear tasted as palpable as the sea water that still clung to his clothes.

"But we were not," he muttered, relieved. He had never liked boats, but it'd been the only route. The only way to Israel. "Did you come on a boat?"

She shook her head.

"How did you not?"

She glanced down, a frown tugging her once-smiling lips.

Had he asked something wrong? It seemed right and normal to ask, but he could see he'd somehow made her sad. "Slicha," he whispered, an apology.

Her mouth curved upward again, looking at something she nudged toward him. A wrapped bundle. "You are hungry?"

It was a peace offering. Whatever mistake he had made—she had forgiven him. When Benyamin took the bundle, his fingers brushed against hers, small and cold. His gaze flipped to hers. And locked into place, like the double lock in the synagogue where they had guarded the Codex.

But he shouldn't think of that. Or of the beautiful girl helping them start their lives over in this new state.

Dawn crouched along the walls of the great city, allowing Benyamin a peek at this new home for his people. As they wound their way through the narrow streets, safety felt near. Hope . . . closer.

Warm hands closed around his. "You should eat it"—a bird squawked overhead—"Benyamin."

He started and stared into brown eyes. "How do you know my name?" How had the sun risen so quickly, when they were still in the car? "It is so bright." Darkness faded like a curtain pulled back on a stage production.

"It's morning light, Sabba. Eat, then we'll head back home."

Sabba? He blinked. Yes, light—and the present. Awareness flooded him as the same eyes—yet not the same—gazed back. "Alison."

"Yes." His *nehda* smiled, lifting a foil-wrapped hot dog. "It's very good." She wrinkled her small nose. "Though not very healthy. We won't mention this to your nurse. Eat, Sabba."

In his hand, he held not the linen-wrapped bundle from the beauty, from his Gratzia, but a hot dog from his granddaughter. Kosher hot dogs, no less. He chuckled, partially at himself, but also at the irony. Of the food and secret he held.

On her phone, Alison turned away, talking quietly. Most likely hoping the noise around them drowned her words. They did not. She spoke with her father. His son. "I'm afraid he's getting worse," she mumbled. "It won't be much longer."

Until his death? Benyamin touched his chest. With a steadying breath, he nodded. Let them think him a deranged, dying fool. He cared not as long as the secret was safe.

14

Gunfire strafed the air. The ground shook beneath the detonation of grenades. Dirt pittered and pattered against her shoulders and helmet as Tzivia crouched over her work. They'd been attacked yesterday but held off the looters. She shouldn't have been surprised there'd be a more coordinated attack later.

Broken remnants of the ancient city wall dug into her knees as she hurried to hide the remaining censer behind the loose rock where she'd discovered the codex leaf. Thank goodness Dr. Cathey had taken it and the fourth censer to Israel to authenticate. With a sigh, she ignored the sealed-off area beyond grid C23.

As she hurried back to the sorting tent, her flashlight flickered, the beam shaken by the rattling chaos aboveground. At shouts from the sorting tent, she quickened her pace.

The meaty sound of a fist colliding with flesh thudded through the air. Metal clanged. A shape fell into view, a dark form splayed across the tunnel entrance. Tzivia sucked in a breath and pinned herself to the tunnel wall. The plastic barrier fluttered, giving her a view into the sorting area. Dr. Ellison lay on the ground, a red knot rising on his temple. His gaze met hers for a second, shoving fear down Tzivia's throat that he'd betray her location. Betray the entire site. He'd made it clear his priority was medical, not archaeological.

"You did good, but not good enough, doctor," an authoritative voice said as a blurry form drifted into view. "What are you looking at?"

The plastic thwapped back, exposing Tzivia.

"Out! Out!"

She needed them to underestimate her, give her the upper hand. Making her hands tremble, she peered up with widened eyes so she looked terrified. "Please," she whined. "Please don't hurt me."

The muzzle of his AK-47 wagged. "Out."

"No, no," Noel said, his voice both placating and warning. "You don't want to do that. The tunnel has the contagion. If she was in there, she's probably infected!"

The man stared at her. Then glanced to the side, where Noel stood out of sight. The soldier clearly didn't believe him. And the questions forming in his dark eyes were enough warning that he'd figure something was up. Someone behind him spoke in Arabic, saying the tunnel would be sealed off if the disease was a threat.

"It *was* sealed," Tzivia said in Arabic, motioning to the plastic, as she emerged from the tunnel with her hands up. She took in the scene—three armed men, Noel on a stool to the side, his hands up, and Ellison at her feet.

Surprise marred the soldier's face. "Then why were you in there?"

"I'm immune." Tzivia nodded to the doctor, slowly bending to help him to his feet. She deliberately leaned in closer. "You betrayed us."

"It's bigger than you." There wasn't an ounce of regret in his words.

A blur of movement spiked dread through Tzivia. She shifted. Her arm came up, blocking the man's punch. Rolled it away as she threw her own left hook into his jaw. He fell backward.

A second gunman lunged. Tzivia nailed his face with a round kick. It snapped his head back. His legs tangled. He flipped onto the ground.

A gunshot cracked the air.

Tzivia flinched.

The man in charge gave a cockeyed nod. "Are we done?"

Breath heaving, Tzivia waited, ready. Behind the leader, his men came to their feet, proverbial tails between their legs.

Scar tissue folded his ear in half and gave the leader a terrifying demeanor. He jerked her forward, hooked nose against her cheek. "Where is Aaron's censer?" he hissed.

Her heart skipped a beat. Then two. "I don't know what you're talking about."

Cold steel bit into her temple as he pushed his weapon against it. He fisted her hair and jerked backward. Fire lit down her neck as he ripped her gaze to the ceiling. "You are lying!"

She caught his hand, whimpering as if he was killing her but silently preparing a good enough grip and angle to break his hold. When he came around, she saw a tattoo on his forearm before he shoved her aside.

"Th–there's no reason to do that," Noel stammered. "Those censers are connected to the plague." His face shone with urgency. "You don't want the artifacts, or you'll end up like them, so just . . . leave her alone!"

Crack!

Noel flipped off the stool. Blood splattered the clear plastic wall. It took a second for what happened to register. They'd shot Noel!

"No!" She lunged toward her friend, who writhed on the ground, then grew still, a pool of blood spilling from his side.

Strong hands hauled her backward, off her feet.

The leader turned to Dr. Ellison and aimed the AK-47 at his head. "Who else must die?"

Tzivia straightened. Tightened her jaw, furious. Would he shoot the man who'd called them?

"Aaron's censer!"

How did he know about it? "The censers were stolen—"

"You think me a fool." He smiled at her. A leer, really.

"Yes," she said defiantly. "Do you think we'd keep them here, something so valuable and important?"

Recognition glinted in his dark eyes beneath that thick unibrow. Yes, they were very important to him. But why?

She had to know. "You're willing to kill people for artifacts?"

"Not just artifacts—and yes, I will kill whoever I need to." He waved the gun. "Now, the censers or the doctor dies."

"He's one of yours. Do you think I care what you do to him?"

"Yes." He almost seemed gleeful.

If she could just drive her heel into his stomach—

More men milled outside the tent. Armed. Heavily. There was no way she'd make it out of here alive, even if she could take him down. What were her options?

The leader stormed at her. Grabbed her hands. "What is this?" He shoved her dirty fingers into her own face. "You were digging!"

Tzivia felt sick.

"Mahmud, take her to the tunnels. Make her dig until her fingers bleed or she shows you the censers."

"But the plague is in there," Tzivia muttered. She pointed at the scarred leader. "It's a high honor to be a martyr, yes? Perhaps *you* should come with me."

He leered. "My time is not yet come."

Before she could object, the tall man urged her on with the business-end of his AK-47. Defeated, she folded herself into the darkness and headed, it seemed, to her death.

"Reynaud sends his thanks, Ellison." The man's words chased her into the tunnel. A second later, a gun fired.

*   *   *   *

— TWO KILOMETERS OUTSIDE JEBEL AL-LAWZ —

"This is Robbie Almstedt with Special Activities Artifact Recovery and Containment," MacIver said as the team gathered at the Muwaffaq Salti Air Base in Jordan.

Red-haired and stocky, the woman must've been in town for a while, because there was no way she could've gotten there in the time parameters of their mission. Cortes stood beside her with her guard-dog agent and Chiji. His friend helped Tox gear up.

"Spooks," Ram whispered.

Almstedt glowered. "What's happening down there—it's impera-tive you protect that site, protect the artifacts."

"What about the people?" Cell injected, his sarcasm thick.

"Of course, the people," Almstedt said, clearly used to dealing with smart-mouths like Cell. "Do not let those hostiles take anything out of there. And make sure what Ms. Khalon found isn't tampered with."

The team jogged to the waiting Black Hawks and boarded, Tox more than a little relieved to have Chiji back while Cortes and Wallace were tied up in diplomatic pandering. Another diversion to make everyone look the other way while Wraith finished this.

On the Black Hawk inbound for the archaeological site, Tox glanced at Ram. His friend bore the concern Tox expected to see about his sister. Comms piece snug in his ear, Ram stretched his neck and adjusted his HK416. Tox gave him a look that asked if he was okay, and almost immediately, Ram nodded.

Then Tox turned to his conscience. In the full battle dress, Chiji looked impressive. Massive. "You okay?"

"I would prefer my sticks," Chiji said, looking at the Glock 22 they'd given him.

"Use whatever you need to stop the enemy."

"Body cams hot now," MacIver ordered.

Tox turned his on. "Command, what is the sitrep on the ground?" Wind ripped at his feet and legs as he sat in the jump seat. Buzzing the treetops, the helo worked to stay off radar to avoid detection. They needed to insert fast and silent.

"More than two dozen hostiles," said a rote military voice from SAARC, who watched via satellite feed. "Heavy firepower in Blue Three."

Tox consulted the small map strapped to the forearm of his tactical shirt. Blue Three was the main sorting and medical tents. Was Tzivia in there?

"Wraith Six" came the strong, commanding voice of Major General Rodriguez. "Be advised there are UN personnel onsite and the site is hot. Repeat, the site is hot."

UN? Tox exchanged a look with Ram. What had Tzivia discovered to draw that attention?

The helo crested a small knoll, the ground blurring beneath his feet as they raced up on the site. He'd jump in three . . . two . . .

Tox leapt from the chopper, rolled, and came up on a knee. He aimed his M4 at the archaeological site. Dust whipped around him, but his shatterproof glasses protected his eyes as he checked for hostiles. "Wraith Actual on the ground," he subvocalized, knowing his mic would filter out noise and deliver his words to Command. Scanning right, he noted Maangi sprinting toward a portable building for cover, Thor on his heels. Ram and Cell hustled up to a tent on the left. Chiji hugged Tox's six.

A dark shape popped from behind a mud structure then vanished.

Tox took a bead on the location. Slowed his breathing. Waited for a reappearance.

The man stepped out. Tox identified the gun, the keffiyeh. *Terrorist*. Eased back the trigger. When the terrorist collapsed, he waited for another to show. "Hostiles engaged," he reported.

A slap to his back told him MacIver had joined him. Tox pushed to his feet and hurried straight toward the body. Tucked himself against the wall. MacI rushed up next to him. Gave a nod, then went to a knee and peered around the corner. Fired several short bursts.

Tox swung out, took up suppressive fire as he and MacI advanced between the two tents. Approaching windows presented unique dangers, so they slowed and angled away and down as they continued on, Tox and Chiji with their backs pressed together to provide cover to the six and twelve.

"Tango down," Cell called. Then Maangi. Several times.

Dirt crunched beneath his boots as he advanced, targeting the center of the site. Tox angled out and rushed up to a portable building.

"Wraith Four in position, with advantage." Maangi. Their sniper had high ground.

Thwank!

The unmistakable heat that streaked past his cheekbone told Tox he'd nearly eaten a bullet. He yanked back, spine to the wall, M4 aimed down.

Plaster exploded, peppering his cheek in a stinging rage. Tox rolled away from the corner, urging MacI back. "Four, we have a shooter pinning us down. You got eyes on him?"

"Wraith Actual, be advised," Major General Rodriguez interrupted, his voice nearly drowned by the chaos of firefights. "It looks like your target from Jurf is packing up an SUV in Blue Three."

Tanin. In other words, Wraith needed to get their sorry butts moving. "Copy," Tox said, on a knee. "Four—we need this shooter neutralized."

"Working on it," came Maangi's way-too-calm voice. "Want to stick your head out again so he'll show his mug?"

Tox nearly smiled. "I like my head where it is."

"Just asking."

Nearby—couldn't be more than a couple of meters—came a flurry of gunfire. Handguns. Close quarters. Who was in trouble?

With Chiji, Tox started back the direction they'd come, MacI hot on his trail, and banked left to come up the other side of the structure. Farther from Blue Three but more cover. They snaked between the portables, sidling up the corner. Tox slid down against the wall and drew out the small mirror from his pocket. He eased it around the corner.

Glass shattered.

Tox bit back a curse and jerked away. The shooter had been waiting for them, knew they'd moved. Probably watched them do it.

The thunderous crack of a sniper rifle sizzled the air. "Tango down," Maangi said. "Thanks, Wraith Actual."

Heart still in his throat, Tox adjusted his brain bowl. "Anytime." He shook off the adrenaline.

MacIver tested the corner, this time with a rag. When nothing happened, Tox hustled out, his weapon secure against his shoulder as he sidestepped, sweeping. Scanning. Bodies and vehicles littered the open area. He advanced, rushing toward Blue Three.

Movement snagged his attention. He whipped to the right. Ram and Cell were closing up their quadrant with speed, tightening the knot on the target.

"Wraith Actual approaching Blue Three." But as he homed in on the designated area, Tox couldn't help but notice the multi-tiered tent and self-contained ventilation system.

Ram came up on his left, indicated the tent with a scowl.

Tox nodded. "Command, we have a medical isolation unit in Blue Three."

"Move!" Rodriguez said. "Get around it and stop that vehicle, Wraith!"

Tox stalked in that direction carrying a mammoth-sized bad feeling—and Command was ignoring it. What was he walking the men into?

"Death breathes here," Chiji muttered.

"Don't." Tox focused on the target. "I don't need that stuff right now."

Shouts and shots peppered the chaos.

"Wraith Actual! Hostiles on the north side. Repeat. North side," Maangi reported as the booming crack of his sniper rifle echoed.

Tox pivoted and raced back with MacI. As they came around the tent-and-wood structure, two men darted out. Advancing, Tox fired and nailed the first guy. Then the second, who threw himself back into the tent.

Thermals would be perfect about now. Tox sidestepped, angling in front of the flaps where the man had vanished. Blood smeared the plastic. Knew he'd tagged the guy.

MacI was there, reaching for the flap to give Tox a clean line of sight inside. Cell slid up behind him. Tox nodded.

MacI whipped it open.

Tox rushed in to the left, pieing his weapon to the right as he moved. His line of sight crossed MacI's, who'd gone to the right and pied left. They traced the walls and came together in the middle, scanning tables and equipment.

Empty. Where was the hostile?

The main hub contained rows of tables and trays holding shards of history and archaeological equipment. Straight ahead, beyond a tarp-like divider, a chambered environment lurked. His gut twisted as he negotiated a tangle of lockers, metal tables, and a grease board with a map to pass through the heavy divide. He waited to get his bearings, noting an opaque tarp covering an entrance on the right. Dark. As if it led underground.

He came around the corner of a shoulder-high stack of crates and found a body laid out. Tox nudged the man with his boot. When he didn't respond, Tox slowly crouched, never taking his eyes off the environment, and touched the guy's neck.

"Got another one over here," Ram said.

Too many bodies. What went down before they arrived? "This

wasn't just artifacts." Tox slid his gaze to the multi-chambered area. "That's a decontamination tent." And beyond it. "There are people in there."

"Quarantine," Ram muttered.

"Can you smell it?" Chiji's voice, serene and smooth, whispered to their fears. "Death."

Weapon at the ready and eyes out, Ram worked his way over to Tox. Held out his phone. Tox glanced at the screen which held one name: Tzivia. He frowned at his friend. "She's here?"

Ram nodded.

Where?

Grunts and thuds erupted from the dark cave behind the flap. Pivoting, Tox snapped up his weapon and readied himself.

A man burst through the plastic, pulling it down and tangling himself in the tarp. When he saw the team, he shouted and raised a weapon at them. Chiji whacked the guy across the head with his Glock.

Movement in the cave. Tox swung his weapon and SureFire torch at it.

Tzivia appeared like a specter, rushing and frantic.

MacIver sprinted toward her.

Boom!

Fire and dirt vomited from the cave.

15

Tox twisted away from the explosion and dove toward safety. A wave of heat washed over him. Tiny needles of fire prickled the back of his neck and hands. He hit the ground hard, head cracking against a table. He waited for the backdraft or a secondary explosion or falling debris, then shoved to his feet.

"Tzivia!" Ram threw himself at the collapsed entrance, digging into the rubble.

Memories flooded Tox. Of Kafr al-Ayn. Of the tunnel collapsing on him. Of suffocating. Fading into the darkness. Then the man showing up in the fire.

"Dig!" Ram shouted.

The command yanked Tox out of the past. He grabbed loose debris. At his side within seconds, Chiji and Cell worked like crazy to clear the opening. "Wait." Tox looked around. "Where's MacIver?"

"Boot," Ram snapped, nodding to a man's black tactical boot sticking out of the rubble.

"Wraith! Report!" came Rodriguez's urgent demand.

"There's been an explosion," Tox panted out as he hurled a piece of lumber to the side. "An archaeologist and one team member trapped inside." He knew to keep names off the comms.

"What about the isolation chamber?" an unfamiliar voice asked.

"Foot!" Ram resumed digging.

So did Tox. Urgency sped through his veins, knowing her time was limited. If she didn't have air . . . if she had internal injuries . . . "We need medevac!"

"Already en route," Major General Rodriguez said, his voice preternaturally calm. "Wraith Actual, we need to know the condition of the containment unit."

Ram pushed to his feet, inching back. He motioned to a large rock, and Tox bent in and hoisted it free. He cringed, calculating the thing had to have been right over Tzivia's back. She could have spinal damage.

"Wraith—report."

"Digging the archaeologist—"

"The containment area. Now!" Rodriguez shouted. "Is it intact?"

Tox hesitated. Tzivia's leg moved. His heart leapt in his chest. Ram saw it, too. Then dug harder, faster. Chiji and Cell were in on the action, trying to extricate MacIver, but he looked lower. Under Tzivia.

"Tzivia," Ram shouted, "hang on!"

She couldn't die. Not here. She'd miraculously survived Kafr al-Ayn. Tox hoisted rocks again, refusing to let her die now.

Rock seemed to rumble. Her legs shifted. The dirt fell away as her arm broke through.

"Don't let her move," Ram ordered. "Tzivia—don't move. Stay still." One wrong shift and she could permanently paralyze herself. Ram brushed her face clear. She blinked. Then coughed. "Does anything hurt?"

She groaned then coughed again. "Everything." Blood trickled down her temple and left nostril. Despite her brother's order, she came upright.

"Easy, easy!"

"Hey."

The gruff voice at Tox's shoulder made him look back, still moving rock to reach MacIver.

Thor stood over him, motioning him to the side. "Command needs you."

"We have a man down. They can wait!" Tox went back to work. A large section lay over MacI's torso and head. "Heave!" he groaned, working in tandem with the Chiji and Cell to hoist the massive chunk.

Finally, the rock slid away. "Get him out!"

MacI was dragged clear of the rubble. Someone uttered an oath.

Tox glanced down and winced. MacIver's head lay at an odd angle. His eyes open but lifeless. Mouth trickling blood. The cave-in had broken his neck. Crushed him.

"Augh!" Tox growled, turning away. Rubbing his face. He took a few steadying but angry breaths. Keyed his mic. "Man down."

"Wraith Actual, visual confirmation on the integrity of that isolation chamber is imperative."

Disbelief choked him. "Repeat man down—MacIver's . . . gone."

"Understood but get to that chamber!"

Disgusted, Tox tapped Cell on the shoulder and headed for the double-walled, double-chambered containment area. But he didn't need a close inspection. "Command, first wall of left front chamber with zippable door has been ripped from the supports."

"What about the inner wall? There—there are two inner walls," another voice asked. That sounded like Almstedt. "One belonging to the decontamination chamber, another to the secondary chamber with the patients. Are they intact?"

"Do we need hazmat suits?" Cell whispered as they inched into the first chamber.

"Wrong question," Tox said. "Command, what's going on here?"

"Forget the decontamination chamber," Rodriguez barked into the conversation. "What about the last wall, the one that separates the isolation area from decontamination?"

"I'll check it out, but how about you tell me what we just walked into?" Treading a fine line between life and death had never been so obvious as Tox stepped over the plastic tarp and poles to examine the double walls on the far side. He carefully traced each seam, corner, and zippered area. "Visual inspection reveals no holes or tears."

A slap against his arm made him look at Cell, who held a pencil through the wall of the first chamber. Then through the second.

Tox bit back a curse. "Decontamination chamber may have been compromised. Small hole, size of a bean." He angled so his body cam recorded the hole.

"Son of a blister," Cell muttered. "The bodies . . ."

Tox's gaze hit the row of cots. Large growths on the neck. Blood seeped from blackened appendages. But— "They've been shot." Disbelief rattled him as he looked from one body to another. All the same. All with a single entry wound to the head. "They killed the victims."

Tox and Cell shared a look and stepped back, but it was too late. They had already been exposed.

"Until hazmat clears the area."

"But there isn't a hazmat team here, sir."

"Hazmat is en route. ETA forty mikes," Rodriguez said. "Secure the scene. Nobody leaves."

"What are we dealing with?" Tox's heart jammed between his ribs. "What have you sent us into?"

"Worry about that—"

"I'm standing in front of a compromised isolation chamber. *What* am I exposed to?"

But there wasn't an answer. The comms had gone silent. Tox tugged out his earpiece and released the oath he'd swallowed several times since landing in country.

"It's a plague."

He turned, surprised to see a dusty Tzivia with duct tape in hand, looking annoyed. She wedged past him and patched the holes in the isolation chamber. A temporary fix that did little to reassure anyone.

She turned and met his gaze. "Tox?" Her eyes widened. Lips parted. "You're . . . alive."

Tox glanced down, embarrassed for some reason.

"That's what we all said," Cell groused.

Three years vanished. Tox remembered the last time he saw her. Their "picnic date." Hurt in those brown eyes as he said good-bye.

Ram hovered, touching her temple. She swatted his hand away.

"I'm fine." Hair askew and dusty, Tzivia had more fire than all the women he'd met combined.

They didn't have time for a reunion. Tox stepped closer. "What kind of plague?"

She blinked. Frowned. "Uh . . . unknown." Her finger flicked toward the man in a white lab coat on the ground. "Dr. Ellison said it was a cross between the septicemic plague and the Black Death."

A new Black Death?

* * * *

"The patients . . ." Tzivia walked to the chamber, trying to shake loose the shock that gripped her—both over the murder of the infected and the fact that Tox Russell hadn't died three years ago. "But . . ."

"Someone had to be in that chamber to execute them." Tox sounded haunted.

Her head bobbed almost of its own volition, then an idea infused her. Tzivia hurried to her work area. She powered up the main computer. "We've been recording since patient zero," she said, hammering on the keys. "If the shooter didn't suit up . . ." She accessed the video surveillance of the room and pulled up the last hour of footage. "Okay."

With Ram and Tox hovering, Tzivia fast-forwarded the video. Watched the entire scene play out as a man stepped into view and hesitated, head down, before the decontamination bay. "Please tell me you put on a suit," she whispered, watching, waiting.

"Can't see his face," Ram said.

"Is there another camera?" Tox asked.

"No, be grateful we have this one." Her pulse slowed in disbelief as the man moved forward, toward the door. "No, the suit. Pick up the suit!" Her breath whooshed out as he lifted one of the suits hanging on a rack and donned it. He entered the decontamination bay, then the isolation area. "At least he was smart enough to guarantee his own safety, which means he's not spreading this sickness."

The gunshot happened silently. But the burst of red that erupted around the victim's head shoved Tzivia back. She clapped a hand over her mouth, watching as he moved to the next bed. Aimed. Fired. Horror gripped her. The tiny explosions were silent but startling.

A warm hand came to her shoulder. She looked up, surprised to find Tox there. His eyes asked if she was okay. Sighing, she glanced back to the feed.

"He's like a freakin' robot. No feelings," Cell said.

"Is that Tanin?" Maangi asked.

Removing his hand from her shoulder, Tox bent closer. "Could be."

Tzivia couldn't fight the tears. It was a mercy, if she were honest. "By shooting them, he stopped their pain." But it was still murder. "I heard those shots—trapped in the tunnel, when they forced me to retrieve the censer." She brushed her dirt-clumped hair from her face. Her eyes burned. Exhaustion and defeat tugged at her, pulling her to the ground. She leaned against the crates.

On the video, the man turned and headed out of the chamber. This time, the camera caught his face.

"Bingo!" Tox tapped the screen. "It's our guy."

Tzivia didn't care if they had found their guy. Her friend . . . Grief tore at her as her gaze fell on Noel's body. She lifted a lab coat from his table and covered his body, his face. She didn't want to keep seeing those eyes staring at her. And Dr. Ellison—shot. Hiding in the tunnel had saved her life from—

She spun. Thought back to standing in the tunnel. The man lunging out after tossing the grenade. "I chased him back up the tunnel. He—" She stalled. Glanced to her left. Then right. She got up and searched the other side of the crates.

Ram reached for her. "What's wrong?"

"Where is he?"

"Who?"

"The guy who tried to blow me up in that tunnel! Did he get away?"

Tox shifted, his hand swinging to a corner and pointing. But he hesitated. "He landed right there. Chiji knocked him out." He traced a path around the sorting tent.

Ram went to the medical area. "He's not here. Why were you even in the tunnel?"

"I tried to hide the last artifact we found—a censer. But he forced me to give it to him in the cave." She nodded to Dr. Ellison's body and her gaze again fell on Noel, remembering . . . "He—he said something . . ."

"The doctor?"

"No, the man who shot him." She motioned to her ear. "His head was scarred."

"Definitely Tanin," Tox said.

She flicked him a look, the name meaning nothing and her thoughts tangled up in the memory. "He said something about a message—or no, Reynolds or someone sent his thanks." She looked at the men, thoughts clearing. "Dr. Ellison called someone yesterday. It was the man who killed those people. Had to be—because they showed up today demanding the censer. That's the only way your Tanin could've known what we'd found. Dr. Ellison told him it was here."

Ram moved in front of her. "You found it?"

Tzivia met her brother's gaze with a half smile. "We found three. Two were stolen before these guys showed up. Now they're all gone, except the fourth."

"Miktereths." Understanding tumbled into confusion. "But you said a fourth—"

"Aaron's censer." She smirked. "I found it a week after the first three were discovered." She tried to tamp down her excitement, remembering people, friends, were dead. "It'd been buried apart from the others with a leaf of the Aleppo Codex."

"The Codex?" Ram's question pitched with excitement. He looked out of the tent, and she knew he was visualizing the mountain in the distance, the scorched summit. Moses. "Then this . . . "

Raising her gaze to the ceiling of the tent, she shrugged. "It seems to be."

"Seems to be what?" Cell asked.

"Though bathed in controversy," Tzivia began, "it seems we've proven this area is where the Israelites of the Bible encamped before entering the Promised Land." She ran her hand through her hair, digging out the knots with a grimace. "But my brother believes also in the curses, plagues, and power of an almighty God. He clings to fanciful tales."

136

"It's no tale. It was in a scroll."

"What was?"

"The story that the three censers were swallowed up," Ram explained. "And that when Aaron presented an offering, the plagues were checked. But if those censers were found . . ."

"It's absurd, Ram!"

"And yet, we stand here where four miktereths were unearthed and now a plague has struck."

"Cell, Thor, Maangi, secure the site," Tox ordered, in command as always. A tall black man remained behind Tox like a shadow as the others filed out. Tox liked being in charge and didn't talk much. He'd been that way three years ago when they'd met, and apparently still was. However, there was a change. She just couldn't put her finger on it.

"Maangi. The cut." Ram pointed their combat medic toward her.

He wouldn't let it go, so Tzivia hiked herself up onto a table.

"How did you find it?" Ram asked.

She watched the soldier sling a med kit off his shoulder and onto the table beside her. "First week onsite, the ground caved in and revealed an underground spring."

The medic dabbed her forehead with a cool liquid, cleaning the wound, and she detected the distinct odor of peroxide.

"From that, we found another level to the walls. We were afraid the rest would give way, so we reinforced the tunnel"—she nodded to the caved-in area—"for safe passage. When we did that, we found it! An entire people group there. Chaotically arrayed," she whispered. The excitement thrumming through her veins was mirrored in Ram's hazel eyes.

Her brother said, "' . . . and the earth opened its mouth and swallowed them and their households.'"

"It'll take months to excavate their bodies."

"But the miktereths—"

"Yeah. Strange that they were found separated. Someone from centuries past. Templar—"

"Templar?"

"The chest had their cross."

Maangi applied a butterfly bandage over her brow. "Done."

Close again, Tox angled in. "How are you?"

"Bruised." Talking about her feelings was as natural as turning herself inside out. "Ticked."

His cheek twitched in a near-smile and brought those soulful eyes back to hers. "Why are you ticked?"

Right. Always business. He might have changed, but Tzivia wasn't convinced it was for the better. "They took the artifacts, the miktereths."

"And there's a plague." He pulled up a chair and spun it around. Straddled it, arms folded over the back. "We've got forty minutes. Why don't you fill us in?"

She snorted. "Don't you already know? I mean, you wouldn't be here if—"

"Tzi," Ram said. "We need to know."

She nodded. "Yes, you do." So she relayed the full of what had happened, starting with Basil's death, then the next worker who stumbled out with a nosebleed. The stolen miktereths. The men who murdered everyone in the camp. "We sent scrapings of the censers to Johns Hopkins, and Dr. Cathey took one to Israel for study. It'll probably be a few weeks still, but I'm at least eighty percent certain they're Bronze Age."

Ram nodded, pleased.

"You said you're immune," Tox noted. "Again."

She narrowed her eyes. "You have this amazing way of making me feel guilty about that."

"It's . . . notable."

"No, what's notable is that my friend and partner is dead." Tzivia's heart hammered. "That the WHO doctor sent to stop the disease turned out to be a traitor. That some freak assassin just walked in here and murdered fifteen infected!"

"We lost a man, too. We get it. But we need facts to stop that assassin."

She stilled. "He's why you came?" So it wasn't because of her, though she'd sent as many hints to her brother as she could that help would be appreciated.

"Been tracking him. Killed an ambassador and a general."

"Yeah, well, if you don't find him and get the censers back, Dr. Cathey is convinced the plague will ravage our world."

16

— DAY 8 —
JEBEL AL-LAWZ

Being locked away in an air-conditioned metal coffin that doubled as a quarantine chamber was no different than the time Tox spent in a ten-by-twenty in the federal pen. He sat against the wall, remembering how he'd gotten himself into this mess by busting Galen's lip. Small joy now as he felt the embers of frustration and agitation weakening his restraint. Chiji hovered nearby, his very presence soothing. Tox was glad his friend had come. He could've stayed in Nigeria, where it was safe—safe from the U.S. government, anyway.

"How much longer, man?" Cell knocked his knees against the walls, sending vibrations through the whole tin can.

"I'm about to put you out of your misery," Maangi warned, "if you don't quit rattling the cage."

Cell punched to his feet. "Yeah?"

"Sit down," Tox said in an even tone.

"I'm going out of my mind in here," Cell growled.

"We all are. That's the point. They're testing us," Thor said. "Lock us up, monitor our reactions."

"Why'd they put us in here, but not that hot chick?"

Ram lifted his head, which had been cradled in his hands, and slid Cell a glare.

"Might want to sit down before he ends you," Maangi said. "And I'll help."

The door groaned open. Light stabbed the dimness, making them wince. A man stepped up into the coffin, flanked by three others in tac gear. Behind them, at least a dozen more.

Tox stood, ready for a fight, but paid attention to the instinct that said one wouldn't happen. He felt the team behind him as he moved to the middle of the tank.

In his mid-forties, the man had salt-and-pepper hair trimmed short and clean. He wore a tactical shirt and pants, a weapon holstered at his thigh. "Thank you for your patience. The containment unit"—his gaze swept the container—"has reported no contaminants. You're clear to leave."

"Leave?" Tox glanced around for Tzivia. "Where's—"

"She's helping the team sent in to clean things up, locate what they can, and work on other things."

"What things?" Ram came forward, his arms out to the side, ready for a confrontation.

"Mr. Khalon, your sister will be fine. I assure you."

That the man knew Ram and his connection to Tzivia unnerved them. Tox wasn't going to let this slide. "Who are you?"

"Arthur Connors." Again, he glanced around the room, settled a little longer on Ram than Tox would've preferred, but it wouldn't be the first time an in-field agent had contact with a Special Forces operator.

"Another spook," Maangi said.

Connors didn't acknowledge or deny the accusation. He angled his head to the side and held out a hand. One of the soldiers behind him placed a sat phone in his palm, which he extended to Tox. "You and your team are headed to New Delhi."

Cell and his colorful language argued.

Connors smiled. "Thought you might like that." He nodded to the device. "Call your people. Verify it. They're the ones sending you." Connors had one of those gazes that spoke more than he did. "You're wheels-up in fifteen."

"You so anxious to get rid of us?"

Hopping out of the box, Connors shook his head. Then looked back. "Fewer bodies for me to count after the next strike."

"Not real fond of India," Maangi muttered.

"Better than some backwater village in Syria," Ram countered, grabbing his ruck. He shot a look to Tox. "You making that call?"

Tox turned from the expectant eyes of his team and faced the steel walls as he called. Something didn't seem right. Seemed too convenient, all these assets in place. They just happened to be here? Connors was close enough to come in and clean up? Or maybe this was just more of the short stick Galen had stuck them with.

"Code in," came the stiff, monotone voice on the other end of the line.

"Charlie-Kilo-Romeo-Romeo-November-Six-Two-Nine," Tox said firmly.

"Please hold."

A moment later, "Tox, that you? This is Almstedt."

Tox met Chiji's calm gaze. "You sending us somewhere?"

"Yes. We—"

"New Delhi," barked Rodriguez, intruding and taking control of the conversation. "It's quite the mess down there in Jebel al-Lawz, Russell."

Accusation laced his words that Tox had created the mess. That, true to his name, people died wherever he went. "Not my mess, sir. It was already here when we put boots on the ground."

"Well, we have to stop this thing."

"Tox, the man you're going after," Almstedt said, "Bhavin Narang—you'll have this information soon—is infected, so we must locate and contain him—yesterday!"

"Understood," Tox said, trying to tamp down his frustration at being forced off mission. This was just like when they sent him to Kafr al-Ayn, where a guy wielding a mace believed himself all-powerful as he spread a deadly toxin. But in this case, the guy was just trying to make a fast buck . . . or thousand. "Why are we breaking mission to go after a diseased subject who'll likely be dead in a few days?" He checked the buzz of medical teams outside the containment unit.

"Isn't that what's been happening? Dead guys aren't hard to find or stop."

"But diseases like the septicemic plague and the Black Death are," Almstedt said. "If he's out there, he's infecting people. I don't need to explain how bad that could be, do I?"

Tox ground his molars, noting the groans from the men around him.

"Listen," Rodriguez said, "it's not beyond the realm of possibility that Tanin goes after this thief."

With a cockeyed nod, Tox considered the general's words, the truth behind them. Tanin came here to steal the artifacts. If he knew Narang had stolen one, Tanin was probably crazy enough to risk a plague to get it back. It wasn't just about the artifact now. Men like Tanin took it personally. It was about conquest.

Tox felt the guys watching. Felt their probing gazes. Their concern. He turned and hopped out of the container. Wandered around the side. "What about the disease?"

"It's one ugly mess."

"Yes, sir, but my team"—Tox glanced back to be sure he was alone—"you're asking me to willingly and knowingly put them in the path of this deadly virus."

"It's the same as you leading your men into a line of fire with bullets, IEDs, and bombs, Russell. Containment is out of our hands. This is no different than combat."

It *was* different. How, he didn't know. But it was. "They didn't sign up for this."

"No, *you* signed them up. Remember? What was it you said? 'My team, my men.'"

The det cord in him sparked. Backed into a corner, Tox fisted his hand. "Sir—"

"Find your manhood and get on that plane."

The line went dead.

Tox threw a punch into the metal wall. Pain spiked through his knuckles. He punched it again, growling as he did. Both hands on the steel, he drew in a breath. Let it out. Drew in another.

"'We battle not against flesh and blood—'"

"Not now, Chiji."

"Especially now, Ndidi." Voice as smooth as satin, as thick as chocolate, Chiji insisted. "*Especially* at this hour when the demons are many."

"I'm leading them to their deaths."

"You are not God," Chiji whispered, his words fierce. "Do not think yourself so great that their lives rest in your hands."

"They're *my* men." Staring up at his friend, Tox hoped to drive home his point. "*I* chose them. Insisted on them—those men. Each one." Major General Rodriguez had been right about that. Tox had nailed each one to the cross of this mission. "So, yes—yes, they are in my hands. If they die—their blood is on my head."

"If God says they die—you can no more stop it than start it."

"Don't. Don't sanitize this." Tox huffed, his heart pumping hard. "If they die, it's on me. I won't let you wash that guilt away with some platitude or Bible verse."

He'd accept penance. Live with it. It was his. Letting it wash away was to dishonor the memory of those who trusted him. The men at Kafr al-Ayn. Brooke . . .

"Then it is *you* who strangles mercy." Chiji bent down, his dark brow mottled with sweat and dirt. "God, He brings you here."

"No, I—"

"*You* are his warrior. He put your foot on this path. He guides you." Chiji shifted the angle of his head.

He wanted to believe that. Believe God actually had purpose for him.

"Tox?"

He pivoted and swallowed his frustration as Ram joined him. Counting rocks beneath his feet gave him a few seconds to regroup.

Ram waited, quiet. Enough worked through his clear eyes to know he'd heard the conversation. "What'd SAARC say?"

"New Delhi." Tox drew in a quick breath and spit it out before he could alter course. "Track down the guy who stole the artifact from Tzivia."

"And Tanin?"

"Unknown. Possibly going after the thief, too."

Ram adjusted the beanie on his mop of curly hair, then nodded. "Tzivia was relieved Dr. Cathey had left the site before Tanin showed up. He's in Israel verifying a parchment and that censer. She'll stay here until he returns."

Tox smiled. "She's not waiting on an old man."

His friend laughed. "No, she'll find any reason to play in the dirt again."

It was one thing Tox admired about her. "So, the parchment— significant?"

"Perhaps." Ram stared out at the mountain in the distance, deep thought sparking in his eyes. "But the censers—possibly the biblical find of the century, likely proving where Moses and the Israelites encamped." He stared at the scorched mountain. "Imagine Moses there, receiving the Ten Commandments."

The words forced Tox to take it in. To consider the possibility that he stood on ground Moses and the Israelites had walked. Heady thought.

"If true, this will give her some badly needed credibility after Kafr."

A Black Hawk showed up a half hour later, and they raced out of Saudi and into Beirut, completely bypassing the FBI agents, who were given orders to meet up in New Delhi. In Beirut, Tox and the guys boarded a jet for India. He checked his phone every five minutes for the information Almstedt had promised.

In a notebook, he sketched out the information they knew so far:

→ archaeological site contaminated
→ plague-like disease killing people: protrusions, bleeding tissue, Black Death
→ artifacts stolen
→ Tanin—Why?

What was going on? Were the artifacts tied to the disease? It seemed logical—and yet, entirely illogical. This wasn't some op with a supernatural twist. He was fighting for real lives, the lives of his men.

"SAARC send that info?" Ram's question carried just loud enough to be heard.

Tox tugged out his phone and double-checked. "Not yet."

Ram indicated the notebook. "What're you thinking?"

"That it"—Tox shook his head—"doesn't make sense." He scanned the jet. "SAARC knew about the plague."

Ram's intuitive gaze probed Tox's face.

"When we found that site, they immediately asked about the isolation tent, about its damage. Before we could even figure out what was going on."

"So they knew there was a deadly plague when they sent us down there." Ram scratched his thickening stubble. Looked at the notebook. "Why would they?"

"Exposure . . . ?"

"Think it's hit more than just that village and New Delhi?"

"If it did, we're in a boatload of trouble." The phone buzzed in Tox's hand. He checked the screen and saw an email with an attached file. "Here we go."

"Group up," Ram said, circling his finger in the air.

The others gathered as Tox opened the file. It came through quick. Too quick. He scrolled down. "Only two pages."

"Keep intel close to the vest."

Tox went back to the first page. "Thief is Bhavin Narang, age twenty-three. Not married." He kept reading, then summarized. "They suspect Tanin is going after him, but assets there report no sight of him." He processed the next paragraph of information. "Bhavin has one brother, Chatresh Narang. Thirty, unmarried . . . and he's missing, too."

"Get me a computer," Cell said, annoyance bleeding into his words, "and I'll find him."

"What," Maangi said, "you think SAARC and DoD haven't tried?"

"*Tried*. That's the key. They tried and what do we have? Bupkus." Cell stabbed a finger against the top of the seat. "Everyone hiding comes out at some point. For small things—food, mail." He scrunched his shoulders. "This brother comes out? I'll bop him on the head."

"No bopping," Tox said. "If we find him, he can lead us to his brother." A second of weightlessness tugged at him. He eyed the name one more time, as well as the address of the safe house, then passed the phone around. "Memorize it. I want to find this guy and get back to the original chase."

"Tanin," Ram said, scanning the page as the plane began its descent.

By 2200, they'd landed and worked their way through the tangled streets to a swanky hotel that towered over the bustling capital city and served as a safe house. The team showered up, ate, and then grabbed rack time.

On first watch, Tox stood at the window, staring down at the tangle of cars and bodies swarming the late night. Thousands could become a thousand corpses in a matter of days if this thing broke out . . . if they missed this guy . . .

He should do this on his own. Protect the team. The men. Nobody else needed to get hurt because of him. There had to be a way to get around this.

Never should've asked for the team.

But he had. So he had to gut it up. He'd wanted to operate seamlessly and without hesitation. For Tox, that level of trust only came with the men in this safe house. But chasing a man infected with a deadly plague . . . Roughing both hands along the sides of his head, he pivoted and grabbed his phone, glad Ram's shift had started.

"Going down to the vending machine." He was halfway out the door before his sentence finished. He wasn't hungry. Didn't care about food. He had to get out. Get walking.

What you run from is responsibility.

Tox groaned. His own conscience now sounded distinctly like Chiji. Maybe he should go for a run.

And where would you run to?

Was there no peace to be had in this world? He rounded the corner.

A man stood there. His face went white—which, for an Indian, was saying a lot.

Tox stopped, his anxiety forgotten. His anger shed. A claxon went off in his head. Trouble. This guy was trouble.

The man straightened. Reached for something.

Tox threw himself at him. Slammed his forearm into the guy's throat, pinning him against the wall and catching his closest arm. "Who are you? What are you doing here?"

"P-please," the man struggled, his dark brows etched into a knot. "I—you are the soldiers?"

Tox applied more pressure. "Don't move."

"No, no," he muttered. "I came—my brother. He was my brother." Tears spilled over his brown cheeks. "Please—please help me."

Things started coming together. His words making sense. This was Bhavin Narang's brother. Pupils tiny. Eyes red, puffy. Crying. He looked tormented.

"Chatresh," Tox said.

The man's eyes widened. He almost smiled. "Yes. I am Chatresh."

Could he trust this guy? No, but he could take him. "I'm going to release you," Tox said, wishing Agent Cortes was here to tell him if he was reading this guy right. "But don't test me."

"I want help, not trouble."

Tox eased off very slowly. Released Chatresh's hand at the last second. "Start talking."

* * * *

— JERUSALEM, ISRAEL —

"Did you find out anything?" Dr. Joseph Cathey asked, unable to restrain himself any longer.

"Yes, yes." On his knees before a long, oak cabinet in his home, Rabbi Akiva opened it and pulled the rear panel of the cabinet aside then reached even farther—right into what must've been the wall itself. He drew out a flat tray and passed it to Joseph before climbing to his feet. "It is not easy to get anything pertaining to the Codex these days."

Akiva tucked on a pair of glasses, angled a light toward them, then slid a grooved lid from the box. "The page is indeed from the Aleppo Codex."

Excitement thrummed through Joseph. "I knew it!"

After putting on a pair of blue cotton gloves, Akiva laid out the leaf. "First—look at this." He lifted a black-and-white photograph from beneath the parchment, separated by an acid-free piece of paper.

Joseph donned his readers. With the lettering and curses at the top . . . "From the Codex?"

"Yes—it's the only image of this leaf that exists—well, this is a copy, to be precise." The rabbi pointed to notes in the margin. "See this?"

Joseph leaned closer, straining to make it out. He saw an unusual combination:

‏אחרי עקוב‏ †

"'Follow the . . . cross'," he read the words in place of the symbols. "What is it?" The lettering seemed lighter than the rest, the edges almost black.

"I have no way to know for sure . . ." His friend rubbed his beard, squinting in deep thought at the piece of history.

"But you have an idea."

Akiva looked up, hesitation darkening his face. "Yes." He sighed but said no more.

"My friend, this is important."

"Mm," Akiva murmured, his gaze not leaving the leaf. Then another sigh. "I have heard a rumor that within the Codex there are dozens of odd cantillation marks, along with many cross symbols, though some say it's not a cross but the letter *T*." He shook his head. "I probably should not be telling you this—"

"Wretched conspiracy of silence."

"It is said that when you"—he traced a gloved finger over the cross—"'*follow the cross*,' there is a hidden message."

The words, the very thought, pulled Joseph closer to the parchment. He homed in on the symbol and scanned across the columns and line. "So this one . . ." Which cantillation didn't seem to fit? "This? The mark over 'censers'?" For the mark to be over a censer, which they'd found with the leaf . . . "This isn't a coincidence. It's a message."

"Part of a message," Akiva agreed.

Joseph waited, half expecting Akiva to go on, because something in his words or demeanor—Joseph couldn't decide which—gave him the impression he wasn't done. "Do you know the message?"

Akiva's eyes widened. "Why would I?"

"You were hesitant to share your knowledge—"

"Simply to protect the Codex." He seemed affronted. "Why would you think I know the message?"

"It just seemed you had more to say."

"Bah, it is only a rumor, as I said." Akiva turned back to the leaf and huffed. "Another rumor floating around is that while ben Asher and the Swift Scribe labored on the Codex, a man named Thefarie paid one of them to conceal the message in the pages, but I cannot believe that. Ben Asher worked far too hard, as did the Swift Scribe.

"A story is told," Akiva went on quietly, "that when the Aleppo synagogue was attacked after the UN vote in 1947, the Codex was nearly consumed in flames before the rabbi's son plucked it from a burning pile of scrolls. Why it was not in its safe, one cannot say, but the boy sprinted out of the flames and delivered it to his father. They delivered it safely to Israel . . ."

Joseph could not help but notice the sadness, the confusion furrowing the man's dark eyes. "Rabbi? What is it?"

"That is when they were noticed."

"Who?"

With a shuddering breath, Akiva hunched his shoulders. "Not who—*what*. The odd marks. They weren't there before the fire."

"Or they weren't noticed."

"No," Akiva snapped. "They were *not* there. It is said that when the Codex nearly burned, the heat exposed marks written in invisible ink." Sorrow threaded through the lines in his face. "A great story, no?" He blinked and his sorrow vanished. "But . . . it cannot be true."

"Why not?"

Recoiling, Akiva gaped. "Because the Codex is then discounted. Thrown out. Useless—all by one wrong cantillation mark." His brows knotted. "Do you know how many codices and early Masoretic texts were verified using the Codex?"

The ramifications would be catastrophic for Judaism. Among the scribes who worked the texts there were strict, nearly obsessive rules and practices regarding the copy of texts. That painstaking and meticulous detail meant it took years for texts to be created. They were written, checked, rewritten, rechecked.

"You see why even I am reticent to join your chase of these pages, to verify this leaf."

"Of course." Harangued by guilt, Joseph knew for the sake of hundreds, if not thousands of lives, he could not abandon this effort. He must push his friend, even the whole Jewish community, if necessary. "But as I have told you, it must be pursued until an answer is found."

"What answer?"

"How to stop this!"

"Stop it? It's a disease, Joseph!" Akiva waved a hand. "The doctors will see to it. Besides, nearly two hundred leaves are missing," he snapped. "What can be done?"

"Find them!"

"You do not think we have tried? We have—for decades!" Defeat punched away the rabbi's spryness. "A leaf here, a fragment there, but no great number." He flapped his hands at him. "It is a lost cause."

"I won't believe that. I can't." Joseph pointed to the page. "People are dying because a plague has been unleashed and the censers are tied to it—just as Aaron checked the plague in the book of Numbers. Then we find a censer with that leaf?" He shook his head. "No coincidence. The chase cannot be abandoned. I must find the others."

At this the rabbi laughed. "All of them?"

"But I only need the ones . . ." The enormity and absurdity of finding the right leaf, containing the right mark, smacked Joseph in the gut. "Augh!" How was he to know which ones in the nearly two hundred missing leaves to even search after? He lowered himself to the rickety chair and moaned miserably. "It *is* a lost cause."

Chatresh glanced around, his bloodshot eyes looking dry and desperate. His white shirt was dirty, rumpled, and buttoned wrong, a spot gaping. "It's not safe out here. We should go to your room."

To Tox's room? Why? Was he scouting the team for someone? Maybe he worked for Tanin. Assigned to kill the team.

"Not yet." Tox stood back, awareness blazing—this was the victim's brother. And Tox had touched him. His mind rifled through what was known of the plague. They hadn't sorted how it was transmitted. He knew the first signs—a cough, itchy eyes . . . He reassessed Chatresh's bloodshot eyes. How could he tell if that was from tears or a virus?

"How'd you know to come here?" Was Chatresh here to infect the team?

"Shanay's brother told me you are here. He works at the desk."

So much for "safe" house. "Who's Shanay?"

Chatresh shook his head, apparently struggling to work through things. "What was that noise?" He jerked to the side, staring with bulging eyes. "Someone is coming."

151

There wasn't a noise. "Nobody's coming." Tox held out a hand to stop him but avoided touching him. "We're alone. It's okay."

"No, it's not okay. They know—they always know." He wrung his hands. "They knew Bhavin came back. They knew about the lamp." He dug his dirty fingernails into his face. "They know everything!"

"Whoa, easy. Let's take it slow." If he didn't get this guy unwound, he'd detonate. Freak and run. "Why don't you tell me why you're here?"

The clang of steel in the stairwell startled him. Chatresh whipped toward the sound, his dirty white shirt fluttering. He jerked back to Tox. "You see? We must hide!" When he lunged to pass Tox, he crossed the line.

Instinct shoved Tox back and pulled his Glock from its holster. He cradled it with a firm grip between both hands. "Chatresh," he said, calm and firm—his swift reaction and tone capturing the man's attention. Wide eyes told Tox his message had been understood. "We stay here until you answer my questions. Okay?"

Lanky like Chiji, the Indian man couldn't tear his eyes from the weapon.

"I do not want to hurt you." Tox gave him a firm look. "But that's up to you. Don't give me a reason to use this." He shifted, still not convinced the guy was legit.

But if he was—then the terror in his expression was real. And the gun wasn't helping. Tox angled sideways. Lowering the gun in his right hand out of sight, he used the other to pat the air between them to both calm Chatresh and distract him from the weapon.

"Who? Who is coming for you?" Tox asked. Weeding through the guy's accent made conversation tough, but add the panic and terror, and it was downright futile.

"I don't know!"

"Where's Bhavin?"

"He's dead. Dead!"

Tox stilled. "Your brother—Bhavin is dead?"

With a sniffle and swiping a hand beneath his nose, Chatresh nodded. A door in the hall opened.

Chatresh sucked in a breath. "They found me!"

"No, it's okay." Tox fought his own frustration and fear. "Easy.

I'll check it out. Wait here." Tox held out his palm as he slid around the corner and peered down the hall.

Weapon in hand, Ram was scurrying toward them.

Tox flashed a palm. "Not too close."

Wariness stilled Ram. "Who?"

"Target's brother."

Eyebrows knotted. "How'd he find us?"

"Knows someone at the front desk."

Ram processed that with a disapproving shake of his head.

The lanky Indian poked his head around the corner, which made Tox mad. "I said wait!" He showed the weapon to let Chatresh know he was prepared to use it. He wasn't about to let anyone compromise another member of his team. "Stay!"

Tentative hands snaked up in surrender, shaking.

"Infected?" Ram asked, watching the Indian.

"Unknown." Tox sighed, his head pounding. Twenty-eight hours and counting without sleep.

"Looks pretty spooked."

"Which makes him twice as dangerous. I need to get him out of sight."

Ram nodded. "A certain Nigerian is making his way up the stairs."

Surprise rippled through Tox and he mentally looked to the rear stairwell. He hadn't even heard Chiji as he had Ram. "Good to know. Find us a room."

Ram backtracked toward the room. After he closed the door, Tox took a second to compose himself. Group his thoughts. Strategize. He returned to Chatresh, who now crouched, elbows on his bent knees and head back against the plaster.

The guy was clearly grieving and maybe even in shock, but Tox needed answers. "Bhavin just came back?"

Chatresh considered him. Nodded.

"Was he sick?"

Confusion flickered through Chatresh's gaze. "You know?" He scowled. "How do you know?" Alarm etched the man's face as he changed Tox from "ally" to "enemy."

"Hey," Tox said softly. "It's okay—"

Shadows shifted in the stairwell. Chiji strode out.

Chatresh jumped to his feet with a yelp.

Tox shoved him back against the wall, breaking the no-touch policy. Then he saw Chiji's face. The set of his jaw. The tightness in his brow. "What?"

Chiji never broke stride, swiftly moving past Chatresh and closing in on Tox. "Visitors," he whispered.

Normally, for security reasons, Tox would haul Chatresh to the room with the others, but he could be infected. He grabbed his cell phone and dialed Ram. "Visitors. Get ready. I need a room."

"I'll notify SAARC. Room 431 is vacant."

"Thanks." He hung up, not wondering how Ram knew the status of 431.

"I will go down a couple of floors," Chiji said. "Come up behind them."

"Good."

The Indian looked pale. "Someone is coming? We should go to your room."

He was too anxious to get in the room. "Your brother was infected. I'm not risking anyone else."

Tox crossed the hall and made quick work of the lock on 431. He opened it, cleared it, and drew Chatresh inside. Securing the door, he pointed Chatresh to the hall that led to two bedrooms. "Lock yourself in one."

The Indian didn't have to be told twice. As he hurried out of sight, Tox made another call. Coded in. "Get me Rick Hamer or Dru Iliescu."

* * * *

— SOMEWHERE OVER INDIA —

"Leave immediately."

At the ominous words booming through the feed, Kasey closed her eyes, fingers threaded as she listened to the call between Cole, CIA, DOD, and SAARC. She and Levi had just entered Indian airspace— apparently too late.

"Negative," Tox barked. "We have an asset who can provide valuable intel on Bhavin and what happened. And did you miss the part where he's probably contagious?"

"Didn't miss anything," Hamer spoke through the line. "It's too hot. If you stay, you won't be alive to sort anything."

"And if I leave and he goes back into the streets, thousands die."

Stomach squeezing, Kasey tensed. What an impossible situation! Her mind fishtailed on the slippery possibilities. Stay and die. Leave and thousands die. A no-win scenario.

God, watch over him. Grant him wisdom.

"Tox," Rodriguez said over the phone, "the men coming into that hotel are heavily armed. And by their pattern and movement, skilled."

"Yeah. I can see that."

Kasey looked to the side, her mind tripping on his words. Could he actually see them? Did that mean he was in their line of sight?

"Got six—make that seven heavy hitters . . . Kalashnikovs . . . old school but effective." The silence on his end proved nail-biting. "Is a QRF en route?"

Kasey glanced at Levi, who had scrambled the quick reaction force, and he leaned forward and keyed a microphone. "Roger. QRF ETA: five mikes."

Cole cursed. "We'll be dead in five." He huffed. Went silent. Cracks and pops peppered the connection. "I have to deal with this."

"Tox, do not engage."

No response.

"*Do not* engage. Your priority is to *secure*." A pause, then Rodriguez spoke again. "Secure the witness and wait."

Crack!

Kasey jumped, locked onto the phone as if she could see what was happening. Was that a gunshot?

Pop-pop-pop!

"Tox, what is your situation?" Rodriguez sounded both upset and worried. "Tox, report. We have no eyes."

The *tat-a-tat-tat* of fully automatic fire rattled the feed. Elbow on the armrest, Kasey covered her mouth and listened. Prayed for Cole. Prayed for the team. Prayed this wasn't real.

"He engaged," Levi muttered, his thumb pressed against his lower lip.

Of course he engaged. Cole was a fighter. Always had been, and right now, he was fighting for his life. Fighting for his men. He could die.

"Tox?" Robbie Almstedt asked, leaning forward at the table. She'd connected with them in Jordan. Her face was a mask of concern.

Staring at the phone console on the small table, Kasey willed Cole to talk to them. Let them know he was still alive.

"*Tox!*" Rodriguez cursed. "Someone get me a feed in that hotel!"

Chaotic chatter buzzed both on the plane around her and on the communication channel, one person ordering Tox to talk, another demanding the location of the next nearest safe house. Someone promised operatives were en route and would assist. A profusion of conversations tangling the air.

Kasey pushed out of her seat and paced. A bitter, metallic taste glanced across her tongue. The taste of fear.

Meaty thuds and grunts pervaded the connection. "Hand to hand," someone muttered.

It was unsettling, what those men had to do to save their own lives. Kasey felt out of her depth again.

"Feed coming online," a droning voice reported.

Robbie, who sat across from them on the plane, turned her laptop around and showed them the screen.

Chaos. Utter chaos. Tables were overturned. Men tackled each other. Had to be six or seven in the confined area. It looked like a sophisticated barroom brawl. One between men in tactical gear and men in dark camo.

A uniformed shape swooped in from the side, lunging at a black-clad figure who used the attacker's movements against him. Flipped him onto his back. Now half-kneeling over the uniform, Shadowman coldcocked him. Another uniform rushed him from behind. But Shadowman turned. Came up. Slammed his elbow into the man's gut, then snapped up his fist and punched the uniform in the face. The uniform went limp, dropping like a wet rag. Two down.

Kasey hoped Shadowman was one of theirs, because he was eliminating a lot of men. Turning, the Shadowman focused his skills on another uniform, who was punching the daylights out of someone on the floor. Shadowman's hands went to the uniform's throat—and only then did Kasey see the knife. She drew in a sharp breath. The uniform froze, stiffened as the knife penetrated. But his hand was already coming up with a gun.

Shadowman stumbled back. His expression calm, focused. His eyes—

"Cole." The realization jolted Kasey. "Did he—" Had Cole just been shot?

"He's been hit," a voice shouted.

"QRF has entered the building."

"Copy that."

"Catalyst is on-site."

The voices drowning the feed did nothing to buffer the shock speeding through her system. She couldn't tear her attention from the monitor. Cole was shot. But it hadn't stopped him. A few more moves that happened so fast, Kasey couldn't tell what he did, and the puncher fell to the side.

"Kasey." Levi stood and touched her shoulder.

"Shh." She waved him off, staring at the monitor. She searched the people still moving. Everything went eerily silent. Men drifted around the room, removing weapons, checking pulses. Another hurried from one spot to another, gathering items. "Did we lose sound?" she asked, looking to Robbie. "What's going on?"

Robbie shook her head.

Cole reappeared, a sack slung over his right shoulder, his left covered in blood. Six men grouped up around him with weapons and gear. "Command, this is Tox." Cole was unnaturally calm and focused. "Targets neutralized. We need QRF exfil."

Pain sliced through Tox's shoulder and arm from the bullet wound. He cringed, hand going to his right pectoral. He gritted his teeth and worked his way out of the hazmat suit he'd been stuffed into before boarding the chopper. Skin clammy, head light, he lifted his leg free. Hopped to the side, his balance shifting, then kicked off the suit. He dropped against the inches-thick glass wall of the sophisticated isolation chamber and took a minute to regain his strength. He peered over at Chatresh, who was also disrobing.

A glass divider slid down between them, pushing Tox farther to his right as it spliced the chamber. Air hissed through a vent. He turned and squinted past the glare into the semidarkness of the warehouse-turned-safe house.

"Just extracting the air and refreshing with clean O_2," a man said as he adjusted dials. "Let me know if it's too cold or hot."

Right, because comfort was important when you were possibly infected with a deadly plague.

"Soon as Dr. Benowitz"—Ram indicated a man standing in a hastily assembled medical area—"clears you, we'll get that bullet out and patch you up. The risk of exposure to the rest of us was both second-ary and minimal, but we're still doing blood work."

"Good." Anger churned through his veins. He turned to Chatresh. "My men just got put through the grinder to save you. What do you know?"

Still disentangling himself from his hazmat suit, Chatresh met Tox's gaze. Then went back to changing.

Tox stabbed a finger at him. "They risked their lives for you, and now you play dumb? We need answers! Tell me what you know."

Sitting, Chatresh curled away from him, his dark hair mussed and clumped to the side, and tugged the suit from his legs. "I told you they were coming after me."

"Who? Who were they?"

Brown eyes widened. "I never met them before."

"Why?" Tox held his shoulder. "What do you have that they want?"

"That's what I'm telling you, I have nothing!" Chatresh held out his arms. Stood and turned a circle. "See? Nothing!"

"Infor—" A stab of pain nearly dropped Tox to his knees. He growled through it.

"Tox, you okay?" Ram asked.

Sweat slipped down his forehead as he nodded.

"SAARC and FBI are onsite," Thor announced, the wash of a blue laptop glaring on his face.

Hand on the cool glass, Tox braced himself. Looked across the twenty-three feet to a monitor that showed the perimeter of the ware-house. A half-dozen shapes closed in, then broke out of view. He glanced over his shoulder as the main door squeaked open.

In walked Robbie Almstedt, two tech geeks, that suit from DC—Wallace—and Cortes. Her gaze swam across the warehouse and quickly came to rest on Tox. Something about her green eyes twisted him inside out. Was it his imagination, or did she seem relieved to see him alive?

"Hey," Ram said, standing in front of the wall again. "How you holding up? Want ibuprofen?"

Tempting. "I'll wait," he gritted out, pulling his gaze from Kasey Cortes. He sat for another twenty minutes, eyes closed. Trying to rest. But he followed her voice. It was soft. Not like the guys or even Almstedt. Hers was low and lulling.

"He's clear," the doctor called. "Go! Get him on my table."

Locks cracked back. The door swung open. Chiji was the first one hovering over him. Tox gritted through the pain. "Make him talk."

"Don't worry," Ram said as they hoisted him up.

"I can walk," Tox argued, hating that they carried him.

Cell snorted. "Like a drunk pelican."

Ram and Chiji ushered him out of the chamber to the table waiting beneath a blinding industrial light. The doc numbed his shoulder then dug around for the bullet. It felt like a knife fight going on inside him.

Finally, the doctor stitched him, then had him sit up. On the edge of the table, Tox endured the bandaging. He noticed SAARC and the FBI agents had set up equipment and settled into the digs.

Tox accepted four ibuprofen from Ram. With a bottle of water, he dumped back the pills and swallowed. "You get anything out of Chatresh?"

"He won't talk to anyone but you," Ram said. "And you might want to get dressed. Seems your bare chest is distracting certain people of the female persuasion."

Tox glanced at Almstedt.

"Not her," Ram said quietly.

Tox's gaze slid to Cortes, whose head was down. Low. In an awkward, trying-not-to-notice way. "Where's my gear?" He came off the table to get another bottle of water.

"Should you be moving around yet?" Square-shouldered and with his white sleeves rolled up, Wallace appraised him.

Tox stopped. "We still have a mission?"

The suit nodded.

"Then yeah, I should be moving around." Tox grabbed the water and twisted off the cap. Gulped. "Where's my gear?"

"You're over there," Thor said, pointing to a cot against the far wall.

Tox grabbed a tactical shirt from his ruck then threaded his arms through it. When he hooked it over his head, pain wrestled him. He ground his molars and tugged it down before rejoining the others around the long row of tables. "Do we know yet if Chatresh is infected?"

"Doesn't look good." Ram sat back in a chair. "There are abnormalities in his blood work. Benowitz recommended keeping him in there until a detailed analysis comes back from a UN lab."

"Hey," Cell said with a lopsided grin, "I got shot, too." He pointed to where his shirt sleeve had been rolled up over his shoulder and a Band-Aid glared back.

Tox snorted. "My grandma's butter knife would've left a bigger scratch."

"Man, why you hatin'?"

"Because you make it so easy." Maangi strolled to a chair and straddled it, arms folded over the back.

"Any word from Tzivia?" Tox asked.

"Actually," Almstedt said, finally looking up from the mound of machinery and paperwork spilled over the tables, "I spoke with her. And Dr. Cathey."

"Why don't I like the sound of that?" Tox mumbled, quickly making the connection between SAARC and Tzivia's censers.

"Because we all know they're going to make us go all Indiana Jones again," Cell complained.

"Because after nearly blowing you guys to a thousand pieces in Syria, they want to make sure they don't miss this time?" Thor's humor was even darker than Cell's.

"*Because*," Almstedt snapped, then took several calming breaths. "Because you signed on the dotted line, Russell."

"We were sent here to track down an assassin. Then we're reallocated to track down an Indian with a virus." Tox wagged his eyebrows toward the isolation chamber. "His brother says he's dead, so are we done here?"

"Until we locate the body and missing censer, you're not done." Almstedt drew off her glasses. "What did you find out from Chatresh?"

"Little," Tox said with a shake of his head. "He got spooked. When we got back here, he went silent."

"Silent how?" The voice was softer, but no less direct. Cortes tucked back a strand of her sand-colored hair.

Was there another kind of silent? "As in, he wasn't talking."

She pursed her lips. "His words may have stopped, but did his body

161

language?" She turned toward the isolation chamber. "Because I see a man waiting to talk."

Tox turned, too. Brown eyes were locked onto him.

"Notice how he's sitting. He's watching you, Mr. Russell."

*   *   *   *

Kasey felt the tug of Cole's eyes come back to her, but she kept hers on their prisoner.

The tall Nigerian strolled up next to Cole. Chiji's gaze was earnest. "*Nwaanyi muta ite ofe mmiri mmiri, di ya amuta ipi utara aka were suru ofe.*"

Cole nodded, obviously understanding the foreign tongue, then navigated the chaos of cables, tables, and equipment. He made a quick diversion for another water bottle, then went to the isolation chamber. He drew out a steel drawer, dropped the bottle in, and slid it closed.

Chatresh Narang unfolded himself and retrieved the water. It was gone in seconds. He dried his mouth then nodded to Cole. "Thank you."

Kasey shifted forward and joined the tall black man. "What—what did you say to him?"

Chiji looked down at her, and she would've sworn he could see into her soul. But then his expression softened. "It is an Igbo proverb—*If a woman decides to make the soup watery, the husband will learn to dent the foofoo before dipping it into the soup.*"

"And why do we care about soup or froufrou?" Cell shrugged.

"Foofoo," Ram corrected absently from where he sat on a table, monitoring their team leader. "It's a staple in Central Africa, like mashed potatoes to Americans."

"And the point?" Cell asked.

"Switch tactics," Chiji said. "The gist of the proverb means to let the situation dictate which tactic to use."

"Whatever he knows," Almstedt said, "we need to get it out of him."

Kasey couldn't afford to miss anything, not with Cole's trust dangling before her. "Is this being recorded?" she asked Steve Vander, one of Almstedt's techs.

"Everything here is recorded," he responded.

That was a bit disconcerting, but also reassuring. She would need to go back over videos a few times, listening, watching, then listening again if she wanted to be of help to the team.

"Information." Cole planted his hands on his tactical belt, then slightly adjusted his left arm. "You have information they want, is that right?"

Chatresh merely stared.

"I have to confess I'm getting pretty fed up with the waiting game, Chatresh." Tox held out his hand. "You came to us, remember? We can't help you—"

"Help me by putting me in here?"

"That's for the rest of the world, to make sure you aren't infecting them."

Chatresh snorted, shook his head, then sighed. "Those men found me very quickly when I came to you."

"They did," Cole agreed. "And you think that's our fault?"

"Just as you think it is mine."

"Fair enough," Cole said. "Tell me how your brother died."

Chatresh stilled. Then looked down. "He died in my arms." So the guy was most likely infected, too. "Bhavin was very sick. Things sticking out of his neck. He made me promise to take care of our parents." He hesitated, eyes swimming in grief. "He told me he stole something, that men were coming. He said I must get help." After a moment of silence, he nodded around a sigh. "That's about all."

Kasey grabbed her spiral-bound journal where she recorded information and scribbled in it.

Cole continued, "Did he have anything?"

"Not that I could see."

"He told you he stole something, though?"

Chatresh blinked. Pulled his gaze back. "All I can tell you is that I was more concerned with his failing health. He was my brother."

He wasn't telling them everything. It was obvious Cole knew it, too. "Look, if you don't have anything for us, this game is over. We're gone. And you can find someone else to play with."

A phone buzzed. Ram hopped off the table as he answered the call and stalked to a far corner.

163

In the cage, Chatresh returned to the chair and sat, rubbing his thumbs over the plastic bottle.

"It's like he doesn't care," Cell groused.

"He's not worried, that's for sure," Thor muttered.

"You're right," Kasey said, her voice and thoughts firming. "He's not worried—not about himself."

Cole's head angled to the side, almost over his shoulder. He'd heard her. Considered her words, apparently. Then focused on Chatresh.

Bhavin Narang had already died. Was Chatresh not worried he might be infected? A thought pushed Kasey toward Cole. "Only a greater fear could mute the panic of a plague infection," she whispered.

Cole didn't acknowledge her. "You're not worried about yourself . . ."

Chatresh looked up.

"Your brother had a deadly virus, and it could be infecting others, but that doesn't worry you."

Chatresh played with the bottle again.

"We need to know where his body is."

"Buried," Chatresh said, still fidgeting with the plastic.

"He took something from that archaeological site he worked. We need that back."

"As I told you," he said, holding out his arms, "I have nothing."

Wait. That—that wasn't quite true. Something . . . Kasey chewed her thumbnail, thinking. "Not the full truth," she whispered. "Either he doesn't have it on him, or—"

"Information, then," Cole snapped. "What's in your head that makes you not worried?"

Chatresh pushed to his feet, and Kasey's stomach squirmed. Ram hurried toward Tox and whispered something in his ear. Cole's head came up, his shoulders squared. He considered Chatresh.

With a sardonic smile, Chatresh nodded. "Now you understand. Brain cancer," he said, pointing to his head. "I will be dead within a month, they tell me."

Ram muttered an oath. "It explains his messed-up blood work." He turned away, lifting the phone to his ear. "Tzivia, he confirmed it . . ." His voice faded as he stepped out of range.

"So you have nothing to lose," Tox said.

Sorrow lanced the man's brow. "My family does."

Again, an extended silence. It felt like hours were falling off the clock as they played this game.

"The longer you wait, it won't be just your family with something to lose." Tox stepped closer to the glass cage. "I get it, when you're hurting and scared, nothing matters except what you're protecting. But"—he shook his head, pleading—"my job is to protect you and everyone else from whatever killed your brother."

"Men killed my brother."

Tox frowned. "The plague—"

"He was sick, yes, but men came. They shot him with a sparkling arrow."

"Am I supposed to believe that? Come on," Cole said, his tone incredulous.

"No signs of deception," Kasey whispered from behind.

Cole stilled, glanced at her. Frowned, questioning her words. After she nodded, his shoulders deflated a little and he turned back to Chatresh. "So, they shot him with a sparkling arrow. What else?"

Lazy shoulder shrug. "That is all."

"You didn't see anything else?"

Chatresh looked down. "That's about it."

"He's whacked," Cell muttered.

The team grouped up around Cole, effectively sealing Kasey outside their tight-knit perimeter. She watched and listened closely, and Levi joined her.

"This makes no sense," Tox said. "Bhavin was as good as dead. Why shoot him with an arrow?"

"To make sure he died?" Levi offered.

Cole shook his head. "Plague means death. Tanin knew that already—he saw it in Jebel al-Lawz." He rubbed his jaw. "It's not adding up. Chatresh must know something."

"What makes you say that?" Levi asked.

Cole met his question with a stare. "Gut instinct."

Levi grunted, mocking him.

"Most times," Kasey spoke up, "gut instincts have legitimate reasons behind them that we just can't identify at the moment."

Cole studied her for a long second.

"Hey," Ram said, catching Cole's arm. "Let's talk."

Their quest for privacy cut through her as they slid off to the side, but Kasey refused to feel excluded. Besides, there was something bugging her about Chatresh . . . she just couldn't pin down what.

She turned to one of Almstedt's techs. "Can you send me the recording of the interview Cole just did?"

"Sure." It took him a few minutes, but he sent it to her laptop.

Hand guiding the mouse, she pulled back the chair and slid into it. She started the video over. Watched it. Tugged out her field notebook and made notes in her standard format of things observed and things questioned. Paid attention to the way he sat. The things he did. Something . . .

"What're you doing?"

Kasey started when Cole towered over her, hands on his belt. "Reviewing."

"Why?"

His question wasn't particularly terse, but she felt like she had to prove herself to him. And she hated that. She'd done it all her life. "Remember your gut instinct?"

"Yeah."

Kasey eyed the screen. "I've got it, too. Which tells me there's something to it." She listened to the interview again and tried not to freak when Cole slid into the chair beside her. *Pay attention to the interview. Not who's next to you.*

"Glad you showed up," Cole said. "Need your skills."

Her heart skipped a beat. But she refused to look into his blue eyes. "Skills?"

Tox wagged a finger to the monitor. "This. The deception thing. It's pretty—there!"

"What?"

"I . . ." Frowning, he sagged. "Never mind. Maybe it's just me."

Kasey ran it back. Paid more attention, made notes in her field notebook. Then smiled. "No, it's not just you. Look. Right here, he's giving three kinesic signs. Notice that when you pointed to him, he crossed his legs, leaned back, and broke eye contact."

"So he knows something?"

She smiled. "Definitely. He answered the question by saying 'that's about it.' Which means the opposite."

Tox nodded, amusement prying a smirk from his lips. "There's more information."

"Ask him again what happened before and after the arrow. I want to see his reaction."

"Okay." Tox touched the back of her shoulder as he pushed up. "Can you watch as I talk to him?"

His touch sent a thrill through her. "Yes, but I find more things when I can review it." She braved looking into his eyes and nearly drowned. *Focus, Kasey.* "Easier to study, analyze. I could probably give you more on what he's already said, once I ran it through a program or two."

With a hand on the table and one on the back of her chair, Cole shifted his gaze to one of his guys—Cell. "Make sure it's recording." After confirming Cell had taken care of that, he strode to the cage. Placed his hands on his belt and stared down Chatresh.

The man pushed from his spot on a cot and stumbled forward. "Yes?"

Cole stood in silence for a second. "That girl there is an expert in signs of deception. She knows when people are lying." He tilted his head. "She says you're not telling us everything, Chatresh."

The man flicked his gaze back to her, making her heart race, then tugged his earlobe.

"I'm wondering why you would do that, since you came to us. See?" Cole rubbed his jaw again and readjusted his stance, folding his arms. "That makes me question everything you've told us. And that makes me think you're not friendly." He could probably drill holes through Chatresh with that glare. "You're an enemy!"

"No! They killed my brother. I want them stopped. I'm telling you this. Those butchers need to be punished."

"That's true," Kasey whispered. "But he's leaving something out."

"You're not giving us a lot," Cole warned. "At this rate, we'll just have to hand you over to the authorities. Or better yet, we'll just turn you loose. Then those men who were after you—they'll see we're done with you. And since you're still alive, they're going to assume you talked. That family you said had a lot to lose? I'd be afraid for them, Chatresh."

Indecision flickered through the man's eyes. Twitched his cheek. The team waited, and it seemed as if the warehouse itself held its breath for his answer. "I will tell you this, my brother had a journal."

"Why would I be interested in a diary?"

"It had information." Chatresh smiled. "About the artifact and the men following him." He put his hands together in front of his mouth as if praying.

Cole squared his shoulders. "Where?"

19

— DAY 10 —
SWAMINARAYAN AKSHARDHAM, NEW DELHI

The one-hundred-acre complex welcomed more than five million visitors each year, and Tox was sure at least half of those were onsite right now. He made his way beneath the fronds of the palm trees. The swanky trees lined the perimeter of the sandstone and pink marble temple of the Swaminarayan Akshardham.

A shoulder slapped his. Though it'd been a day since he'd been stitched up, it still screamed in pain. But he rolled with it and even muttered an apology to the person as he kept moving. Too crowded. If it was this crazy out here, how was the main mission going? "Cell?" he subvocalized into their comms. "How's it going?"

"If I touch anything in here, someone's going to see," Cell said, sounding irritated and paranoid. "I just passed the stampede of elephants, and it's shoulder to shoulder."

Usually more bodies meant less chance of getting noticed, but in a sacred place like this, people noticed when you started messing with their gods. But this was where Chatresh said he'd hidden the journal. They'd spent the last twenty-two hours getting rested and planning this insertion, making sure to come near closing time.

"Just get to the audio animatronics," Tox said.

It was brilliant, really, hiding the journal in plain sight. It was also insanely crazy—how were they supposed to retrieve it with thousands of visitors at the sacred temple? Added to that, Chatresh couldn't remember which audio animatronics exhibit. Just that a man was sitting at a table and had a book in front of him. Great help.

"I'm in position on the northeastern tower," Maangi reported. "Getting some weird looks hanging out up here." In other words: drawing attention. "I've got Six and One headed up the main path," he reported, referring to Tox and Wallace. "Five and Two taking a stroll through the south gardens." Five and Two were Ram and Thor. Cell was Three, and Maangi was Four.

"Copy," Tox muttered as he banked right. Looked over his shoulder. The FBI agent had done okay so far. Didn't stick out. Tox glanced around, keeping a finger on his surroundings. A quick movement to his far right set off alarms in his head. After another dozen steps, he paused. "Just act like I'm showing you something," he muttered to Wallace as he pointed to the gardens. Behind the dark tint of his sunglasses, he searched for the black blur he'd noticed. Sure enough, a man quickly pivoted. Bent down.

"Keep moving," Tox said to Wallace. "Heads up, Wraith. We've got company."

"You mean like five thousand?" Cell muttered.

"Four, you got my twenty?" Tox continued toward the animatronics for backup.

"Roger that."

"To my four o'clock, black shirt and pants. Five-foot-eleven. Dark hair." Tox had deliberately slowed, forcing the man to stay in place so Maangi could snap some pictures, while pretending to be an amateur photographer. Wallace leaned closer, nodding as if they were talking to each other. The guy might survive this mission after all.

"Got him. European, definitely not local," Maangi said, the sound of the shutter clicking through the feed. "Definitely eyes on you. Methods are stiff, patterned. Armed. Handgun beneath left arm. Leg holster." Probably one at the small of his back.

"One on me, too," Ram said. "African male."

"Copy." Tox's mind pinged through possibilities. Variables. "You

170

know what to do. Take your time. Just buying time right now." The beta plan was to split up into units, make it harder to follow them or guess their objective. Get the journal and make it back to the warehouse. "We're in no hurry. Three, find it—but if you have a tail, leave it."

"The journal or the tail?"

"Both."

"Roger."

With hand signals, he sent Wallace left, while Tox took the turn toward the right corridor that would lead to the exhibits. As he hustled up the steps, he slid a surreptitious gaze back and down. A distinctly Caucasian male rounded the corner. He looked straight at Tox, then mounted the stairs.

Two tails?

He was now out of Maangi's line of sight, but since Maangi wasn't operating as a sniper, it did little good anyway. They'd gotten photographs of the tails. They'd work those to find out who was following them.

Forget following. How had they found Wraith in the first place? Were they monitoring the warehouse? That would mean they'd been on them since the hotel safe house. And that the warehouse could be in trouble.

"SAARC," Tox subvocalized.

"Go ahead" came Robbie Almstedt's ultra-calm voice.

"We have tails. Your location might be compromised."

"Understood. We'll stay eyes out," she reassured.

It was a load off his mind.

"I think I see it" came Cell's quiet but excited voice. "It's sitting right in front of this wax thing." Did Cell just curse? "Man, this is *sick*."

About time something went right. "Can you retrieve it?" Tox asked, walking around a column and admiring the reliefs of the deities and stories—but really waiting for his tails. Not because he was worried about them taking him out. He had to keep them away from Cell. Away from the objective. Confuse and distract them.

"I . . . don't think so. There are guards and people. Too many eyes.

And son of a—they're wax." A hissed curse. "Have I mentioned how much I hate—and I mean that four-letter word *hate*—wax figures? Their lips move exactly in sync with the narration. It's crazy. Jacked. Get me out of here."

"Baby," Maangi taunted through the comms.

"Dude, when this stuff melts, there are skulls—"

"*Three*," Tox bit out, insisting he get focused. He rotated and slipped to another column, eyed it for a second, then continued down the outer perimeter, his gaze momentarily surfing the open courtyard to the real splendor of this site—the mandir. Incredible. He wished he had time to appreciate the enormity and beauty.

Tox spotted the Exhibits door. "Three yards from the exhibit hall."

"Let me try something."

Tox cringed at the words that sounded too much like, "Watch this, y'all!" and kept moving toward the doors that hid Cell and the wax animated figures.

"This is muffed with these wax people moving," Cell muttered. "Might as well be zombies."

"Three—"

"Almost—"

A shout rent the quiet din.

Tox hesitated, watching the doors. Rumbles, murmurs, and yelling seeped between the jambs and threshold.

"Okay, that didn't work," Cell said. "I'm coming out."

Tox flexed his fists, advancing. "What happened?"

"I think"—Cell's voice faded—"we should probably—"

Tox veered left. Expecting the doors to fly open at any second, he followed the half-wall of the upper balcony level that overlooked the gardens.

"Guys." Warning sailed through Maangi's voice.

Tox saw them at the same instant.

Twenty to twenty-five camo- and red beret-clad soldiers scurrying up the wide paths between the arched walkway that enclosed the perimeter of the mandir. Coming toward the upper exhibit.

Mission: failed.

"Stay calm and clear out," Tox subvocalized. "RTB."

172

Behind him, the doors burst open. He looked just in time to see Cell sprint out. Two guards shouting in Hindi raced after him, knocking aside women and children to pursue.

This had gone six feet under in a split second.

Screams and shouts added to the chaos. Some people fled the scene. In their panic and fear to get away from the danger, others plowed right into the soldiers. Blocked their path.

Surrounded by chaos, Tox pivoted and headed into the exhibit for a last-ditch effort to retrieve the journal. Cool air bathed him in sweet relief from the Indian heat as he entered the darker environment. Soft lights glowed along the walls and on the exhibits, their temperatures no doubt closely monitored to protect the wax figures that had freaked out Cell. Tox hurried on, eyeing each exhibit. Moving swiftly. Purposefully.

Until he rounded a corner.

Seven guards stood talking with three suits. A few patrons hung around, idly chatting and mumbling. Rubberneckers in every culture. He couldn't make out what the guards talked about, but their tone and grave expressions told him whatever had happened had upset them. Tox got closer, glad it was no act to seem surprised or curious at the goings-on.

Peering over heads and shoulders, he saw the display. Five turbaned animatronic figures sat cross-legged on a dais. Each held an instrument, except the fifth, positioned in front of a table.

A table with a journal on it. Tox's heart thumped a little harder.

"Amazing, isn't it?" came a voice tinged with a British accent.

Tox didn't make eye contact, but he felt the presence of the man who'd come after him on the stairs. And the guy was confronting him? Nerves thrumming, Tox eyed the guards. Still involved in discussion with the suits, who pointed toward the exhibit, their faces as absurdly animated as the figures on the dais.

"That someone would actually try to steal from a place that teaches everlasting happiness based on spiritual truth . . ." The Brit clucked his tongue. "A pity, that."

Tox gave a nod to no one in particular and took a step back.

"I would not do that," the Brit warned. "Not just yet."

Tox skated a sidelong glance at the guy, who was peering over his shoulder at something behind them.

"Who's with you, Six?" Ram asked through the comms.

Like he could answer.

Tox braved a look and found soldiers flooding the room. Crap. Trapped. Should've left when he had the chance. Not only would he not get the journal, he might not escape without handcuffs and a black eye or two. And how had the man beside him known to warn him? "Who are you?"

The Brit bent forward and pointed to the first animated figure. "That's Brahmanand Swami plucking a devotional on his stringed instrument for Lord Swaminarayan. The other saints, Premanand Swami and Muktanand Swami"—his long finger, marked with a jagged scar, moved from one figure to another—"also prepare their instruments to accompany Brahmanand Swami."

I really don't care. Go or stay. Those were Tox's options, each equally dangerous. If he stayed, he risked being questioned or captured. If he went, the same.

"*Aut viam inveniam aut faciam.*"

Was that supposed to mean something? Scanning the walls and corners for hidden doors heightened Tox's fears—no visible exits, save the main one.

"You should see this place in the evening," the Brit said, his back to Tox. "They close it up at eight. But the lights are on and it glows!"

Was there a reason this man was rambling in the middle of a crisis? Tox needed an exit strategy. Right now, his priority was evading the watchful eyes of twenty-something Indian soldiers.

"*Aut viam inveniam aut faciam.*" The Brit said the words in a way that made Tox realize they were a repeat of the earlier gibberish.

"Six." Ram sounded panicked. "Six—that's Latin."

Still didn't help.

"'Either find a way or make one'," Ram said. "That's the translation. Do what he said. Get out of there."

The Brit tucked his chin, again cleverly concealing his face. But then he turned. Locked onto Tox—his gaze so fierce, so forbidding, it seemed fire spiraled through Tox's chest and into his toes, pushing him back a step. It was instantaneous. Horrifying. Thrilling.

Tox sucked in a hard breath. "How . . . ?" No, it couldn't be. The man from the flames . . . How was this possible?

"Don't think to steal it now. They will notice and capture you." The Brit whirled, then stopped and looked over his shoulder. "Israel has the Crown. Find it." And with that, he dove headlong into the unit of soldiers with buoyant laughter and camaraderie, his linguistic skills exploding in Hindi fluency. He pointed toward a corner, laughed, shook his head, then said something else. It was enough to send the soldiers darting through the door.

"Six! Move!" Ram shouted.

His mind jumbled with memories of a raging inferno from three years ago, tangling with the current images of Cell fleeing, the soldiers hustling in rigid formation toward the stairs, and the Brit.

"Get out!"

But the journal. They needed it. How did the Brit know what they were after?

As the visitors were shuttled to safety, Tox ducked and rolled his shoulders, bringing himself to the side of the tumbling crowd. Locked onto the prize, he moved swiftly.

A guard stepped into his path, shouted as he two-handed Tox around and shoved him in the other direction. Tox could take him. Bring this guy to his knees, to the grave if necessary. But there were too many innocents and witnesses. Thrown into the sea of bodies, Tox let it take him like a tide to the other side. But another shove told him the guard wasn't letting him out of his sight.

When he spilled out of the Exhibits wing, sandstone spit at him. Smacked his cheek. Tox flinched, instantly recognizing that a bullet had struck the column. He ducked, his instinct searching for the shooter. He crouched.

A guard yelped and pitched forward. Blood spurted from his neck. Like a broken dam, the sea of bodies flooded down the steps. Screaming hysteria washed over the people. Women tripped. Children were trampled. Screams rent the once-quiet mandir.

Tox broke into a run, half-bent and using the wall of the upper balcony to shield him as he rushed for safety. He zigzagged across an open area. Bullets ripped through the sandstone, cracked the marble. They had waited for him to come into the open.

Why? What were they after? Him or the journal?

He diverted from the throng and found a side door. He punched through it, the wood thudding back against the wall as he threw himself down the steps. Raced around the next landing and leapt to the lower level. He eased open the door to verify he had a clear shot. Mentally, he traced the layout of the temple. The quickest route. Thought through the angle of the bullets.

The shooter had to be on the opposite wall that traced the expansive perimeter. Which meant the door would provide extra protection. He peered down the covered walkway that led out to the gardens. An eight- to ten-foot gap with nothing to hide behind stretched wide and shouted, "Shoot me!" He had to make it to the gardens. If he could, with the tree cover he had a chance. It'd be intermittent, but each step he moved away from the mandir and main structures, the less likely the shooter could nail him.

Always better the odds.

Eyes on the goal, Tox puffed out three quick breaths as he drew his weapon. He rammed his shoulder against the door. His first step felt as if it'd been suctioned in mud like a nightmare, his legs working against him. His calves burned as he pumped his arm for the second step. His pulse thudded in his head. Three . . .

Sandstone exploded at eye level. His cheek stung.

. . . four . . . five steps, then he sailed into the air. Dove for the last section of covered walkway.

Fire sizzled across his thigh. He shut out the pain as the path rushed up to meet him. He braced. Captured his breath. Hit hard. Shards of pain clawed through his shoulder. Knocked the wind out of him. Momentum carried him several feet. He rolled, angling for the wall and staring down the length of his Glock, ready for assailants. Mentally assessed his own injuries, the graze on his thigh. The stickiness in his shoulder—must've torn the stitches.

His head thudded into something hard. Next thing he knew, a hand reached over his shoulder.

Tox grabbed it, primed to kill the person. He was not dying now.

"Ndidi." Chiji grabbed his shirt and dragged him backward.

Sweet relief. "The gardens," Tox hissed, scrambling to his feet. He sprinted for the vegetation. Heard the crack of weapons' fire. Shouts of soldiers. Shrieks as people flooded the carpet of grass, seeking shelter. They could get lost in the chaos, so Tox slowed marginally, but focused on the end goal: the gate.

Trees batted them. Branches smacked his head and face. A few grabbed his shoulder. The limbs were moving because bullets pelted their waxy leaves. Tox kept hustling.

Crack. Thud!

Behind! Tox spun. Towering over his opponent, Chiji with his lightning-fast reflexes delivered lethal blows to a small man in tactical gear.

Another attacker surged from between two trees.

Tox steadied himself. Let the man bring the fight. As soon as he threw the first punch, Tox blocked it, deflecting the momentum and putting the man off balance. Tox countered with an uppercut, nailing the guy's solar plexus.

Suddenly, his attacker arched his back, arms winging out. Something protruded from his chest. The air glittered like some twisted fireworks show as the man screamed—primal and loud. Flesh sizzled. He crumbled, smoking.

Ten, maybe twelve yards away, the assassin's mangled ear and unibrow glare were unmistakable. Leering, Tanin lifted a crossbow.

"Come!" Chiji shouted, grabbed Tox's collar.

Startled that he'd frozen, Tox raced unyielding to the end of the temple grounds, anticipating the arrow Tanin would lodge in his back. Each step felt like his last. Each breath weighted. Safety hovered closer—yet the tricks of adrenaline made it feel an eternity away. Why hadn't the arrow hit yet?

When he rounded the corner, he skidded to a stop, glancing back. National police were in pursuit of Tanin. And the man he'd struck instead of Tox? Smoke rose from the body. What on earth . . . ?

People rushed across the lush gardens, faces awash in the horror of the attack. Some screamed. Many were injured. A few seemed to have taken bullets meant for Tox. In the trunk of a tree, another arrow. How many had missed him? Was Tanin that bad of a shot?

The howl of an emergency vehicle pushed Tox to go. But in the midst of it all . . . at the top of the center mandir, amid the heavily carved columns and darshans, Tox saw him. The Brit who'd spoken to him. Standing there, hands in his pockets, watching.

Tox hesitated. He wasn't just a man. He'd walked amid fire in the tunnel collapse.

Not possible. Yet . . . he was there. How? Why?

"Ndidi," Chiji said, his voice rumbling.

Eyes on the man, Tox nodded, patted his friend, then glanced at Tanin. Then back to the mandir. Now empty of the watcher.

I'm missing something.

Kasey hit REPLAY and leaned back in the chair, headphones on, reviewing the interview with Chatresh Narang again. Maybe she was overthinking things. They were getting the journal. What else would Chatresh hide from them?

A light tap against her shoulder drew her out of the analysis. She slipped off the headphones and looked up.

Robbie nodded to the video. "Why are you watching him again?"

"Something's bugging me. I think he didn't tell us something."

Robbie considered the possibility.

"Ma'am, we have incoming," Vander announced.

Both their gazes swung to the surveillance feeds.

"Male and female, according to thermals," Vander reported. "Running the vehicle . . ."

Robbie waited at Kasey's chair.

"Car's a rental. Running . . . Ah!" He peered over the rim of his glasses at them. "Dr. Joseph Cathey and Tzivia Khalon."

Robbie moved closer to the feeds. "Perfect timing. Let them in."

They watched the archaeologists park and climb out. Tzivia Khalon went to the professor's side. Together, they walked toward the camera until they stepped out of sight. Levi, hand on his weapon, punched in the code on the keypad then swung open the steel door.

Tzivia entered, her gaze sweeping the warehouse.

"Welcome, Ms. Khalon," Robbie said, arms folded. "Is there a reason you aren't at Jebel al-Lawz?"

Tzivia stared. "And you are?"

"Shut the door," Robbie said, waiting for Levi to secure the area before continuing. "Robbie Almstedt with SAARC—we spoke on the phone."

Tzivia glanced around again. "Where are my brother and Tox?"

She knew Cole? Something in Kasey bristled.

"They're fine," Robbie said.

Tzivia's finely penciled eyebrow arched. "Just because you know our identities doesn't mean we trust you."

"Likewise," Robbie said, her tone evening out. "They'll be back soon."

Tzivia clenched her jaw, then gave a slow nod. "Jebel al-Lawz was bombed. There's nothing left."

Robbie scowled and turned to Vander, who muttered, "on it."

She straightened. "I assume your brother instructed you to come here?"

"He said Bhavin's brother was here." She nodded to the glass interview room. "That him? Did he talk?"

"Yes. We got everything out of him," Robbie said, her gaze drifting to Kasey.

"You don't sound too sure about that," Tzivia said.

"Agent Cortes just told me she felt like we were missing something. The team went after a journal Mr. Narang"—Robbie nodded to Chatresh—"said his brother kept."

Tzivia's keen, perceptive eyes shifted to Kasey. "You think there's more?"

"That's just it." Kasey bunched her shoulders, hoping she wasn't about to make a fool of herself. "I saw signs of deception, but I figured it was just about the journal."

"Like what?"

With a click, she advanced the video. "Here, where Ram is talking to him—I wasn't here for it, but listen." She pointed to the screen as it played. "Phrases like, 'That's about it,' 'that's all I can say,' 'that's what I'm telling you,' 'I'm telling you'—they're signs that there's more information the person isn't sharing."

It should be enough to satisfy her that they'd caught him in his lie. But . . . "There's also steepling the hands, which is a sign of superiority. Doing so in front of the mouth is saying, 'I'm superior to you, I know more than you, and I'm not going to say it.'"

"So he's high off himself." Tzivia looked at the image of Chatresh, his smile frozen against his dark features. "That all?"

They shared a glance. "No," Kasey muttered. Hit PLAY again. Watched. Rewatched. Then—"There." She pointed to his smiling self. "That."

"You don't like happy people?"

Kasey sniffed. Then had an idea. She went back to the video the tech had sent her and played it. "I—there!" She practically broke her track pad stopping the video. "Right there." By placing the two images side by side, exultation spiraled through her chest. "Knew I wasn't imagining it."

Tzivia leaned closer. "What?"

"The last smile," Kasey said, tapping the right-hand image, "is a lying smile. The corners of his mouth turn down in that one, which they normally don't do."

Tzivia's wide eyes came to hers slowly. "Impressive. And that means . . . ?"

"He knows something—something *else*. Even after he tells Cole about the journal, he's still smug, and that's when he gives that smile." She shuddered. "He has more information in his possession."

"Think he knows the location of my stolen censer?"

"I wouldn't be surprised."

Tzivia started toward the glass wall.

"What are you doing?" Robbie called after the take-charge woman.

"Having a friendly chat," Tzivia said as she entered the halo of light from the chamber. "Mr. Narang."

Chatresh rolled over and looked at her. "Yes?"

"I'm Tzivia Khalon—the site your brother worked was mine." She took in a breath. "Do you know what happens to any person who touches the censer without protective gear?"

He stilled, worried.

"Every person who has touched it unprotected has died." Tzivia stuffed her hands on her hips. "I need to know where my censer is, Mr. Narang."

The rock-hard walls slammed back up.

"His family," Kasey whispered. "They're important to him."

"I hope you didn't hide it in your home or in a place where anyone you love could touch it. It's cursed."

Cursed? Kasey frowned, eyeing the woman whose black hair was coiled into a messy knot at the back of her head.

But the man's posture hadn't changed.

"How much do you want, Mr. Narang?"

He came off the cot.

Tzivia sighed. "What will it take to buy your soul?"

21

One million dollars.

Guided by a GPS device, Tzivia drove through New Delhi faster than she would've driven anywhere. "I will never understand people," she muttered.

"He wanted to protect his family. Desperate people do desperate things," Dr. Cathey said, gripping the dashboard and roll bar as they rounded a corner, the tires squalling in protest. "Like drive too fast and cause an accident."

"Am I making you nervous?" She grinned and gunned it through a light as it changed to red. Horns blared.

"Always." Dr. Cathey shuddered. "Even when we're not going ninety kilometers per hour in a sixty."

"Well, then you should've stayed home in London."

"And miss this adventure and the chance to die of an ancient plague?" he said with a chuckle.

"It's not the same plague from the Bible," she clarified, wanting to be sure he didn't have a path to get religious on her. "Dr. Ellison verified that—it's both septicemic and Black Death. And Benowitz thinks that

183

being exposed to our air in this century altered its makeup. I gave him some blood before we left. He hoped to figure out an antigen with it."

"Bah, Benowitz would say whatever you want him to say," Dr. Cathey said. "But this *New* Black Death—have they discovered how it was released or activated?"

"No—"

"Aha—"

"Don't start." She tightened her grip on the wheel.

The GPS guided them to the building, and she parked along the curb then fed the parking meter. She eyed Dr. Cathey's cane. Its hollow core allowed him to store things but it could also be a great fighting tool if they encountered unfriendlies.

"You have gloves?" he asked as they approached the multistoried building that held a shopping center. Like an American mall but in a skyscraper.

"Of course." She also had a baggie and a keen awareness that they could be followed or attacked—or both—at any second.

They entered through a department store as Chatresh had instructed and made their way to the mall concourse. Tzivia moved to the balcony, a sense of dread heightening as her gaze rose several levels. "Think of all the people . . ." She didn't want to utter the words. The ones who could die.

"Yes, think of them and get going," Dr. Cathey said, not stopping to gawk with her. He turned the corner and was out of sight.

"Hey," Tzivia hissed, skipping to catch up with him. "I was also looking for tails."

"Just assume they are there and walk quickly," he muttered, using his cane to pull himself forward.

"Yes, sir, Mr. Bond."

His gray eyes chided her.

She shook her head, but then saw it. "There. The masseuse."

In a wider opening in the concourse, a row of black leather chaises were occupied. Every last one of them. Chatresh had said he'd laid on one, trying to hide from the people hunting down his brother.

"He said the third or fourth one from the end."

Tzivia groaned as the full set-up revealed itself. Not just one row—

184

there were three! All chairs surrounded by black mats. "What do we do?"

Dr. Cathey tapped her arm. "Gloves." He started toward the first row. "You check the far one, I'll check the closest. Whoever finishes first goes to the middle."

At first, his method didn't make sense until she remembered Chatresh had said he'd been hurrying down the concourse. What he hadn't said was that he went to the middle. It would've been significant enough for him to have mentioned. At least, Tzivia hoped her logic was sound.

"That's a lot of time."

"Only if you keep talking." Spry for a sixty-something man, Dr. Cathey went to the far row and used his cane to tug the black mat away from the chair.

Tzivia started her hunt, muttering an apology to the masseuse and the client as she knelt and lifted the mat. Nothing.

She scuttled to the next. Nothing. And moved on. "Nothing."

"Hey," the masseuse shouted, "leave my customers alone!"

"Sorry." Tzivia shuffled over to another chair.

"No! You leave!"

Tzivia managed a weak smile and returned to the side, where Dr. Cathey joined her. "Nothing?"

"I even got halfway down the middle row," he lamented. "Was he lying?"

"I think that deception expert would've known." She shook her head. Discouraged. Frustrated. "Come on." She tugged his arm and pivoted—

A massage patron lifted his phone from a compartment beneath the chair.

"What . . . ?" She hurried closer, scanning each chair. They all had a hollow space built into the chair, perfect for keeping belongings while getting a massage. She raced to the other side and scampered along the perimeter, searching. Both sides. Then stopped short. Backtracked.

She squatted four feet from the table where she'd spied a discoloration. Bent, she moved in. Saw the handle of a censer peeking out of the shadows. She put on the glove and reached in.

"Is that it?" Dr. Cathey sounded breathless.

She slid it into the plastic bag and stared at it. "You little trouble-maker."

"Tzivia," Dr. Cathey called, his voice distant . . . panicked.

She looked up and saw two cops jogging down the concourse. "Time to go."

* * * *

Waiting for the team to return after they'd split up to increase their chances of making it back to the safe house undetected proved excruciating. The two hours droned by, especially once Chatresh Narang had been removed by a hazmat team to a quarantined location. Kasey was at the end of her rope when the perimeter alarm of the safe house finally went off. The first to return was Ram Khalon, Tzivia's brother. Then over the course of forty minutes, the rest of the men returned. All except Cole and his Nigerian friend.

"Where's Russell and Okorie?" Almstedt asked, her voice masking what Kasey saw on her face. Concern. Fear. They needed Cole.

"En route." With another look at Kasey, Ram Khalon joined his men against a wall, silent. They had, without a word, drawn a line in the sand, creating sides.

Silence could be painful. Especially when it was coming from all sides. Like they all knew a terrible secret. And suddenly, that secret became a thousand different terrors, all drenched in what wasn't said as much as what was. Cole was en route.

The last they knew.

What if he'd been captured *en route*? What if he'd been killed? What if . . . ?

Kasey gripped her upper arms, squeezing away the dreadful thoughts. Regardless of the outcome, Cole was out there. Ten minutes struggled on. Then fifteen. Nerves frayed and wits whittled down by the pressing quiet, she wandered the room, inwardly begging Cole to silence her fears and step beneath the beams of the streetlamp that captured trespassers.

"Something's happened," she muttered to Levi.

"Stop. He's fine." His tone bordered on acerbic.

She checked the monitors again, irritated Levi chalked up her concern to romantic interest in Cole, not to her ability to read a situation.

"Movement!" Vander announced. "One newcomer."

A presence formed behind her, but Kasey begged the monitor to reveal Cole. "Who is it?"

"Chiji," Ram said.

Kasey deflated.

"Why's he alone?"

"Because he vanishes like a ghost," Cell taunted from the far wall. Once Chiji entered, they all grouped up on him.

"Where's Tox?" Ram demanded. "He was with you."

"We fought our way out, but it was very bad. They pursued us. We had to take different routes." Chiji shook his head, sweat gliding from his temples.

"Did any of you get the journal?" Robbie asked.

"Things got too hot too fast," Cell said.

"So you *didn't* get Mr. Narang's journal." Robbie folded her arms over her bosom, consternation knitting her penciled-in eyebrows.

"No way to get it." Ram shrugged. "Tox knew that. He ordered us to return to base to regroup and plan."

"Your sister showed up," Robbie said.

"Tzivia? Here?" Ram's gaze surfed the room. "Where?"

"Out," Robbie growled, then nodded to Kasey. "Through Agent Cortes, we discovered our guest had more information. He knew where the censer was."

Ram's eyes widened. "She went after it?" Distress colored his question.

"Left almost immediately after she arrived," Robbie said. "That was two hours ago. Haven't heard from her since."

With a muttered oath, Ram turned away, the team following him.

At the table with Levi, Robbie, and the techs, Kasey bounced her legs through another ten minutes. First time in the field, and she would not let them see her sweat. God had her here for a reason, and she was convinced it wasn't to bring Cole home in a pine box.

"You worry for him" came the low, gravelly voice of Chiji.

She managed a smile. "Will you tell me it's silly, too?"

Chiji folded his lanky frame into a chair and threaded his fingers on the table. "Worry shows concern. Why would you not worry?"

"Because I know God's got this, got him."

His satiny black skin rippled with an amused arch of the eyebrow. "You believe?"

It was almost a crime these days, but yeah. "I believe . . . help my unbelief," she said, her voice fading at the end as she referenced the Bible verse.

"Ah, you are wise, Agent Cortes, to ask Him to help when you struggle." His dark eyes drifted away from her. "I have spent many days and nights asking His help for Ndidi."

"Ndidi?"

"The name my mother gave him."

She shifted, surprised. "You don't call him Tox."

"Neither do you." With that, he pushed from the chair and went to a cot, where he stretched out. Without looking, he dangled his arm and dug into his backpack on the floor below him. He drew out a small leather Bible and began reading.

Another fifty minutes fell off the clock in a weighted, aching silence. Her mind pinged through a million different, deadly scenarios, until the quiet and inaction pushed her to Levi. "How long do we wait?"

He looked at her, his gaze pensive. "All night, if necessary."

"I mean, before we go looking for him."

"We don't." His eyebrows tangled. "Kase, if he goes missing, we put out feelers, but we don't launch a rescue op. Not without intel. Not without an idea of where to search. Doing so puts him in more danger. We wait."

The fear and pain must've bled into her expression because Levi bumped her shoulder. "You should get some rest."

"If only," she murmured, then moved to the table and opened her secure laptop.

Buck up. God had not given her a spirit of fear, the Bible promised. And this was Cole. A skilled operator. He'd hidden from intelligence networks around the world for three years. She'd seen his self-defense handiwork on the video feed.

She checked email. Found one from another agent, asking her to

188

view a video. Slipping on her headphones gave her the appearance of not obsessing. But . . . what if Cole had been compromised? What if something awful—

Stop!

This was Cole, remember? Seasoned soldier. Fierce warrior.

She glanced at the digital clock. Fifty-eight minutes and counting since Chiji returned. She couldn't stand the thought of sitting here all night waiting, wondering, worrying.

Warmth covered her hand. Kasey glanced down, realizing she'd been snapping her pen against the table. Robbie smiled and shook her head.

Kasey gave a nervous laugh. "I've never been good at waiting."

"Why don't you work on transcribing the last report—"

An alarm pierced the air.

"Breach! Rear door," Vander shouted.

"Why didn't the monitors pick up movement in the lot?" Robbie asked.

"No idea."

The warehouse came alive. Cole's team leapt to their feet—weapons ready. Levi pulled his gun, and even Kasey had hers in hand. She jerked in the direction the men raced. Took a step forward.

Robbie straightened. "I have a feeling our phantom has returned."

"Hands! Hands!" Ram shouted.

"Friendly" came Cole's strained voice.

The men muttered as they made their way back to the main area, a flurry of comments and questions flung at Cole. Kasey didn't dare move, her nerves buzzing and jangling against her confidence.

Robbie started toward Cole.

"How'd you get around surveillance?" Vander demanded from his station.

"Blind spot." Cole's words arrived shortly before he did. His left cheek sported a cut atop a red, swollen knot. Blood smeared his jaw and neck. He swiped his thumb up his temple, smearing more blood, then winced and rolled his shoulder.

Chiji was at his side.

"Glad you're alive, Russell," Robbie said.

"Makes two of us, ma'am." Cole looked at Kasey and hesitated. His gaze skated over her, then shifted to Wallace, Vander, and Lewis.

"Is that another bullet graze?" Thor asked, pointing at the bloodstain on Cole's leg.

Cradling his injured arm close, Cole nodded. "We had a shooter."

"And a hunter," Chiji agreed. "He shot flaming arrows."

"Did you get the journal?" Robbie seemed hopeful as she pressed into the center of the throng.

Fire ignited Cole's eyes. His hands clenched. "Things went sideways. Authorities, soldiers, Tanin."

"You had a mission—"

"Yes, and I about died trying to do it." He flung his hands out. "Guess I failed."

"You didn't fail," Kasey muttered. "You just found a way that didn't work."

Cole's gaze snapped to hers.

Too late, Kasey realized her mistake. Remembered all the times she'd heard that saying so many years ago. From the lips of Cole Russell.

"You didn't fail, son. You found ten thousand ways that won't work."
His father practically browbeat Tox with that Thomas Edison saying.
The words rang through his mind as he met the green eyes of Kasey
Cortes. It collided with his previous hackles that rose while listening
to her talk, watching her move. There was something . . .

She curled her hands toward her stomach, then turned away. Her
actions screamed of guilt. Nerves.

"You said something about an arrow?"

Tox flicked his attention to Almstedt. But he couldn't help skating
another look at Cortes as she made her way to the tables in the middle
of the warehouse and slid into a chair, wavy blond hair concealing
her face. Familiar. Somehow, she seemed familiar.

"An arrow?" Almstedt repeated.

Tox shook his head to dislodge the denotation from the past. "It
struck a guy who'd attacked me. Next thing I know, everything's burning like it's on fire."

"Burning arrows?" Cell taunted.

"I know," he said, shaking and nodding his head at the same time.
"It was crazy. Went through his chest. Flesh sizzled like bacon." Tox ran

a hand over his head. "But Chatresh said something about a sparkling arrow." He looked to the isolation chamber, now empty. "Where is he?"

"Taken to a quarantine facility," Almstedt said.

Ram shouldered into the conversation. "Hey, Tzivia is in town with Dr. C. They went after the censer Bhavin took."

Tox lifted his eyebrows. "Anything?"

"Not yet."

"Russell, have a seat." Sitting at the head of the table, Almstedt motioned him to the chair on her left. Directly across from Cortes. "Brief me on what happened at the temple."

Too many unknowns there at that table. The interrogation tactics of Almstedt and the unsettling nature of Cortes. But noncompliance would only inflame things.

"Can you identify anyone involved in the attack?"

"Just Tanin." Tox lowered himself onto a folding chair, his thigh still burning from the bullet that had nicked it. He held his arm close as his gaze veered across the paper-scattered surface to the thin but athletic agent who'd helped him sort Chatresh earlier. Something about her . . . "Happened too fast. The other shooters were out of visual range."

What was it about her? He searched for an answer in Cortes's features. Straight, average nose. Killer green eyes. Wavy dark blond hair. She shifted and bent over the pad, writing. Then set it down and massaged her left shoulder.

That buzzing at the back of his brain returned, mingling with his own nerves. He adjusted and felt the sting in his leg again.

A med kit slid onto the table, compliments of Ram. Two antibacterial wipes would work for cleaning the cut on his forehead. But what would it take to clean up the mess at the temple?

"Think anyone identified you or any of your team?"

"Possible, but unlikely. Too chaotic."

"Unless they have cameras," Almstedt suggested.

"Again, possible but unlikely." He leaned forward and tapped the table. "Look, I'm—"

"Please, continue," Almstedt said, then froze when their words tumbled over one another.

Right. Finish the story. He noted the upside-down words Cortes had scrawled. She'd copied his report verbatim. The realization made him swallow his agitation. That was impressive, her ability to recall all the facts.

He dragged the wipe over his bloodied knuckles, backtracking mentally to the temple. "With Cell's distraction, I took a chance to get the journal."

"That wasn't a distraction," Cell injected. "I was running for my life."

"It's why you make good bait," Tox teased, then refocused. "Inside, I spotted the journal—"

"On that dais with those five freakish wax dudes with instruments."

Tox ignored Cell's second interruption and the image of the Brit that melded with the fiery inferno at Kafr al-Ayn. "I went for it, and a Brit comes out of nowhere. Starts saying weird things."

"Latin," Ram said.

"Right. Latin. Whatever." Tox used another wipe for his temple and face. The burn in his cheek let him know it'd been cut.

"Did the Brit know why you were there?" Cortes's voice was like silk. "Was he trying to distract you?"

Tox met her gaze and felt another implosion of time at the back of his head. Something—there *was* something familiar about her. Green eyes. Tilt of her head. "Yeah," he said, trying to keep his mind above the churning whirlpool of thoughts. "He knew *exactly* why I was there. But I don't think he was trying to distract me."

"Did he try to stop you?" Wallace hovered behind Cortes again. Like a protector. A possessive one.

"Yes and no." Tox glanced between the two. "Like Ram said, he muttered something in Latin—"

Ram nodded. "He told you to find a way out or make one."

"Right. He knew we were in trouble." Fire seared his skin as the antiseptic went to work. "Then he whips around and distracts the security and suits guarding the room after Cell's incident."

"Running for my life."

"I move in to get the journal when all . . . heck . . . breaks loose." Tox held out his hands, remembering the moment. "Army shows up.

Guard sees me. I get pushed out by the crowd. Next thing I know, someone's taking shots at me."

"Indian Army shooting at you?" Incredulous, Wallace snorted. "How would they even know to target you? How could they get there so fast?"

"Negative." The suit had some attitude and Tox was glad to put him in place. "Shooter was concealed. Army and local authorities had no reason to hide." He nailed Wallace with a look. "And they were tipped off. As I said—someone did not want me getting that journal. They were willing to kill me to make sure I didn't."

"And kill five hundred innocents at the temple," Cortes added.

"What I want to know is how they knew we were there," Tox said as he applied a patch to the graze in his leg.

Almstedt slid a piece of paper across the table toward him. It was a printed email. "Indian Embassy is already asking why American soldiers were there."

Why hadn't she shown him this already? "Any other intel you want to share with me or my team?"

"I think you should dial back that anger—"

"What we should be doing is finding that journal," Ram snapped. "Not sitting here through an hour-long interrogation."

"Excuse me?" Almstedt demanded.

"This has to stop," Tox said. "We need to work, be active."

"I hear you, Russell."

"Good." He let out a short breath.

"The team will work on a plan to get the journal," Ram said.

Almstedt gave a clipped nod. "And we're waiting on Miss Khalon and Dr. Cathey to return."

Following Ram to the back of the warehouse, Tox's thigh burned again. Gripping it, he glanced down. Saw the edges of his scorched pants. "I'm going to change." He grabbed his rucksack.

"Aren't we supposed to be working on a plan to get the journal?" Thor asked.

"Get started. I'll be back in five."

As he aimed for the bathroom, Tox noticed Almstedt, Cortes, and Wallace huddled. He hoisted the ruck over his shoulder and deliberately made his way to the showers—via a wide route that took him near the trio.

194

* * * *

"He's not who you remember, Kasey."

Kasey flinched at Levi's words. But he was right—the Cole she knew and remembered probably wasn't the man standing in this warehouse.

"He was in Leavenworth with good justification. He got people killed—President Montrose died." Levi stabbed a finger toward the computer screen. "Now things are heating up. A man got out of the dig site with the virus, and because Tox wasn't able to intercept him in time, it spread it to India. Add to that the attack on the hotel, which left a half-dozen innocents dead—"

"Not his fault."

"Absolutely his fault—his team led the guns there." Levi huffed. "Letting Tox loose to run this mission as he sees fit is not in our best interest. He's a wrecking ball. Anyone who thinks otherwise would be a fool."

His words, unusually harsh, warned of stronger feelings that were personal. Not professional. His jealousy was getting involved in this conversation.

"Almstedt?"

"Yes, Vander?" Robbie turned to a tech, who handed her a piece of paper. She glanced at the report and shook her head. "Two patients admitted to New Delhi hospital with plague symptoms." She sighed. Her tired gaze drifted to Kasey. "You're quiet."

"'Better to remain silent and be thought a fool'"—she deliberately met Levi's gaze—"'than to speak and remove all doubt.'"

"Abraham Lincoln."

Kasey jerked, a wave of heat splashing across her shoulders as she met Cole's narrowed gaze.

Where had he come from? Why hadn't she noticed him standing off to the side? He stared at her, his blue eyes darting over her eyes, nose, mouth, and back to her eyes. Over and over.

"Can we help you?" Levi asked.

"Sorry." Cole blinked. Almost seemed abashed. "Passing through. Heard Lincoln's quote." He paused. Then continued his course.

But she saw it. Saw the recognition in his eyes that wasn't there before.

"What was that?" Levi planted his hands on his hips.

Galen had told her not to tell Cole her real identity. If he'd figured it out, would they remove her? "Nothing." She focused on Robbie. "I think he's right."

"Who?"

"Russell," she said, forcing herself to use his last name for safe distance. "If we don't trust him to do this, then we need to put him back in the tank." She nodded to Levi. "And Agent Wallace is correct as well—we need to exercise caution."

"Espionage and black ops don't work that way. There's oversight for a reason, to protect him and those men." Robbie's tone did not betray her feelings. "Besides, I can't cut him loose—his record speaks for itself, I'm afraid."

Kasey sighed. "With respect, if there were options other than Russell, would any of us be here talking about him? But he is here because he's our best bet. And apparently the president and his chief of staff believe that, too. They chose him. We either trust their decision or we don't." She held up a hand so she could continue. "People are coming down with the plague. That means word's getting out. And if Cole is right, then someone else is after this journal. We need to find out who and why."

Levi and Robbie held a silent dialogue, right in front of Kasey as if she weren't standing there. She suddenly knew how Cole felt when they did that to him. But clinging to that Abe quote kept her mouth shut.

"Agreed," Robbie said.

Levi shook his head. Annoyed. Angry.

What was this? Did he trust her so little? Not value her thoughts?

Robbie nodded. "Kasey, contact the Saudi Commission for Tourism and National Heritage and the Israeli Antiquities Authority to find out what they know about that dig site bombing. It wasn't us who hit it, so who did? Levi, get a tactical plan going. Work with Wraith. I want them heading out in a few hours to find that journal."

Levi snapped his head and pivoted. His actions were so stiff, so robotic, Kasey couldn't move at first. Then after a brief shrug from Robbie, Kasey went after him.

"What was that?" she demanded.

He rounded on her, his frown tight. "You have no idea—"

"Educate me."

"He's dangerous."

"And 'dangerous' is what we need out there right now." Though Levi towered over her, she stood her ground. "He knows his stuff. He can do it, and there are lives depending on someone like him doing what he does best."

"You sure are gung-ho about him, Kase. Is this your professional opinion, or is it that you're glad to see him again?" He dug in closer. "I just want to protect you from him. You shouldn't be here. This is a mistake."

She snorted. Stepped back. His words, his lack of trust in her skills pushed her away from him. "The only mistake was thinking you might be someone I liked."

"Hey—"

She waved him off and went to her laptop. Seated and temples throbbing, she refused to let anyone see her as weak. *Review the files, look busy.* Headphones on, she was ready for some quiet time. *God, I'm losing myself.* This case, Cole being alive, had turned her world upside down.

Heartache came barreling at her from the past. Brooke's constant belittling because Kasey was a tomboy. Because she wasn't into makeup and flirting. She didn't want the silky dresses and bows. She wanted hiking boots and jeans.

Work. *Get to work.* She dug through the mound of files to find information about the Saudi site and Tzivia Khalon's dig. After retrieving contact information from Vander for the two organizations, Kasey dialed the first contact, a cabinet member of the SCTH.

Identifying herself, Kasey moved onto the meat. "I'm calling about the Jebel al-Lawz archaeological site."

"Yes, a historic discovery."

"Definitely, but we're looking into the bombing—"

"What bombing?"

Kasey hesitated. "The one that leveled the dig site."

"There has been no bombing!" He shouted something in another language to someone else, then the line went dead.

Kasey stared at the phone. Maybe he just hadn't been informed. Or maybe the site *hadn't* been bombed. Could they pull up satellite footage of the dig? It made no sense, but she'd call the Israel Antiquities Authority and see what they said. Then try the SCTH again, and talk with someone higher up. She'd need—

"Haven."

"Yeah?" She turned.

The world whirred to a stop in a stunned, slow-mo second. Staring into Cole's blue eyes, she realized her second mistake of the night. Haven. He'd called her Haven. Nausea coursed through her as he stepped into her personal space.

When had his chest filled out so much? Laugh lines pinched the corners of his eyes. A deep tan made his blue irises glow.

She couldn't breathe. Couldn't move. For years, she imagined this moment. When he would step into her space and take command. When he'd finally *see* her.

The left side of his mouth lifted in a partial grin. He gave a small shake of his head with a breathy snort. "Unbelievable."

She struggled to smile, knowing guilt hung on every inch of her body. "I knew you'd figure it out eventually."

But then his gaze went . . . weird. "Was it Galen?"

His words made her feel like she'd stepped from a hot summer afternoon into the middle of an icy, cruel winter. Her mind tripped over his question and whiplash change of direction. "Was what Galen?"

"Why did he hide you from me?"

She swallowed. *Hide her?*

Hurt flickered through his eyes that now so closely resembled cold steel. He nodded. Backed up. "Good to see you." He retreated another step and turned away.

She caught his arm. "Wait."

In a split second, Cole pivoted. His expression hard.

Kasey drew up. *Be strong. You've got this.* "Please. Just listen. I . . ."

"Why are you here, Haven?"

"To catch Tanin. And stop this plague."

He indicated over his shoulder. "Almstedt and Wallace can handle that."

"I have a part in this, too—I helped you earlier. At your request." Did he not remember that? Was she really so . . . forgettable? Easily discarded?

Stony and implacable, he stared at her. Then finally said, "He's right."

Kasey frowned. "Who?"

Cole looked away, his fingers thumping the table. "I'm dangerous."

She drew in a quiet breath—he'd heard Levi.

"Go home, Haven."

AND CURSED BE HE WHO SELLS IT

Light may shine brightly through the curtains of his home, but it had shone brighter through the lace ones handmade by Gratzia during their first six years of marriage in Israel. Benyamin smoothed a hand along the arm of the chair. It had been her favorite, their first piece of furniture when they'd come to America. She'd loved the richly embroidered tapestry. It was beautiful to the eyes. Painful to the backside. Lumpy and lopsided after all these years, it put a crick in his back.

He grunted. Bracing his hands on the chair, he pushed himself up enough to shift. His body collapsed against a new bump in the seat cushion. He sniffed, recalling how he'd wanted to buy her a whole houseful of nicer, better furniture—anything for his Gratzia—but she refused. Comfort, she said, dulled the senses. The chair reminded her of the rocky shore upon which they'd met. Of their first years married, and their grand adventure moving to America, where they worked hard and laughed more.

He looked across their living room to the front door. A sigh sifted his joy, remembering . . .

In awe that they had their own place with three bedrooms, they stood there for a long time simply holding hands, Daoud in her arms, Yitshak toddling around the empty living room. Benyamin was still amazed that she had saved so much money, never once telling him. Had it not been for that money . . .

"What is that?" Gratzia asked, nodding to a chair that seemed illuminated by the morning sun.

"It is a gift," he murmured. "For you."

Gratzia gingerly made her way across their new home to the lone chair basking in the sunlight. "The tapestry!"

Benyamin could barely suppress his excitement. "It shows your favorite passage."

Her eyes rimmed with tears. "You?" She swallowed. "You made this?" He lifted his shoulders and chin. "For my beloved."

"Oh, Ben!" She ran her fingers over the fabric then lowered herself into it. "It's wonderful."

It wasn't, really. He'd known even then, but at that point in his career, it was the best he'd ever made. The cushion was lumpy. He could perfect the wood and carpentry elements, but a seamstress he was not.

"Is it really all ours, Abba?" five-year-old Miriam asked about the home.

"Yes, little one. It is. Yahweh has blessed us."

With a squeal she went running through the house, checking each room before rushing back and throwing her arms around his legs.

He smiled at Gratzia, but even then, she had the weight of worry rimming her eyes. "We will make it," he reassured.

"There is so much to do. Perhaps I should not—"

"We agreed," Benyamin said, bending over and pressing a kiss to her temple. "This is our home. We will do what we must." Hard work had never been a stranger to them. He'd found work here and there in Israel, but he wanted to establish a business, and there were more opportunities in America.

"Will they find us here?"

He went to the window where light glared through. When he stepped into the beams, it felt like a warm embrace. He closed his eyes and drank it in, allowing the heat to wash away the stress. The missing parts of the Codex had created an uproar against their fathers and many elders. Some had said the missing parts burned in Aleppo. Others said the Muslims had torn the Codex apart before it could be rescued. How was he to know? He'd last seen it when he was but twelve. What could a boy of that age remember?

"Benyamin?"

He let out a breath. "Yahweh knows." Turning, he met her gaze. "We cannot let it devour our lives. We—"

"Wow, Abba! Look how many cars are down there," Miriam said, her voice awe-filled. "Do they all live here like us?"

"Indeed." Down the street beckoned a playground. A little girl with a red coat ran for the swings. She thrust herself into it, arms splayed, and rode it as if she were an airplane. Benyamin lifted Miriam into his arms and pointed. "Look, a little girl just like you."

Miriam's brown eyes brightened. "She has a red coat. I want a red coat."

"Perhaps you will have one," he said as Yitshak slapped the window in excitement.

"Do not make such promises, Benyamin," Gratzia chided as she set Daoud at the window, helping the baby grip the ledge and look out.

"Oh, tsh," he said, smiling at his beloved. "It is good to dream."

"Abba must find a job, first, Miriam," she told their daughter. "We must pay for this home and our food."

"And a car!" Miriam's wide eyes followed a black Chevrolet down the street.

"Definitely a car," Benyamin whispered conspiratorially to Miriam.

Gratzia sighed heavily, and when he looked at her, his smile faded. What he saw there was more than matronly annoyance with his dream-building. A weight lurked behind her brown eyes. Pulled on her shoulders. He set his daughter down and urged her toward the rooms again. He turned to his wife. "What is it, beloved?"

She shook her head. "I am only tired."

He frowned. The trip had been long, but they'd rested well and eaten before coming to the house.

Her smile was weak but endearing. "I think we should have asked for four bedrooms."

Benyamin again frowned at her—then gasped. "Fo—you are . . ." He could scant hope for the news. The cost.

She nodded and sighed again.

"When?"

"By Purim."

He folded her into his arms and breathed of her beauty. "Another blessing of the Lord!"

Daoud tugged at them, whining for attention, too. Gratzia drew out of his arms and lifted their son. "I will visit Devra," she said, speaking of their lone friend, who lived two buildings down. She started for the door to the small hall.

"Gratzia." His heart was full. Life was full. Yahweh was good.

Silhouetted in the doorway, she looked back.

"It will be well. You will see."

"If you say it will," she said and left the apartment.

He returned to the window, breathing in the new air. New life. They had a few friends in the city and a job. It would be enough to get them going, but he dreamed . . . oh, he dreamed of his own shop. Providing for his family. Helping their relatives come over as well.

A shape in the door drew his attention. "Oh, back so soon?"

"So soon?"

Life flipped, then flopped. Shaken, he waved at Alison. "Time is but a blink to an old man like me."

A man appeared behind her, and she shared a look with him. One that warned Benyamin she now had more faith in this stranger than in her sabba.

The memory of Gratzia, the ache of that day, pulled him into darkness. It had been the last day he saw her healthy and happy.

23

Three years ago, Tox's life had been cleansed of soft targets because of his innate ability to destroy. Things were better that way. Everything had changed now that he knew who she was. Her true identity.

He stalked back to the SAARC corner. "I want her out of here."

Almstedt looked up from the planning station where she and Wallace bent over a map. "Excuse me?"

"Cortes. I want her out of here." Tox nodded to where she sat at a computer.

"No," Almstedt said. "She's a deception expert. With the language barriers, we need her now more than ever."

"She's the president's sister-in-law." Tox pressed his lips into a thin line. "But you knew that. She's a risk!"

Shoulders squared, hands on his hips, Wallace shifted around and faced Tox. "*Former* sister-in-law."

So the possessiveness Tox had noted before was real. "Get your girlfriend out of here. If you cared for her at all—"

"You know nothing!"

"Get rid of your ego and protect her!"

"That's not—"

205

"Remember?" Tox took a step forward to amplify his point. "I'm dangerous!"

"Hey!" Almstedt snapped. "Enough." She breathed out heavily. "Kasey stays." Weariness weighted her shoulders. "Those orders come from above."

Exactly the information he'd needed. With a nod, Tox pivoted—and saw *Haven* staring at him, hurt etched into her pretty face. Exactly why he wanted her out of here. He strode . . . to where, he didn't know. Just had to keep moving. Outside wasn't an option. Not now. He walked from one end of the warehouse to another, his anger bubbling.

Galen . . . Galen had deliberately put Haven in his path. Why? Did he want him to kill her, too? Why keep her identity hidden? What purpose could that serve?

He turned.

A stick sailed at him.

Tox caught it before his mind registered Chiji tossing another. Armed with two thirty-six-inch kali sticks, Tox rolled his shoulders, stretching. Adjusted his stance. Within seconds, a natural rhythm clacked through the air as they went through several drills. Twisting with the right stick and connecting with Chiji's, then following that path, letting it rebound from his waist to a low strike.

Clack! Then with the left. *Clack!* Back and forth. Each collision of wood jarred his injured shoulder, but also invigorated him. Their speed picked up. As did the complexities.

It didn't take long for his arms to ache, but Tox pushed himself. Sweat drenched his shirt. He'd need another shower, but he didn't care. The physical exertion stimulated him. He fought through the knot of frustration and anger. His brother . . . always running his life. *Ruining* his life.

But putting Haven in his path . . .

Hiding her.

Pain exploded across his temple. Tox bit back an expletive, pressing the back of his hand to his head.

Chiji lowered his sticks. The surprise rippling through his friend's eyes was enough chastisement. Awareness rushed through Tox that he wasn't focused.

"You are not here," Chiji said.

Tox sighed. Used the tail of his shirt to wipe the sweat from his face.

And like that, Haven was there. Holding a towel. "Not sure there's a dry spot left on your shirt." She extended her arm. "Thought this might help."

He accepted. Didn't trust himself to speak. Truthfully, he had no idea what to say. This person, this *woman*—*Kasey* Cortes—he didn't know. But Haven Linwood, the twelve-year-old little sister of his then-girlfriend, that girl he knew. He moved to a small plastic cooler and perched atop it, toweling off.

"It wasn't your brother."

Scruffing the back of his neck with the towel, Tox peered up.

"When he told me you were alive, I didn't give them a choice. I threatened to make your presence public." She shrugged as she stood over him. "I never would have, of course, but it was the only flashbang I had to get their attention."

He smirked. "You haven't changed at all."

Hurt splashed across her cheeks, the blush fading. He remembered—*painfully* remembered—all her doe-eyed looks, the way she followed him around when he was at their house to see Brooke.

"I meant that in a good way." He stood, noticing she only came up to his chin. "Haven, this isn't good, your being here."

"I'm a deception expert with the FBI." She had changed—there was a lot more *woman* framing her green eyes now. "This is what I do. And you have to admit I've helped already."

"But you're not combat trained. I can't worry about you while we're out there."

"Worry about me?" Anger reddened her face. "I'm not out there in the field. I'm here in this dull, maddening warehouse behind a laptop and my notebook. And my status isn't in your hands." She breathed out. "But yours is in mine."

The pardon. "You always knew how to get one over on everyone." He looked down because he *would* worry about her. Especially because it was Haven. He couldn't handle another death on his conscience.

He ran his hand over his head and glanced at his team. They were working hard to act like they weren't listening. But they were. Every one of them. "What's happening here—your parents would kill me if anything happened to you. And Galen—"

"Hey, at least *I'm* not going to run off with him."

Tox flinched.

Haven hung her head. "Sorry. That was—"

"Expertly delivered." Somehow he had to convince her that going home was the right answer. "Haven, this operation—"

"Is my job." Her words were soft but ardent. "I know you only remember me as—"

"Tox!"

At Ram's shout, he pivoted and saw his friend's expression. He was instantly in motion. "What's wrong?" Wait—Haven. He shot her a glance and knew instantly his priority shift to Ram had hurt her. But bigger matters were in play. This was why he didn't want her here. "See?" he said and held out his hands. "Worrying." He headed toward his friend.

Ram nodded him to the side. As they moved, it seemed their presence had a magnetic pull, drawing the team.

"What's going on?" Tox shouldered in, getting the vibe Ram had some stiff news.

"A friend called—IAA is going ape over Tzivia's dig."

"Why?"

"It's about the leaf she found."

"Dude, I can send them a bag full of leaves from my backyard," Cell smarted off.

"A leaf—a page from an ancient manuscript." Ram pushed on. "If Tzivia found one from the Aleppo Codex, IAA wants it. But so do a lot of other organizations who will do whatever it takes to get it from her."

"So she's in trouble?"

"Most likely." Ram adjusted his beanie. "When dealing with the Aleppo Codex, you get a lot of silence from pretty much everyone. There are those who want it to go away at all costs."

His intensity and confidence warned Tox this was a classic Ram scenario, where he knew more than he was letting on. And Tox knew to trust his friend. "And the censers? Tzivia's out there looking for the one Bhavin stole, right?"

"At this point, censers are secondary. A concern, but not like the

Codex. I mean, this thing is holier than holy to my people. And if Tzivia has a piece of it . . ." Ram glanced at the SAARC assets. "I have connections who say the underground is lit up like Times Square on New Year's Eve. They know she found this leaf."

"What are you saying?"

"We need to get to Israel," Ram said. "The leaf belongs to them and needs to be safeguarded."

"I thought you said they would destroy it."

"I said there are those who want to destroy it. But there are also those who can guard it—the only ones I trust. They know this leaf, which was with a fourth censer, just as has been written in ancient texts."

Tox frowned. He was missing something again.

"The censers and the plague are connected, and this leaf is connected to the censers."

"Connected?"

"The censers unleashed the plague. The leaf can tell us how to stop it, I bet."

Tox nearly laughed. "You're saying this is supernatural?"

"I'm saying we need to get to Israel."

* * * *

They're hiding something. Why would Cole not trust her? Did he still see her as just the little sister? The huddle around him tightened, the men intense, focused. Their gazes were down—what was he showing them? Their body language. . . .

"Kasey," Robbie called, "were you able to reach the SCTH or IAA?"

After glancing back to Cole, bent over a table with his team, Kasey joined her. "I reached someone at SCTH, but I don't think they were well-informed. Do we have another contact there?"

"Not a friendly one," Robbie said. "Why do you think they weren't well-informed?"

"He didn't know about the bombing. Went into a rage and hung up on me."

Robbie mulled over the information, then lifted her chin. "Try again." She looked to Vander. "Any word from Tzivia and Dr. Cathey?"

"Negative."

Robbie scratched her scalp frantically with a growl. "I need something, guys. Something to get us past 'stuck.'"

"Trying SCTH again." Kasey tugged her phone free and dialed. She set it to speaker and placed the phone on the table. It rang six times then went to voicemail.

Levi jutted his jaw to Vander. "What about IAA? Did you reach them?"

"Not yet."

Robbie nodded to Vander. "Get Ariel Bloomberg. And Levi—how's that plan coming with Wraith to get the journal?"

"Waiting on a source for the layout of the temple and its security. Once we have that, we can put things together."

Vander pointed to a phone cradled on the table. "Secretary's putting us through."

"Hello?" Robbie hit the speaker button. "Ariel, it's Robbie Almstedt."

"Shalom, my friend. How are you?"

"A little left of center. Listen, we needed to talk to someone with knowledge of the site at Jebel al-Lawz."

Hesitation gaped over the line. "Terrible tragedy that. Looters have no respect for history," Ariel growled.

"So you think it was looters?"

Kasey wished for a live feed to read his facial expressions and body language. Instead, she listened to what he didn't say as much as what he did.

"It is reasonable. A report from the DoD said the dig site was robbed, yes?"

Robbie swallowed. "Yes."

"There you have it."

"But how many looters do you know who can bomb with missiles?"

"Missiles?"

"Don't patronize me, Ariel. The satellite images show impact rings consistent with an air strike."

"You think we have done this thing?"

"An artifact was recovered, one believed to be important to your country, then suddenly the site is bombed." Robbie drummed her fingers on the table. "A little too coincidental for me. We need to stop this, Ariel. There's a plague—"

"I hope you do. A plague—there is already enough trouble in this world."

Was he toying with them? Why would he, when lives were at stake? Eyes darting back and forth, Robbie sat with a smile half frozen on her lips. "I realize we all walk a tricky path with anything related to—"

"Sorry, Robbie. Wish I could be of more help." He hung up.

* * * *

"We don't need to go back to the temple." Tox directed the team farther into the corner and away from the prying eyes of SAARC.

"Why's that?" Ram asked.

From beneath his belt, Tox withdrew a small leather-bound note-book. He held it close, so only his team could see it. Chiji leaned in, awe in his face.

Ram smirked. "That's why it took you so long to get back here." Shouldering to the side to block SAARC's view, he accepted the jour-nal and untwined the thin cord around it. "D'you read it? Copy it?"

"Took pictures with my phone." Tox pointed as the guys huddled around. "There's some interesting stuff. Sketches are important, I think."

"It's not even in English," Cell complained as he peeked over Ram's shoulder.

"Arabic and Hindi, mostly." Ram flipped another page, his finger tracing the script back and forth, right to left, then left to right. He paused over a spot, a flash of uncertainty or concern in his expression. He resumed reading. "He was looking to make some quick money. A French guy recruited him, offered payment for information about what was discovered at Jebel al-Lawz. Bhavin took the censer and fled while the others were distracted by the sickness."

Ram kept reading, pushing the beanie back from his forehead. The casual demeanor that so often marked the Israeli fled. In its place came a stern mask, one that didn't seem to like what it had seen.

Tox waited, though he itched to ask what was wrong.

"He came home—here, India—and was followed . . . evaded them . . ." Ram swatted another page, frowning. Reading. Scanning. He flipped back a page. "He speaks of a guardian." He shook his head, scowling as he continued reading.

Tox couldn't wait. "What?"

"Stranger things," Ram muttered.

"Hey. Fill us in," Thor insisted.

Holding up a hand, Ram read: "'I'm sick. I have no idea if it is what made the others sick, but I hope not. I heard they are dying.'" He turned a page. "'I was very frightened tonight. Two Western men I'd seen earlier in the market were in our building. I got away, but I am scared for my life.'"

Eyebrows climbing into his hairline, Ram widened his eyes. "'Now that I have met with Ti, I believe the danger is much greater than I thought. He says this artifact is related to'"—Ram's face fell—"'the Codex.'"

"Just as you thought," Tox whispered.

Alarm rang through Ram's eyes as he brought them to Tox. "This Ti showed him a text that says the fourth censer and leaf were to remain together. That without them within proximity to the other three, the plague would go unchecked."

24

Jealousy poked hot daggers into Kasey's conscience as Vander announced that Tzivia Khalon and Dr. Cathey had returned to the warehouse. Tzivia held a large black satchel, moving with confidence as she threw a flirtatious smirk at Cole. "Still alive. I'm impressed."

"No thanks to you." Cole closed the door and secured the locks.

Their easy, casual relationship smothered hope that he might see Kasey. As it had done all those years ago with Brooke. But it was time to put away childish things, wasn't it?

Robbie joined the group. "Ms. Khalon, did you find it?"

"The censer?" Ram asked, sidling up next to her.

She slid a coy smile at her brother. "Safe."

Robbie shifted. "I'm sorry? Where is it?"

Lifting her chin, Tzivia looked coolly at Robbie. "It's safe."

Robbie frowned, more severe than usual. "That's government property."

"Actually," Tzivia said, "it's not. Right now, it belongs to Saudi Arabia. Technically." She wrinkled her nose. "But we aren't letting them know just yet that I've recovered it."

Dr. Cathey shuffled forward. "We believe it in the best interest of stopping the plague that we find all the censers first."

"All?"

213

Dr. Cathey scratched his salt-and-pepper beard. "Yes, all three of the originals. I have contacts in Israel I'd like to talk to since you're headed that way."

"We are?" Robbie's voice pitched.

"You should be sure Mr. Narang is secured," Dr. Cathey said. "Especially after what Tzivia learned from Dr. Benowitz."

Bristling, Robbie clearly wasn't used to having her operations overrun by so many rogue elements. "When did you speak with him?"

Kasey eased into the conversation. "What did you learn?"

With a smile, almost a collusion against the Alpha personalities, Tzivia homed in on her. "They've verified the markers for the cancer, but there's still much unexplained." She sighed, looking to where Chatresh had been in the isolation chamber. "He's gone?"

"Quarantined," Robbie said.

"No visible signs of the virus?"

"General malaise and a headache."

Tzivia gave a shake of her head.

"You think he had the virus?" Cole stuck close to Tzivia. Too close, within personal space. What was their history?

"I'm no physician or virologist," Tzivia said, "but yes—that's what we were seeing at Jebel."

"Your report says the time from exposure to onset of symptoms for the other patients was four to five hours." Robbie stole back control. "Chatresh was with us all night without any visible symptoms."

"I can't explain it," Tzivia said, "but yes—four to five hours was normal. Viruses can mutate. Some are more potent as gases, some more so as liquids."

She turned to Cole and touched his arm. Which drew him even closer. Was that really necessary? Their words dropped to hushed whispers. Wreathed in shadows and mystery, they wandered to the corner with her brother, talking quietly.

"So much for that openness and honesty," Levi said, standing beside her with his hands on his belt.

"Because we were so good at it," Kasey muttered.

"Ms. Khalon?" Robbie's voice rang through the warehouse. "Would you care to share with the rest of us?"

Tzivia turned. Her dark eyes spat daggers, but she came to them. "As you know, the site was destroyed, but we'd sent samples to Oxford, some back to Johns Hopkins. We suspect a connection between the censers and the underground springs in the outbreak of the disease." She seemed to draw up at the end. As if she had additional information she wasn't willing to share. "It's more important now than ever that we find the other stolen censers."

"They were all stolen?"

Tzivia acknowledged with a nod. "By different men, so the challenge is great." Her dark eyes shifted to Kasey. "But we've already recovered one, thanks to your lie detector."

"Deception expert," Kasey corrected.

"At least at this point the contagion hasn't spread," Tzivia continued. "But according to my brother and Tox, it's even more dire than that."

What was Cole's relationship with this woman? Why would he trust her with information, but not Kasey and SAARC?

"It is normal to protect a site against the elements and treasure hunters," Tzivia said. "But not every dig hits a gold mine. Or a significant one."

Curiosity piqued, Kasey forgot her jealousy. "The censers were significant?"

"Yes, and somehow, Bhavin Narang knew it."

"What is the significance?" More Clark Kent than Kasey had seen him before, Levi narrowed his eyes.

"To be honest," Tzivia said, "even with my degree and experience, I'm not sure I fully understand the significance—or implications. That's why I've asked Dr. Cathey to join me in the hunt."

"We're running out of time." Cole positioned himself at the head of the long tables that bisected the room. "Circle up."

"What's going on, Tox?" Levi asked from the rear of the group.

"We have new intel. We need to break into teams and tackle this in a two-pronged approach." Cole was used to being in charge, and he did it naturally. "First—the intel." He nodded to Tzivia, who drew in a breath and faced the others.

"As you know, at our site we dug up artifacts dating back to the Bronze Age. Some of them were typical finds. Nothing to draw attention." Tzivia glanced at her brother, who stood with one hand over his chest and another stroking his stubbled chin. He gave her a nod. "There were, however, artifacts that appeared to be consistent with the biblical story of Moses and Joshua, when the earth swallowed men involved in a rebellion."

"Uh, which story is that exactly?" Cell asked with a lazy, apathetic shrug. "Not all of us are Bible scholars."

"None of us are," Cole clipped.

"Except Dr. Cathey," Tzivia added, the older man inclining his head.

"Korah's rebellion," Kasey said, thinking of the passages she'd studied. When the others looked at her, she shrugged. "Biblical deception is a hobby."

"Biblical what?" Cell frowned.

"It's . . . well, it doesn't matter right now." She nodded to Tzivia. "The story she's talking about is when Korah, Dathan, and Abiram set themselves against Moses, asking why Moses was so special. Korah said they were all gods, that Moses shouldn't get special treatment."

"Right." Tzivia bobbed her head. "The rebellion was a power-grab, and according to the Bible, Moses asked God to answer. So they all burned censers before the Lord in the tabernacle. Then the next morning, the ground opened up and swallowed the men who'd started the rebellion."

"Indeed," Ram said, smiling. "Then a volley of fire rushed out of the Tent of Meeting and wiped out all 250 who followed Korah, Dathan, and Abiram."

"'And they served as a warning sign.'"

The rumbly voice sent chills down Kasey's spine. She, as did most everyone else, looked at the tall black man behind Cole.

"Verse 10 of Numbers 26." Chiji stood tall, resolute. And made a stark impression with that ominous phrase. "But what of Numbers 16, verse 47?"

Tzivia seemed to shift under his gaze.

"'*So Aaron did as Moses said, and ran into the midst of the assembly,*'" Dr. Cathey recited from memory. "'*The plague had already started among the people, but Aaron offered incense and made atonement for them.*' Verse forty-eight says, '*He stood between the living and the dead, and the plague stopped.*'"

216

"This," Chiji pronounced with a nod to Cole, "is your task. To stand between the living and dead. Stop this plague."

Cole seemed to shiver.

Tzivia wet her lips. Interesting—the stories must make her uncomfortable. "We all know the biblical story," she said, "but the context is important—when the rebellion happened, plagues were coming and going in that region. Israelites were dying by the thousands. At the time they were settled just outside what would be the Promised Land, there was a plague—as Chijioke referenced." A faint smile. "I believe the censers we uncovered were somehow infected with trace bacteria from the plague."

"This is what you *believe*?" Chiji challenged.

Tzivia straightened, her jaw set in defiance.

"You tell the story as one reciting the code of a computer program, not as one who *believes*."

"I—"

"If you read the Holy Word, you will see it was God who sent the plagues of which you speak, the ones that came and went, in accordance with the disobedience of His chosen people."

"So . . . what, God sent this plague on these people? On us?" Tzivia's eyes lit with anger. "Tell me how Bhavin's brother was guilty. He came to us to help—"

"Bhavin stole. Chatresh lied. Not one of us is without sin," Chiji said.

Tzivia swallowed. Shook her head with an empty laugh. "If you need religion to make you feel better about bad things—"

"Easy," Cole warned, touching her arm and silencing her in the act. "Regardless of the source—"

"No, Ndidi," Chiji said. "If the plague is otherworldly—"

"We are dealing with a scientific plague in a scientific way," Tzivia snapped. "There is nothing religious about this. It's an archaeological site with historical and cultural value."

"Without its significance to the Israelites—"

"Can we stick to the facts?"

"Okay, hold up." Cole lifted a hand. "Just . . . stop." He placed his palms on the table, took several long breaths, then looked around the room. "I don't have all the answers. Not what started this. Not the source. But I have one answer to the attacks—us." He pinned each person with a gaze. "We're going to stop them. Stop this plague from spreading. And that path starts in Israel."

"Israel?" Levi growled. "How do you figure?"

"Russell," Robbie said, her thin impatience emanating. "I understand you—"

Cole tossed something onto the table. *Thud!* It landed inches from Kasey's fingertips. She instinctively picked it up. Surprise spiraled through her. "Bhavin's journal?"

Why hadn't he told them he had it? He had plenty of opportunity. But she buried the questions as she flipped through the pages. Most of it was in Hindi, which she couldn't read. Every few pages, he drew something—and those were more telling than the Hindi.

"Many of his notes are about his last I-don't-know-how-many years." Ram nodded. "Toward the end, his notes grow chaotic. Disorderly."

"Wait," Robbie said, her expression speculative, "it's in Hindi. How do you know what it says?"

"Lady," Cell snickered, "Ram's like the walking encyclopedia of languages."

Ram's jaw muscle twitched. "I speak several languages, including Hindi—can we focus?"

Arms folded, Cole tossed his chin toward the journal. "Bhavin mentions fearing for his life and a deal he brokered with a Frenchman."

Tzivia drew in a sharp breath.

Cole met her wide-eyed gaze. "Yeah . . . he says the Frenchman was hunting him."

"Yeah, what?" Levi asked.

"Tzivia encountered a Frenchman three years ago on another mission," Cole said.

So they *did* have history. Nudging aside the jealousy, Kasey riffled through the pages. "Is this the censer?" She angled the book to Tzivia, who nodded.

"But there are a few symbols and lines of text in there that lead us to Israel," Cole explained.

"Show me," Robbie demanded, "since I'm *not* a walking encyclopedia of languages."

Instead of a bullet point, Bhavin had drawn an arrow next to a line of script. "What does this say?" Kasey showed it to Ram and his sister. "I assume it's important because—"

Tzivia snatched the journal. "This!" She pointed to the arrow and wagged it at her brother, then Cole. "I saw this tattooed on one of that Frenchman's guards. And also on the man at the dig site, your assassin."

Ram retrieved it, giving Cole a hard look as he passed it back to him. "It is *imperative* we go to Israel."

"Why?" Levi and Robbie asked at the same time.

Ram and Cole went into that silent visual dialogue again for several long seconds until finally, Ram drew in a breath and heaved it out. "That arrow belongs to the Arrow & Flame Order, an organization whose pockets are deep and their connections deeper," he said. "Think of the Freemasons, but with more influence and more power."

"I'm not sure any of us want to imagine that," Kasey said.

Robbie lifted her hands. "But again—why Israel?"

Annoyingly, Ram and Cole did the unspoken alliance thing with their eyes again. An almost imperceptible nod by Ram pushed her attention to Cole.

He glanced at the table, then to the others. "In his journal, Bhavin made a note that had nothing to do with the other things he recorded. Everything else could be connected—the censer at the site, the Frenchmen who'd hired him."

"And the odd notation?" Kasey asked.

Cole's eyes glinted. "The Codex."

Ram pressed three fingers to the laminate surface. "I believe it's a reference to perhaps the most important surviving bound manuscript of the Hebrew Bible. It is the Crown of Aleppo, the Aleppo Codex, the Crown of Jerusalem, the *Keter Aram Tzova*, to list a few of its names."

"And how do we know he meant this codex?" Robbie asked.

"Because of the other notations—the Frenchman, the flaming arrow," Ram said.

Tzivia folded her arms. "And because I found a leaf from the Codex in Jebel al-Lawz."

Robbie scowled at Cole and Ram. "Why did you not tell us immediately that you retrieved the journal? Why are you withholding information?"

"I'm *sorting* information," Cole growled. "Are you going to tell me SAARC had no clue about this organization with the arrow?"

Her supervisor had never seemed so ruffled. "No. No. I haven't heard of it."

That's not true. The realization rattled Kasey.

Cole must've seen it, too. He stepped forward, his eyes narrowing. "My team has been attacked and exposed to a plague. I have every reason to be cautious with information, just as you do." He shifted, his gaze bouncing back to Ram, but not quite. It was as if he was trying to . . . to what? What was going on?

"You're not telling us something," Kasey whispered to herself. Only it escaped a little louder.

Cole seared her with a glare. Huffed before adding, "Someone at the temple told me to go to Israel. I hadn't even looked at the journal yet, but he told me to find the Crown—and as Ram just indicated, that's a pseudonym for the Codex."

"He?"

"It's not import—"

"The Stranger," Tzivia said with a hollow laugh.

"No."

"How do you know?" she snapped. "You didn't see the Stranger. I did. He appeared like a ghoul. Spoke things no human could know. Did things no man should do."

"Point taken." Cole wiped a hand down the back of his neck. "But this guy—I don't know who he is."

"If it's the Stranger—"

"It's not."

"—you need to listen. Last time I didn't go when he told me, that toxin was let loose in Kafr al-Ayn, and look what happened." Tzivia nodded urgently. "You need to go, Tox. If you don't"—she pushed her bangs off her face in a moment of panic—"this plague could explode."

"I think it already might have."

Kasey spun toward Vander, who stood just outside the group with a page hanging limp in his fingers. "What?"

"The virus Bhavin came in with, the New Black Death?" He huffed. "The hospital's reporting at least a dozen more cases."

25

Repacking his gear, Tox marveled at how things had changed in the last seventy-two hours. And in the last week, for that matter. Less than two weeks ago, he'd sat on the cliffs overlooking the plains as cheetahs hunted down antelope. Now he was the hunter chasing down one mystery after another. It was a never-ending loop, feeding back on itself each time they blinked or adjusted their grip.

Now—Israel?

The *clack-clack* of kali sticks drew his gaze to Chiji. His friend gave him an inviting look, but Tox shook his head. No time. Tox rolled a shirt and stuffed it into his ruck, then grabbed the next one, cramming them tightly together so he had room for everything. Shirts, boxers, tactical pants, socks, vest, holsters. It felt good to be back in action, but he'd have never picked this. Never would've pitted his team against a hostile biological threat again. Galen and Attaway had one-upped him this time, sending them after an assassin without informing him what they'd get tangled up in.

But Tox couldn't lay the whole blame at his brother's feet, though he wanted to. Tox had known there was more to this mission than he'd been told. And curse his ego, or pride, or whatever it was that possessed him to enter the fray, risking life and limb for . . . what?

What is wrong with you?

He'd always had a thirst for the dangerous side of life. But the inevitable, the part he never anticipated, always happened. Someone always got hurt.

A voice drifted into his frustration.

He glanced up as he rolled a pair of pants tight. Packed them. But saw no one. He focused on his clothes. But the voice poked the air again.

Tox looked around, searching out what sounded like agitated—but repressed—conversation. A shadow slid along a wall of lockers in the northwest corner. A feminine one.

He checked over his shoulder. Almstedt and Tzivia were hanging over a map or something, talking. That meant . . . Haven.

Tox followed the voice around a stack of crates that served as a divider. She sat at a makeshift desk, a notebook splayed open on the small table, with one hand cradling her forehead and the other pressing a phone against her ear. "No! You can't—" She snapped her mouth shut, drawing up sharp. "I am not responsible for that."

Since her supervisor and handler were on the floor behind them, there could only be one of two people talking to her right now: Attaway or Galen.

"Yes, I know—you allowed—" She sighed and hung her head, rubbing the back of her neck as she did. She jerked to her feet. "How dare you? I have never compromised my integr—" Then she ducked and shook her head, fingers to her forehead. She sniffled.

Something in him awakened. Shifted. Got lodged in his chest. It might have been more than ten years since he'd seen her, but Tox knew one thing about Haven—unlike him, she wasn't easily upset. For someone to set her off . . .

He strode toward her. Had to be Attaway. Galen was manipulative, but he wasn't acerbic. Well, not to everyone else. With Tox, he'd never minced words.

Haven turned and her eyes bulged. "Co—"

He took the phone from her. When she reached for his arm, he placed a hand over hers and held her in place as he rotated his back to her. He lifted the phone to his ear. Heard the voice. "Attaway." With the way he'd turned, Haven was tangled against him, her arm wrapped around his chest. The warmth of her other hand rested on his back.

"Cole," she whispered.

"Tox, is that you?" Attaway sounded strained.

"Is my brother there?"

"He's not."

"Get him on the phone."

"He can't be disturbed right now. He's in a meeting with—"

"Tell you what," Tox said, adrenaline pumping through his veins.

"Cole, please," Haven whispered, drawing his gaze to hers, where he found still-glossy eyes. Like a sea. One he found himself lost and adrift in. Pulling him in. She shook her head.

Two options presented themselves. One, light into Attaway for cutting through Haven's thick padding of sweetness and niceness. But that might not reflect well on her. Two, he could redirect this, completely ignoring the poor treatment of her. "We're heading to Israel. I need Haven with me."

"She *is* with you. SAARC—"

"No. Attach her to my team."

"I . . . I don't think—"

"No, you *don't*. That's why I'm telling you—attach her to my team. I need her." Something strange and frightening shot through him at those words. And the surprise in her green eyes only agitated the heat coursing through his chest. Especially when she moved her other hand from his back to his bicep. All in an effort to stop him, but it just made him press Attaway harder. "She has skills we need." That felt better.

"She's not combat trained."

"But I am." *Stupidest mistake of your life. She'll end up dead like Brooke.* "Make it happen. Tell Galen to authorize it or I'm done."

"You understand your brother has a country to run, right?"

"If I can't stop this assassin, we may not have a president." Haven shifted. Tox needed her to be still. To stop distracting him. "Or a country."

223

She drew up straight, her lips parting in surprise.

"Listen to me," Attaway said, his tone taking on a deathly chill. "Are you forgetting about al-Homsi? About the fallout? The unintended consequences?"

Ghosts of his past sailed through the shadowy passage of crates and steel wall, reaching for Tox. Anger pulsed, but he shoved back the memories. "I never forget." Especially al-Homsi. Biggest mistake—

"Then remember that the next time you start handing me orders." The words, the reminders were a threat.

Mashing the END button, Tox bit down on his frustration. He lowered the phone and stepped back, releasing Haven. Releasing this mess. When he handed the phone over, she had so much concern in her eyes he couldn't stand it. At the same instant he saw that look, the same one he'd noticed years ago when he was dating her sister: Attraction. Embarrassment wrapped up in a schoolgirl crush. Back then, he'd brushed it off. She was a kid. Now . . .

She hugged a notebook.

"What is that?" he asked.

Haven looked down as if she'd forgotten it, then tossed it on a crate. "My field notebook." It fell open. The left-hand page was marked OBSERVED and the right, QUESTIONED.

He traced a finger down it, reading. "From Chatresh's interview?"

"Yes."

He remembered something she'd said. "You said he might have stopped lying with his mouth . . ."

"Yes. Our bodies often betray us and our lies."

"'What are the worthless and wicked people like? They are constant liars . . .'"

She tilted her head. "What?"

He shrugged. "Nothing. Just something my mom used to say about my dad's friends." Though he snorted, he had to admit that was how he felt about his dad's circle—constant liars. He fought the urge to look at her again. "It was in the Bible."

"That almost sounds like biblical deception." She laughed, but she had her phone out, thumbing a browser. She tapped quickly on the screen.

224

"You mentioned that earlier. The Bible teaches how to deceive?"

She smiled, not quite lifting her gaze to him. "Not exactly." She swiped a screen. Then slid the bar up. "Here." She scanned. With a quiet gasp, she lifted a pen. Turned a page in her journal and started writing. "I was right."

Cole felt exposed. Had he just betrayed himself somehow? He leaned over her shoulder as she wrote. "What?"

"So . . ." she said, still writing and distracted by the forming list, "there must always be three forms of deception for it to indicate the person is deceiving you. Right here—it's Proverbs 6:12, by the way—listen: *What are worthless and wicked people like? They are constant liars, signaling their deceit with a wink of the eye, a nudge of the foot, or the wiggle of fingers.*"

"And that means they're lying?"

"Wink of the eye—that's classic breaking eye contact. People do that when they aren't telling the truth. It can even be rubbing the eye—anything that removes the gaze." She pointed to the second one, then turned the page back to Chatresh's notes. "Here—he was shuffling his feet as he broke eye contact with you. It was one of the ways I knew he wasn't being totally honest. Proverbs speaks to the nudging of the foot."

"And the wiggle of fingers?"

"Classic nervous tension release." Her grin was wide, her eyes vibrant. "The most fascinating thing is that I've always been taught that signs of deception are culturally based but the cultures of biblical times are vastly different from today's—yet these truths are still there. The three-rule test is still there."

Cole wasn't sure what to say. It was strange seeing her so animated over a lie detection method found in the Bible.

"Sorry," she said, her embarrassment plaguing her face, "I get a little excited. It's thrilling to find another instance of biblical deception."

"Is that an official specialty?"

She wrinkled her nose. "No, just a hobby. But fascinatingly, it almost always lines up with what I see in the field."

He nodded. "Chiji would really like you." Something in her gaze

225

felt like a life preserver thrown to save him from being adrift. Calling to him. Asking him to come in from the storm.

Reality check: *She* was the storm. He was toxic. "I need to pack up." The surprise and disappointment in her face pushed him around and toward his ruck.

"Cole."

Don't stop. But his body disobeyed the direct order. He clenched his teeth and hesitated. Turned back.

The muscle beneath her left eye twitched, showing confusion seconds before her eyes narrowed. "Why did you tell Attaway you wanted me attached to your team?"

"Attaway needed to be put in his place."

She smiled and gave a breathy laugh. "It was nice to see someone do that—Galen is far too lenient with him . . ." Confusion didn't become her, but she'd worn it often since they'd been reintroduced. "What . . . happened?"

Dread shot through him, remembering the way Barry had brought up al-Homsi and Brooke. Had she heard that? "What do you mean?"

She never took her eyes from him. "He said something to you, something that made you angry."

No, he couldn't go there. "Him being alive makes me angry."

She smiled but started to shake her head.

"Leave it, Haven. Please. Focus on the mission."

26

On the fifth floor of a hotel in Jerusalem, Tox let himself into a suite with that renovated-but-old stench, one of mingling mustiness and carpets heavily sanitized to rid the fibers of cigarette smoke. He closed the door and quietly dropped his duffel, his gaze sweeping the room. Five paces delivered him into the small kitchenette with vinyl flooring and an anemic-looking stove and sink. He crossed the space, lifted the paper towels from their holder, and tested the weight of the holder in his hand. Satisfied it'd work, he stalked out of the kitchen and hesitated, glancing left and right, where the hall jutted off into two rooms. In the middle, a sitting area occupied the majority of the space.

Tox slipped into the first room. Paisley polyester bedspreads draped two full-sized beds, separated by a pathetic-looking table. He slid up alongside the closet door, hoisted his makeshift weapon high, and flipped open the door.

Clear.

He repeated the same in the second room. Back in the living area, he eyed the balcony that afforded a view of the Old City. A small wrought-iron table and two chairs consumed the space. He returned the holder to the kitchen, retrieved his duffel, and tossed it on a bed in the room with the north-facing wall.

Fifteen minutes later, Levi showed up, followed closely by Ram and Chiji.

"She's an FBI agent, Tox. Not a soldier," Levi said. "Why did you send her with the others?"

It only took one glare to silence the agent. Tox stood by the door as Ram drew out a small box, hooked it up to a tether, then walked the rooms, searching for listening devices. The crackle of the box proved comforting—no bugs.

"Clear." Ram headed for the bedrooms to ditch his ruck.

Tox turned to Levi. "Next time, make sure the room's clear before you start giving out info on us and our game plan."

Ram returned, tugging his beanie a little tighter around his face.

"Have you made contact yet?" Tox asked him.

"No, but we'll head to the synagogue. He's always there."

"Is that normal?" Levi asked, his voice strained. "Not to hear from your contact? Is there a reason I'm not being filled in?"

"Yes, and yes." Ram nodded to the door the same moment Tox heard people coming down the hall. He stepped aside, listening.

Laughter, quiet but noticeable—Haven's. How he knew, he couldn't say. He just did. At the noise of their key cards sliding into the reader, he moved out of the way.

Click.

The door opened. Cell entered, his keen gaze taking in the room before shifting to let the women and Maangi, who watched the hall, enter. Tox appreciated their careful insertion into the unknown.

"Tzi, you and Cortes to the right," Ram said, taking their bags and setting them inside the bedroom. "Rest of you, duke it out for the rollaway, sofas, and floor."

"What about the beds?" Cell asked.

"Tox and I took them," Ram said.

"What is this, finders keepers?"

"Yes," Tox and Ram answered at the same time.

Grabbing a bottled water from the counter, not minding that it wasn't ice cold, Tox glanced around. Took a swig as the others dropped their gear. He took another gulp and motioned them into the living area. "Gather up. We need to get things in play." Once they were together, he turned the convo over to Ram.

"Tonight, order in. Stay low," Ram said. "Tox and I are heading to a synagogue." He nodded. "We should be back in a couple of hours, but we'll keep you posted."

"If you don't hear from us, you know what to do," Tox said.

"Um, no, we don't." Tzivia straightened. "And Dr. Cathey will be contacting me. I need the freedom to go with him."

"You have it, but limit the in-and-out." Ram adjusted his beanie again, nodding to the men. "Until then, just follow their lead. They know." With that, he started for the door.

As they made their way to the rental car, though modestly dressed, Tox felt naked beneath the glares of the suited and bearded Jewish *haredim* and Muslims. Or maybe that was his distrust of those he didn't know. In the Old City, walking beneath the warmth of the sun and their glares felt like the longest twenty minutes of his life.

Tox quickly grew tired of the monotony of Jerusalem stone covering nearly every visible surface—walls and sidewalk alike. Occasionally grass would stab defiantly through the mortar or a weed would launch upward, as if it too praised God from rocks.

Everything felt the same. Low arches, short doors, and narrow passages. It'd be easy to get turned around and lost, especially for someone who couldn't read Hebrew. While some words had a marginal similarity to Arabic, of which Tox had a passing knowledge, the letters were harder to sort.

He scanned the narrow street for signs of a large synagogue. He'd loved the soaring architecture and incredible mosaics in many of the mosques across Afghanistan and Iraq. The artistry and extravagance there knew no limits. Well, until it met with the head of a two thousand-pound JDAM. But here—here he found only simplicity.

Ram banked right between two stone columns and pushed open a wrought-iron gate. He ducked beneath its scrollwork. Brass lettering on the—*surprise!*—Jerusalem stone clung to the building, probably the name of the synagogue.

Ram reached for the door and swiped off his beanie.

Surprise lit through Tox. He stopped. Stared at the small round cap that seemed glued to Ram's brown curls. A yarmulke? "Since when?"

"Shut up and go inside."

"You been wearing one the whole time beneath that beanie?"

"In," Ram growled then pushed past him and entered.

Tox grinned. "How have I missed that?"

"Shabbat shalom." Ram was speaking softly to someone within the synagogue.

Tox hurried in but suddenly felt out of place. He took a second, glancing around to gain his bearings and adjust to the dimmer light. In those seconds, he noted three men huddled near a small alcove. Others were scattered around the synagogue's interior. Just beyond the foyer, Ram stood in quiet conversation with a rabbi. Body language conveyed little. Respect. Reverence. But it didn't seem Ram knew this guy.

Not their contact?

Tox glanced back to the doors, gauging his best route of escape, and counted only one door to his right. Two on the left. Within the synagogue, a raised section cantilevered over the rest. Rows of chairs mirrored the rows of stained glass. Ironic how the simplicity of the building made the stained glass seem more elaborate.

Ram pivoted on his feet, his head slightly bowed still, and motioned to a small bench. "We wait."

Wait? Tox looked at the bench. Then the door. Back to the theater-style seating of the main area. Ram sat on the thin pad, his back pressed against the wall.

Tox folded his arms. Stayed on his feet. In his experience, sitting implied submission. Implied he wasn't in control.

"Sit," Ram said. His tone wasn't combative. But it also wasn't placating.

"I'm good."

"Tox"—Ram skated a glance around—"sit."

Teeth clenched, Tox let out a huff. Planted himself on the bench. He felt like a freakin' kid at the principal's office. "I don't do this well."

"I know." Ram twisted the beanie as if wringing water out of it.

Tox didn't have anything to wring—except Ram's neck. Did they have a contact to meet with or not? Didn't sitting here compromise them? Put them in the open too long?

The door opened, light fracturing the dim void of the synagogue. A man entered with his son, whose ringlets around his face reminded Tox of something from that prairie show with the little house. He wouldn't say anything. Not here. But the inappropriate comment sat on the tip of his tongue. A defense mechanism to shift the focus from his discomfort.

The silence, the gaping void of activity, pelted Tox's nerves like tiny needles of sleet. How he could sit on the cliffs overlooking the African savannah for hours on end without a problem but not sit here in a synagogue defied explanation. He needed a distraction. "So, the yarmulke . . ."

"So," Ram said, his voice quiet, "Haven."

Silenced, Tox nodded. "Fair enough." He pushed to his feet and paced to the doors. Glanced at his watch. Twenty minutes. How long were they supposed to wait for this guy? "Did—" His friend's grin stopped him. "What?"

Ram smirked then shook his head. "Sit."

"Don't you have an appointment?"

"Right, I called and said I'm an American black ops soldier and need to talk to you about a deadly plague that may or may not have supernatural—"

"Might've been faster," Tox muttered sarcastically.

"And deadlier."

"There is that." Tox shifted back to the door with stained glass, then swung around to check the offices for movement. With a grunt, he dropped onto the bench again. "This place is driving me nuts."

"Guilt in a synagogue could imply—"

"Too much. I know."

"You call her Haven."

Tox had known this was coming at some point. "That's her name." He didn't like the other one. It had too much attached to it. Like a dead husband.

"Not according to her. And nobody else uses it."

Tox lifted a shoulder. He checked the offices again. "Aren't we supposed to be meeting someone?"

Again, that smirk. "She likes you."

"What do you want from me?"

"For you to—"

"My apologies" came a deep voice.

Tox punched to his feet and muttered, "About time."

"Shabbat shalom," Ram said, inclining his head to the black-clad rabbi. "We are looking for Rebbe Baum."

The rabbi, wreathed in both solemnity and severity, glared at Tox then dragged his attention back to Ram. "Why do you look for him?"

"Regarding the Codex."

The rabbi scoffed. "You are wasting your time with Rebbe Baum. The Codex is in the Israel Museum."

"Yes, we were informed, but we had questions for him."

Hands held out, the rabbi said, "Truly, I am sorry, but Rebbe Baum is not here."

Ram cocked his head. "You told us he was in a meeting."

"Yes." He managed a flat smile—they didn't need Haven's deception skills to know it was fake. "There were several rebbes in the conference room"—as if to confirm his words, a sea of black swept past them and into the afternoon sun—"but I was wrong. He was not here." He chuckled. "How silly of me."

Silly? Tox would put silly through his skull.

"Do you know where he is?" Ram asked.

"Yes." He motioned to an office door. "I have just learned he went to the Great Synagogue."

Ram hesitated. Frustrated. "The Great Synagogue."

"Yes. There is a bat mitzvah there." The rabbi was trying too hard to make it convincing. Or maybe Tox was overly paranoid. "A friend of a friend, I hear."

"Thank you. Shabbat shalom." Ram started for the door.

Outside and bathed in the fading warmth of the Jerusalem sun, Tox waited until they were back in the rental car before speaking. "You said he was always there." He fisted his fingers. "Is this . . . normal?"

"What *is* normal here?" Ram pulled into traffic.

"But you're bothered." In fact, Tox would say very bothered. Skeptical and maybe annoyed. But Ram wasn't saying anything. Hadn't confronted the rabbi. Was it a mutual respect? What?

"Time's been wasted," Ram replied.

"Is this other synagogue far?"

"By car, about ten minutes."

"I feel like we're getting strung along." They'd lost forty-five minutes waiting. But they'd endured worse beneath pelting live fire. Or a ball of fire like at Kafr al-Ayn.

Tox kept track of the streets and turns in the off-chance he had to find his way back to the hotel alone. He used landmarks as a guiding beacon. They headed down King George Street. Two very large Jerusalem stone buildings surged from the monotony. They might use the same material, but there was nothing blasé about these buildings. "Now that's more like it," Tox muttered.

"What?"

"This—it holds its own against the great mosques."

Ram glared at him.

"What? I only mean that all the mosques we saw in A-stan and Iraq were filled with gold and glitter. Here, things are . . ." He waved his hand, not sure how to word it.

"More concerned with the heart than the suit the man wears."

Tox nodded. "Whatever. I only meant—"

"Here." Ram whipped the car into a spot and parked. He was out before Tox could finish his sentence.

Normally Ram wasn't easily offended, and it bothered Tox that he had somehow irritated him. He huffed before opening the door. He hurried to catch up with Ram, whose pace was clipped and fast.

A blur of white snagged his attention. He glanced to the side. And stopped cold.

His hearing hollowed. His mind powered down, his brain processing only one thing: the man standing at the end of the walk.

Not just a man.

The one who'd reached down to him in the fireball in Kafr al-Ayn. The one who'd spoken to him at the temple in India.

"Tox!"

He jerked, eyes on the man. "Who are you?"

"Tox! What are you doing?" Ram. It was Ram talking to him.

His Israeli friend stepped in front of him. Tapped his shoulder.

Tox blinked. "That man"—he glanced around Ram, only to find the stone path empty—"What?" He turned a circle. "Where'd he go?"

"Who?"

"The man. The one—" Tox bit down on the words. He'd recounted the story about that man in the fire only once. He'd never do it again. Saw the *His mind went outside the wire and didn't RTB* racking up. "Nothing." A heavy weight thudded against his gut. *Shake it off.* "Let's get this done." He shifted toward the building. Two entrances presented themselves. "Which one?"

Ram frowned but hooked a finger at the building on the left.

"Let's go." Tox marched to the thick wood doors, leaving behind the empty sidewalk and gut-churning experience.

Inside they were greeted with more of the alluring simplicity—and incredible beauty—of the stained-glass depictions that were prevalent.

Ram headed to a bank of doors and rapped on a jamb. "Shabbat shalom," he said to a rabbi Tox could not see.

"Shabbat shalom," a voice intoned.

"Forgive the intrusion," Ram said, "but we are looking for Rebbe Baum."

Tox angled to see farther into the sanctuary. Split in two levels, the splash of color from the stained glass never ceased. A veritable rainbow—and in fact, a legit rainbow hung over the ark and seemed to divide the glass mural into two halves.

"Ah, well, I'm not sure he's available right now. Let me check." A short, rotund rabbi emerged from the office. He made his way down the hall, his gait crooked, probably from arthritis.

Tox waited as Ram crossed the hall. "This Baum seems rather . . . busy."

"Mm, or—"

"Might I ask what this is about?" a voice called from a long, dark hall. The same voice, Tox believed, that belonged to the rotund rabbi.

"It's very urgent," Ram said, moving toward the voice. "We need to ask him about the Aleppo Codex."

Shuffling was the only answer, the shadows darkening again.

"Maybe next time," Tox said, feeling exposed beneath the murals, "we should say he's come into a wealth of money."

"That wouldn't matter to a true rebbe."

"*True* being the operative word."

"Mm."

The second usage of that word tugged at Tox's brain. Ram was going internal, processing. That meant something was up, a sentiment nagging with doubts.

Heavy feet pounded down the hall. Different person. Maybe the contact was here after all.

A younger, stouter man emerged from the shadows. "I am Rebbe Gershon. How can I help you?"

Or maybe not.

"I need Rebbe Baum," Ram said, his tone firm. "We were sent here by a rebbe from Or Zaruaa."

"Oh. Well." The rabbi slid Tox a gaze that felt more like oil being poured over him than a friendly gesture. Slimy. "My apologies."

"For what?" Tox pulled forward, his irritation obvious.

Ram held up a hand. "It is very important, Rebbe, that we speak with him. Lives are at risk."

The man swallowed. "Of course." He shrugged. "But . . . I am sorry. He is not here."

Patience wasn't Tox's strong suit. "We were told he's doing a bat mitzvah. Those are pretty important, right?" He wasn't leaving without checking this place.

"Those—those aren't done here." Sweat dotted the man's olive complexion. "They're in the banquet hall—"

"Good, we'll look there." Tox started walking and felt assured when Ram fell into step with him.

"But you can't!" the man squeaked as he hurried behind them.

They banked down the hall, Tox letting Ram lead, since he could actually read the signs on the walls that led to the banquet hall.

"Please. You can't do this!"

To the right. It was a rush to sidestep obstructions and get on with finding answers. What was going on? Why were they getting the royal runaround?

"Please wait. There's—"

Ram tugged open a door. They stepped inside.

A swath of ribbons and flowers. Laughter and merriment. A shout went up, followed by more laughter. A bride . . . and groom. A wedding reception.

Gasps rippled through the hall.

Tox backed up, right into the rabbi. He spun and barely resisted the urge to grab the rabbi by his jacket. "What are you hiding? Does Baum even exist?"

"Hey, hey. Easy." Ram stepped between them. Gave Tox a firm look before focusing on the religious man. "Please. It's important. People are dying. Rebbe Baum may hold the answers."

"Dying?" He shuddered through a breath, easing away from Tox with bulging eyes. "I shouldn't . . ." He glanced to the side, as if afraid he'd get caught. "O-okay. Hecht."

Ram muttered something and shook his head. "You're sure?"

"Of course, of course."

"Who's Hecht?"

"Not who. What." Ram pivoted on his feet. Stomped down the hall and back out the route they'd come.

Tox trailed him closely, agitation churning into anger. "Where are we going?"

"Hecht Synagogue."

"Are you kidding me?" Rage flung through Tox. "I thought you knew this guy. Knew where he was. And why are you being so nice to them?"

"Respectful," Ram corrected, stalking down the sidewalk. The sun now hid behind walls and multistoried structures.

"Ram."

In the car, he pulled back into traffic. Focused on traffic, lights, pedestrians.

"What if Baum doesn't even exist?"

"He exists."

Maddening. "Have you even met this guy before?" Tox motioned to the streets. "We're chasing our butts and getting nowhere fast."

"Just trust me."

Tox snorted, yet Ram's words stemmed some of his frustration. He *did* trust Ram. Almost more than anyone. Except Chiji. "I need to know the plan."

"I know."

"You haven't told me that plan."

"I can't."

"Why?" He'd known Ram Khalon for nearly ten years. Worked with him for six. And the guy was the truest soldier he'd ever met. But he'd always had "insider knowledge," especially pertaining to things he shouldn't know. This wasn't the first time Tox wondered who—or what—Ram was behind his stoic demeanor. "If you put us in danger, I will kill you."

Ram smirked.

* * * *

— THE ISRAEL MUSEUM —

The eyes of an FBI agent were keen and alert, a veritable detector of deception and criminal activity.

Except when distracted by a beautiful woman. And Joseph Cathey used that to his advantage. While Wallace and Cortes were engaged in a discussion, he slipped to the side and stared at a brightly lit vase dating back to the days of David.

"You are making much noise," a stiff voice said from beside him.

Joseph tilted his head, focusing on pottery striations, careful not to look at the man. The "noise" he referred to were the rumblings within the secretive community. "Noise must be made to be heard. The leaf—"

"Many would be very eager to take it from you."

It was a common tactic to ascertain where the artifact was and who had it by insinuating a threat. Joseph knew better than to play into the hands of mysterious persons. "Three miktereths were stolen from the site in Jebel al-Lawz. I think it would be in everyone's best interest if the remaining miktereth could be verified. And the leaf must be verified."

"Then you have it."

Joseph bristled. "*Whoever* has it must verify it. There is a plague sweeping our world." He bent closer to the brown pottery, lifting his glasses for better inspection. "Unless you are as Moshe and can persuade Yahweh to stay this one."

"Yahweh used Aaron to check the plague of Korah's rebellion."

"I would not waste any more time trying to ascertain its location, Akiva," Joseph said, watching in his periphery as the agents' discussion grew more agitated. "I need to speak with them about the Codex. We need to see it."

"Careful, Joseph," Akiva whispered as he turned. "I'll convey your request, but be warned—this may be an invitation to death."

"They're toying with us." Tox stood in yet another foyer. An empty foyer. He stared at his yarmulke-capped friend. "Third synagogue where Baum is supposed to be. And surprise—he's not here."

Jaw muscle popping, Ram stared into the sanctuary.

"How long do we wait this time?" Tox was sure he could have dug a trench several feet deep with his pacing over the last few hours. For what? To be made a fool of?

"You aren't very patient."

"I do patient just fine—when it has a point." Like waiting out a terrorist in a village. Or waiting out an asset until he had enough information. Or watching Kasey until he had more certainty than doubt that she was Haven. He stabbed a finger toward the floor. "*This* has no point. Except to make us look stupid."

"There *is* a point." Ram's ferocity bled with frustration.

With a questioning look to his friend, Tox just as quickly saw the expression—the same one Ram plastered on every time someone approached the vault of his past, his secrets.

Tox shook his head. "This secrecy of yours . . ."

"No worse than the last three years of your life."

"I told you about the last three years."

"Not everything."

Tox glanced up, ready to object, but the challenge in Ram's eyes silenced him.

Okay. True enough. There were things Tox hadn't told anyone.

"Whatever you did," Ram said, "whatever they made you do, they also silenced you."

Tox ground his teeth.

Steady, quiet eyes held his. "The same is true for me."

"They silenced you?" It made sense. "Mossad."

Ram didn't deny it. Or confirm it. That was an admission in Tox's book. The steady clop of shoes distracted them both. Down the hall strode a *haredi,* an Ultra Orthodox Jew. Tox stood.

When Ram let out a heavy sigh, Tox knew it wasn't Baum. Again.

"Forgive me for making you wait." The rabbi gave a slight bow.

"It seems to be a practice with your kind," Tox said. "What, did they call ahead from the other synagogues?"

"Tox," Ram chided. He turned back to the rabbi. "Forgive him. He is tired from our travels."

The rabbi frowned, glancing between them, then focused on Ram. "I am truly sorry for your troubles."

"Troubles?" Tox snorted. "We've been on a wild-goose chase. All we want is to ask questions about the Aleppo Codex."

The rabbi went white.

That. That right there was what rankled Tox the most. They were all kind and humble until the Codex was mentioned. Then suddenly, *You're at the wrong place.*

"Tox. Stop," Ram said, his voice thick.

"Yes—and that is why I am confused," the rabbi said, shaking his graying head. "The Crown is not housed here, nor at any of our synagogues. And Dr. Baum's office is at the Israel Museum. That is where you should go, if you want to talk to him."

"Unbelievable." Tox wasn't surprised. Should be, but really, had they expected anything in Israel to be easy?

Ram scowled, nudging Tox backward. "Thank you, rebbe. We will look there."

But Tox didn't budge. He'd been played. By these rabbis. Men he'd instinctively had a pretty stiff level of respect for. Until now.

Ram stepped into his path. "It's not a long trip." But something in Ram's expression shot warnings at Tox. With gazes locked, Ram eased to the right just enough to clear Tox's line of sight.

A shadow shifted behind Ram. Adrenaline spiked, but Tox quickly dismissed it. Just tree limbs dancing behind the stained-glass window. Had to be. No need to be jumpy.

Except the sun had gone down.

That shadow wasn't a branch. A person stood in the darkened passage.

"Ready?" Ram asked, his tone light. Almost happy.

Warning received. "Yeah." Who was enough of a threat to worry Ram?

Outside, the cool breeze did nothing to soothe the anger coursing through Tox. He trailed Ram a few feet, noting his friend's squared shoulders. Clipped pace. "What was—"

"Not yet." Ram folded himself into the rental and turned the key.

Tox climbed in. The car pulled forward, pressing him backward as he struggled to close the door, cement blurring beneath them. Though it took everything in him, Tox waited five minutes before probing for answers. "Anytime you're ready." Because this was messed up, seeing Ram scared.

"Mossad."

The lone word zapped Tox with enough fear to silence him. "I thought you were . . . acquainted with them."

"To them, I'm an American operator."

Read: not Israeli. Not trustworthy.

And somehow Ram and Tox had their attention. Did Tox have a red dot on his forehead right now? The urge to duck grew surreal. But what? What had lured them out of their dens? "This about the Codex?" It was the only thing that made sense. "Or the plague? Censers?"

"Any and all." Ram sighed. "But this—this silence, it is normal when you inquire about the Codex. There are too many mysteries about it, and nobody is so expertly prepared to protect a national treasure than the IAA or Mossad." He nodded to Tox. "Ask questions of them, get silence."

"And a maddening wild Codex chase."

Ram nodded. The car rounding another corner exerted the force of gravity on Tox—and his mind. He noted the buildings. The streets. Wait. They weren't headed back to the hotel. "Why are we going to the museum still?"

"He told us to."

"But we're compromised!"

"We were compromised as soon as we boarded the plane to Israel."

Tox bit back a curse. More secrets. More Ram couldn't say. "This is—" He shook his head. Then nodded. Unbelievable. He'd done his best to shut down his questions and theories about Ram's connections. But with his racial background and tactical experience—more like excellence—there weren't many theories remaining. Tox just wasn't ready to accuse Ram of treason.

"They are testing me." Ram turned the wheel hand over hand as they took another corner. "If I don't go, then they will say I am scared or impatient."

Neither would be a lie.

"And if I am scared or impatient, then I am not worthy of whatever truth they can reveal."

"You mean whatever they are hiding." Wrapping his mind around the fact that they were dealing with this secretive, deadly, and highly effective organization was hard. It created a whole new pucker factor. "How'd we tick them off?"

Ram gave a caustic laugh. "I think it is in my blood," he said, referring to his family's long history of drawing the wrath of the Israeli agency.

Tox didn't know the whole story, and Ram wouldn't tell it, at least not every detail. Only that his family fled Israel in the middle of the night because his father wouldn't do something. Then his father died under mysterious circumstances, and their American-born mother raised them in New York, quietly and humbly. But Ram had never forgotten. Or forgiven.

"Think they realize who you are?"

"They *know* who I am." No merriment or laughter in his voice. Dead serious. "We're here."

Looking out the window, Tox sagged. Another place to wait. Find out they'd been baited. "How long do we sit this time?"

Ram shrugged. "At least we won't be bored here."

Tox was forced to study the building, a 1960s structure if he ever saw one with its long, clean lines and little but nature to accent it.

"This is the largest cultural institution in Israel." Ram almost smiled. "It's ranked among the world's leading art and archaeology museums. Tzivia loves this place."

"I imagine her professor does as well."

"Indeed. In fact, Dr. Cathey has cooperated with the institute and been here on numerous occasions to work with or see the scrolls and codices." Ram's cheek twitched. "Our problem is knowing where to look for Baum on the twenty-acre complex."

"Information desk?" It was meant to be funny, but really, where else would they start? The rabbi hadn't given them instructions.

They made their way up the path with its intermittent pegs and stairs. The far quarter actually had steps of light, providing ample illumination as dusk pushed away the warmth of the sun and the serene glow from the steel and glass structures. Tox tried not to stare at a giant apple core, a sculpture that must hold some importance. His mind wandered to Adam and Eve, but who knew why there was an apple core on the path to the museum entrance.

Beyond the plates of glass and translucent walls, they found the entrance. Ram strode to the information booth in the middle of the grand foyer. He palmed the counter, and Tox turned a slow circle, taking in the museum, artifacts, patrons, and exits.

Ram spoke in Hebrew to the woman, and while Tox didn't speak the language, he heard Baum's name. She replied quickly and quietly, drawing a long, dour look from Ram. He finally sighed and shouldered Tox.

"Let me guess—not here." Although he didn't directly eyeball them, Tox noted the half-dozen security cameras peeking from the ceilings like black eyes, monitoring the museum that perfected the art of cement, steel, and glass for a cool, retro-classy look.

"She's never heard of him."

"But he's your contact—and he does exist, right?"

"My contact exists. But his name"—he shook his head—"is whatever he needs it to be."

"So you don't know him?"

"Not personally."

Tox blew out a frustrated breath and probed farther into the galleries, all littered with remnants of history. Some open and unprotected, others in glass cases. A conglomerate on shelves.

Recognition flared. The man by the statue—Maangi. What was he doing here?

Another man stood with a woman, inappropriately close in this cultural climate. He had a possessive hand at the small of her back. He bent his dark head toward her as she spoke into his ear. Weren't there laws or something here about that kind of PDA?

But then the woman laughed. Tox started. Haven. And Wallace. Something in Tox twisted and clenched.

"Tzivia." Even as Ram named his sister and stalked toward the gallery where she stood with the others, Tox spotted Cell and Chiji across the gallery, hovering over a sculpture. Buzzing with a truckload of annoyance, he couldn't decide if they were subtle enough in their presence, even though the gallery was heavily populated with tourists of all ethnicities. They weren't sticking out.

A huddle of visitors off to the left muttered quietly, looking at a brochure. Tox saw a blur of flesh—bald—and let his gaze drift around the gallery.

Wait. Tox stopped, his mind pinging back to a second ago. Not a bald head. He pivoted. Craned his neck to search the crowd across the way.

"What?" Ram asked, his voice quiet.

A man stepped into view. Definitely bald. But that—that wasn't what Tox saw. "Tanin."

"Here?" Ram breathed.

Darting a look around disproved his thought. "Maybe not." One more long, probing check didn't reassure him despite finding nothing. "Guess I'm imagining things."

"Either way, let's move." Ram strode toward his sister. "What are you doing here?"

Tzivia might be small and look demure, but she was a tightly coiled rattler. She drew up straight, her eyes blazing. "Research."

Tox knew Ram could handle his sister and the absent-minded professor, so he maintained a watchful eye. Had he seen Tanin or not? He aimed toward Haven and the too-slick-for-reality Wallace. But just as quick, a dark wall slid between them.

Chiji towered over Tox, his presence like a cloud in the blazing heat. "Dr. Cathey told us some good news."

"Yes, yes," Dr. Cathey said, hurrying closer. "The Aleppo Codex—it is here." He shook his head. "Not in this building but in the Shrine of the Book, which is on the property." He swiped a hand through the air. "Well, actually it's not even there. Not really."

Had he taken his medication? "Is it, or isn't it?" Tox asked.

"Yes and no." Dr. Cathey smiled. It seemed the brainiac was enjoying the moment where he knew more than everyone else. "In the Shrine of the Book—" He huffed and scratched his head. "Come. Let me show you."

It was better than standing around waiting for a rabbi who probably didn't exist, or for Tanin to prove Tox right and put an arrow through his chest. Seven headed out with the doctor, Ram at his side. But Tox drifted back, watching their sixes, watching Haven, stuck at the hip to Wallace, who obviously had a thing for her. Did she share the interest?

Tox worked through the way she'd responded to him, to his touch, when he'd talked to Attaway. Had he imagined that? The distance between her and Wallace suggested he had. They trailed the professor from the glass and steel structure into one with a white domed ceiling and a basalt wall. The dichotomy of black and white was stark.

"A contrast of colors representing, most likely, the War of the Sons of Light"—without slowing, Dr. Cathey pointed to the white dome—"and the Sons of Darkness."

"What war was that?" A military history buff, Tox didn't recall that conflict.

"Not a war. A scroll," Dr. Cathey corrected as they entered the unique building. "A manual for military organization and strategy discovered among the Dead Sea Scrolls."

That would explain why Tox hadn't heard of it.

"These scrolls contain an apocalyptic prophecy of a war between the Sons of Light and the Sons of Darkness. The war is described in two distinct parts, first the War against the Kittim, which was purported to be a battle between the Sons of Light, who are the sons of Levi, Judah, and Benjamin, and the exiled of the desert, against Edom, Moab"—he waved his hand as if to say so-on and so-on—"and those who assist them from among the 'wicked who violate the covenant.' The War of Divisions is the second part of the war and is described as the Sons of Light, now the united twelve tribes of Israel, conquering the nations of vanity. In the end, all Darkness is destroyed and Light lives in peace for all eternity—at least, that's what the prophecy says."

"What about the Codex?" Tzivia, eyes wide with wonder, slid up alongside Tox. "Just listen," she whispered to him, threading her arm through his. "It's incredible."

"Ah!" The older man's face lit beneath his bushy eyebrows and rimless glasses. "Isn't it a beauty?" He nodded to a display built into a stonelike alcove. The rectangular enclosure held a propped-up book that looked ancient and thick.

It made Tox curious. "How many pages?"

"They're called *leaves*, not pages," the professor corrected. "And there are only two leaves there right now."

Tox frowned at the protected book. There had to be easily a couple of hundred.

"What you see on top is the only real leaf. The rest are props to make it appear real."

"Where are the rest?"

Dr. Cathey smiled. "That's the question, isn't it? Because even that first page is not real. It's a copy."

Tox leaned closer, intrigued.

"Seriously?" Cell muttered. "It looks legit."

"The real Codex is too valuable to display, even in a protected case. There are many threats against the Codex." Dr. Cathey sighed. "Terrorists are brazen. Treasure hunters ruthless."

"Where's the real one?"

He stroked his beard, thoughtful. "They keep it hidden well below the city."

"Where?"

"That is another question," he said around a smile. "Ask them and you will find yourself engaged in a conspiracy of silence."

"I think we already have," Tox muttered. But then frowned again. "So why are we here? Why did you bring them out here and endanger—"

"They weren't in danger," Agent Wallace said. He really wanted his face rearranged, didn't he?

"We came because I wanted to meet a colleague," Dr. Cathey said. "And I did."

Wallace scowled. "That's not what you said."

"We're out of time." Ram had that look again, the one that put Tox's hackles up. The one he'd had in the last synagogue when the Mossad agent appeared.

Nerves thrumming, Tox motioned the others to the door. "Move out. Time's up."

"Oh, we don't need any more." Dr. Cathey strode confidently toward the front entrance. "I already met with my friend."

Silence cracked the normal but quiet thrum in the museum. The others were looking at each other, then back at the doctor.

"When?" Wallace demanded.

"While you were talking with Agent Cortes." He patted Levi's shoulders. "You were very good to be distracted so my friend wouldn't feel threatened."

Tox pivoted toward the agent.

Chiji's hand fell on Tox's shoulder and redirected him into the balmy evening.

Tox nudged it off. Glared at Wallace. "If you can't handle protection when you're—"

"I had eyes on her at all times."

Rage lit through Tox as he lunged at Wallace.

Arms hooked beneath his. "Easy, easy." Ram drew him backward.

Tox reeled in his anger. A little. He pointed at the agent. "You fail her again, I can't promise you'll wake up alive."

Wallace drew up straight. "Kasey and I were doing just fine before you showed up."

Tox balled his fists.

"Hey," Ram snapped.

"Doing fine?" Tox said, feeling a thud in his chest. One that warned him his heart was about to climb out. "You didn't even see the professor make contact!"

"*Hey.*" Ram's voice was tight as he grabbed Tox's arm, urging him down the path.

Somehow, the tension in his friend's voice registered. Not tension as in trying to stop Tox from taking a piece of Wallace, but trouble. Tox recalibrated. Flashed a questioning look at Ram.

"We have a problem."

"What?"

"Tanin."

Needling sensations rippled through Kasey as she watched the transformation come over Cole. As if a storm had moved in. Subtle. Startling. Knowing his skills, his capabilities, it was alarming.

A few paces later, he sidled up to Levi as if he hadn't just been within inches of punching him. "We have shadows," he said, his voice stiff, quiet. "Keep moving."

Shadows? Someone was following them? Kasey's stomach roiled.

Levi's hand engulfed hers and squeezed. It should've been reassuring, but her awareness had keyed into Cole, who was falling back again. Behind them. Out of sight. Though she kept walking as ordered, she also noticed the silence. The lack of conversation. Cole's absence proved the most unnerving. She flicked her gaze to the side.

Tzivia had her arm through Dr. Cathey's, heading toward a small compact car. Though they looked casual, an intensity had plastered itself onto the woman's face. A key dangled from her hand. Cole's friend, Chiji, was with them, assisting the professor as if he were elderly and needed help. Kasey understood the scenario—if they were being followed, Dr. Cathey would be the slowest, which meant he

249

needed the car. The rest would be on their own, navigating back to the hotel.

As she surreptitiously scanned the night-darkened lawn, she found it empty. Was she just not seeing the team? Or the threat?

Levi tugged her closer and put his arm around her shoulder.

Her muscles tightened but Kasey didn't pull away. "Where are the others?"

"Scattering for better positions," Levi muttered, his lips against her temple, lingering a little longer than appropriate. Not out of affection. He was using it to scan their surroundings. Mostly. "If we have to run . . ."

"Like the wind," she whispered.

A strange whistling carried through the still night.

"Get down!" Cole shouted.

Arms wrapped around her, dragging her to the ground.

Crack! Hissssssss!

"Go go go!"

Tightening her against his chest, Levi flipped them over and rolled across the lawn . . . sidewalk . . . They fell into the grass on the other side. Hit hard.

Kasey grunted. No time for pain. They landed on their bellies, and she scrambled for orientation. To see where Cole was. Where the others had taken refuge. She spotted him behind a tree, shoulder to the bark, ready to shoot. Did he have a weapon?

Cole scowled. "Get her out of here!"

Rebellion stabbed Kasey. She didn't want to leave him and the others. But what could she do? She wasn't armed. Best to follow orders.

"Run," Cole barked.

She came up, Levi pulling her away from Cole. They took off toward a covered breezeway of the main Israel Museum. Darkness cocooned them. Shielded them. She slowed and glanced back.

In that instant, she saw two things: The first—Cole hunkered behind the sculpture of an apple core and aiming a gun. Tiny bursts sparked from the muzzle as he confronted an unknown assailant. The second, a glimmering metal arrow spiraling toward her, the feathered tail like a child's pinwheel.

Thunk! She glanced at the wall and found a glowing blue arrow. Not a foot away. A rancid smell seared her nostrils.

Sparkling arrow. Kasey let out a strangled yelp, only to be yanked away by Levi. He pitched her forward.

Crack! Boom!

The explosion blasted her spine with heat. Kasey stumbled, but ran. As hard as she could down the sloping hill away from the museum. Away from Cole.

*   *   *   *

Crack-crack-crack-pop. Pop! POP!

Light vanished. Darkness fell like an obsidian orb. In the distance, the lights of the city twinkled. Whoever was targeting them had hit the power supply. Dropped them into a blinding darkness. Shadows crept and leapt along the grass and gnarled tree trunks.

Chest pressed to the steel sculpture, Tox aimed into the black, at the spot where he'd seen the second blue arrow erupt. Tanin. This was his chance—nail this guy, mission over. Team still alive. His mind buzzed, skipping from Mossad to the Arrow & Flame Order. Were they both after the team? How'd Tanin and the AFO find them? How had any of them gotten so close? What did Ram know?

A yelp snapped his attention to the fifteen-foot space between two buildings. Protected by an awning, the space was pitch black. Then a cloud shifted and moonlight stroked Haven's form as she raced away with Wallace.

He'd better keep her safe. Tox had made a promise three years ago to protect those Brooke loved. It was what had drawn him out when Evie's life had been pawned in Attaway's sick scheme to lure Tox into the open.

Fiery shards splintered off the sculpture. Seared his cheek. Tox jerked back, searching for his team. Maangi, Cell, and Thor had scrambled, taking up strategic positions, no doubt. But where?

A museum patron darted across the path, leaving the safety of the museum and sprinting for the parking lot. No! Tox sucked in a breath and held it, anticipating the man's death.

A flash of light erupted, hissing.

Thunk! The meaty thud ended in a flash. Blue glowed through the night. The man screamed as he tumbled forward. Horror-stricken, Tox watched him writhe on the ground, knowing there was nothing he could do to help. The man's arms constricted in agony, curling in as his howl pierced the night. A gurgling noise came just seconds later.

Agitated by the sight and smell, Tox let it burn into his mind as a reminder that the victim could've been anyone on his team. Or Haven.

"Wraith Actual, coming up on your six," crackled through his handheld. Thor dropped against the retaining wall. "Just before"— breathing hard—"lights out, I saw them." He gulped air. "Three o'clock. On the roof."

Tox peered out over the grassy area, straining to see against the black of night. Moonlight did little to help, partially hidden by another drifting cloud. "How many?" He wracked his brain to remember what building lurked over there. He'd seen shops, but wasn't that side of the street residential? He needed to know possible casualties when they went in after the targets.

"Don't know." Thor blew out a breath. "Enough to notice—three, maybe four."

Which meant at least a half-dozen had hit them. Why? What did they want? Tox scanned the field and saw movement. What he wouldn't do for his tac gear, a pair of binoculars.

Tiny bursts of gunfire erupted milliseconds before the boom of the weapon reached him. Return fire came from the roof, just as Thor had reported. But taking cover here, they were too far away to hit the target.

"Move in." Tox rushed around the sculpture and ran, hunched, to a tree.

Behind him, Thor thumped against a trunk. "Go."

Cars whipped around each other in the parking lot, racing for the exit. Taillights bled across the darkness. He started over the grass. A vehicle turned toward him. Headlamps splashed him in a glow of white.

Exposed, Tox ducked.

Shots peppered the night. Dirt spit at him. He dove to the ground, scrambling for the sketchy protection of a hedgerow that lined a southern path. Ignoring the ache in his shoulder, he hunch-ran, heading to the parking lot. He'd get to that shop or house and stop them. Whatever it took.

An engine revved. Lights sprang to life. An older model. Noisy. Perfect.

Tox eyed the vehicle as it rattled closer. Darted behind another car, lining himself up with the noisy one.

Crack. Crack!

Tox glanced back and saw Thor coming up, providing a distraction. Tox refocused on the noisy car. The small sedan wheezed and whined as the driver put it in gear and gunned it.

Tox launched up. Sprinted toward the rusted body. Bullets nipped at his heels, pushing him faster. When the car slowed to round the corner, it afforded him the safety he'd sought. Bent, he ran alongside as it navigated the parking lot, then turned onto the street. When it veered right instead of left, Tox was exposed again.

Bullets peppered the air. He threw himself toward the nearest building—a grocery. Skimmed the shadows. Rushing west, his gaze rarely left the rooftop targets trying to pick off his team.

Lights at the intersection bathed the night crimson. Then green, which splashed over him like a homing beacon. Tox dove behind three trash bins. Without slowing, his sole purpose to neutralize the threat, he leapfrogged from one car to the next.

A van squeaked at the corner then chugged toward him. Tox hurried to stay aligned with it, using the size to block his advance on the building. Thirty feet now.

As the van picked up speed, he hustled. Twenty feet.

At ten, he jumped out of traffic and dove against a half wall. Heart pumping hard, he felt along the plaster until the gap between the buildings yawned, revealing an alcove. He slipped in. Plunged into deeper darkness, he squatted. Lifted his handheld. "Wraith Actual in position," he subvocalized, then sucked in a breath. Exhaled. "At the building."

"Wraith Five north ten yards."

Tox searched the darkness for his team, glad Ram was close. The others reported in, Maangi and Cell moving in from the northwest.

Thor reported complications trying to cross the street without eating lead.

Shouldering the wall, Tox peered around the corner. Plotted the course he'd take. He rushed the five feet to a half wall in front of the target's building, aiming his weapon as he stretched to see over the wall and clear the area behind it. A perfect hiding spot.

Then he saw it. A boot. The toe rested just in sight. The lookout, no doubt. Dead? Alive?

Rocks crunched as the boot adjusted. Alive then. And within spitting distance. The only protection between them, a stone wall. Silently, adrenaline coursing, Tox expelled a breath.

Nothing like a stiff risk.

Muscles taut and with painstaking precision, every movement, every contraction of his ligaments tightly controlled, he eased around, careful not to grind rocks or dirt beneath him. Eyes never leaving the boot, he whipped around the corner.

The man jerked. Tox double-tapped him.

Silence dropped, the target crumpling in a whoosh of defeat. Breathing out, Tox crouched and snatched up the man's weapon. Pressed his spine against the wall, expecting someone to respond to the sound of his weapon. His gaze rose to the shadowed alley where a stairwell climbed the north wall.

Peppering gunfire rattled the night. The targets were still up there. Maybe too focused on killing Tox's men to hear him. Since they weren't coming to him, he'd have to go to them. He traced the walls. Walked backward to a corner, eyeing the road behind him. Plaster dug into his shoulders as he hiked a boot onto the stairs, covering the street.

A shape coalesced in the darkness. Tox snapped his weapon up.

"Friendly," Ram hissed as he joined Tox amid the wail of sirens in the distance, warning them time was short.

Time to move. "Wraith Actual and Five going in," Tox radioed as he turned to the stairs.

With Ram walking forward, Tox climbed the steps backward, watching their six. The rustle of Ram's clothes seemed to scream in the deafening silence. Ram not only covered the top of the stairs but the side of the roof, where someone could easily aim a weapon down. They'd be fish in a barrel.

A hand on his shoulder made Tox crouch as they ascended the last few steps. Below, a black mass shifted into the courtyard. His eyes must've adjusted or the moon hung naked again, because he could make out Maangi situating himself to protect the entry point, leaving Tox to cover Ram as he rounded the rooftop corner.

Ram jerked back, firing. Answering gunshots raked the night.

Pop-pop-pop!

A meaty thud and *oof* sounded from up top.

"Clear," Ram said.

Tox hustled onto the roof. Two men lay in a huddle, both missing chunks of their skulls and bleeding a river. Tox's stomach churned as he and Ram advanced on the man slumped against the wall facing the museum. The shooter was in his final, wheezing moments, the injury and his breathing proof he couldn't be saved. However, Tox kicked away the man's weapon as Ram squatted beside him.

"Who sent you?"

The man's eyes shifted to Ram, then slowly unfocused. He slumped in Death's grip.

"Dead." Ram rifled through the shooter's pockets. "Nothing. No wallet, no ID."

"Where's Tanin?"

Ram shrugged. "Lost him."

Tox lifted his handheld and radioed the team. "Rooftop is clear."

"Main level clear," Cell reported.

Tox growled. "I want Tanin dead."

"Maybe he cleared out before the action started." Ram thumped one of the bodies.

"How did the AFO find us?"

Ram straightened. "Who knows?"

Tox sighed. "Let's regroup with the team." He hustled down the darkened stairs, iron rattling beneath his boots, and hit the street.

Ram put his phone to his ear, muttering. He ended the call. "Tzivia and Dr. Cathey are fine. They made it to a safe place."

Tox shouldn't be surprised at Ram's efficiency. "What about Chiji?"

"Didn't mention him," Ram said as they assessed the damage and monitored their team grouping up. "Wallace and Cortes?"

"Last I saw, they were headed east behind the museum."

Ram glanced in that direction, shifting the beanie on his head. "Warehouse district."

Thor limped toward the rest of the team.

"Too much fun for you?" Tox asked.

Thor grinned. "Needed to slow down some bullets so you could escape."

"Thoughtful." Tox keyed his handheld. "Wraith Actual to Eagle One and Two, report." His gaze hit the parking lot, waiting for a reply. Since the rental had been used to ferry Dr. Cathey to safety, the team had no vehicle to make a quick exit. He repeated the request.

Sirens wailed and shrieked, lights whirling as the authorities surged onto the street, seventy yards down.

Ram started walking. "Warehouses?"

Tox nodded, but then glanced to Thor. "Can you—"

"Yes."

Tox admired his men. Admired their tenacity. "Let's do it." Though he hated tangling them up with this nightmare, he wouldn't want to face it with anyone else.

They negotiated the traffic cluttering the street and crossed the lawn of the museum. It was an expansive area but not too open to make the trek foolish. As his foot hit the cement sidewalk, light erupted around them.

One of the guys cursed.

"Easy," Tox said. "Power grid's up."

Artificial light glared as they ran in the direction he'd seen Haven and Wallace flee. Halfway into the breezeway, he saw the glint of steel. Glowing, blue.

Tox diverted for it.

"Don't let it touch your skin," Ram called. "Hold on."

Tox knelt in front of the arrow embedded in the ground. The shaft near the arrowhead was black. Not blue. Why had the arrows been blue when they struck? The earth around it was blackened.

"Here." Ram offered a scarf that had been shed in the haste of the museum patrons fleeing.

Tox wrapped it around the arrow and lifted it. Strangely heavy.

"Here," Cell said, angling sideways to aim a backpack in his direction.

Tox stuffed the arrow in the bag, and they hurried off the property. He tried Wallace again, to no avail. Why weren't they answering?

"Maybe he forgot how to work his radio," Cell muttered. "He's an FBI agent, after all."

Not a comforting jibe when Haven's life was in his hands. They crept along a rocky stretch lining the first row of warehouses. Metal structures loomed like menacing giants in the cloudy night.

"Maybe they can't," Maangi said. "If they're pinned down—if someone's on top of them . . ."

Again, not comforting.

"Too bad I don't have my thermals," Maangi said. "Heat-seeking nocs would be handy about now."

"Yeah," Cell said.

Tox glanced at Ram. If he was truly well-connected, could he recruit some help? Get this sorted for them. Get their people delivered to them safely and without further incident. SAARC wouldn't be happy about tonight. They were supposed to be finding answers, stopping a plague, not racking up body counts.

But Ram walked without conversation, his gaze on the buildings.

To stifle his frustration, Tox keyed the radio again. "Wraith One—"

His words crackled back to him like an echo. But not. Tox stilled. Turned in a circle and pressed the button again.

More crackling.

Maangi followed the sound and bent down.

"Did the FBI agent drop his radio?" Cell taunted, his words tinged with aggravation and patronization.

"It's pretty scratched." Maangi flipped it over. "I'd say he was in a scuffle when he lost it."

Tox stiffened. "Spread out. Let's find them."

They headed down a street and Tox stopped. Stared. There had to be at least twenty to thirty warehouses nestled in the dark night.

Occasional lamps spotlighted corners and entrances. How were they going to find Haven in this aluminum and steel mess? Tox wiped a hand over his mouth, fighting off the frustration.

"You have got to be kidding me," Cell whined. "We need help. There is no way . . ."

"Agreed," Maangi said.

Mumbled words carried to Tox. He glanced back and found Ram with his beanie in hand, covering part of his face, a nearly invisible wash of light across his mouth as he concealed the glow of his phone.

Tox paused. Watched. Knew his friend had some powerful friends. Hoped he was talking to them now. The others watched as well, apparently with the same expectation.

When Ram ignored them, quietly engaged on the phone, Tox said, "Eyes out. Cell, get on the sat phone. Notify SAARC. See if they can send—"

"No," Ram snapped, the phone still pressed to his ear. His expression a mixture of alarm and warning. "Not yet."

Tox jerked, half-angry Ram countermanded the order and half-praying he had good news. When his friend lowered the phone and tugged the beanie onto his mop of brown curls, Tox stopped. "Well?"

"Two more streets," Ram said as he jutted his jaw to the right. "Three buildings down—heat signatures."

"Dude," Cell said, "you have more connections than a motherboard."

Tox had focused on that direction. A dull glow of streetlamps spilled an ominous haze over the district. Though Tox couldn't see the street Ram referenced, he mentally searched for Haven.

"We need to hoof it. Company coming from the north." Ram patted Tox's shoulder. "We'll find them, but we have to move fast."

"Someday you need to let me in on your secret." Tox smiled, his heart charged by the intel. "Move!" He swept up to Thor and hooked his arm beneath his.

"No, no. You go." Cell came alongside on the right, and Maangi took up the slack on the left.

"Go. Find her!" Thor said.

Her. Not them. Tox felt the same way. With a nod, he and Ram sprinted off. Weaving in and out of alleys, they narrowly avoided a couple of encounters—one with a delivery truck and another with a security guard.

"Here," Ram said, pointing to a street hedged with shrubs.

Tox banked right—and slammed headlong into someone. The force knocked him backward. He hit hard, both the person and the cement. Instinct flipped him around. Brought him forward. Fists and training ready.

"Whoa! Friendly!" the man said as he peeled himself from the ground.

Confusion choked him. "Wallace?"

"Yeah." Wallace's hands went to his head, apparently where he'd collided with Tox. Or the ground.

Alarm shot through Tox. "Why are you alone? Where's Haven?"

"She—"

A scream rent the night.

Wallace spun, sucking air. "Kasey!"

Ram was a blur of motion—a warrior rushing into the fray instead of away from it. Tox threw himself after him, his mind registering the men swarming out of the building. Secured between them, a bloodied Haven.

29

Six. There were six men surrounding Haven.

Glock up and hurrying forward, Tox took aim at the farthest target. Eased back his trigger. Allowed the kick. Acquired his next target as he heard the crack of Ram's weapon.

And then it was like a tornado whirled into the chaos. A blur of black and tan. Chiji! His Nigerian friend had a stick in each hand. Arms moving with such speed they looked like propellers, he quickly advanced on two attackers, taking them out almost simultaneously. Kali sticks still whizzing, he turned toward another. Where had he come from?

Tox homed in on the men wrestling Haven between them. "Let her go!" he shouted in Arabic, Farsi, then heard Ram repeat the command in several other languages.

The captors hesitated. A weapon peeked from behind a long cloak.

Tox fired once, twice, three times, closing the distance. He advanced, focused on one threat, registering Chiji behind the threesome, taking care of another. As the shooter folded to the ground, Haven stumbled backward, her knees buckling. She fell back against Chiji, who cradled her in his arms.

260

Relief, sweet and sharp, rushed through Tox. It wasn't the first time he'd thanked God for his friend.

Car tires pealed. Tox whipped toward the threat as a silver van burst around the corner, fishtailed, then caught purchase. It lurched toward the remaining trio, followed by a black sedan.

"Stop the car," Tox said.

Ram walked across the street, firing on the vehicle.

The windshield spider-webbed. The car twitched. Lurched right, straight into a building. Smoke and dust plumed, creating an inadvertent shield.

Tox sprinted toward it to make sure the driver didn't get away, but as he did, he noticed Levi running to Haven, wrapped in the arms of Chiji, her attackers like a dark sea at her feet.

With Ram on his right, Tox rushed the car, slowing as they came upon it. Engine fluids leaked from beneath the crumpled hood. A hazy shape shifted in the dust cloud. A dazed man wobbled. Then swung at Tox.

Instinct made Tox squeeze off three rounds. The man collapsed, tumbling out of the haze onto the ground, an AK-47 just beyond reach. As with the men on the roof, this one had no uniform or identifiable marks.

Except . . . Tox crouched. The man's sleeve had tugged up, revealing an arrow, the tail feathers engulfed in flames. "AFO," Tox huffed. What did this group want? What were they about?

A heavy sob reached through his questions and brought him back to the moment. To Haven. On his feet, he pivoted. Saw Ram and the others circling up on Chiji, who held Haven and smoothed his long, dark fingers over her waxy-blond hair. Her sniffles cuffed Tox by the throat.

Wallace stood behind her. Touching her shoulder. That screw-up of an agent had left Haven. *Left* her during an attack. Ran away . . . left her in a warehouse and ran, putting her in danger.

Something exploded in Tox.

"Tox."

What kind of coward did that? And the punk stood there caressing her now?

"Tox!"

Only when his gaze struck Ram's did Tox realize he'd closed the fifty feet between them. Anger pulsing. Rage roiling. Tox quickened his pace, hiked across the back of a small sedan blocking him. Drew back his right arm, hand fisted.

As Tox went airborne, Wallace turned. His eyes widened.

Tox's fist connected with his face.

Wallace dropped like a rock.

"Tox!"

Kasey turned at the shout, her vision blurred by stupid tears. She shouldn't be crying. She was an adult, an FBI analyst. Sure, the AFO men had threatened to kill her. They'd used her as a punching bag until she'd stopped fighting. But she was alive—that was what mattered, right?

She wiped her eyes—wincing at the tenderness of her cheekbone—and stared down the dark street, trying to makes sense of what was happening.

Shouts and men moving quickly. The tangle of arms and noise diverged into two groups. One huddled to the right. Another over a body.

She gasped, a twinge of pain rushing through her side. "Levi!" He lay on his back, unconscious, blood running from his nose. Carefully, she knelt beside him. "Levi."

Terse words snapped her attention to the other crowd, where three of the team herded Cole away. He wrested free and stabbed his hands in a placating manner. He walked off, shoulders hunched.

"What happened?" she asked.

263

"Tox coldcocked the son of a gun," Cell muttered, his gaze flitting over her face. "How are you?"

Kasey frowned—a dull ache in her head brought her focus back to her ordeal. She pushed aside the thoughts. The images of those men kicking and punching her. "I'll be fine."

"Your face doesn't look fine," Cell said.

"Hey," Maangi snapped.

"What? I'm just saying—"

"Shut it." Maangi shoved the guy away. "I should look you over."

Levi groaned, his eyes fluttering. His nose was crooked. Puffy.

"Easy, Levi. Easy." She cringed at the swelling of his nose and brow. "Are you okay?"

"He's conscious," Maangi said in a dry voice. "He'll live. It's you we're worried about."

Kasey looked up, scowling. "I said I'm fine."

Beyond the crowd, Ram argued with Cole, who jerked toward him and shouted something she couldn't hear because of the din of chatter around her. Ram reached for him, but Cole shoved him away. Ram shifted. Cole did, too. A fight seemed inevitable.

"Oh crap," Cell muttered. "They're going to blows."

A gurgling-choking sound pulled her back to Levi, who lifted his head, moaning. Curled onto his side as he came up, he spit into the dirt, blood dripping from his nostrils. Cole did this to Levi? Why?

A couple dozen feet away, Chiji strode toward Cole with long, determined strides. But again, Cole warned him off with angry words.

Kasey gritted her teeth, frustrated she couldn't hear over Maangi telling Levi to take it slow and easy. Cell suggested Levi could have a concussion. That he needed to have his head assessed.

Apparently, so did Cole. What was with him attacking Levi?

Levi dragged himself off the ground. He turned to Kasey. Touched her face, wincing. "I'm sorry."

She drew away. "It's over. I'm fine."

"Yeah," Cell snipped, "no thanks to him."

Levi met her gaze with a cringe. "They really did a number on you."

"Feels that way, too." A busted lip stopped her smile.

They'd been tracked from the moment they left the museum, so

Levi muttered something about splitting up. It'd made her sick to think about being on her own, but their training said it was better to be captured alone than to be used against each other. So she'd agreed.

He'd used his exit to give her the chance to slip away. But it'd backfired—the men were too close. They saw her. Caught her.

Rumbling filled the night. Black vehicles streamed into view between the buildings. Vehicles without head lamps on. Why? The lead SUV paused at the top of the slight hill—were they after Ram and Cole?

Kasey pushed to her feet, watching as more vehicles shook loose behind the lead and stalked toward her, Levi, and the rest of the team. Fear, reminders of what happened in the warehouse, sent Kasey scurrying into the shadows as Cell, Maangi, and Thor arced out to meet the oncoming SUVs.

Only about halfway down the street did she realize her instinct carried her toward Cole. A presence loomed from behind. Kasey braved a glance back. Her stomach dropped then vaulted into her throat as a tower of darkness whooshed toward her from the side.

When she recognized the gentle face of Chijioke, she let out a shaky breath. "You scared me." Kasey kneaded an ache in her neck, which felt like a full-on migraine coming. She strained to see around the black Suburban. "Where . . . where is Cole?"

Chiji pointed not toward the SUVs but to his right, where buildings blurred into each other. A shift in the grays quickly became Cole as he stepped out from between two buildings.

"How'd you find us?" Cole asked his friend.

Chiji pointed to the sky. "I prayed."

Cole stared at him.

"And followed the gunfire."

Cole snorted and met Kasey's gaze. "Time to go." A silent exchange happened between Cole and Chiji before the Nigerian turned and headed toward the other vehicles.

"What's going on?"

Hooking her arm gently, Cole led her toward the lead SUV. "They'll clean up, and we clear out."

"Who are they?"

"Don't ask." As they reached the Suburban, a man with a fully automatic weapon dangling from his chest opened the door. Tox ushered her inside.

Nerves wracked, Kasey slid onto the seat. Tox's leg hit hers as he climbed in after her, forcing her to scoot over. He shut the door.

"You trust them?"

"No." He looked through the back window. "But Ram does."

Kasey peered at the heavily tinted window but only saw their reflection because the dome lights hadn't dimmed.

"How are you?"

His question pulled her attention back to him. But he wasn't looking at her. He was looking at his hands. He rubbed a thumb over his bloodied knuckles.

"I'm okay," she whispered. "A little banged up—"

"You call that 'a little'?"

She loved that he was worried, that his protective instincts drove him. But . . . "You shouldn't have hit him."

His eyes narrowed. "He shouldn't have left you," he growled.

"We agreed to split up. It was the only way—"

"It was stupid, and as an agent with field experience, he should've known that."

"Please tell me this isn't because I'm a girl."

"You're a girl?" Cole laughed at his joke. "No, this isn't about you being female. This is about experience, about numbers being on your side in unfriendly territory. About abandoning protocol and leaving a man behind." He covered his bloodied hand. "He had one task—protect you—and he didn't do it. He's lucky I didn't do more."

"Protect me? Excuse me, but we're both agents. We're both attached to this team."

"Please," Cole said, "do not make this a thing about equality. That works in an ideal society, but this isn't ideal. And none of us has the same skills or expertise."

"I don't need to be babysat or treated differently just because—"

He shifted toward her, his arm stretching over the back of the seat behind her as he stared her down. "You're in a position of concealment, and you observe two four-man teams approaching in a defilade configuration. What is your best counter?" He hesitated just long enough for her silence to betray her. "What's the proper order to give coordinates to call in an airstrike?"

Embarrassment pushed her gaze away.

"If you had the tactical expertise, I wouldn't care if you were a ballerina and on your own." Intensity radiated through Cole's words. "But you don't. Wallace does, to an extent, so he failed—and as a direct result, you were harmed. You've never been in the field. There is nothing wrong with protecting our own."

"Okay." She hadn't meant to snap. "I get it." Sitting back, she worried her lip—and felt the pinch of pain. Then warmth sliding down her chin. "Shoot." She cupped the heel of her hand below her lip.

The daggers in Cole's blue eyes over her injury didn't help her annoyance. Which annoyed her more—because she didn't want to be annoyed with him.

"Let me see."

"Just leave me alone."

He smirked and tugged the bandana from around his neck. "That's the Haven I knew. Here."

She rolled her eyes and snatched the bandana, pressing it to her lip. And trying to ignore the scent of Cole clinging to the fibers. Well, and sweat. There was that, too.

Ram climbed into the front passenger seat, closed the door and looked back. He was about to speak when he saw Kasey. He frowned but directed his words to Cole. "Hotel is compromised. They're taking us to another location." He handed Cole a device.

Kasey glanced at the screen, noting bright, colorful splotches moving around a blue-schematic-looking structure. Heat imaging? Was that their hotel room?

"Who are they?" Cole asked

"Unknown. My friends are working on it, but they've relocated our things to a warehouse."

* * * *

The warehouse was definitely that—soaring ceilings, roaring fans for heating, cement floors, steel stairs, and catwalks. The north wall supported a second level of offices and larger conference rooms. Below it, bathrooms, showers, and a kitchenette. East side sported a line of twenty bunk beds with gray plastic mattresses. In the center, a hub of desks, workstations, six-foot tables, plexiglass wall maps and grease boards, and whatever else a black ops team might need.

It was handy. And disturbing, especially the cozy area on the west wall with three couches, two recliners, and a large-screen TV.

As the team filed in, Tox kept tabs on Haven's location. Their conversation wasn't finished. He'd upset her—no surprise there—and wanted to remedy that.

"Home away from home" came the sultry voice of Tzivia Khalon as she entered with Dr. Cathey.

He wondered who'd found the pair and directed them here. Ram wouldn't be crazy enough to give her the address over a wireless device that could be intercepted.

Tox made his way to Ram, who was at his bunk, digging through his ruck as he talked with his sister. "Got a second?"

Ram adjusted his beanie, a set of clean duds in hand. "Sure."

"So this warehouse—Mossad?"

Ram didn't answer. Just held his gaze.

That was his answer. Tox ran a hand down the back of his neck. "Will they monitor us in here?"

With a snort, Ram smirked. "You won't take a breath without them knowing."

Defeat soaked Tox's muscles.

"It gets worse. AFO has long-range listening devices. Another reason my friends intervened."

Long-range listening devices? That was some serious equipment. Hefty costs. That meant the people spying weren't worried about cash flow—they were loaded. "So that's how they've been ahead of us all this time."

"One of the ways." Ram shrugged. "They're well-funded and clearly well-connected." He started backing away. "I'm going to shower up."

Tox nodded, chewing the news update. Hands on his belt, he looked across the open space and saw Haven on a bunk by herself. He shifted his gaze to the hall that led to the bathroom and saw Wallace with a towel in hand.

Cole crossed the warehouse with quick strides. Haven saw him coming and lowered her gaze.

He eased onto the mattress beside her, noting the Bible in her lap. "Going to beat me with that?"

"I should."

"My mom would've." That thought was a dagger to the heart.

Haven brought her soulful expression to him. "She misses you, you know."

He swallowed. Studied his boots, his pulse skipping a beat. "I'm sure she's glad I'm gone. No more embarrassment."

"No," Haven said, vehemence thickening her answer. "Galen invites me to family events so I can see Evie. This past summer, for Evie's birthday, your mom invited me out to the estate for the weekend."

Tox ran his thumb over his raw knuckles.

"The party was big."

He sniffed. "She doesn't know how to throw a small one."

"True," Haven said. "But you know what I noticed in every single room?"

Unable to bring his gaze to hers, his mind slogging through the halls of the ten-room house he'd grown up in, Tox waited. Found himself anxious to hear. Remembered running hard and fast down the long hall, Mom shouting to stop running before he broke his neck.

Haven hadn't gone on, so he looked at her.

Her smile was serene, soft. "Pictures of her hero. You."

She hadn't forgotten him. The thought relieved him. Tox bent forward, forearms resting on his knees. Rubbed his knuckles. If he could ever go back, it'd be for his mother.

"She's still grieving you."

Guilt choked him. He straightened, but couldn't dislodge the bitter truth of deception from his throat. "It was better this way."

"Believing you're dead? No, that's not better."

"You don't understand—"

"You're right." Her words were edged in hurt, but were also soft.

Haven was always soft. Everything about her. "Maybe someday you can help both of us understand."

Tox shook his head. "I can't go back home."

"Because of your deal?"

After an almost imperceptible nod, he cleared his throat. Had to get out of this quagmire of the past. "Look, I just—"

Her touch was light against his hand. Warm. Her hands were small and porcelain against his tanned and bloodied knuckles. Fire shot through his gut as she gently traced the scabbed spot. "Your mom saw worse than this from you, and she still loves you."

Tox stilled. She meant the trial, imprisonment. He swept his thumb over hers. For a split-second, entertained something he shouldn't. Especially when she leaned into him. She was smart, beautiful, connected to the world he couldn't be a part of. Sweet. Innocent. Beautiful. Those green eyes of hers had telegraphed her attraction when she was twelve. And still did.

"I know what you want, Haven."

He heard her quiet intake of air. Noticed how her palms grew warmer, sweaty. Again, he traced the smooth spot between her thumb and finger. A scrape on her skin snapped him back to reality. To what had happened to her now that she was in his world. She'd been captured, beaten.

"But I can't."

"Why?"

He lifted her hand, set it back on her knee, and held it there. "I'm . . ." Tox pushed away from her, ignoring the raw ache to stay and talk. To catch up. On his feet, he forced his gaze to the warehouse. To the others pretending they hadn't noticed him talking to her. "I'm no good for you."

Haven stood. "You can't look me in the eye? Say it to my face?"

Tox stopped, knowing what had happened the last time he'd done that. He already had one Linwood death hanging over him. He wouldn't risk hers, too.

Haven stepped forward and caught his arm. "I want to be your friend, Cole. Always have."

He shook his head. "You've wanted more than that, Haven." He looked down at her for several long seconds. "I see it in your eyes every time I look at you, especially now."

Color stained her cheeks "Maybe," she whispered, "but I have always been willing to simply be your friend. You just couldn't see me or that."

Couldn't see her? How could he not? Even when she was twelve, she stood out. "I made a promise." He gritted his teeth. "I won't break it."

"Promise?" She frowned. "To whom?"

"Brooke. I promised I'd protect you and Evie."

She snorted. "Even dead, she haunts my steps."

"She just wanted you safe." And so did he. "Haven, I'll just hurt you. There's a reason they call me Toxic."

"Cole is a man, a hero. A friend. Toxic is a choice."

31

Some people had emotional baggage. Cole Russell had an entire department store.

Anger clutched at Kasey, taunting her. Telling her he only saw her as trouble. Hugging herself, she sat on the edge of a cot across from Levi, who was stretched across it, his back propped against the cement wall. The swelling was pretty hideous, his blue eyes glinting beneath an angry reddish-purple knot.

Tzivia joined them, handing Levi an ice pack. "What'd you do to tick him off?"

Stunned at the woman's directness, Kasey hesitated.

Levi's hand stalled halfway toward the pack. Then he glared and snatched it. "Thanks."

Tzivia grinned. "I've never seen him get ticked enough to do that."

"And you've spent enough time with him to see him angry often?" Kasey hated the shrillness of her question.

Cell passed behind Tzivia. "Tox coldcocked him because Wallace left her alone when we were under attack." He kept moving.

"Well, that was dumb." Tzivia had the beauty typical of Israeli women—much like actresses Gal Gadot and Natalie Portman. In

272

fact, she favored them right down to the dark hair, facial structure, beauty, and poise.

"No, it was strategy," Kasey countered. "Together, if we were captured, we could've been used against each other. It made . . . it made sense to split up."

Tzivia smirked at her, eyes dancing in some sort of victory. "Tox might not have punched him if you actually believed that."

"Tox—Cole," she corrected herself, "had no idea what I thought when he hit Levi."

Tzivia's eyes sparked. "I meant—if it'd truly been a good idea, then Tox wouldn't have been angry. But it wasn't. You were in trouble. He wasn't there." She bounced her head from side to side, then pointed at Levi. "Tox could've put his nose through his skull. Be thankful he didn't."

As she wandered off, Levi groaned and lay against the cot, the pack over the bridge of his nose. He let out a hissing breath.

Kasey's heavy thoughts made it tough to cheer him up. She struggled around the weights anchoring her heart to the pit of her stomach. "I hate that our decision got you punched."

"Don't." Levi dragged one leg up on the bunk, the other dangling off the edge.

She swung over and sat on the edge of his mattress, staring down at him, the blanket still squeezed between her hands. "How can you say that? Everyone thinks you're this coward or something."

"They're right." His puffy stare held her. "I shouldn't have left you. Tox was right—he entrusted you to my care."

She groaned. "Not you, too."

"What?"

"Nothing." Kasey frowned. Would she never be . . . enough?

"You okay?"

She managed a smile, cringing at the tug of pain in her lip. "Sure." Knowing her actions weren't convincing, she shrugged—an ache in her shoulder pushed a throb up the back of her skull—because she wasn't up to dialoguing about the new hole in her heart. "Just tired."

"Man, my head is pounding." Levi downed two ibuprofen with a gulp from his bottled water. He closed his eyes.

"I'll let you rest."

He wrapped an arm around her waist. "Please . . . stay. Talk to me. The light hurts my eyes, but your voice is soothing."

At least someone wanted her company.

"And . . . I am sorry, Kase, for leaving you."

"That was our—"

"Let me apologize," he said. "And I'm sorry for . . . being jealous. For arguing with you."

"Jealous?"

"My eyes might be swollen shut, but I can see your feelings for him."

Kasey swallowed, pained that her heart had not only been laid bare, but trampled. "He has only ever seen me as Brooke Linwood's kid sister, and that's all I'll ever be to him."

With his other arm propping his head, Levi kept his eyes closed. Maybe it wasn't right to talk or mope about Cole to him. "I hate to say it—"

"What? That I'm stupidly naïve?"

Levi huffed. "You sell yourself short too often. No," he said, his hand gently rubbing her back. "No, I think . . . I think he sees you as much more. A guy doesn't lay another guy out over someone's kid sister."

Heart skipping a beat, Kasey turned and looked down at Levi, though he didn't share his gaze with her. What was he saying? "I . . . I don't understand."

"Good." He chuckled.

"No, tell me."

He sighed. "He likes you—or at the very least, cares about you. A lot."

She shook her head and settled back against his propped-up leg. "Only because he made my sister a promise to look out for me." She patted his arm. "Get some rest. It's late."

Kasey lay on her bunk and pulled the blanket over her shoulder, trying to shut out the body aches and the heartaches. Sleep snatched her quickly, shoving her into the darkness of her subconscious. Dreams filled with memories of Duarte and Brooke—even Evie—flitted and sparked. She snapped awake, the strange, somber glow of sunrise fighting through the grimy warehouse windows.

Kasey made her way to the bathrooms then showered. She felt refreshed when she emerged. Tzivia stood on the upper level at a filmy window, her arms wrapped around her waist. She looked . . . sad. The metal walkway clanged as she joined the Israeli beauty.

"'One doesn't go to Jerusalem, one returns to it.'"

Kasey hesitated, wondering if Tzivia thought she were someone else. But as she stood behind her, Kasey saw a spot had been cleaned in the filmy window that provided a view of the Old City. The rising sun bathed Tzivia's olive skin and the city in a warm glow. Her still-damp hair hung straight and dark, almost black.

"'That's one of its mysteries.'" Taking in a long breath, Tzivia smiled at her. "Elie Wiesel said that. And it's true. My parents grew up here, but I was young when we fled, so I don't remember it. Yet . . ." With all five fingertips touching, she tapped her heart. "I remember it all. Here." Her gaze roamed the white structures littering the hills and valleys. "I am home."

Longing spiraled through Kasey. The words, the sentiment, the sincerity stirred a deep ache. Kasey's own parents had been good parents. They'd loved and provided for her and seen to her education. They'd also tried to see to her relationships—naturally, she refused. But things were lavished on her as long as she stayed within the lines they'd drawn. Lines of cooperation. Lines of compliance to their well-laid plans for her life. Life as a senator or congressman's wife.

Which she'd shattered when she chose Duarte. It was bad enough that she had dated someone with no wealth or notoriety. Then they discovered he was a Navy SEAL. The horror! But she still committed the unpardonable and married him.

Their support fell away and the distance grew. It wasn't that they disapproved. But saying they *approved* would be going too far. Duarte had given her total acceptance, love, laughter—all without expectations. Then he left her.

"Tzi. Cortes."

They both turned at the gruff voice of Ram carrying through the door to the balcony where they stood. "Breakfast. Day's already running," he said in a way that told them this wasn't a choice.

"And it begins," Tzivia muttered as she stepped after her brother,

Kasey following. Dr. Cathey and Chiji were chatting animatedly as they waited near a table that held large aluminum trays of food.

Kasey slowed. Took in the view. It was odd, maybe even weird, to see Cole in a black shirt and jeans. Not geared up in camo and intensity. Here, talking with Ram, he seemed so . . . everyday.

But she knew the warrior within was never more than a blink away. That part never rested. She only had to remember the confrontation from the live feed.

As the others formed a line for the buffet, Kasey couldn't help noticing how everyone paired up. Not in a romantic way, but in a friendly way. Guys chatting and laughing. Camaraderie built though years of missions together. Tzivia had her brother, though they were sometimes like oil and water. Kasey started toward the table, but Dr. Cathey, engrossed in conversation with Chiji, stepped in her path, cutting her off. She said nothing but appreciated the apologetic look Chiji offered.

When Tzivia and Ram did the same, Kasey couldn't help the grunt as she narrowly avoided a collision with Cell's very full plate of food.

Cole shot a glance over his shoulder.

"You okay?" Levi guided her into line before him.

But her gaze had locked with Cole's. "Fine." She lifted a styrofoam plate and peered at the catered food.

Tzivia and her brother fell into quick, tense dialogue—in Hebrew. What didn't they want everyone else to know?

Cole fell back, now just ahead of Kasey. He didn't speak to her— probably wouldn't after last night. It was all or nothing with Cole. Ahead of them, Chiji and Dr. Cathey moved through the line, scooping up food, hotly engaged in chatter that never stopped.

Levi's phone rang. "Almstedt?" he said as he answered. He focused on his conversation, slowly drifting out of the line.

Kasey sighed, rubbing her temple.

"You look lost," Cole said, lifting a spatula and sliding some sort of casserole onto his plate.

"Is that your way of saying I don't belong here?"

"If I wanted to say that, I would have."

Kasey swallowed.

276

They reached the end of the food line, grabbing bottles of orange juice and water. He nodded to the right and followed her to the tables where the others sat, already digging into their food.

With Ram and Tzivia still rattling in their native tongue, Kasey reached for a chair. So did Cole. The same one. She drew back and went for another, but Cole pulled the seat out and motioned her into it.

Surprised at his manners, she sat and thanked him—trying not to make a mountain out of this anthill. Or when he took the chair beside her and not the one next to Tzivia. That really gave her too much pleasure.

"Here," Levi said, handing her a napkin out of the blue.

"Thanks." Why did it feel like she had two guys fighting over her? That was . . . wishful thinking.

Ram folded his arms on the table and leaned closer. "It is said the prime minister has food from this restaurant"—he jabbed his fork at his plate—"catered in all the time."

"If he liked it that much, he'd recruit the cook out from the place," Tzivia said with a laugh.

"I don't care what the prime minister eats," Cell said. "Can we talk about the arrow?"

"SAARC assets secured it from us this morning." Maangi threaded his fingers over his food. "They delivered it to a lab at the university, where they'll analyze it."

Ram had fallen into dialogue with his sister again, this time lifting a shoulder in a lazy shrug, nearly grinning. He seemed to take joy in annoying her.

Kasey focused on her food, not really sure what she was eating, except that it involved eggs and vegetables. How bad could it be?

"So, Cortes," Ram said, suddenly propping himself forward. "You knew Tox while he was wet behind the ears, huh?"

Of its own will, her gaze slid to Cole, who scowled a warning at Ram. "I'm not sure Cole was ever wet behind the ears," she said, alluding to the warrior spirit he'd always had, sure that was a safe enough answer. "But yes—I've known him for a while."

"What was he like back then?" Tzivia's brown eyes glinted with entirely too much amusement and interest.

The question, the probing intrigue that radiated through the group, made Kasey close the book on that part of her life. On the knowledge and experience of Cole Russell. Then guilt swarmed her, but she had reasons for not wanting to share those pages of her life: One, she didn't want to embarrass him; two, it wasn't her story to tell; and three, since it was something Tzivia didn't know, Kasey wanted to keep that to herself. Guard it.

That was jealousy, Kasey knew. And she should feel bad. Maybe. But she didn't.

Cole rapped his knuckles on the table. "Leave her alone."

"Why?" Tzivia said with a chuckle. "What do you have to hide?"

"A lot, especially from you two." He craned his neck to look around. "Don't we have intel to work?"

"What do you mean, *from us two?*" Tzivia's voice pitched, but she smiled and reached across the table for Kasey. "Tell us about him. Everything. Don't leave anything out."

An uncomfortable knot threaded through Kasey's stomach. She shrugged, the knot tightening, annoyed because it seemed Tzivia wanted the dirt on Cole. "He wasn't much different than now—intense but committed."

Tzivia widened her eyes. Swallowed. "Committed?"

Kasey realized her mistake. "He was committed to my sister. They were dating."

"Interesting," Ram said.

"No, it's not." Cole's tone severed any argument or persistence in pursuing this conversation.

Tzivia hunched her shoulders. "Tell us how you met your husband."

Again, Kasey nearly choked. "How do you know about Duarte?"

Tzivia's interest again had been sparked. "He was a Navy SEAL, right?" Dark brown bangs framed glittering eyes as she angled closer. "My roommate dated a SEAL once. It was the only time I was tempted to steal her boyfriend."

"You should be ashamed of yourself," Ram said.

"I said *almost*." Her laughter carried through the warehouse. "And don't get all protective, big brother. You know I don't date military." But even as she said that, her eyes drifted to Cole.

"Duarte was a good man, right?" Cole's question felt more like a challenge. As if he'd hurt Duarte if he wasn't.

Water bottle in hand, Kasey hesitated with it halfway to her lips, then set it back down. Their love had been deep and true. The ache of his death still raw. "One of the best men I've ever known."

Cole stared for a few seconds, then slowly nodded. "Never imagined you marrying military."

You imagined anything *about me?* "He was gorgeous and had integrity that bled into everything, including his dedication to God, country, and to me." She tried to hide the smile. "And he was everything my dad didn't want."

Cole laughed as he slouched back. "*That* sounds like you. Always bent on getting your dad riled." He tipped his water bottle at her. "Haven wanted to go skydiving with me because her dad said it was too dangerous."

No, I wanted to go because I would have been with you. "My dad coddled me. Wanted me to be a debutante like my sister and marry money or politics."

"So you married a SEAL." Ram guffawed. "Awesome." He slapped Cole's shoulder. "I like this girl."

"Did you ever go skydiving with Cole?" Tzivia asked.

"No, not with Cole." Kasey almost flinched when he shifted to her, and she realized she should've just left the last part off. She shrugged. "Duarte took me up on our second date."

Cole grunted and shook his head. "Surprised he didn't take you swimming."

What was that? Sarcasm? Annoyance? "We did that on our third"—she shook her head—"*fourth* date."

Cole's blue eyes settled on her, his expression stony, which felt almost as frustrating and punishing as every other conversation with him. On the surface his gaze seemed as deceiving as a riptide—little warning what lurked beneath the surface. But get caught in it, and she'd drown. That danger with Cole rose every time she looked in his direction.

"So." Ram glanced at Cole. "You dated her sister." His words came out like a slow leak, weighted with thought. "Isn't . . ." He pointed to Kasey, then wagged his finger. "Wasn't she . . . ? Her sister—"

"My brother's wife." Cole's answer was monotone and devoid of the animosity that Kasey knew roiled through him.

Ram's eyes narrowed for a second, then he nodded. "Yeah."

"Wow!" Tzivia laughed at Cole. "How crazy—your brother stole your girlfriend then became president. How do you compete with that?"

"Tzi," Ram hissed.

Gaze down, Cole snorted. "I couldn't. She dumped me while I was in Basic."

"Ouch," Cell chuckled.

Now they were all staring at Kasey, and she felt the need to explain about her sister. "With Brooke and Cole, it was always about the tension. My sister was addicted to it."

"*Tss.*" Cole rolled his eyes. "Among other things."

"Like?" Tzivia asked.

"Power," Cole said.

"Money. Anything that put her on a higher rung." Kasey felt bad for talking poorly about her sister, who could no longer defend herself, but it was true. "Brooke really cared about little else, except Evie."

The pain of that truth lingered in Cole's baby blues. That Brooke had married his brother. Bore his brother's child.

"Who's Evie?" Tzivia asked.

"Her daughter." Cole stared at the table. The chasm that stretched between them seemed like a mile and yet not long enough to bridge the years or her sister's actions.

It would always be like this, wouldn't it? Cole brooding over Brooke. People finding out about it, which only reminded him of it, keeping the distance stretched wide. Kasey forever Brooke's little sister.

"What is this food anyway?" Maangi said, frowning down at his plate.

"Shakshuka," Tzivia said. "A Bedouin dish of eggs poached in a sauce of tomatoes, chili peppers, onions, and spiced with cumin."

"The spicier the better," Ram muttered, lifting his fork.

"No, no," Dr. Cathey said as he delivered a new tray of French toast to the table. "This option was hidden and might have more appeal."

Half the team abandoned the spicy food for the drizzly goodness of French toast. Thick slices of bread piled nearly three inches high and soaking in a generous pool of syrup.

"Now *this* is a breakfast." She smiled.

"Bah," Ram said, digging into his shakshuka. "This is a meal for a *man*." His boast was a challenge. "A real man."

Snorting, Cole shook his head as he cut into his syrup-drizzled toast.

"He wouldn't eat that anyway," Kasey said. "He doesn't like spicy food."

"What? How can you call yourself a man and not like spicy food?" Ram demanded.

"Quite easily." Cole folded a piece of toast into his mouth, his cheek chipmunked, and grinned at his friend in foolish pleasure. After he swallowed and started cutting more, he added, "I don't need spices to tell *me* I'm a man."

Ram froze. "Did you—"

"I did." Cole still hadn't looked up, but there was a smile as he lifted the next bite to his mouth.

Ram's hand flicked toward Cole. But with a lightning-fast move, Cole blocked.

"Just wait till you're in a dark alley."

"Chiji will protect me." Cole mopped the syrup off his plate with a chunk of toast. "He's always around."

"But if the trouble is of his own doing" came the clipped, accented voice of his tall shadow, "I will let him learn."

"Ha!" Ram finished his shakshuka. "Hear that? You're mine, Tox."

"Bring it."

Metal grated against cement. Dr. Cathey was on his feet, his expression stricken.

"Oh, this is not good," Cell said.

Cole shoved upward and pulled the doctor aside. "What's wrong?"

"India." Phone in hand, Dr. Cathey covered his mouth, eyes wide. "Two more have died and even more are turning up with the plague. It's spreading." He tugged off his rimless glasses and set them atop his head as he tapped the screen. "I . . ." He tapped some more. "Yes, I should."

"You should what?" Tzivia was at his side, her tone placating and concerned.

He blinked. "Weren't you listening?"

"You didn't finish your sentence."

Again he blinked then grunted. "I need to go to university. Find my old friend. Yes, yes. He will know what to do." He turned in a circle, searching for something. "Ah. There. I must go."

"Whoa, wait." Cole gripped the fabric of his shirt at the shoulder and stopped him. "Hold up. Nobody leaves alone." He turned to his friend. "Chiji."

The Nigerian gave a slow nod as he rose, apparently not needing Cole to say any more. He strode out of the warehouse with the professor, and Kasey couldn't help but watch as Cole monitored their progress.

"Now who's going to watch your back?" Ram taunted.

True enough. Without the tall Nigerian around, Cole almost acted as if he'd taken off his tactical vest in the middle of a firefight.

* * * *

"My contact wants to meet with Tzivia, too."

Tox met Ram's hazel stare. "Now?" They'd barely finished breakfast when Ram's phone had buzzed.

"Yes." Ram checked his watch. "We should hurry. And split up. They won't like so many people."

"They?"

Ram gave him a look.

"Okay," Tox said with a sigh. "Cell, Maangi, and Thor—stay here with Wallace. Be alert and watch your phones."

"Wait," Wallace said, "what about Kasey?"

"She's coming with me."

Wallace's jaw muscle popped but he was smart enough not to argue.

They headed out, and Ram led them to a tangled mess of a market, where Haven hesitated with a groan.

Tox grinned. "Still hate the city?"

Her left eyebrow winged up. Was she surprised he remembered that? "Hate's a strong word."

Wares hung at every possible height—above the head, shoulder

282

height, and even at hand level. Shops were no more than partitioned sections. Bronze vases and lamps stacked so high, they leaned. One wrong bump . . .

Ram trekked up a slight incline, then cut through another cluttered market.

Feeling more suffocated than when he'd been imprisoned, Tox worked harder to monitor individuals. Watch for threats. This place had his nerves vibrating, like a live wire crackling against a steel pipe. He stepped to the side. Haven kept stride but then spotted his move and slowed.

Tox touched her back. "Keep moving." He wanted her and Tzivia in the middle. She didn't have the training that he, Ram, and even Tzivia had. He half cursed himself for letting her come, and then *did* curse himself for keeping her lackey boyfriend with Team Two. Not that he wanted Wallace around, but he wanted eyes on her at all times.

Haven only glanced back once as they pushed through the crowds. Why had Ram chosen this route? Surely there was a less populated one. Less to worry about. Less to monitor.

Then again, they'd be alone. Easier to ambush. Easier to attack.

Which was the better of the two evils? Tox didn't know, but right now he was in complete agreement with Haven about hating cities. Give him a mountain or country farm—minus the zero-dark-thirty chores and barn mucking—any day.

Through the bright fabrics waving and snapping came a cool breeze. A spiced breeze. As they navigated the market, Tox appreciated the effort Haven gave at keeping up. Not complaining. Then again, she never had been the type to complain or whine, unlike Brooke, who'd had a complaint about everything. At the time, he'd thought it simply because she was a girl who needed protecting. Turned out, she was just high maintenance.

For the most part, Haven had been a quiet kid who watched him and Brooke but said little. Now she had a degree in criminal justice, had married a Navy SEAL, survived the loss of said hero, and trekked through a massive disaster of a mission that included plagues, missing artifacts, and glowing arrows.

How on earth did she remember he didn't like spicy food?

The air cleared, slowly growing fresher, less inundated with body odor, colognes, and spices, not to mention incense. A dull ache pulsed at the edges of his temples. They emerged from the market, a little sweaty and a lot agitated.

"We're too slow," Ram threw over his shoulder. "We have to hurry."

The next ten minutes were spent weaving around cars, shops, and homes. They rushed down a narrow alley, Tox's shoulders brushing the walls. A cat darted across their path with a hiss and shriek, to which Tzivia added her own.

"I hate cats," she bit out.

"They've never liked you either," Ram teased.

Soon they broke into an opening. There loomed the Wailing Wall. Cole felt the need to slow. To study. But there were too many people. Too many things that could go wrong in this crowd. And Haven was already starting to slow. Her shoulders sagged. They were falling behind, so he kept moving.

Ram led them up an ugly walkway and straight into the Old City. "We might make it," he tossed back as he banked around a multi-storied building. Wedged between the plaster façade and the fence, they hurried, though it felt like the walls closed in.

The scritch of shoes hit his ears seconds before Tox bumped into Haven.

"Sorry," she muttered. "I'm not used to this."

"You're doing fine," Tox said.

"Liar. But sweet." She trudged on, her feet dragging, yet somehow managed to stay tight with Tzivia, who stuck close to Ram.

Thud!

Tox spun toward the sound, snatching his weapon out and bringing it up.

Two men stood in the alley, wrapped in shadows and ferocity. Black eyes, black beards, black clothes. Mysterious. Intense. No hesitation in their fierce expressions.

Tox shouted, "Back off!"

A yelp from Haven forced him to look over his shoulder.

Four men crowded the other end of the alley, blocking Ram, who lifted palms in surrender.

Tox whipped around to the men and backed up until he felt Haven's hand on his shoulder, surprised at how that reassured him.

A string of Hebrew flew off Ram's tongue. His tone was confident, authoritative—harsh—as he conversed with the shadows.

The closest black shadow shouted at Tox.

He firmed his grip.

"Tox, no!"

But he took aim.

Dead weight slammed into his shoulder. He went down hard. Head bounced off the plaster wall. His vision blurred. He bit his tongue. Felt the crushing weight of a body pressing him to the ground. He managed to flip himself, struggling not to end up with a broken nose or concussion. As he fought the man, in his periphery, he noted Haven looking up.

That was how they'd gotten the drop on him—they had literally dropped on him. From trees or a balcony, he wasn't sure. But they'd had high-ground advantage.

Hands pawed at him. A boot pinned his hand to the ground. "Augh!" Tox ground out. His grip broke. His weapon clattered across the road. With everything he had, Tox scissored his legs, catching his attacker off guard. The man flipped back.

Tox hopped to his feet in a ready stance. Ready to fight. To keep his people safe. Two men moved in at once, both athletic and quick, their punches coming fast and furious. He deflected, but they struck him. He used their momentum to throw them off. It didn't work. They kept coming. He could not let these men get to Haven or Tzivia.

One grabbed at him. Tox caught his arm, hooked his over, and secured it beneath his armpit. He drove a palm-heel strike into the man's face.

A side blow surprised Tox, but it shouldn't have. They were both skilled fighters, and so was he.

"Tox, don't. Stop!"

But his fist was already airborne. It never made contact. A rifle butt nailed him in the temple. The world tilted. Thrown off balance, he twisted. Went down on a knee. Caught himself, plaster scoring his palm. Tried to come up, clenching against the pain.

A firm touch came to his shoulder. "Cole, wait . . ." Haven's voice felt like silk against his buzzing brain. "Ram."

Her words turned his attention to his friend, who stood as a barrier. A fire dug into Ram's expression as he flashed his arms out to each side, staying the shadowy executioners. But he remained locked onto Tox, his pale eyes blazing until Tox offered an almost imperceptible signal that he'd yield. Lowering his hands, Ram focused on someone behind Tox and muttered in Hebrew.

Tox followed his gaze, surprised to find a haredi, complete with black garb from head to toe and a wide-brimmed hat. The man's dark eyebrows were a sure indication that the silver beard had been near-black in his youth.

The haredi stood in icy silence as he studied them. Hebrew sailed through the air and somehow felt like daggers.

Ram spat back in Hebrew, his tone harsher than normal. "We're to go with them," he said, the planes of his face hardening.

Tzivia started, then tucked her chin in deference.

Unease slithered through Tox. He could fight. Would fight. But while he saw the tension and anger in Ram's face, he also noted that his incredibly skilled friend *wasn't* fighting.

Body aching, Tox looked to Ram. "What's going on?"

"Don't freak—they have a lot to protect."

It wasn't just a statement. It was an explanation—for the thick, wool hoods the shadows produced.

Tox stiffened. He could still feel Haven's touch against his shoulder, so he reached back and caught her hand. He'd play this game. For now. But if they crossed a line . . . if Haven got hurt . . .

All bets were off.

AND CURSED BE HE WHO PAWNS IT

Pain. So much pain. In his blood. In his heart.

Benyamin writhed, drawing his shoulders up to his ears. Had he not endured enough punishment? Enough heartache? Despair wrapped him in a thick cloak, fiery and restrictive. The agony in his bones went beyond old age. Life without Gratzia. . . . cutting his heart out would have hurt less!

Miriam had her faith and family—but far away in London. His sons had moved away as well. Were it not for Alison, he would be alone. "Thank you," he whispered, teeth gritted against the fire consuming his body. She had earned a full scholarship to a school in New York and spent her free time with this old fool.

"Sabba?"

Ah, the voice of the angel soothed the ache enough for him to force a smile.

"He's so bad," she whispered.

She had that friend with her again. There was something about the man he didn't like. However, there was something compelling about him, too. How he towered over her, protecting. At the same time, he seemed indifferent.

"Do you love her?" Benyamin asked.

"Who, Sabba?"

He fastened his eyes on the man, growing agitated when he did not answer. "Do you love her? Do you think because I am old, I cannot call the power of heaven?"

"Sabba!" Sitting on the hospital bed they'd brought in for him, Alison leaned on the edge of the mattress and cut off his view. "You must rest. You're not well."

"I am well enough," he said, trying to look around her.

"I think he needs to go to the hospital," Alison muttered, turning toward the man. She hesitated, then they went into the kitchen. There, Alison sat at the table with a pad of paper and pen. She tapped something into her cell phone.

The man turned his eyes to Benyamin.

And he remembered. His heart jolted at the realization. "*You!*"

Ruddy-faced Ephraim came into the world kicking and screaming. Benyamin had been at work when news came. He rushed home, worrying for his wife. For their unborn child. Once through the front door, he heard the triumphant howl of their child thrust into the world. The screams were raw and demanding.

Staring at their bedroom door, he listened, exultant in the cries that marked his fifth child's arrival. The door opened. Devra whirled through, a bundle of white in her arms. She closed the door. Her gaze struck his, horror etched into her face.

His breath vaulted into his throat.

The baby's howl startled them. She looked down, then back to him, wetting her lips. "A son again, Benyamin." She hurried the angry, crimson-faced baby into his arms.

Benyamin took him, marveling over his son's outrage at this cold, cruel world. A fist punched into the air, plucking a laugh from Ben. "You are a strong one, Ephraim."

It was then he heard the cries. Not of his healthy, newborn son, but of the women. Ben stilled, his gaze flicking to the door. To the light seeping across the threshold. Shadows skittered. A sob reached from within and clutched him by the throat.

"Gratzia!" He rushed forward and threw open the door.

Women hovering over the bed gasped as they spun to him. They smoothed the blanket, lifted a bundle of soiled, bloody sheets, and hurried out.

Face as white as the clean bedding she lay upon, Gratzia dragged weary eyes to him. A smile shone in her eyes but never made it to her lips. "Ben . . ."

He went to her. "A son," he said, angling Ephraim to her. "Strong, ruddy."

Her eyelids drifted closed.

He held his breath, watching. When she didn't move, he could stand it no longer. "Gratzia."

She breathed heavier. "Forgive me," she wheezed.

"No." He was grateful when Devra took Ephraim, so he could be alone with his wife. "There is no need, my beloved."

Her head lolled to the right. Then the left. She pulled her hand from beneath the clean blanket—over her still-swollen stomach—and handed him a piece of paper. "The curse . . ."

He frowned at the paper, but was more worried about the fading light in her eyes. "Shh, Gratzia. It is well."

"No," she said around a hoarse throat. "The Lord gave me mercy"— she swallowed and wet her cracked lips—"did not deserve." Her hand rested on his. A tremor of strength from her fingers might have been a squeeze.

"Not true. You are the most deserving—"

"No." The word was a rasp. Broken. A tear slipped down her all-too-young face. "I'm so sorry." Her face screwed tight. "I believed it a promise." She breathed a pained, prolonged breath, tensing beneath the effort. "I wanted to bring a piece of our homeland with us."

"What—?"

She nudged his hand.

He glanced down. Remembered the paper. Wait . . . not a paper. It was crisper. Stiffer. He unfolded it. A wave of shock pounded him. He

couldn't move. Couldn't believe what lay between his fingers. No . . .
What had she done?

A board in the room creaked. He looked. A man stood there. His
eyes probing. Penetrating.

Guilt stuffed the parchment out of sight. "Who are you?" Benyamin
demanded. "Get out!"

"You know who I am."

Benyamin didn't. "I said—"

"Please calm down," Devra said from his side.

But Benyamin's outrage was complete at the man intruding on his
wife in her bed. "Get out! You don't belong here."

"But I do."

"Out!"

"It I is need worse you when to you calm are down angry."

Benyamin blinked. The words made no sense. And yet perfect sense.
He heard "it is worse when you are angry" and "I need you to calm
down" spoken at the same time from different voices. But only one
person stood there.

"Sabba?"

He jerked. Saw the young face of his nehda. Again. It had happened
again? He glanced behind her. "Where is your friend?"

Alison slumped, her head lilting to the side with sadness. "Sabba,
no one is here but you and me."

He waved a hand. "Your lover. That's what he is. Am I right? Tell
me I am wrong."

"Sabba, I would never!"

"Then why do you bring him to the house? Do you think I am so
old and blind?"

Her brow creased. "I have brought no one. We must be very careful with your illness."

"Bah!" Angry, he dropped back and looked to the curtains. Yes,
he had an illness. A painful, lingering sickness that had infected his
heart from the day his Gratzia fled the earth.

It was the curse. Because Gratzia had pawned the parchment off
onto him. He welcomed it and the pain. They meant he still had her
with him. He dragged his hand over his breast and let it rest there.
Breathed a little less agony. Yes, he had her with him.

32

Nearly smothering beneath the wool hood and Israeli heat, Tox closed his eyes. Shut down his agitation. Focused on the environment, on the route. They'd been herded twenty-three paces, then banked right. Traveled ten more feet before another right. They were led down sixteen stairs then were stuffed into a vehicle. Diesel, by the fumes and engine rattle.

"Cole?"

The sound of Haven's voice, small and frightened, struck a violent chord in him. "It's okay." The lie tasted weird on his tongue—he always told things straight. But he'd do anything to wipe that sound from her words, the one that reeked of fear. The one that made him scared he would fail her, too. That another Linwood daughter would die because of him. He wanted to touch her. Reassure her, reassure himself that wouldn't happen. "You hurt?" He used the question as a homing beacon.

"Just scared."

He shifted to his left, searching for her. "Trust Ram. He knows Israel." Though while Tox trusted him, he didn't like putting Haven's

291

life in his hands. Brooke would rise from the dead and haunt him if her little sister got hurt. "It'll be okay."

A riffle against his sleeve made him freeze. The pressure grew—fingers crawled up his forearm.

Tox turned in that direction, unable to see through the dense fabric. "It'll be okay." Man, he sounded like a glitching playlist.

Weight pushed against his shoulder. She'd scooted closer. Past the thud of his own pulse, he heard her frantic breath as she leaned against him. With her touch came a strange sense of relief.

The vehicle lurched to a stop, tires squealing. The sound echoed, seeming to amplify. Were they in a tunnel or parking structure? Doors creaked and the vehicle shifted. Another door popped with a groan.

"Out!" a man demanded.

Tox scooted toward the voice, going slow enough for Haven, who kept her hold on his arm. A vise-grip hooked his bicep and yanked him around. Biting back a retort, Tox surrendered that fight. At least, mostly. He wasn't a dog on a lead, no matter the situation. Resisting reminded these people that Tox and the others weren't just going to lie down and play dead.

A door squawked then shrieked, echoing to the right. From that, Tox could extrapolate they were at the end of a passage of some kind. A half-dozen more paces and a gruff voice ordered, "Stop."

Hesitating, Tox fought the urge to reach for the hood. Another weight—someone stumbled into him. Tox caught the person, steadying them.

Without warning his hood was yanked off. Tox cringed, splinters of fire rippling across his scalp at the hair they'd ripped out. The explosion of light was cruel and blinding. Blinking, he took in their surroundings. Hard-packed earth surrounded them, arching overhead and spreading out until darkness swallowed what little light existed. One section of the passageway was lined with stones in perfect alignment. The network of stones swept overhead and rushed down into an intersecting tunnel.

Ram stepped between Tox and Tzivia, whose olive complexion looked more Irish and less Israeli, blanched beneath the situation. "Don't do anything stupid."

"What's going on?" Tox hissed.

With his back to the black-clad men, Ram angled closer. "Just be patient."

"You knew they'd do this?"

Ram met his gaze with a glint of challenge. "We both did."

Tox flinched. It wasn't completely unexpected. The Mossad and many other covert agencies across the world liked the cloak-and-dagger tactics. Tox knew how to play the game to get what he needed. "Is that our contact?"

Ram gave a single shake of his head.

"I believe that would be me" came a creaking old voice filled with age and wisdom.

Ram pivoted. Inclined his head, his broad frame blocking Tox's view. "Shabbat shalom."

"Shabbat shalom, Ram," the man said in a thick accent.

Tox shifted to the side, his shoulder nudging Haven's as he sought a clearer view. The rabbi was at least a half-dozen inches shorter than Ram's six-foot height, mostly the cost of age and arthritis. His gnarly gray beard was tightly trimmed and splotched with pure white.

"Please." He motioned back to the passage, producing a cane from beneath the folds of a black suit jacket that reached to his knees. "Forgive our rather rough methods for secrecy." He huffed out words that were as slow as his pace. His hooklike fingers traced the walls as he shuffled onward. "But that secrecy is imperative for the mysteries we guard."

Ram fell into step with the rabbi, a hand hovering over the old man's crooked spine, as if he could balance him—and yet, afraid to touch him. "Rebbe, we have come—"

"I am aware of why you have come." Though he moved slowly, he did so with familiarity in the dark tunnels, navigating them as easily as if they were fully lit.

Tox kept Tzivia and Haven in front of him. A few mind-bending twists and turns delivered them into a room cramped with wood and parchment. Large beams stretched across the ceiling. Cedar shelves stuffed with scrolls and books of parchments consumed the entire wall opposite the door. A long table hogged the middle of the floor and abutted the left wall. Where Tox half expected to find pots of ink and candles burning, only low-wattage lamps provided the dim glow of light.

With a flick of his hand, the old rabbi sent them to four stools that hugged the thick, long table. "There is little comfort here, including what lies within these leaves and scrolls."

Tox positioned himself so he couldn't be surprised. But the feeling that someone watched from behind the wall of shelving and scrolls had him checking over his shoulder more than once. Finally he surrendered and sat on a stool, folding his arms as the rabbi, with great effort, lowered himself into a rather simple wooden chair with a worn tapestry cover. The thick rug muffled the groan of the wood as he adjusted on the cushion.

A shadow shifted in the corner, and Tox nearly came off his stool to reach for the weapon he no longer had, thanks to the shadowed men. But it was only another rabbi, seated in a corner and hunched over a small square table piled high with books and precariously propped scrolls. The yarmulke-topped head lifted as the rabbi peered at them down his bulbous nose. An overhead lamp caught coils of hair along the sides of his face and his beard, which still held its full color.

"Ah, this is Rebbe Natan Sokolov," the older rabbi said. "He is very devoted to the preservation of the texts, their transcriptions, and translations."

Ram dragged a stool across the room and sat beside the tapestried chair. He leaned forward like a young boy waiting for a story before his grandfather. "Rebbe Baum, you remember my message?"

Baum? This was Baum? But Ram had acted like he hadn't met him. No . . . he just hadn't answered the question.

"Yes, yes," Baum said, waving his hand. "The miktereths. The plague."

Ram tugged out his phone and showed it to the rabbi. "This is what my sister"—he threw her a look over his shoulder—"found at a dig site."

"Jebel al-Lawz."

Okay, the old guy had Tox's attention now.

"Three miktereths, yes, young lady?" Wizened eyes sparked with vibrancy.

Tzivia nodded. "Yes. They were well below the main dig site."

He chuckled. "Of course they were." He laughed again. "And you have them?"

"They were stolen, Rebbe," Ram said. "By different men."

"Oh my." The rabbi steepled his fingertips. "That's quite a shame." He focused on Ram again. "You came because you think they belonged to Korah and his rebel leaders, Dathan and Abiram."

"Yes."

"Always knew Eli had good blood." Baum struggled to push from the chair, and Ram came forward to assist.

Tzivia twitched. "You knew our father?" she asked, her voice unusually high. Her face piqued.

Rabbi Baum made his way to a shelf and pointed to a scroll, which Ram removed. They turned together, and Baum motioned to the long table. Haven was on her feet, facing the men as they laid out the scroll.

Hands propped on the wood, Rabbi Baum smiled. Fondness filled his gray eyes as he peered at the parchment. His fingers wavered as he reached for the text. He swallowed then opened it. The scraping of pages seemed to scratch against the very fabric of time. "What you are looking for is written in Numbers chapter sixteen."

"And that's in the Aleppo Codex?" Tox asked.

Rabbi Baum turned to Tox, his eyes now piercing. "What do you know of the Keter?"

"The what?"

"The Keter Aram Tzova."

Ram nodded. "It means 'the Crown of Aleppo.'"

"What do you know of it?" Rabbi Baum challenged again.

Tox shrugged. "Not enough. Which is why we're here."

"A quiet fool is half a sage."

The remonstration was subtle yet clear. Annoyance spilled down Tox's spine as he clenched his jaw—they needed answers, not a lecture.

Baum raised his eyebrows, pleased his message for Tox to stop interrupting had been received. "Now, Numbers relates the story of

Korah and those who mounted the rebellion with him." He nodded to Tzivia. "You found the site below ground."

"A good half mile, if not more. It was submerged near a spring." Tzivia was on her feet.

"Of course." His hand took on a life of its own, sliding along the columns of neat script as he rolled the scroll apart in one direction, closing the other at the same time. Fingertips trailed over the parchment columns of Hebrew script. "Yes, here. '*Korah son of Izhar, the son of Kohath, the son of Levi, and certain Reubenites—Dathan and Abiram, sons of Eliab, and On son of Peleth—became insolent and rose up against Moses.*'"

"Is that the Codex—er, the Crown, or whatever it's called?" Tox asked, leaning over Haven's shoulder.

"Heavens, no," Rabbi Baum said with a laugh. "This is a scroll."

That was supposed to imply something, and apparently Tox wasn't the only one confused by the old rabbi pointing out what was obvious.

Haven shook her head. "I don't under—"

"The Codex is bound," Tzivia said, with a bit of exasperation. "In fact, it was the first of its kind. The first full Masoretic text bound as a book."

"I've heard that before—Masoretic," Tox mumbled.

"It's the Hebrew text of the Tanakh approved for general use in Judaism," Tzivia explained.

"It comes from *masoreth*, meaning tradition. Therefore," Rabbi Baum continued, "it is the *traditional* Hebrew text of the Jewish Bible."

Tox rubbed his forehead. "And the Masoretic text is the Aleppo Codex?"

"No, it is *a* Masoretic text. One of the oldest, most complete texts of the Hebrew Bible," the rabbi said. "The Aleppo Codex was a full manuscript of the entire Bible, which was written around 930. For more than a thousand years, the manuscript was preserved in its entirety in important Jewish communities in the Near East: Tiberias, Jerusalem, Egypt, and Aleppo."

"So if it was in all those cities," Ram asked. "Why is it called the Aleppo Codex?"

"That is one of its many names. Around 930 AD in Tiberias on the Sea of Galilee, sages led by the ben Asher family assembled all twenty-four holy books and painstakingly hand copied each one into a single bound book—the Codex, which is the first definitive Tanakh, or Hebrew Bible. Besides being the first complete text to be bound as the Romans had done, the Codex also contained the cantillations, which are vocalization marks. This was very unique and very helpful."

"Again," Tox asked, "why is it called the Aleppo—"

Baum held up his gnarled hand. "'Patience is bitter, but its fruit is sweet.'" He smiled, his beard almost hiding the smirk beneath it. "Aristotle."

Tox pinched the bridge of his nose. The rabbi seemed bent on annoying him, or melting his brain with too much information.

"In 1099, the Crusaders laid waste to Jerusalem," Rabbi Baum continued, "and it is they who removed the Codex from the Holy City. They held it ransom, and the Fustat Jewish community in Cairo paid an enormous ransom for the Codex. In the twelfth century, Moshe ben Maimon—also known as Maimonides—was a great medieval Sephardic Jewish philosopher, astronomer, and one of the most prolific and influential Torah scholars and physicians of the Middle Ages. In creating his Mishneh Torah, he used the Codex, which he regarded as one of the most accurate and holy texts. Decades later, his grandson migrated to Aleppo and took it with him. It was safely guarded there for six centuries."

"So that brings us up to our day." Ram was bent over the scroll but watched the rabbi, who had eased onto the stool Tzivia scooted over to him.

"Mystery surrounds the current condition of the Codex and how it came to be in Israel. There are many stories of its journeys over the last seventy-nine years. One particular story is that it was secreted out of Syria in 1947."

"The UN vote to divide Palestine," Tox suggested.

"Precisely," Rabbi Baum said. "There was great fear of backlash against the Jews after the vote. Some say the Codex was smuggled out before the vote in anticipation of riots and attacks, while some say it remained hidden in Aleppo." He shrugged and pursed his lips. "Who can know?"

In the alcove of the other room, the younger Sokolov lifted his head from his work and stilled. A moment later, he gave a sidelong glance at the elder rabbi, then met Tox's gaze and quickly returned to his work on the scroll.

"But it reappeared in Jerusalem," Tzivia said, her tone . . . off. Stiff.

"It did—"

"Missing nearly forty percent."

Baum lowered his head, his expression grave. "Yes."

"What happened to it?" Haven asked, her green eyes darting between them.

"That is the mystery," Baum said. "For years we all believed the leaves were destroyed in the fires when the Jewish quarter was attacked, but there were witnesses who claim to have seen the Crown—complete—months afterward."

"So how did forty percent go missing?"

"Who knows?" Baum shrugged again.

Again the yarmulked head in the corner lifted, but not as high this time.

Tox shifted. "Okay. This is a great history and Bible lesson, but—"

"But what does this have to do with the censers and plague?" Baum finished his thought. At least they understood each other. "In Aleppo, where the Codex was safeguarded, the Jews believed it possessed magical properties. It was said that women who looked upon it would become pregnant, that those who held the keys to its safe—"

"Safe?" Tox asked, his attention again sliding across the room when Sokolov stood from his station, rested his hands on the wood surface for several long moments, then shuffled to the wall of scrolls and books. The rabbi moved without drawing attention from the older rabbi. He could probably do anything he liked as long as he didn't interrupt Baum. The younger rabbi plucked a book and returned to his station. His gaze darted toward the others, then rested on the unopened book.

Baum nodded. "Yes, yes. The Jews were so concerned about protecting their national treasure, it was kept locked in a safe and took two keys to open—each held by a different rabbi. Those who held the keys were blessed." His index finger didn't point—it almost looped as he stabbed it in the air. "And the opposite: Anyone who stole or sold the Codex was cursed." His expression went grave. "They believed a plague would wipe out the Jewish community if it were removed from the synagogue.

"At the tops of some of the pages, the Aleppo elders inscribed a warning to ward off thieves: 'Sacred to Yahweh, not to be sold or defiled.' And elsewhere they wrote, 'Cursed be he who steals it, and cursed be he who sells it.' Among some Jews, especially the Aleppo Jews, those fears persist even today."

"This is asinine," Tzivia said. "A curse didn't cause the outbreak we saw in Jebel al-Lawz." She brushed her bangs off her face, knotted with frustration. "We aroused some latent bacteria. This has nothing to do with the Codex."

"You must read Tiberius" came a soft voice from the alcove—Sokolov.

"Bah!" Baum scoffed. "Why send them to chase fairy tales, Natan?"

"His writings are—"

"Myth! In fact, *Tiberius* is a myth," Baum said. "His writings are just recitation of lore, nothing more. It would be a fool's errand to track them down."

"His writings are founded in fact and proven time and again." Sokolov spoke with conviction.

Face red, Baum shook his head. "Only if you have had too much wine!"

"No, it—"

"Silence, Natan! You know not of what you speak." Baum glowered at the younger rabbi. With a weighted huff, he looked back to Ram and Tox. "Forgive him. 'A wise man conceals his intelligence; the fool displays his foolishness.'" He gave a final *harrumph*, then added, "Tiberius is a myth!"

Dejected and frustrated, Sokolov reached for a small jar. Opened it, then turned toward them and blew across the top.

Almost immediately, Rabbi Baum sneezed. Coughed. He scowled at the younger rabbi. "Must you use that? You know it aggravates my sinuses!"

"My apologies," Sokolov said, hurrying to a small fan, which he turned on. Penitence was as far from the rabbi as arrogance.

Eyes watering, Baum sneezed again. Then coughed. And coughed again—and again . . . until his face was turning red.

Tox shifted and unfolded his arms, ready to administer CPR or a trach if necessary. "Rabbi . . . ?"

Baum struggled to his feet from the stool before shuffling toward the door. "Forgive me." Through another cough, he added, "I will return."

Why had Sokolov sent the aging rabbi into a coughing fit? Tox glanced at Ram and saw the same question on his face. They both focused on the younger rabbi.

"Listen." Sokolov scurried toward them with the book he had retrieved a few minutes earlier and spread it on the table. "'*Though I am no physician, it would seem from the writings I have collected that there is some link between the plague the Hebrews experienced and the plague I witnessed with my own eyes after my brother-knights plundered Jerusalem.*'"

Quiet mushroomed over the room, silencing even the storm in Tox's mind.

"See?" Sokolov, his eyes bright with excitement, smiled at Tox. "Ti Tzaddik has the writings of Thefarie of Tveria, the Templar Knight who faced what you are experiencing. You *must* find Tiberius's Writings—"

Tox pointed to the book. "That's not it?"

Brown hair dusted the man's forehead as he shook his head. "This is only a copy of a fragment. Find Tzaddik and Tiberius's books, and you will find the answer to stopping the plague."

Tox roughed both hands over his face. To Ram he said, "This is like a black hole. Every time I think we might get answers, we only find more questions."

He planted his hands on the table, staring down at the scroll. Felt Haven watching him. How did he always get tangled up in messes like this? Why couldn't soldiering be as "simple" for him as it was for most? Find the bad guys. Neutralize the bad guys. Go home.

Tox turned to the rabbi. "Where do we find this Tzaddik?"

Rabbi Sokolov widened his eyes. "Find *him*? You do not find *him*." Of course not. That'd be too easy.

"I know where to find him," Ram said.

"And even with that, unless Tzaddik wants to see you, he will not be found. Ti Tzaddik only makes himself known to those whose lives are tethered to God's will," Sokolov said. "Just as the angels and demons are."

Right. Great. Tox pushed off the table and paced, hands behind his head to keep them from throttling someone. He felt Haven's gaze and saw concern in those rich, green eyes.

"The book," Sokolov said, nodding to the one lying between his hands, "was written by a man named Tiberius in Byblos. It is a history of—"

"Bah! Why are you bothering them with this? Confusing them?" Rabbi Baum rushed into the room with more speed and power than a man of his age and condition should have. He flapped a hand again at Sokolov. "Be off! Back to your scroll copying. Enough with your fool-speech."

Baum stood over the younger rabbi as he scuttled back to his station, head down. "Forgive him." He sighed, his face a lighter shade than when he'd left. "Do not listen to his ramblings. He has been too long with the parchments and ink." He laughed.

Tox was beginning to identify with Sokolov, going crazy trying to sort out this mission. Though Kafr al-Ayn had made him believe he was losing his mind, this mission convinced him he had. What was he doing chasing artifacts? He was a soldier, a warrior.

From somewhere aboveground drifted the Muslim call to prayer. A chill skidded through his veins. The permeating, haunting sound of the muezzin was an odd and unsettling intrusion, considering where Tox stood, surrounded by the inked history of the Jews.

"Ah, and that tells me I must go." Baum inclined his head. "As you must."

Shadows seemed to peel off the walls and manifest in the forms of well-muscled men. Mossad. Tox's gut churned—why hadn't he sensed them before now?

"They will see you out," Baum said.

"You haven't given us answers." Tox glanced at the men. Groaned at the hoods in their hands.

"You know entirely more than you should," Baum said, his tone no longer friendly and accommodating. "Shabbat shalom."

It'd been a long day, but they were getting nowhere fast. Finding more questions instead of answers. Time to change that. After briefing the team, Tox headed toward Cell, who sat at a bank of computers in the warehouse. "What're you working on?"

"Everything," Cell mumbled, his right hand working one mouse and his left another as his eyes bounced between the two monitors. "Setting up a date with an Israeli soldier-hottie I met in the market, planning a family reunion, getting my dog groomed." Even with his sarcasm, Cell never stopped clicking or tracking.

Tox pushed into a chair beside him at the table. "I need you to do something." He rubbed his lower lip with his thumb. "Off grid."

Cell glanced at him. "Ooo-kay."

"Find whatever you can on the Arrow & Flame."

"And while I'm at it," Cell said, his words monotone and lifeless, "I'll start planning my funeral."

"Well, you're so good at multitasking . . ."

"Now you grow a sense of humor, when I'm dying."

"Nobody's dying." Tox edged closer. "Find names. Find *something* we can track. We need to get them off our back."

Cell scribbled some code on a piece of paper, then tossed the pen down and continued. "Shouldn't SAARC be doing this?"

Tox squinted. "They should—so why haven't they?" It bugged him.

"Maybe they have."

"Never knew you to be a devil's advocate."

"Hey, if the devil keeps me alive, I'll be his best friend." Cell grunted. "Heck, I'll even marry him."

"Yeah, well, I'll probably judge you for it."

"Hardnose."

"You know it." Tox slapped his shoulder and stood. "Let me know what you find. And Cell?"

"Yeah?" Brown eyes pulled away from the computer.

"Be smart about it."

"When am I not, Sarge? When am I not?"

Tox patted his shoulder again and strode back to his work station. He snatched a folder from the table, some tape, and headed to a wall at the far end of the building. There was little light, but that was all he needed—well, that and some isolation to get perspective on this mission.

In the center, he taped a paper with the word PLAGUE on it. Around it, he added: JEBEL AL-LAWZ, TANIN, RABBIS, TIBERIUS, INDIA, CHATRESH/BHAVIN, ARROW & FLAME, CENSERS/THE CODEX.

Tox worked it, making a note here and there, but mostly, he stared. Let the words, the locations connect. Cross-connect. Explore possibilities. He'd been doing this without the data wall for the last two weeks as they worked to stop what was happening. But the tangibility helped.

At least, he hoped it did. He relaxed into the problem-solving but unfortunately felt no closer to solid answers.

"Want some food?"

"Not hungry," he said, only peripherally aware the question had been asked. His brain energy diverted into finding solutions.

Hours later, Tox leaned back against the table, squeezing a hand over his mouth and dragging it down over his jaw. *What am I missing?*

Someone walked in front of his data wall, saying, "We have a problem."

Tox blinked.

Cell stretched up to one of the pages taped to the wall and started writing on it.

"Hey!"

Cell rotated. A symbol now glared back from the page marked Arrow & Flame. "We have a problem," he repeated, this time more ardent as his light brown brows knotted.

Tox scowled, tugging his gaze from the flaming arrow symbol. "What?" Then his brain caught up, his gaze once more on the drawing. "Where did you see that?"

"C'mere." Cell returned to his station.

Dread simmered in Tox's gut. He followed the communications expert, and though he sensed eyes watching them, he did his best to play it cool. Cell's monitors were dark, oddly turned off, making the dread roil as the techie scooted in his chair and jabbed the monitors on.

Tox glanced at the first—CANNOT FIND PAGE. Then the next. And the next. On every monitor. "These—"

"Every one is a different system, self-contained." Cell flicked his finger backward at the monitor directly in front of him. "This is what I get when I hunt around for you-know-who." He pointed to a task bar at the top. "Different search parameters." He tapped the screen. "Same result—page couldn't load."

"Is our ISP being blocked?"

"Negatory." Cell tucked his pencil in his mouth and typed LYNETTE EASON into the central monitor. A screen splashed to life with hundreds of listings for the author. "I can look up everything and anything *except* the Arrow & Flame."

How did that even make sense? "Did you try glowing arrows?"

"Yep. And fiery arrow organization and terrorists . . . every combo you can imagine." He arched an eyebrow. "I haven't just been sitting here for the last four hours."

"What's going on?" Ram asked.

"I even tried digging around that error message, but it's"—Cell shook his head—"it's impenetrable. Anything related to Arrow & Flame comes to this."

"What?!" Ram shouted, lunging forward. "*What* are you doing?"

Tox jerked up. "Working this mission."

"If you look for them, they—" Ram yanked off his beanie and spun in a furious circle. "You stupid—" He flipped out his phone. Started dialing. "Everyone, pack up! *Now!*"

"No!" Tox surged after his friend, motioning to the others. "Disregard that!"

Wild, angry eyes met his as Ram spoke a series of unintelligible words.

"Who are you talking to?"

Tzivia was at his side. "Hebrew."

Tox lunged. "Mossad? You're talking to Mossad?"

With a glower, Ram shoved him off and jogged toward his bunk. He threw his gear into a sack, Hebrew spewing still.

"What's he saying?" Tox asked over his shoulder to Tzivia.

"'We're compromised,'" Tzivia whispered, her voice trembling as she translated her brother's words. "'Orders were violated.'"

Orders? Dread washed over Tox, the wave scalding and terrifying as he saw the expression on Ram's face. That wasn't just anger—it was terror.

Crap. "You heard him. Pack up!" Tox glanced at Tzivia again, who stood watching her brother, shock riddling her features.

"He's following something called Joshua Protocol," she said, lifting her shoulders in apparent confusion and shaking her head. "'Chances of survival'—"

"Go!" Tox knew she didn't need to hear the rest. "Get the professor!" He swung her in the direction of Dr. Cathey, who was moving as fast as he could.

Tox sprinted and grabbed his ruck. Then ripped the pages from the data wall before herding the others, unnerved, toward the exit.

"What was that?" The gasp in Ram's word caused a hush to fall over the entire warehouse. He whipped to Tox. "Incoming!"

"Go go go!" Tox sprinted toward the door, ruck over his shoulder. He spun, scanning the warehouse to make sure everyone was out. Ram had swept the professor into a fireman's carry and hoofed it out the door with Tzivia on his tail.

Tox whipped around, eyeing the exit. Bodies bottlenecking to get through. Adrenaline spiraling through his veins pushed him hard.

Drove him forward. "*Go!*" He plowed into Cell and Maangi, who were pushing Haven and Wallace out the door.

Compression and release. He shoved, their arms and legs tangling. Maangi and Cell broke free. Ran hard.

Over the drumming of his heart, the whoosh of his breath, Tox heard the unmistakable, high-pitched scream. A missile. His tactical mind knew he wouldn't clear the building or blast radius in time. Safety hovered out of reach. Too close to the target. Just . . . too close.

The ground rattled. Shifted. His feet twisted and turned. Pavement scored his knee. He reached down to brace himself.

Thunder cracked against his ears. Vacuous silence suffocated his hearing. He was lifted off the ground. Feet came up behind him. Flipped over. He sailed through the air. Scalding air that felt as if it were on fire. It rushed around Tox and swallowed him whole.

Numbing vibrations wormed through Tox's skull. He blinked and groaned, the pain akin to a skewer driving through his temple.

"Sarge." Cell's voice plucked at him.

Tox peeled himself off the ground. Blinked, confusion acute. He looked around—flames roared from a pile of rubble. Chiji rushed toward him. "Haven." His head pounded.

"Got her," Cell said as he and Chiji gripped his arms. "Let's go."

They ran away from the missile strike and caught up with Ram, who was in a light jog. "Where are we going?"

"SAARC wants us at Fiq Airfield. Forty-minute hike."

They moved silently through the night, rattled by the explosion but determined to make it to the jet alive and unharmed. When they arrived, the jet was waiting as promised. They boarded, and Tox zeroed in on the long, thin conference table flanking a forty-inch monitor.

The plane raced down the airstrip. Turbulence jostled them, pitching him forward. Tox planted a hand on the curved hull to brace himself.

Ram went to the monitor and tapped a button. The wall sprang to life with the faces of Robbie Almstedt and Barry Attaway. "Great balls of fire!" Almstedt exclaimed. "You boys left a mess for us to clean up."

"Wanted to make an impression, ma'am," Cell muttered.

"Well, you did that and then some."

"We need to know about the AFO," Tox said, leaning to the side to mitigate the ache in his ribs and head.

Attaway bent toward the camera, his graying hair and Italian features making him appear forbidding. "Russell, the first thing is that you opened a boatload of trouble digging around for them."

Tox lifted his chin. "Kinda figured that out already. But I have a mission—to find Tanin and stop this plague. And when someone gets in my face about it, I need to figure out why and how to stop them. Standard MO."

"Which is why you aren't on the first jet back to the Leavenworth."

Tox curled his fingers into a fist. "A threat?" After what they'd been through? After the insane parameters of a mission involving a plague?

"Easy, boys," a voice came from off-screen. Dru Iliescu moved into view. "Russell, the AFO has been on our radar for decades."

"Tell me what you know."

"Little." He nodded into the camera. "Each time we thought we were getting close, the smoke screen would blow over and we'd be left standing there, holding our butts." He huffed. "They date back centuries—their mark found even among Templar seals and letters. We haven't proven it, but I think they were even mentioned among the Saracens."

"Who?" Wallace asked.

"Dude—only the fiercest Muslim assassins known to history," Cell said. When Tox looked at him, Cell shrugged. "I play *Assassin's Creed*."

"The Templars were known to war with the Saracens," Iliescu explained, "yet there was a great respect between the two breeds of warriors on holy missions."

Tox's stomach knotted. Not only were they not finding answers, they were falling back in history to dark, deadly times. "Are you saying the Saracens were part of the AFO?"

"Honestly, we don't know. There are indications they infiltrated both the Templars and the Saracens—and political seats all the way up to the thrones of some countries."

"Wait—you mean there were kings or queens who were AFO?"

"That is our belief," Iliescu said with a sigh. "And we suspect they still hold great power and influence throughout the world today. For centuries, they have had some of the best fighters and assassins."

"Like Tanin."

Lips tight, Iliescu nodded.

"Obviously not," Maangi said. "We're still alive."

"Maybe they want us alive," Tox muttered, not buying into the arrogance of thinking they'd escaped those arrows out of sheer luck. "Where are we headed?"

"Syria."

"What's in Syria?"

"Ti Tzaddik," Ram interrupted.

"The guy Sokolov mentioned."

Ram nodded. "He has more knowledge on historical events than any encyclopedia you could pick up."

Tox eyed his friend, wary that Ram knew of this guy. "Wait—" He wagged a finger. "In Bhavin's journal, he mentioned meeting with 'Ti.' Could that be the same guy as this Tzaddik?"

"Possibly. Maybe Tzaddik asked him to steal a censer?"

"Maybe he was trying to find them like your sister was."

"Maybe." But Ram didn't look convinced.

"Okay, listen," Iliescu said, "Robbie will get you up to date. Keep us posted. I've got a meeting."

The screen blanked out, the wall of the plane regaining its presence. Tox roughed a hand over his face, then glanced at Ram. "Fill me in. Ti Tzaddik."

"I met him on a mission about three years ago. His knowledge is"—Ram shook his head—"there's no explanation for how he knows what he knows. But he knows."

"Sort of like you." Tox let the words hit then went on. "So we hope he knows something about this plague and the censers?"

"And the AFO." Ram lifted a paper from the printer and held it up. "This symbol—the one Cell kept running up against, that we found in Bhavin's journal. The arrow you collected outside the museum had this symbol. I've seen it before, too, on a ledger in Tzaddik's possession."

"So he knows about the AFO."

"Probably."

"Speaking of the arrow," Thor spoke up loudly, "initial reports are that it might have phosphorus or something in the shaft."

"That's sick."

Maangi huffed. "Iliescu said the AFO were deadly. So if they wanted us dead—how'd they keep missing at the museum?"

"This path," Dr. Cathey mumbled from the far end of the table, "it leads to Resheph and Sheol." His keen eyes looked around the table, and he shrugged. "That's what the Israelites believed."

Ignoring the professor's words, Tox leaned forward. "Where's Ti located in Syria?"

"The Citadel of Aleppo."

"The Aleppo Codex," Haven said.

Tzivia sighed. "But ignore Resheph and Sheol."

"What are they?"

"Resheph was the figurative personification of death," Tzivia said, her tone flat, annoyed. "Sheol was the name for hell."

"Manuscripts, scrolls, codices, and people do not agree that Resheph was *merely* the name for death," Dr. Cathey countered. "Some words used around it indicate the possibility it was a spirit, or even a real person."

"Stop it," Tzivia snapped. "It's bad enough you lure them with taunts of miracles and curse-inducing plagues—do not insult our intelligence by suggesting Resheph is a *person*."

"I have seen many Westerners discount the supernatural, reducing God to what they can explain and hold in their hands," Chiji said, his long, ebony fingers forming a cup before him.

"And how is it our beliefs are insulting but yours are intelligent?" Ram asked Tzivia, his calm nature exuding confidence.

"Mine rest in science."

"So you have found the source of the plague?" Ram challenged, not with malice but with more of that confidence.

"Okay, enough." Tox had been on the receiving end of Ram's maddening confidence before. He smoothed a hand over his short crop, noticing a tender spot. He winced and refocused. "When do we land?"

As if to answer, the plane began its descent. "We're landing at a private airstrip under a faked transponder," Ram said. "We'll split up and head into Aleppo. It's a hot spot for extremists."

"Why?" Haven asked.

"They're demolishing anything cultural—including many attempts on the citadel itself."

"So it's not safe?"

"Most of this region isn't safe." Cell gazed out the window as the ground slowly became closer.

A tone sounded on a phone, and Tox glanced over. Haven lifted her smartphone and swiped a finger across it. A moment of confusion rippled through her thin eyebrows. She covered her mouth as she watched something, her expression still a mask of confusion.

Haven's eyes went wide. She yelped.

Something primal in him detonated when she lurched back, holding her phone out as if it had a disease. "What?"

She jerked to him, eyes pools of a turbulent sea. She shoved the device at him with a strangled cry.

Tox braced her, afraid she'd collapse as he glanced at the screen. A video. He thumbed it.

Quiet . . . a broad sidewalk . . . the buildings were European. Someone walked into view. He couldn't gauge age because of the perspective, but he guessed it to be a young person. A teen in uniform. School uni—

"No." Tox's heart slowed. His mind powered down, recognizing the form.

Beside the person filming, a crossbow glided into view.

"It's her, isn't it?" Haven whispered. "It's Evie." She pressed against his side, her face in his chest.

A hand with a flaming arrow tattoo in the crook between the thumb and forefinger. The arrow launched from the crossbow.

The camera never wavered as the arrow sailed across the distance. Haven cried out and Tox held her tighter.

Thud!

In his arms, Haven jerked when the arrow pierced Evie in the back. His niece pitched forward with a scream. She lay on the sidewalk, unmoving.

A voice demanded, "You failed our first warning. Stop before more die."

Tox wrapped his arms around Haven, a piece of him tearing at the brokenness in her sobs. At what he'd just witnessed. He cupped the back of her head, wanting to give her reassurance. Wanting to say it wasn't Evie. Wanting to promise she wasn't dead. But he'd seen his niece. Seen what those phosphorus arrows did to a body. Over her shoulder, he met the grief-stricken gaze of Chiji.

Ram lifted the phone from Tox's hand and glanced up, his own phone to his ear.

"Please," Haven sobbed, her forehead pushing into his chest. "Please tell me that wasn't her. Tell me she's not . . ." She shook her head, her body trembling.

Tox tucked his chin, his cheek against her hair. "We're going to find out."

Her fingers coiled around the sides of his shirt, twisting and squeezing. "I can't . . . I can't . . ."

"Hey." Tox adjusted his hold. "Hey." There was one reassurance he could give her. It was the only one he had. He slid his hand along the side of her neck and used his thumb to push her gaze to his. He

312

hated the rawness, the vulnerability there. "I promise you . . ." Breathing was a chore, staring down at her innocence with a lethal vow. "I promise," he whispered again.

Her breaths came in gulping spurts and struck his cheek as she searched his eyes for some hope.

"Whoever did this . . . I'll hunt them down."

She slumped against him in what felt like a whoosh of relief. Her arms encircled his waist, and she clung to him. Tox held her, startled. By how much that promise to her fueled him. How much he didn't want to let her down. Or let her go.

"I'm sorry," Haven whispered through her tears as she drew back. "I'm sorry."

Tox peered at her. "For what?" Her eyes were streaked, hair mussed, but Haven owned a natural beauty.

Her chin dimpled as she fought more tears. "For losing it."

He almost snorted. "We got blown up. Raced through Israel. Then saw an awful video of my—our niece . . ." The words tasted like bile and he found he couldn't finish them, not gazing into her eyes like this. "I'd be ticked if you didn't lose it."

A smile tugged her lips up.

"Tox."

He looked up and found Ram staring, a solemn expression gouged into his hazel eyes. That wasn't good. Immediately, Tox knew the video was no illusion. Evie had been hit. He mustered strength from the dregs of his courage, from having to see Haven's grief when the news was delivered. He slid his gaze to the side, where Levi Wallace stood, hands on his belt, head tucked. Angry. Grieved.

Tox caught his gaze. Gave a thrust of his chin. Levi straightened.

"Haven," Tox said, angling back. "I need to address this." He held her shoulders, guided her to Levi. Something in him twisted as the agent stepped so easily and seamlessly into the hole Tox had left.

That . . . that was where she belonged. With someone who wouldn't bring her hurt and pain. Someone who had no history or bodies in his wake. Someone who didn't put her in the path of explosions and dangle her life within Death's grasp.

He made his way down the aisle to Ram. "What'd you find?"

Holding Tox's phone, the mute feature selected, Ram said, "It was her. The president got word as my call was put through."

Tox covered his eyes, as if he could shield himself from the tragedy. "Is she dead?"

"No."

Practically tasting the hesitation in that clipped answer. he glanced at Ram.

"But it's not good." He handed the phone to Tox and stepped back, tapping his Bluetooth, indicating he'd be making calls.

Roughing a hand over his face, Tox blew out a breath. Canceled the mute and lifted the phone. "Galen."

"I don't have much time. I'm flying to England. She's critical."

Tox squeezed his eyes shut. Shook his head. *Breathe.* "I'll find them."

"You'd better," Galen ground out. "I want them dead."

"For once, we agree." He really had no right to ask, but Tox had to. "Keep me posted?"

Silence gaped, then, "I will. Oh, and Tox—you've got whatever you need to hunt them down."

The call ended. Tox balled his fist. He leaned back against a seat and closed his eyes. He needed that image of Evie on the sidewalk in the front of his mind so he could work with focused determination. But he desperately wanted that image seared *out* of his mind. He didn't want to think of her like that. Of her being boiled alive.

"You okay?"

Pulled straight by Haven's soft voice, Tox did his best to avoid her eyes. "No. But I will be." Once he gave a double tap to whoever had done this.

"You talked to Galen?"

This time he met her eyes. And felt that vortex that'd erupted when he'd held her. It sucked him in like deadly backwash from a jet. "Yeah."

She inched closer, her dark blond hair loose around her shoulders. "What—" She swallowed. "What'd Galen say?"

"She's alive." He nodded, trying to reassure himself Evie would stay that way. "Report is that she's critical. But alive. He's flying out to be with her."

"Good." She breathed and laughed. Trembling.

The plane dipped down, marking its descent.

"Heading into Syria." Tox grabbed the distraction and touched her shoulder, concerned this leg of the mission might be too much too soon for her. "You up to this?"

She lifted her chin. "More than ever." Though Haven had pulled herself together, it wasn't hard to see she was on the verge of collapse. That the strings holding her together were thin and frayed. She was strong but not designed for combat.

"It's okay if you need a break."

Haven frowned at him.

"Tox," Tzivia called. "We're landing. Ram wants you."

"Yep." Tox looked over his shoulder and gave a curt nod, then turned back to Haven.

"Go." Haven mustered a smile, but they both knew it was fake.

Tox felt like a heel leaving her and making his way to Ram, who was on the phone. But he also felt a huge dose of relief. Things were getting too weird with Haven.

Ram glanced up as he pocketed his smartphone and Tox slid into the seat beside him. "Contacted SAARC. The AFO made a mistake targeting the president's daughter. Every agency, both American and British, is tracking down those responsible for this. ICE and NSA are on alert."

"They won't find them." Tox knew that in his bones.

With a solemn nod, Ram agreed. "They seem to have amazing luck escaping attack sites."

"This Tzaddik . . . you think he'll be much help?"

Snorting, Ram shook his head. "I know you think I'm being under-handed, but there's a limit to what I know. And I can only hope he'll be the help I want him to be."

"That makes two of us."

The tires screeched as they hit the tarmac. They jerked forward as the reverse engines roared, the plane's tail wiggling as it strained to slow the momentum. The aircraft lumbered to a stop.

"Here they come," Cell announced, watching a herd of SUVs tearing up the tarmac toward them.

"Yeah," Maangi said, "but are they ours?"

Either way, they were sitting ducks on the plane. "Everyone to the door," Tox shouted, pushing out of his seat. Herding them to the front of the plane, he kept an eye on what was happening through the windows. Two of the vehicles swung around, facing away from the plane. Another pair broke off, one going to the front, one to back. "Protective perimeter."

"They're ours." Ram hurried to the hatch and opened it.

Light exploded across the interior. Pain stabbed Tox's eyes, the agony probing into the dark recesses of his brain, then punching into his stomach. Nausea churned. This was going to be a lot of fun—being in a desert with a borderline migraine. His shades cut a lot of the glare, but not enough to completely eliminate the pain.

Tox noted Haven watching him seconds before Wallace urged her out of the plane, followed by Cell. Wallace glanced at Tox, his eyes looking more like a raccoon with each passing hour. Tox had really messed up his nose. Maybe he owed the agent an apology.

"Want a push?" Wallace asked. "It's only a ten-foot drop."

Forget the apology. Yet the humor from the agent was unexpected. Anger. Animosity. Jealousy, Tox expected. But this?

"Sarge, I could break his legs to match his nose," Thor offered.

"You were right." Wallace pointed to his bruised face. "I shouldn't have left her."

What was Tox supposed to say to that?

"I'm glad you were there for her when that call came in about your niece," Wallace continued, "but . . . if you hurt Kasey . . ."

That sounded like a challenge. A game of one-upping. And Wallace stood there staring him down, something in his eyes. Tox nearly laughed when he finally realized the FBI agent wanted a piece of him. "Try." Because if the guy didn't, he'd be itching for it the rest of the trip.

The broad-shouldered agent stilled, locked on Tox, who waited, knowing full well Wallace would take the opportunity. "You're a legend," Wallace finally said.

"Remember that when you fail."

The fist came from Tox's right—flying hook at his head. Tox caught it, twisted the arm, and threw Wallace up against the hull of the interior. Pinned him to the gray vinyl, knocking a meaty *oof* out of him.

Tox released him, nudging him aside, out of strike range, then hopped from the plane into the truck bed. "Try a little harder next time."

Dark clouds seemed to have invaded her life, even if the sky over Aleppo was startlingly blue. With the threat against the team and Evie in a hospital fighting for her life, Kasey felt like she sat in a vehicle made of paper rather than armor-plated, reinforced steel. They lurched away from the tarmac, away from the others, and rushed into a gnarled city littered with debris and destruction. The heat was insufferable, especially beneath the hijab they'd handed her as soon as she'd left the plane. It was designed to make her blend in, not suffocate, but she was sure one less female wouldn't bother any of these men.

The devastation of the city proved heartbreaking—but what hurt more was the people. They walked the streets, oblivious to the giant craters and crumbling buildings. And yet—they were affected. The women walked a little quicker. Held their children closer.

Kasey ached to hold Evie, for her niece to once more be the little girl who rushed into her arms and squealed in delight.

Only as she was able to watch a mother and son reach an intersection did Kasey realize how slow the vehicle was going. She checked the speedometer on the dash. Forty-five. It didn't feel fast enough.

317

Until the next corner threw her into Maangi's arms. "I'm so sorry," she muttered, pushing herself free.

"I promise not to tell Tox."

Surprise spurted through her at the teasing, partially because it insinuated she was Cole's girl. But she wasn't. She shot the olive-skinned Maangi a look, only to earn a wink from him.

She adjusted in her seat between him and Levi. "Are we sure they're taking us to the right place?" Through the back window, only dust and more buildings.

"Look." Maangi leaned forward, pointing beyond Levi's window. "Watch down the alleys to the parallel street."

Kasey peered out of the trouncing SUV. In between buildings and down an alley, a blur of black whizzed in and out of view in a heartbeat. She held her breath. Was that . . . ? It happened again. "That's them—the other vehicle?"

"One of them," Maangi said.

The revelation distracted and calmed her. Minutes later, after a few more jarring turns, they glided to a stop in front of a long line of squat dwellings. Levi climbed out, blocking her view as he checked their surroundings. He finally stepped back and offered a hand.

Kasey ignored it and exited. "I'm not incapable of watching out for myself."

"He just doesn't want another black eye or broken bone." Maangi pointed to a path that rose up a slight hill. "This way."

She wasn't stupid enough to guess whether that was true or not. She just started walking. And as soon as they crested the incline, Kasey saw another group coming toward them: Tzivia, Chiji, and Dr. Cathey.

"Keep moving," Maangi said. "No need to draw attention."

Prompted by his warning, she fell into step behind him, more than half wondering about Cole and Ram. They rounded a bend, Maangi navigating as if he'd lived here. As if he knew this area. Ahead, down the sloping footpath, Cole folded his large frame through an arch and vanished. Reassured by the sight of him, Kasey quickened her step and arrived at the arch a few seconds later, just as the front door of a home opened.

Cole's gaze struck her—and she felt it to her core. She wished he'd open up to her, not shut her out. Especially when he looked at her like that.

The team filled the courtyard as the door opened wider, a woman's soft voice welcoming them.

"We're looking for Ti Tzaddik," Ram said.

She bowed in acknowledgment.

"Are—are you his wife?"

The woman laughed. "He would no sooner take a wife than a mistress." She waved a dismissive hand. "I'm his housekeeper. He is where he always is."

Ram and Tox exchanged glances.

"The citadel." This time, she snapped her hand in the direction of the great stone fortress towering over the crumbling, bombed city. "He sits up there, as if king to rule it."

"Thank you," Ram said with a sort of bow.

They crowded out of the courtyard, Cole and Ram talking quietly. Finally, Cole stopped right in front of Kasey and turned, towering over her just as the citadel did. "Stick to your teams. Make your way into the fortress. Don't cluster. But stay where you can see us."

His blue eyes met hers. He hesitated, then angled to Levi, and though she couldn't be sure, it seemed a stern warning sailed from those ocean depths.

Levi's arm came around her shoulder. "This way," he muttered.

After an almost imperceptible, approving nod, Cole pivoted and strode away with Ram, leaving Kasey tugged in the opposite direction between Levi and Maangi.

"You know," Kasey said, irritation piqued, "I am not a child."

"Good," Levi replied. When she looked at him, he smirked. "I'd have a hard time explaining that I dated a child."

Maangi skirted a glance between them, his brow knotted. She recalled his promise about not telling Cole when she fell into his arms in the car. Now Levi had implied they were dating. She hadn't really *dated* Levi. But she couldn't lie to herself or anyone else—she allowed his interest. They did things together. And she'd kissed him.

"I meant, you do not need to hover like some protector."

"Wrong," Maangi said. "If we want to live, we will."

She frowned at him.

"Tox will kill us if anything happens to you."

"*That!* That's what I'm talking about." She bristled. Hated that she was being treated like an incompetent member of the team. "I'm with the FBI."

"And you've never been in the field," Levi said.

Movement snagged her attention, her heart in her throat as she spotted Cole stalking up around the bridge, entering the main area where they stood. And he strode right past them, as if they were strangers.

"This way," Maangi said, aiming them more to the left.

It took only a few minutes to come around the side, lingering on a level lower than where Cole and Ram were searching for their contact.

"We'll keep walking." Maangi guided them along a series of stepped walls that had at one time been dwellings. Rooms, though they didn't look big enough for a single person to sleep in. She couldn't imagine living like this . . . cramped. Shoulder to shoulder not just with stone walls but people.

Blue eyes slid into her visual path. Kasey swallowed, realizing Cole watched her make the circuit around the citadel. Should they break away? Drawing attention would be bad.

"Keep walking," Maangi said, his voice really close.

Kasey erased the half-dozen feet between them, noting that Ram inclined his head to someone hidden by a half wall.

Cole angled toward Ram, then visibly jerked. He stumbled backward—right into Kasey. "You," he breathed, the word filled with disbelief and fear as he stared at someone. He shook his head. "No. Can't . . ." He pivoted, eyes in a wild panic.

"Cole?" As soon as his name slipped between her lips, she knew she shouldn't have said it.

"*Walk*," Maangi hissed, prodding her along like a reluctant child.

But she wheeled after Cole. He ducked around a corner. When she turned it, he was gone. The crunch of rocks pulled her to the left, behind a crumbling stone wall. Bent in half, Cole gripped his knees, his eyes closed, as if he might vomit.

"Cole?"

He snapped up, startled. Then relaxed. "You shouldn't be here," he whispered, his voice barely audible.

"What's wrong?"

He stood, his thumb pressed to his temple and finger to his forehead. "That man . . ."

Kasey glanced back, though the wall blocked her view. "Tzaddik?"

"Can't be."

"Why?"

"He . . ." His gaze grew distant. "I met him before. He was the man at the temple."

"In India?"

"But he can't be." Again, he shook his head, but she saw the uncertainty. "I . . ."

"Did he scare you?" It seemed impossible that anyone could scare Cole.

"He just keeps showing up . . . the temple . . . here." Cole's gaze fell to the ground, his rapid eye movement seemed to search for answers his head couldn't find.

Cole was a rock, a fortress of his own. It terrified her to see him distressed. Kasey touched his face, hoping to draw his attention, help him focus. "Cole."

Those beautiful blue eyes locked onto her. So hard, so fast, she felt it deep, as if he'd dropped anchor in her soul. Drawing her in, deeper.

"Talk to me."

Torment wormed through his expression. Fear lurked there. Haunting. Desperation. It surprised her that she could practically hear his thoughts, his anxious heart thundering one question: *Can I trust you?*

"Let me help, please."

But he pulled free. And in the space of that heartbeat, Cole the Warrior was back. "I need to talk to Tzivia."

Kasey started, her heart thumping in hurt.

"Tox." Ram's voice intruded. "This is Ti Tzaddik."

* * * *

"We should go to the top of the citadel." Neatly trimmed gray hair framed a face that seemed no more than fifty or sixty years old.

Tzaddik stood even with Tox's six-foot-two-inch height. Muscles filled out his chest and arms—not like a powerlifter, but like someone who knew the value of hard work and embraced it. Yet for all the man's fitness and vitality, there was a hint of something . . . off. Something not right about him.

Tox had to talk to Tzivia. Ask her about the Stranger—if this was him. It was the only thing that made sense. And yet . . . it made no sense.

Ram and Tox flanked Tzaddik as they headed up another level of the citadel, tourists cluttering various sections and clamoring for the high vantages. As a cool breeze traced Tox's shoulders, he looked out over the one-hundred-fifty-foot rock that loomed over Aleppo and saw the horizon blending into the sunset.

"Fortresses have risen and fallen above the old city," Tzaddik said in a soft British accent, sweeping his hand over the citadel. "Layer upon layer of civilizations—ruins of Ottoman palaces rest here, nestled below the walls from the times of the Crusades."

The words stirred within Tox a new respect for the hill.

"And over there, beyond the amphitheater"—he motioned to a Roman-era stepped theater—"a sphinx and lion guard one of the oldest great religious centers of ancient times." Tzaddik seemed to revel in his storytelling. "The sanctuary of the storm god, Adda."

"We really aren't here for a history lesson," Tox said, scanning their surroundings, those nearby. He spotted some of his team loitering, trying to blend in.

Tzaddik stood tall over the fortress. "'Those who don't know history are destined to repeat it.'"

Edmund Burke. "'History does not repeat itself. Man always does.'" Tox had long loved that quote by Voltaire.

"'To be ignorant of what occurred before you were born—'"

"—'is to remain always a child,'" Tox finished.

Tzaddik almost smiled. "Good." He gave a solemn nod. "You know Cicero, and apparently history."

"We're here about—"

"Not yet," Tzaddik said as he thrust a finger upward, then shifted and peered out over the expanse, hands behind his back.

Agitation ate at Tox. Playing word games after appearing like a ghoul in so many places? "Look, we—"

Without a word, Tzaddik walked away.

In disbelief, Tox turned to Ram. "What's with this guy?"

"He's . . . particular. Has rituals."

Interesting answer. A defense. "How do you know about him?"

"He's a legend," Ram said. "Friends talk." And by friends, he no doubt meant Mossad. That seemed to be the fare of the day when it came to Ram. "Half the stories they tell"—he shrugged—"seem too incredible to believe. The things he knows or can find out . . . one would think he had been there himself."

"Then why didn't you suggest him in the first place?"

"Because his knowledge is specific. Artifacts, history . . . the Levant."

"Levant?"

"The historic name given to the entire region east of the Mediterranean from Egypt to Iran." Ram glanced toward the old city. "Cyprus and parts of Turkey sometimes."

Tzaddik faced them, his expression betraying nothing. "We should go."

About time.

Tzaddik's gaze swung to Tox, who surveyed the path they would take to leave this place. Anything to avoid eyes that felt like a truth probe drilling right to his core.

Tox shifted to walk next to Ram. "Where's Tzivia?"

"Down at the base with the professor. Seems he got distracted with inscriptions or something," Ram explained.

Tox needed to know if this was the same Stranger she'd seen in Paris while chasing down the mace that had devastated Kafr al-Ayn. "I'll track them down. Meet you at the foot gate."

He hoofed it away from them, putting as much distance between himself and Tzaddik as possible. Tox had killer instincts and they'd rarely been wrong. He could sense in his blood something was off with Tzaddik.

He hustled down the stepped path, scanning for Chiji, who would stand out with his six-five height and dark features. But at every turn, Tox only found more locals and frustration. "C'mon, c'mon," he muttered, rounding a corner, visually sorting those in his path into groups—tourists and locals.

A boom of laughter plowed into his hearing. Chiji.

Tox wheeled around, scanning . . . local male, hijabbed woman . . . another woman, younger. A man, possibly tourist, possibly local. Hard to tell with the olive complexion. Another woman in an orange hijab. An older man—

Professor! Tox threw himself in that direction, realizing before he took the second step that the woman in the orange hijab was Tzivia. Chiji emerged from a shadowed alcove, his white teeth bright in the afternoon sun as he smiled and spoke.

Tox swept up to the trio.

Tzivia flinched at his sudden presence, then smiled. "What—?"

"Can we talk?" He gripped her elbow and guided her away before she could refuse.

"What are you doing?"

He angled her into a corner for privacy, then skated a glance around to be sure they were alone. "Kafr al-Ayn."

Eyes narrowing, Tzivia adjusted the hijab, careful to make sure her hair wasn't showing. "What about it?"

Tox huffed, hating that he had to cough this up now. But it had to be done to get to the bottom of this. "There's something I didn't tell anyone."

Her irritation slid into rapt attention. "Is something wrong?"

He couldn't help but draw a comparison to the way Haven had instinctively and immediately known something was wrong, very wrong atop the citadel. The way she'd reached for him out of concern.

Then again, he'd been acting the fool, running from Tzaddik, though Tox Russell never ran from a fight. "In Kafr al-Ayn, when I was trapped in the tunnel after the missile strike—"

She nodded, her brows knitted together now.

Do or die, Russell. "—I saw . . . something."

Tzivia's mahogany eyes widened. She went three shades paler than her normal, glowing complexion.

Tox frowned, wondering how she could know what he was going to say already. But then he realized her gaze had shifted. She was focused over his shoulder. Tox turned. Tzivia grabbed his forearm, her nails digging into his flesh as she slid closer to him.

Ti Tzaddik emerged from a passage with Ram, Haven, Maangi, and Wallace.

"That's him," she breathed, all color now gone from her face. "That's the man, the Stranger."

This was neither the time nor the place to be jealous. With Evie in critical condition, a plague devastating India, and an organization hunting them down, Kasey knew she should be focused on those things, but all her brain could notice was that Cole went running to Tzivia. And the Israeli-American had latched onto him like a bee to honey.

Kasey looked away, unable to watch Tzivia cling to Cole in front of God and everybody. At least they hadn't stopped to dialogue. The team and Dr. Cathey kept moving, Mr. Tzaddik leading them back out of the citadel and through the crowded city to his home. There, the woman who'd met them earlier delivered a tray of fruit, dates, figs, baklava, and other sweets before bustling away. Dejected, Kasey sat on a cushion in the corner, ordering herself to tamp down misplaced feelings. All these years later, and the end result with Cole was the same—he didn't want her. He wanted someone older, with a little more experience . . . a little more . . .

What?! What did Tzivia and Brooke have that she didn't?

Levi lowered himself to the cushion nearby, hand resting on the floor behind her. "What's eating you?"

She snorted. How did Levi always know? And why was it him who noticed while Cole remained oblivious? If nobody else did, Levi knew. Always knew. But she gave herself away when she glanced again at Tzivia and Cole whispering in the corner.

"Don't let him get to you," Levi said.

"Those words sound more like 'I told you so,' than encouragement," Kasey said. "I'm fine."

"You're not," Levi said. "And I could kill him for it."

At the venom in his words, she met his blue eyes. Touched by the ferocity she saw there. The mild-mannered agent-boyfriend-who-wasn't-a-boyfriend had transformed into a fierce force.

"I'll give him a piece of my mind when I get a minute alone with him."

"That might not be the best plan," she said, nodding to his nose and puffy eyes. Images of Cole flattening those men in India slid through her mind. "He . . . he doesn't understand. I don't even think he knows . . ."

"That's what ticks me off most," Levi said. "Any guy with eyes—actually, every guy here—can see it."

Guilt churned like thick yogurt through her veins. So everyone here knew she had feelings for Cole. Great. She must look so unprofessional and just plain stupid.

"I'd give my right arm to have you look at me like that."

His words stabbed her conscience, especially since there had been a day she *had* looked at him that way. But the more time she spent with him, the more he felt like a brother.

He shifted, hooking an arm over his leg. "Why? Why on earth do you care about him so much? He abandoned you and your family when your sister married the president, right?"

She snickered. "Galen wasn't the president then."

"What was it about him that made you believe in him so wholly, so much that you'd dedicate your career to clearing him when all evidence points to his guilt?"

"But it doesn't," Kasey said, vehemence the bedrock of her words. "If you saw the documents I managed to get hold of, it's clear he wasn't responsible, not entirely. Facts were redacted. That report had so many blacked-out lines—"

"You're doing it again."

"What?"

"Defending him."

"You don't understand—"

"You're right. I don't." He angled toward her. "Kase, he's everything we fight, everything we as agents work to subdue and restrain."

"Everything we fight? Are you kidding me?" Disappointment tugged at the corners of her heart. "You really need to stop looking at this as us against him. We're working *with* him, and it has to be that way if we're going to stop this threat."

"I didn't mean it like that." He studied the rug beneath them, his dark, strong brow knotted. At this angle, wisps of gray were barely evident in the dying light of the day. "You told me once you didn't want to be like your mom. Isn't that where you're headed, chasing after Russell?"

Breath stolen by the accusation, Kasey drew up straight. "This is light-years from my parents' situation."

"How?"

"My father was a hard man, unforgiving and—" The word *driven* dangled on the tip of her tongue but she knew it would only fuel Levi's stance. But as she scrambled for the right word to describe her father's character, Kasey had the unsettling feeling that maybe her father and Cole were more alike than she'd realized. "My father was cruel. Cole isn't."

"I think your father was just trying to look out for his daughter."

"Maybe." She shrugged. "You asked why I believe in him?" Her heart jostled in her chest, irritated with his tone and cutting comments. "I saw *him*. I saw how he remained honorable and true to his word when my sister was so horrible to him. And during the trial . . ." It surprised her how much the memory of his trial still wounded her. "It frustrates me that you and others can't see what I see in him."

"But that's my point. What if you only see what *you* want to see?"

So she was just imagining Cole's honor? "You're wrong. You don't know all the things he did for me when he didn't have to. When I was twelve, Cole took up a fight with a bully for me. He cared."

"And now he doesn't care, and that's ripping your heart out." Levi sighed. "I can't take much more of watching it happen."

Cole propped up a wall near the door, his arms folded. Tzivia to his left, both staying separate from the rest of the team that gathered on the floor and dug into the food and tea.

The fifty-something Mr. Tzaddik entered, talking with Dr. Cathey as they made their way into the sitting area. Dr. Cathey pulled a book free and moved to a quiet corner as Cole's men made room for Mr. Tzaddik. He had a strong presence and seemed to know it. Broad-shouldered, tall as Cole, he moved with confidence and assuredness. His dark hair was lightly streaked with gray around the temples, and he reminded her of old movie stars like Sean Connery and Gregory Peck.

"You have come about the Codex." Mr. Tzaddik captured the attention of the team, silencing them as he glanced at Cole. It was weird, but Kasey felt there was some unspoken war between the two.

"Rebbe Sokolov suggested we speak to you," Ram said from Mr. Tzaddik's left.

"Ah, Natan." Mr. Tzaddik smiled. "A good man."

"He said we should read Tiberius's Writings." The planes of Cole's face had gone hard.

Chiji edged closer, his demeanor serene. Cole shook his head, as if knowing his friend wanted to calm him.

Mr. Tzaddik shifted, his smile slipping for a second. "Writings . . ." He gave a breathy laugh before wagging his head and stealing his gaze away. "That Natan . . ."

"There a problem?" Hands on his belt, Cole was ready to face off.

Something spirited through Mr. Tzaddik's expression that made Kasey draw back. He and Cole were like two negative sides of a battery touching. They repelled each other.

A compulsion to salvage the situation pushed her into the conversation. "Do you know anything that might assist us, Mr. Tzaddik? We are trying to stop a deadly plague."

"My dear—aren't most plagues deadly?"

"Not all, but with this one"—Tzivia nodded from her post beside Cole—"victims die within thirty-six hours. Our timeline is short."

"Then let's stop wasting time."

Cole came off the wall, apparently upset at the implication that this was his doing.

"Ndidi," Chiji rumbled, touching his arm.

Cole wrangled free. "No." He turned to Tzaddik.

"I am not your enemy, Cole Russell."

As if someone had pushed a button, the tension in the room went nuclear. Team members grew rigid. Cole roiled in fight-readiness mode. Kasey's own heart pounded as she realized why—when had Tzaddik learned Cole's name?

Laughter seeped through the air. "You think I am not aware when a black ops team comes to me?" Mr. Tzaddik chuckled. "Your friend Mr. Khalon will verify there is little I do not know. Even less I cannot find out."

"Why don't you start with why your name was in the journal of a man who stole a censer implicated in unleashing a plague—the same one that killed him?"

"Bhavin?" Tzaddik wasn't ruffled and waved a hand. "Bhavin contacted me about these artifacts. I gave him information."

"Who are you that you have information on what he found and on our identities?" Cole asked, his tone measured. The real question wasn't Mr. Tzaddik's name. It was who he could be that he'd have access to classified information. That he could reach into cyberspace and extract whatever data he wanted or needed.

"Why, Mr. Russell, I am Ti Tzaddik." Chuckling, he waved and stood. "Relax, relax. You have come to the right place. As I said, I am not your enemy."

"Neither are you a friend," Cole countered.

Rustling fabric and squeaks of boots against the floor riffled the air, amplifying the fact that nobody was speaking. Ram said nothing, his posture one of contrition. The others were inching closer to Cole, clearly not pleased with the power grab by Mr. Tzaddik.

Shaking his head as he let out a long sigh, Mr. Tzaddik crossed the room. "I would've preferred, Mr. Russell, that you had said our friendship remains to be seen. In fact, I could even ask, how can I know to trust *you*? In truth, what do you know about *me*? Nothing. I risk much by even having Christians in my home here."

Whispers skittered around the room as he reached for a door and opened it. "But as I realize these are perilous and uncertain times, even friends can be enemies, can they not?"

"An enemy of my enemy is my friend," Cole muttered.

Mr. Tzaddik shrugged as he stepped sideways into the closet, reached up behind a steel pole that held several jackets, and pulled down. *Click!* "Let's get on with things, shall we?"

Cole closed in behind him. "How *do* you know to trust us?"

Mr. Tzaddik turned, something wild and unpredictable in his brown eyes as he smiled. But even his smile wasn't friendly—it was primal, like a dog sniffing out an untrustworthy person. "I *know*."

Tinkling of fluorescents preceded a progressive blooming of light, as row after row of long bulbs sprang to life. Bewildered, Kasey tried to make sense of the revealed room and how there was so much space in such a compact home. They must have built a small bunker into the side of the hill. To enter the hidden compartment, the men had to bend down. Even Kasey felt the doorpost brush her hair as she ducked in. The area was surprisingly lavish. Couch, recliners, and a long table with a half-dozen chairs around it. Green reading lamps cast a warm glow over the rich, dark wood. It felt oddly European.

"My weakness," Mr. Tzaddik admitted with a bashful grin as he crossed the thick Oriental rug to a well-worn armchair. He sat with a satisfied moan. "Nothing like it. Now." He pointed to a shelf lining the far wall. "The books. Bring them."

Cole glanced at him. "There's more than one?"

Mr. Tzaddik laughed. "They span centuries, Mr. Russell. Think such histories could be recorded in a single book?" He smiled, mischief in his eyes. "Pick one."

Annoyance rippled through Cole's stony expression. Locked in a visual duel with Mr. Tzaddik, he reached to the side—without looking—and tugged a book free. He tossed it on the table with a sigh then flipped it open.

Curiosity lured Kasey closer to Cole, who stood over the splayed book. "Tiberius wrote all these?"

Mr. Tzaddik's laugh was almost mocking. "That would make him immortal, wouldn't it?"

"He copied them, then," Tzivia said, browsing the collection, plucking out a book, riffling the pages, then replacing it.

"It is said," Mr. Tzaddik spoke softly, "that he collected them, borrowed some, wrote them by hand into"—he motioned toward the bookshelves—"what you see there."

"Museum-quality lights and tables," Tzivia murmured to Cole, whose gaze slid to a corner where a large, industrial-grade light table devoured space. "What is he hiding?"

"Nothing. Everything." Mr. Tzaddik's tone made it clear he enjoyed their confusion. Capitalized on it. "You are wise to suspect everyone, to not trust easily. The path you tread is filled with rogues, villains, distractions, dangers, and antiheroes."

"How do you have all these?"

"I've been collecting them my entire life." Mr. Tzaddik laughed. "It feels like centuries."

Cole tugged another book off the shelf and shrugged open the cover, which thudded noisily, followed more quietly by the crackling rustle of heavy paper. Not parchment. "What am I looking for?"

"The truth," Mr. Tzaddik said.

Kasey scanned the shelves and dusty stacks of history. "Which one should we start with?"

"Ah, a woman who knows what to ask." Mr. Tzaddik raised his chin, devilry crouching at the edges of his crow's-feet.

Kasey turned to him, drawn by his apparent delight, knowing to get the answers they wanted, they'd have to play his game. "Where would you suggest?"

Behind a smile and steepled fingers, he motioned toward the middle shelf. "The large one, bound in scarlet."

Using both hands to heft the bound pages onto the table, Kasey moved to the chair by his feet and sat. The massive volume consumed her lap, the weight nearly numbing her legs. With care and respect, she opened it. Breath stolen by the archaic script—Latin—she hesitated. Glanced at Mr. Tzaddik, who gave another solemn nod. Had he known she could read Latin? Quiet trepidation sailed through her as she scanned pages that had blurred ever so slightly with age. She read to herself.

"So the others may hear, please." Mr. Tzaddik leaned back, hands still steepled, and closed his eyes.

"Oh." Kasey skirted a look around the room, then took a breath and began aloud:

> "In the year of (Our) Lord's incarnation 1215. I, Thefarie of Tveria, have determined, for the greater glory of God and the protection and safety of the Order—"

"What Order?"

Mr. Tzaddik glared at Cole, then again indicated for Kasey to continue. Surprised at the way he silenced Cole, Kasey hunched over the tome and slid her finger across the words until she found where she'd stopped.

"'safety of the Order, the Brethren—'"

"Brethren."

"In earnest, Mr. Russell," Mr. Tzaddik hissed, "if you are not interested in hearing the words, the door awaits your hasty exit."

"The Templar Knights referred to each other as brethren," Ram put in softly. "Or brother-knight."

"Yes, fine." Mr. Tzaddik growled. "Thefarie was a Knight. The date and wording of the text make that obvious, do they not?" He rolled his eyes. "Must you have everything hand fed to you?" He huffed and shook his head, as if trying to shed their ignorance as well. "Please, Mrs. Cortes."

The way he'd somehow planted her between himself and the team made her uncomfortable. But there had to be a point to reading this, and he hadn't yet lied to them as far as she could tell, so Kasey lowered her gaze to the page once more.

> " . . . and the statutes that I put to parchment these words and accounts. Be it known to all, both present and to come, that with the failure of my strength on account of extreme age and poverty being well considered, I relate the events to follow. I commit to their wisdom these accounts of which I, Thefarie, have given witness to or have received a true and accurate account through writings or oral recitation by those with knowledge impossible to refute. For the protection and preservation of significant treasures, the Lord's holy knight repairs to the cold isolation of his room day and night in the bosom of this cruel winter to secure these facts to parchment."

"Sir," Cole spoke, his voice contrite but edged in frustration. "I appreciate the history lesson—"

"Do you?" Challenge sparked in Mr. Tzaddik's brown eyes.

"I do," Cole said firmly. "But we're dealing with the Black Death." He motioned to the book on Kasey's lap. "As was Thefarie."

When Chiji gave Cole a look, he hesitated. Then his blue irises washed over Kasey and the book. A fraction of the tension in his posture leaked out, and she could only guess he shared her thoughts—there was a point yet to be revealed. He dragged a chair from the table to where he stood and straddled it. His message clear: *I'm listening.*

"Mrs. Cortes," Mr. Tzaddik said.

Kasey twitched at her name and refocused on the book. "'I, Thefarie, have in my possession the parchment detailing the events from the year of Our Lord's incarnation 90 AD. No name is—'"

"Yes, yes." This time, Mr. Tzaddik interrupted. "Skip ahead, please." He stared at the leather-bound book, his gaze seeming to drift somewhere besides the letterings. "In fact . . ." He again fell silent, his eyes narrowing. With a wide swipe of his arm, he grunted and looked to Tzivia. "Miss Khalon." He jabbed a finger toward the shelves again. "Second book, third shelf, please."

Tzivia frowned but did as instructed, retrieving another volume. With annoyance, she delivered it to Kasey.

Mr. Tzaddik smiled at her. "If you please, Mrs. Cortes." Another toothy smile, this time to the others. "I like her voice. It's soothing."

Heat flashed through her face as Kasey opened the book of bound parchments. She cleared her throat and glanced at the text. "Oh. More Latin." Translating it under pressure was exhausting!

"Of course. Please—read."

"Wait. You know Latin?" Cell squeaked.

Kasey shrugged. "Expensive private schools specialize in teaching torturous languages to their students." She wet her lips and looked at Tzaddik, again wondering how he'd known she could read Latin. "Where should I start?"

"At the beginning, I would think."

"Tzaddik, you do understand we're under a deadline, right?" Cole's agitation was back.

"Do you, Mr. Russell? Interruptions cost time. Are you now ready to let the beautiful Mrs. Cortes read?"

Cole stretched his jaw and tucked his chin.

Recognizing the embers of Cole's anger, Kasey read to fill the silent void.

* * * *

"In the year of (Our) Lord's incarnation 1099—"

"The Crusades," Tox muttered, his annoyance with this charade tempering slightly. He'd always had a stiff fascination with the Templars. He listened in rapt attention as Haven read an account of the slaughter in Jerusalem, one Thefarie apparently felt was brutal but justified.

"Ndidi," Chiji said, shifting on his feet, "something is wrong here."

"Tell me about it." Tzaddik both unsettled and drew Tox. It was like the man *wanted* to agitate them.

"Mrs. Cortes, please skip the next two pages."

Haven bounced a gaze to Tox, then back to Tzaddik.

"Second paragraph," Tzaddik further instructed.

She pointed to the indicated section.

"'Encamped in the Holy City, the Brethren attempt to secure the Holy Land for all pilgrims who would journey to the city of our Lord. The decision to hold the Crown and other holy works for ransom angered the Karaites. But it was against these very people that the Crown was removed and held for ransom.'"

"The Crown," Tzivia shifted forward, her hand resting on the back of Tox's chair. "Thefarie writes of the Codex?"

Tzaddik smirked but never looked at them. "Go on, Mrs. Cortes."

"Once more I encountered the Saracen, Ziryan al-Karzan, the bloodiest of them all, who has set himself against our Brethren. He and rogue militia attempted to retrieve the Crown from our possession. In a tense confrontation, Ziryan failed to achieve victory. But his warfare and tenacity have left us with no choice but to remove the Crown from the city."

"Please." Tox couldn't take any more. Time was falling off the clock and people were dying. Maybe even Evie, and he was sitting here listening to history lessons? "If there is a point to this . . ."

"Do you wish to learn from history?"

"I do." Tox worked to tame his frustration that was quickly fanning into anger. "But I don't want to *become* history learning from it."

"Would you prefer to sift through these volumes yourself"—Tzaddik wagged his eyes toward the wall of shelves—"over the next few months?"

Son of a gun.

"Or will you listen to passages I know to be beneficial to your purpose?"

Tox resented the guy turning this on him. "I'd prefer you just tell us what you know. I'm glad to read your collection. In fact"—his need to do something pushed him to his feet—"it'd be an honor. But right now, thousands of lives are at stake. My niece is dying in a hospital, and all I want is to stop the AFO and this plague."

Tzaddik met him.

Fire and rage surged through Tox. Chiji was at his side along with a klaxon warning to stand down. "I thought you were going to help us."

Tzaddik pivoted. Strode from the room.

"Wait." Haven shoved to her feet, tossing the bound parchments at Tox, and hurried after him. "Please wait, Mr. Tzaddik."

"His anger controls him," Tzaddik's voice drifted back into the room. "I will not be a part of that."

The words were painfully true, and Tox balled a fist, then felt it a glaring confirmation of Tzaddik's words.

"I understand," Haven said, her voice soft. Soothing, just as Tzaddik had said earlier. "Cole—all of us—we're just really worried about this plague."

Quiet ruled for several long minutes, then Haven returned, her shoulders sagging. "Sorry. He's . . ." Her gaze hit the book, green eyes twitching. She scowled, peering closer. Attentive.

Tox glanced at the volume, the lettering that might as well be Greek. "What?"

Haven hurried closer. Tucked her blond hair behind her ear. "' . . . an arrow with a faint glow . . . '"

"Dude. Seriously?" Cell popped up next to them. "Read it."

"You see now why I would have you read it?"

Tox shot a look over his shoulder to Tzaddik. "If you knew this was in here—"

"Read it, Mrs. Cortes."

Man, he hated the way this guy lorded his knowledge over them. But curiosity was stronger than his need for defiance. Tox shifted the book on the table and leaned over it. Tzivia was at his right as he scanned the words.

Haven began reading.

" . . . our latest battle with the Saracens has brought us against a formidable foe. An organization so deeply embedded in the fabric of kingdoms across the world that I fear ever driving them from their positions of power and influence. Their signature is an arrow whose shaft is laced with phosphorus. Our Brethren, those not hideously murdered by these glowing arrows, were so startled by the faint glow that preceded the boiling death—"

Someone cursed.

"But phosphorus wasn't discovered until the 1600s," Maangi said, knuckling the table as he glanced over Tox's shoulder to see the text. When the others looked at him, he bounced his shoulders. "What? I know chemistry."

Tox flipped back a page, looking for a date notation. Again, surprise speared him.

"Holy cow," Cell said. "It's dated 1680."

"Who wrote it?" Ram asked.

"It's in the same handwriting." Tox double-checked it against several pages to verify what he'd noticed. "That doesn't make sense. Thefarie was a Templar, twelfth century."

"It is wrong," Chiji whispered, repeating his earlier words.

"Good point. How could Thefarie record events in 1099 and 1215, a hundred years apart?" Ram asked. "Then in 1680?"

"Perhaps the translation wasn't quite spot on," Tzaddik said, giving

Haven a condescending look. "And remember, these are said to be writings *Tiberius* collected."

"You said some were collected, some were his own."

"Yes, but it's not possible, is it, for him to live long enough to have witnessed both?" Tzaddik chuckled, but it wasn't incredulity. It was . . . amusement.

"And the phosphorus," Maangi said.

"Ah, very good." More of that amusement. "So this would mean that either phosphorus was discovered far earlier than expected—"

"Unlikely," Maangi put in.

"—or somehow Thefarie managed to defy time and live a very long life."

"Four centuries?" Tox laughed. "Impossible."

Tzaddik shrugged. "Then it is a mystery."

"Perhaps Tiberius forgot to attribute some of the writings to the real author," Haven said.

Tox stared at the script that seemed to have a poetry to its styling. All in the same hand. "So this Tiberius transcribed Thefarie's collection and messed up."

Tzaddik pursed his lips. "That's most likely, isn't it?"

"The point"—Tox tapped the text—"is that this isn't a coincidence. The Codex, the AFO. I mean, to have both mentioned—the arrow and the Order—back in Byzantine times and to have both surface and invade our lives . . . it's too coincidental."

"Without a doubt." Tzaddik finally seemed pleased. "Are you familiar with the verse about not adding to the Bible?"

"Deuteronomy 4:2," Chiji offered. "'It is written: *Do not add to what I command you and do not subtract from it, but keep the commands of the* LORD *your God that I give you.*'"

Tzaddik smiled. "And what would you say if I told you someone added to it? Added to the Codex?"

"That doesn't affect us, though. Right?" Tox looked around the room. "I mean, isn't there a curse against whoever adds or subtracts?"

"Yes," Ram said quietly, his expression contemplative. Stern. "But if they can prove the Codex has been added to, then it will be deemed corrupt."

Tzivia folded her arms with a sigh. "And that means it's fallible."

"Which, in turn," Ram said, looking miserable, "could be the means to refute the entire Codex."

"Call into question the Bible itself." Tzivia lowered herself into a chair, head down. Though Tox half expected her to look exultant, she seemed as affected by the news as her brother.

"That's crazy," Cell said.

"It's reality." Though Tox struggled in his faith, tattered threads still bound his heart, thanks to Chiji. "But . . . really, how does this affect us now?" He hated that truth, but they had a plague to neutralize. An organization to shut down.

"The Arrow & Flame Order is a two-headed serpent," Tzaddik said. "It affects you because what you need to locate is also being hunted by the AFO—they will stop at nothing to destroy the already humbled credibility of the faith. To stop the plague, you must find the page from the Codex that speaks to that part of Deuteronomy and the censers. All four. They must be brought together."

Tzaddik rose to his feet, but there was something crazy about his presence that seemed to soak in the shadows and crevices of the room, filling every square inch. His face lit with challenge. "You must also confront the two heads: Iomhair Kaine and Nur Abidaoud."

"Wait." Tox held out a staying hand. "Abidaoud?" He glanced at Ram, then back to Tzaddik. "Any relation to Salih Abidaoud?"

"His brother, a black mark on the family. You know of Salih?"

"Tried to capture him."

"'Tried.'" Tzaddik grunted. "That's telling. The family is powerfully connected. Nur will be a greater challenge, especially if he knows you have been after his brother. But Kaine and Nur are as savage as they are ruthless. Neither should be approached unless you are prepared to face severe consequences."

Relieved to finally be on her way to see Evie, Kasey lay awake on the private jet ferrying her and Cole's team from Syria to England. As soon as they'd left Tzaddik's home, Cole had Cell and SAARC hammering away, tracking down the two heads of the serpent: Kaine and Abidaoud. While the latter proved elusive, Cell managed to get a ping off Kaine in London.

Though most of the team slept for the duration of the flight, Kasey only managed to grab two hours of sleep, stress over her niece's welfare and confronting the AFO keeping her awake.

She slipped out of the seat and headed to the lavatory at the rear. Finished, she emerged to a droning voice. She glanced back to the galley and saw Cole at the table, head in hand as he talked on a phone.

"Wheels down at 0900 . . . yeah . . . let me know what you find. Clearly, he's a tricky son of a gun. Such a high-ranking member, I wonder at finding Kaine so easily."

Kasey moved to the coffee percolating in the corner and quietly lifted the pot.

Cole lowered his hand, blue eyes sliding to her. He nodded, though he didn't speak. "Agreed." He scooted upright. "Will do. Keep me posted on Evie." Another silent nod. "Yep. Bye."

Kasey poured the coffee and added the creamer, noting it was barely warm. Cup in hand, she turned and propped her hip against the narrow counter. "Galen?"

Sighing, he set down the phone. "Yeah." He pushed out of the seat and came around the table, lifting a foam cup for himself.

It was crowded when they had a table separating them. Now that he stood next to her, she resisted the urge to ease back and give him room as he made coffee. "How's Evie?"

"They've induced a coma to slow the damage."

Kasey held the cup in front of her face, allowing the coffee-scented steam to spiral around her nostrils. "Is there a lot? Of damage." His presence was tangling her mind again. "I mean—those arrows *killed* people. How'd she survive?"

He leaned back against the counter, too. "Arrow wasn't phosphorus." He sipped his coffee.

She set down her drink. "What was it? Does that mean it's not the AFO?"

After a swig and swallow, he sighed. "They're not sure, but her organs are shutting down. They think the arrow had a virus. Maybe the head was coated with it."

"They injected her with the plague?"

He dumped back the rest of his coffee. Crumpled the cup and tossed it in the bin before folding his arms. "That's my guess. Might have gotten it from the censer Tanin stole."

It took everything in her not to cry again. She deflated beneath the news. "Why would they do that to a child?"

"Because of her father. Because of me." His shoulder lifted. "To make a point."

"Galen makes sense—he's a powerful president. But you?"

He smirked. "Thanks."

"That's not what I meant."

His smile was small but genuine. "I know." He rubbed the back of his neck. "They target those I know because I'm bringing the fight to them. I'm getting in the way. You saw the video—I'm not listening."

Two weeks ago, when their lives had reconnected, that comment might have been laced with arrogance or pride. But now she heard his exhaustion. The weariness that pushed against his shoulders.

"I'm sorry, Cole."

His eyes struck her. Rippled. "Why do you always say that?"

Kasey shrugged and pursed her lips. "I guess because I see how this affects you." She tried to measure his response, but there wasn't one. "You're a warrior, always have been. You do what nobody else wants to do, and yeah—things that affect most of us roll off like water." Still no reaction, flinch, or change in his expression. "But behind that wall of granite is a really great guy who often gets a very short stick." More staring. Maybe some softening. Or was that her imagination?

"I don't get you."

Kasey tilted her head. "What does that mean?"

"You've got Superman there fawning over your every move, but you're talking to me."

Pumping Nutella through her veins would've been easier than trying to get her heart to work right. In her line of work, what a person didn't say was as important, sometimes more, than what they did say. And she heard in the empty space between his words that he knew she had feelings for him.

"Haven, there's a reason I'm who I am. There's a reason I'm alone." He snorted. "Brooke knew what she was doing dumping me."

Kasey scowled.

"I'm no good for you, Haven. You're too sweet. Too good for me."

"I think that's my decision."

Cole watched her for several long seconds. It seemed he stood braced against his own will. As if he was afraid to move.

Why would he be afraid to move? "I scare you."

He snorted again. Shook his head, then nodded. "Maybe. Yeah . . ." He nodded, stronger this time. "Okay, yeah. You do. But mostly because I refuse to screw up your life. No matter what I think about you, I'm not willing to go there, to risk that."

Her heart thrashed against her ribs now, demanding freedom. *No matter what he thought about her?* So he had thought of her. And clearly thought of her in a romantic way. He'd have to do that to decide he couldn't mess up her life, right? But he had it wrong. "That's what a relationship is all about. It's not about guarantees. It's about risks. About a willingness to test those waters."

"I've tested them before. And I end up evaporating them and leaving a desert in its place."

"You're too hard on yourself."

"No." Cole pulled himself off the counter and started around her. "I'm not hard enough. People have gotten hurt. I won't do that to you."

She stepped into his path. Before she could think it through, her hand rested on his stomach. His muscles contracted beneath her fingers, then froze. Surprised at her own actions, she hesitated, then peered up into his bright eyes and suddenly felt herself swimming. "So I'm not worth the risk of finding out you have better in you than you think?"

Cole's gaze traced her eyes, her nose, her mouth. Was he seeing the bruises, the remnants of being beaten? When he bent closer, his intensity squeezed her breath. "I made a promise."

"To whom?"

His knuckles swept her jaw, and Kasey's pulse shuddered. She leaned into his touch and took a breath, one laced with fire and hope.

He shook his head but didn't pull away. "Haven . . ." His warm, strong fingers teased her neck as they slid to her nape. Heat washed over her shoulders and spilled down her stomach then flared across her back.

When his gaze dipped to her lips, Kasey was afraid to move. Afraid to speak. Afraid he'd pull away. That the moment would slam shut. Even as she willed herself not to mess this up, he angled in. His breath slid across her cheek, warm. *Please* . . . The past fell away and her dreams rushed to the front.

He looked at her, his eyelids hooded with desire. Haven tilted her head to receive his kiss. So ready. Finally.

Turbulence pitched him sideways. Bracing himself against the hull, Cole blinked.

Cold wind blasted between them.

"Gettin' kinda hot in here, ain't it?" Cell stalked around them. "Might need something to cool off before we hit London."

Cole glanced at her, his expression inscrutable. He rubbed his forehead. Shifted and tapped the wall before looking at Cell. "Any closer to finding Abidaoud?"

Three signs of deception. He'd just given her three, one right after the other. He wasn't lying to his friend. He was lying to himself.

Tsssk! Soda can open, Cell guzzled. Thumped his chest and belched.

Cole was taking his out. She knew him well enough to know that with the moment broken, he would act is if nothing had happened. She slipped into the aisle. Hand on the dividing wall, she stole one more glance.

His back was to her now.

Pain scorched as she returned to the leather chair and lowered herself into it. She felt Levi's gaze from across the aisle and turned to the portal window, escaping conversation and pity. Sunlight reflected off the clouds, nearly blinding her. Should she cry that the moment had been lost? Or exult that she saw in Cole's eyes the same desire that had churned through her breast all these long years?

* * * *

What was wrong with him? Tox didn't dare leave the galley. Phone on the table, he cradled his head in his hands, staring down at the device. *Idiot.*

He didn't care what Haven awoke in him, he would not go there. Would not destroy her life, too. And if he caved to the attraction, that was what would happen.

"So I'm not worth the risk . . . ?"

She was worth it. And so much more. Which was why he had to say no. Because he knew himself. Knew he was a complete screw-up when it came to relationships. To people. He knew how to run a team, but that was where his social skills stopped.

"What's going on?"

Tox lowered his hands to the table but didn't look up at Ram. He dropped back, feigning depression. "Evie's getting worse."

Ram didn't move. Didn't speak.

"Wasn't phosphorous in the arrow." Tox picked up his phone and pushed from the table. "She might have been infected with the plague."

344

Ram watched him leave but didn't respond.

Tox hadn't fooled him and didn't care. He wasn't going to explain himself. Wouldn't confess his idiocy. Better to just leave it behind. Bury it.

When he stepped out of the galley, something flew through the air. Tox caught it, his brain instantly registering the kali stick his fingers had wrapped around. Dark eyes challenged him. Tox hefted the stick and welcomed the second one Chiji tossed. Enough room existed between the seats and the galley for a decent workout. Might be tight. That'd just make him focus harder. Get his mind off her.

He nodded to Chiji. And swung into the rhythm of stick-fighting drills.

Chiji pushed him hard. In fact, he was unrelenting. The strikes came faster. Harder. Stronger. Though Tox considered himself advanced, his Nigerian friend was the master, the expert.

Tox moved quickly, startled when one stung the air near his ear. Rattled at the aggression, he worked to stay alert. The team gathered, clapping out a fast beat as he and Chiji drilled.

Thwap! Tox's forearm stung. He shot a shocked look to Chiji, who merely gave an acknowledging nod. "What was that?"

Punishment. For crossing a line with Haven, no doubt. Chiji was showing big-brother instincts when it came to her.

The intercom from the captain crackled out the announcement that they were making their descent into London.

"You should buckle in," Chiji said, taking back the sticks. Not a bead of sweat on his dark brow.

Levi Wallace approached. "So you *can* be beaten?"

Tox snorted and shook his head, glancing at the angry knot forming on his arm. Even after they'd landed and made it to the safe house, the arm still ached. Not that anyone would feel sorry for him, including him. In fact, he slowly grew grateful for the painful reminder.

Their safe house was a two-story house on the outskirts of London that provided anonymity and enough space for him to avoid Haven. The team had gone in various directions, chasing leads and opportunities.

Tox clapped a hand on Cell's shoulder. "Find anything on Abidaoud?"

"Only tracks after he left someplace. This is one tough guy to find."

"What about Kaine? Still here?"

Cell cocked his head. "Not a hundred percent guaranteed but very likely. His trail is hidden, though not as well as Abidaoud's."

Tox nodded, hoping it wasn't too convenient that they'd found Kaine, that they weren't stepping into a trap. He glanced at an image on Cell's monitor. "That him?" Fifty-something. Thick head of graying hair. A bit thick through the waist, but not too much. Evidence that he was comfortable enough in his life, in his power, to get a little sloppy with his health. Maybe he was sloppy elsewhere, too.

"Cole?"

He felt Haven's voice rush up his spine and coil around his brain. "Yeah?" He kept his gaze on the monitors, studying Kaine.

"I'd like to go see Evie."

Family entanglements. That meant he'd likely have a run-in with his brother. "I'm not sure that's a good idea."

"I talked with Galen," she said, sounding closer. "He asked me to come. But that you had to bring me."

Tox turned at that. "Why?"

Haven looked down. Swallowed. Met his gaze, her eyes swimming in pain. "They're . . ." She bit her lower lip. "She's not doing well."

Revelation crashed in on him and his defenses vanished. "She's dying."

Her chin dimpled with repressed tears. She nodded.

"But I promised her . . ."

"Promised who?"

"Brooke." He ran a hand over his head. His mind buzzed at the thought of his niece dying. Suffering because her father and uncle pitted themselves against a brutal organization bent on making the world pay for its sins.

"When did you do that?"

"Do what?"

"Promise Brooke you'd watch after Evie."

He didn't have time for that conversation. Ever. "Grab your things." He turned to Cell, relieved when Haven hurried to get whatever she needed. "Should be back in an hour."

Cell nodded, monitoring the data. He pointed to a laptop. "Message from Ram—he wants you to swing by the professor's place."

"Roger," Tox said. "Keep hunting down Abidaoud."

"Uh, aren't we worried about getting bombed again?"

"Every day. But if we stop? They win. We're not going to stop." Tox patted his shoulder. "Besides, you know how *not* to get caught, right?"

"Copy that."

Tox and Haven made the drive to the hospital in silence, his mind hopping from their visit with Tzaddik to the mission ahead—finding Abidaoud and Kaine while Dr. Cathey and Tzivia searched for the missing censers, but it invariably landed on the incident on the plane. Which ticked him off. He didn't need distraction.

Was there time to save Evie, even if they found a cure?

"I shouldn't be doing this." Only when Haven looked at him did he realize he'd spoken aloud. "She thinks I'm dead."

"A certain text of yours changed that."

He smirked, remembering the pseudo-threatening message he'd sent more as a warning to Galen. He'd never hurt Evie. "Forgot about that. Just don't want things to be awkward or weird." But not being in her life since her birth sort of wrecked that.

"Relax," Haven whispered. "She's in a coma, remember? She probably won't know you're there."

Like most of her life.

"Hey." Haven touched his arm. "What's wrong?"

"She found out I was alive two weeks ago, and now she's fighting for her life." Why was that bothering him so much now? It was better for her safety. Tox stretched his jaw as he navigated a roundabout. "If she's not conscious, why are we going to see her?"

"Scientists believe the unconscious can hear us, but even if that weren't true, it's for us, Cole."

He glanced at her.

"Tell me it won't help you to see she's still alive."

"What I'll see is a twelve-year-old fighting for her life because of me."

"No, she's fighting for her life because of the AFO." She braced as they turned a corner. "Besides—as you said—you promised Brooke."

Man, she was good, bringing that up again. "Cheap shot."

"Only if it doesn't work."

He gritted his teeth and spotted the sign for the hospital. As he drove down the street, eyeing the multistoried building, he realized what a perfect death alley the street formed. He scanned rooftops. Perfect for snipers or those with phosphorus arrows. Just like in Israel.

Made sense. Target his brother's daughter. Wait for them to show up. Pick them off. With the way the AFO was connected, they would also escape without notice.

A light touch to his arm gave him a start. He glanced at Haven.

"You're rubbing the wheel," she said, nodding to his hand where he flexed his wrist up and back, over and over as the car glided beneath trees and between cars parked along the curb. "Worried?"

"Always." Tox slid past the hospital, not comfortable with the parking arrangements. As bad as climbing stairs. They'd be fish in a barrel.

"You passed it."

He whipped the wheel to the left and swung around into the emergency entrance beneath the portico. "Wait." Out of the car, he hustled around, scanning the area, rooftops, other cars as he opened the passenger door. He pressed close. Not because he wanted to, but because he wasn't going to give them a clear shot at her. "Okay, quickly."

Haven stepped out. He wrapped an arm around her waist. "Stay close. Walk fast."

"You're terrifying me."

Tox ushered her through the sliding doors of the emergency entrance. Inside, he kept Haven snugged against his side, hurrying into the main portion of the hospital. He called Galen. "We're in the ER. How do we get to you?"

"I'll send a security detail down."

With his back to a wall, Tox turned Haven toward him.

"Did you see something?" Her voice grew husky in anticipation of danger.

"You rarely see it coming." He managed a half smile. "I think we're okay."

"No, you don't."

Tox met her gaze, surprised that laughter hid in her words, yet there was no mirth in her face.

She swallowed. "I see it all over your face. Your body language."

He kept forgetting she was a deception expert. "Always anticipate danger. Stay alert and you have a better chance of staying alive."

"But you went on edge when we drove down the street."

"It was a well—perfect vantage on both sides for snipers, no easy egress. Perfect for Tanin to set up on a rooftop and pick us off."

Haven processed the words. Slowly nodded.

Two suits emerged through a small door. One of them peeled off toward the entrance and Tox's car.

"C'mon." Hand on her shoulder, Tox guided her toward the other Secret Service agent. He wanted out of that waiting area and out of sight. They were ushered to a deserted third-floor wing run by a limited staff. It was creepy. Like something out of a horror movie, with the silence broken by hissing machines. At the far end, his brother turned at the sound of their footsteps.

Haven rushed forward and hugged Galen. Something about that twisted Tox into knots. Wouldn't be the first girl Galen had stolen.

Of course, she'd have to be Tox's to be stolen. And she wasn't.

"I'm glad you came," Galen said, hugging her.

"Me too." Haven stepped back and indicated the glass wall separating them from Evie. "She looks so pale."

Tox moved to the wall. His niece had gotten big. And yet she also looked so fragile lying there, machines and tubes threading in and out of her body.

"How's she doing?" Haven asked.

"With the induced coma, they slowed the progress of the disease."

Tox couldn't help but think of all the doctors and scientists working night and day to stop the spread of the New Black Death. "Any word on an antidote from India?"

"Benowitz said they're getting close—thanks to the blood of that archaeologist." Grief weighted Galen's voice and shoulders.

He heard what his brother wasn't saying. *Close* might not be good enough. Tox looked at Galen, really seeing him for the first time in decades. He had more gray than Tox had realized. A little heavier, but maybe that was just maturity. He was the spitting image of their father, the disapproving, grave man who'd shaped Tox into the rebel he was. Worry lines had carved into Galen's brow after years of being a single father while he ran a country. Without his wife. Without Brooke. How would Brooke handle this, seeing her daughter at death's door? She'd shriek at them both for putting Evie in the hospital.

His mind slid into the past. *Blood gurgling in her throat. Shock bulging her brown eyes. "Promise me . . ."*

Strangling a cry, Tox nodded as he cradled her broken body in his arms. "Anything." Sticky warmth slid through his fingers. Blood. Her blood.

"Watch"—she coughed, red-tinged spittle hitting him—"Protect Evie and . . . Haven."

"I . . . shh. You'll be fine." He couldn't do what she asked. This mission, his actions, dictated his isolation for the rest of his life. But he'd do whatever she wanted if—"Just fight, Brooke. Live!"

"Promise," she demanded, blood bubbling in the corners of her mouth.

"Okay." No, he couldn't release her. "Yes. I promise."

"Cole?" the soft soothing voice and touch called him back to the present.

Broken all over again, he steeled himself as Haven's presence saturated his awareness. She nodded behind him. He gritted his teeth when he saw Barry Attaway coming down the semi-darkened hall.

"Can we talk?" Attaway asked, piercing Tox with a glare.

Bring it, old man. "I'm here for my niece. Then I have to hunt down the dogs who did this to her."

"Yeah, about that . . ." Barry bobbed his head to the side then started walking away.

"I—"

Haven joined him. "Maybe he knows where Abidaoud is."

Tox's fingers curled in. He clenched his fists and conceded the point.

"You don't have to like him to get information," Haven whispered, making him turn from his anger to her. "We have to save Evie. He might have the key."

His gaze flipped to the private hospital room that held his niece, and

350

he nodded. Focused on the empty hallway. Which room? To the right, three rooms up, a door stood open. Tox headed there and checked around the corner.

"We don't have much time," Attaway said.

Tox stepped into the hospital room full of bare beds and curtains flung back. Blinds shut. A black feed dome hung from a corner tile. Not live. "Time for what? Shouldn't you be holding down the fort back home?"

"We were scheduled for a diplomatic trip anyway. Just came a few days early. Besides, I'd think you'd be grateful I could manage things here while your brother worries over your niece."

No way would he give this guy an inch in his life or mind. "You wanted to talk."

Hands stuffed in his suit pockets, Attaway huffed. "I have information."

Wasn't that obvious if he wanted to talk privately? What didn't he want the others to hear? Who was he trying to keep something from? Tox had learned long ago not to give anything away with words. Silence tended to make people uncomfortable, forced them to talk.

"Almstedt said you were heading out to find the members of the Arrow & Flame." Attaway's eyes narrowed slightly, as if he wanted Tox to react.

He didn't.

"I've had people digging into the AFO for years."

This should be telling. If he had people looking into them for years, shouldn't he know Abidaoud's location? "What put them on your radar so long ago?"

"Their fingerprints are on several major events—the bombing of the *Rosenberg*, the collapse of the metro lines two years ago. I even think they might've had a role in Kafr al-Ayn."

Interesting.

Barry shrugged. "Many other major events have been suggested by my task force. The AFO is not above catastrophic results, thousands dead. One might even say that's their signature. The bigger the impact, the more likely it's the AFO. They aren't about flash. Just the aftermath."

"To what end?"

"Power. They have key players in most every government."

"American?"

"Without a doubt." Attaway ran a hand through his thinning hair. "Just haven't figured out who. We're narrowing in."

"Good." AFO members who'd infiltrated the U.S. government needed to be burned at the stake before someone nuked the daylights out of his homeland.

"But like I said, my team has been digging for a while, so trust me when I say I'd be looking elsewhere."

Suspicion crowded Tox. "Like?"

"Naftali Regev."

Tox's phone buzzed and he extracted it from his pocket. Ram.

"Look into Regev," Barry said. "I might be wrong, but I'd wager that's where you need to start." He patted Tox's arm and swept past. "I'll catch you later."

Not if I can help it. He put the phone to his ear and pivoted, surprised to see Haven outside the room. "Ram." Thank goodness he had a reason not to talk to her. He wasn't good at staying within the lines of his own rules, especially when they were alone.

"Where are you?" Ram asked.

"Hospital."

"You need to get back here."

Tzivia wandered into a small room at the back of the farm estate outside London. "What's that?"

Dr. Cathey looked up, delight in his eyes. "When we were at Mr. Tzaddik's, I asked to read a journal. These are my notes."

Sliding into the chair beside him, she eyed the notes. One name caught her attention. "Thefarie. That name keeps coming up."

"Unusual, isn't it? Since we found that mark on the leaf and since Akiva mentioned it when I visited him, I asked Ti if I could look at his copy of the journal." He scattered the pages across the table. "It is as I thought—Thefarie searched for the censers during one outbreak. It took him decades, but he only found three."

"The three we found in the wooden chest! With the Templar cross on it."

"Yes, my belief also. But with only three . . ."

"He couldn't stop the plague."

"No."

"But why did he tear a page from the Codex? I thought he'd have respect for it rather than mark it up."

"I'm not sure he tore it from the Codex."

"Then how did it get there?"

Dr. Cathey pointed to a phrase he'd written.

Tzivia sucked in a breath. "'God knows.'" The words the Stranger had spoken to her before Kafr al-Ayn.

He smiled at her. "He wrote that when he wondered at the fourth miktereth's location."

"That's what Tzaddik said to me in France." Her brain cramped. "Who is he? Why was he there?"

"That's a question for later."

"Is it?"

"Yes. Plague first."

She scratched her forehead, frustrated. Confused. "But—but the fourth censer, the leaf was sealed to it by a red cord and wax with the Templar symbol. If Thefarie didn't do it . . . how'd it get there?"

With a long, frustrated sigh, Dr. Cathey groaned. "Oh, I have no answers for you there, my dear. We have more questions with each step we take." He nodded. "I fear I must speak with Akiva again."

"Why?"

"Something Thefarie wrote in his journals." He shook his head. "It is probably just the imaginings of an old man."

* * * *

Cole emerged from the darkened hospital room like a storm. "Let's go," he said, aiming for his brother. "Got a call. Time to head out."

Galen turned. Something flickered through his eyes that slowed Kasey, but she felt Cole's hand at the small of her back. "Tox—"

"Sorry." Cole nudged Kasey toward the elevators. "To save Evie, we need to get on this."

At those words, anger bubbled through Kasey. It was true, they had to work to find someone with answers to the disease, but leaving here, rushing out wasn't directly related to that.

"Security moved your car." Galen's words were clipped and loud.

Cole stopped. "Where?"

"In the garage." Galen nodded to a suit who stepped out of an elevator. "Mark will take you down."

Kasey removed herself from Cole's possession—for that was what it felt like—and hugged her brother-in-law. "Let me know if there's any change."

Galen lowered his head and whispered, "He's trouble, Haven. Don't let Tox bend your mind."

Heat climbed into her cheeks. She patted his arm then backed away. "Call if anything changes."

They made it down to the garage in two minutes and were pulling into the warm London afternoon within five. Cole navigated the streets like a pro.

"It was cruel to use Galen's concern for Evie to get us out of there," she chided.

"I wasn't using anything. It's true. We have work to do."

"Then you could've just said that."

Cole kept his eyes on the road, one hand hooked over the wheel, the other resting on the gear shift. "Why were you snooping on me and Attaway?"

Surprise tugged at her. "I wasn't—I mean, I didn't intend to snoop." She would not lie to him. "Galen asked for you, so I came to find you. Noticed Barry's posture. Saw the twitch in his face."

"It's his job to lie to people."

"That's a pretty cynical view." Yet he was probably right. "But he wanted you to know something, and I knew it had to be important because he pulled you away from Galen and me."

Cole eased up to a red light, his expression stony.

"What're you thinking?" she finally asked once they were under way again.

He opened his mouth. Froze.

Tires pealed as the car braked hard. *THUNK!*

"Get down!" His hand cuffed the back of her head then grabbed the gear shift.

He rammed it into first and nailed the gas.

Kasey bent away from the windows, her mind registering several things in that split second: someone was attacking them, an arrow had struck the hood of the car, and Cole hadn't flinched once.

"Here," Cole barked as he flung his phone at her, then worked the gearshift and whipped the car around to the right. "Call Ram."

The car veered right. Then left. Her head smacked the console. Right again. The glove box clipped her ear as Kasey worked his phone, trying to find the contacts. Last call—his last one had been from Ram. She pulled it up. "Number's blocked."

Cole rattled off a series of numbers, and she quickly entered them and hit the call icon.

Crack! Another three-sixty, and she was flung against her window. The phone flipped from her hand. Kasey hauled herself upright, reaching for the device, but it slid.

The car spun around. *Clunk-clunk-clunk!*

Kasey whimpered, trying to reach the phone and avoid having her head banged to a pulp. Her fingers grazed the edge of the device. She grunted and pushed forward, stretching. And caught it.

She lifted it. And saw a blur of black.

Cole cursed.

In a dizzying, terrifying instant, she saw the grill of a truck barreling toward her. Kasey screamed.

Metal and glass flung into a whirlwind. Crunching and groaning pervaded Tox's hearing. The world spun into a blur of silver and black. His head felt like someone had taken a hammer to it. With a deceptively soft rocking motion, the car stilled. The world fell out of warp.

Tox peered through the mostly crumpled windshield, surprised to find them right-side up.

Haven. He jerked toward where she sat limp. Her head dangling. "Haven." He reached for her. Panic ripped him a new one, seeing the blood on her temple. No. This couldn't happen. Not again. "Haven! Haven, you okay?"

She moaned, pulling upright. Blood streaked the side of her face, but she opened her eyes. Groaned. Touched her temple and cringed.

As an ounce of panic slipped away, he shuddered. "Anything broken?"

"I . . ." She stretched her back. Rolled her shoulders and grimaced. "No. No, I don't think so."

"We need to get out of here. Can you walk?"

"Yeah."

Through the windshield crushed nearly to the hood, movement

357

caught his attention. Cole snatched the handgun from the console where he'd stowed it and kicked out what was left of the door. He climbed into the open, weapon down and to the side, as he stared across the open field of a park at a bearded man in sunglasses, a Fedora, black pants, and a blue shirt coming toward them. Tox didn't trust him, but then, he wouldn't trust anyone right now.

"You okay?" the man asked.

"We're good." He motioned Haven out of the vehicle.

The man was still coming. "That was some cartwheel your car did. You sure you're okay?"

"We're fine. Stay back. I smell petrol," Tox lied, maneuvering to the other side. The passenger door was banged up. The window missing altogether. He tugged on the handle, but it broke off in his hand. Tox tucked the weapon in his belt, shooting a look to the still-advancing man—and used both hands to pry it open. The door groaned and creaked.

"I could help."

"He's trouble," Haven said, echoing his thoughts.

Tox spun and snapped his weapon up, immediately noticing the other man had reached behind himself. Sunlight struck the side of his face—and his mangled ear. Tanin.

Tox fired.

Tanin dove into the brush as Tox fired off another round, reaching back to Haven and guiding her out of the vehicle.

A firm but gentle touch to his sides told Tox she was behind him.

"Phone." Haven bent toward the car.

"Wait. No—"

A shot pinged off the car. Tox pushed to the side so she could use the car door for cover. He squeezed the trigger, never taking his eyes off the field. He didn't have a clear line of sight, but he couldn't afford to ease off.

"Go go go!" Tox hissed to Haven, motioning her away. "Buildings—!" He hustled backward, taking shots. Watching as Tanin low-crawled away from them along the rolling incline, probably jockeying for better position.

Each time he saw a patch of blue, Tox fired. Over his shoulder, he instructed Haven not to stop. He backstepped toward the sound of her steps, then fired off two more rounds. When he could no longer see Tanin, he considered making a clean run for it. But Tanin was probably waiting for that.

Gauging the distance, Tox spotted Haven vanishing behind a half wall. Good. But where was Tanin? Either way, this wasn't Hollywood—he didn't have an endless supply of bullets. He had to get to cover. About to pitch himself toward the building, Tox spotted him.

His heart slowed, the moment frozen as Tanin emerged from between two trees with a rifle. Sniper rifle. Where had he gotten that? Must've made it back to his vehicle to retrieve it.

The distance was too far for Tox to hit him. But not too far for Tanin to take a sniper shot. *This is it*. He was going to die. Get Haven killed just as he had her sister.

Sirens screamed through the day.

Tanin hesitated, his gaze shifting marginally in the direction of the emergency vehicles. Tox seized the distraction. Threw himself to the wall. Even as he did, his periphery recorded Tanin snapping up the rifle. Taking aim.

Wind roared against his ears. His pulse skyrocketed. Each breath thumped. He expected a bullet to shove him into the ground. Faceplant him into cement. Any millisecond now . . .

Another step. It felt like a nightmare slowing him. Another breath. Wind. Step. Breath.

Crack! The report of the weapon reached his ears.

He dove for the wall. Rammed hard against it. He rolled and pitched himself down the alley. How he hadn't eaten lead, he didn't know. But he wouldn't stop to figure it out.

A dozen feet ahead, Haven skidded to a stop and glanced back at him.

"Go! 'Round the corner."

She lunged that way without complaint. Three bounding strides carried him into her. Momentum threw him against her. He crushed her. Rotated away and dropped against the wall. With a strangled cry, Haven lunged into his arms. He caught her, hugging her tight, cradling her head. Breathed her in, startled at the immense relief spiraling through him. She wasn't dead. They couldn't stay here, but he was selfishly unwilling to let her go, having felt Tanin's scope burning into his skull.

"We should go," he said, wrenching himself from her arms and the guilty pleasure of holding her.

She gave a shaky nod, and they hurried on, weaving through shops and streets. Ten minutes later, he tapped her shoulder. "You have the phone?"

Haven handed it to him as they continued, making several dizzying turns just to keep the pattern chaotic and untraceable.

Tox dialed Ram. "Tanin just tried to take us out."

"I'll meet you at the cemetery." Ram gave him directions to the site.

"Copy."

Walking through a parking structure, he ended the call, removed the battery—tossed it. Then the SIM card. Cracked it. They stepped into the sunlight and he spotted a fountain. He hurried over and tossed the SIM card in. After a nod to Haven, he hesitated when he saw the bloody spot on the side of her head. Touched it. "How's this?"

"Painful," she murmured, wincing. "But no worse than a migraine."

He cupped the back of her neck, feeling for heat and swelling. "Your neck hurt?"

"A little."

Holding her head between his hands, he thumbed her eyelid up. Stared into her pupils. Good reaction. *Probably too much*. But he also saw the exhaustion, the adrenaline dump from the accident. She was barely holding it together, and it tugged on his conscience. "Hey."

She met his gaze and almost instantly her eyes glossed.

He cupped her face. "We're going to be okay. But we have to keep moving."

She nodded, squeezing away the tears.

Though he'd like to give more reassurances and take time to recover, the clock ran against them. "We'll have a lot of company soon." Sirens shrieked closer as if confirming his words. "We need to cover about three klicks. Can you handle that?"

Again, she nodded, and they headed southwest, aiming for the old cemetery. Forty-five minutes later, they passed under the ornate scrollwork of an iron sign heralding the name of the graveyard. Tox aimed for a crypt and guided Haven onto a small stone bench. "Rest."

Haven shuddered. "Graveyards creep me out."

"Won't be long," he said, eyes on the road. Silence hung between them as Tox monitored every car that passed.

"Last funeral I attended was yours."

He shifted, his gaze yanked from the road for a second.

"Your mom . . . I always saw her as a woman of iron—so strong. A lot like you." She sighed. "But the way she clung to my hand that day . . ." She shook her head, wiping the blood from her fingers.

His mom had always favored him, though nobody looking in on their family would've known. She was truly an iron woman. She'd been hard on him most of his life but nothing like the driving force that was his father.

"Why was your death faked? You were already in prison."

What would it be like to off-load the anvil of the past? Live without it pressing in on his every thought and move? If anyone in this world could be trusted with the truth of what he'd done, it'd be Haven. She could probably forgive him for most of it. But not all. And telling her would violate the conditions of the contract. "I can't answer that."

"You struck a deal, right? For your team?"

Surprise stabbed him. How could she possibly know that?

She smiled with a lazy shrug. "I followed your case . . . very closely. It was interesting that you were dead one day and the men had their records expunged the next."

"It wasn't quite that fast." Tox stared at the pebbled walk, trying to shove the past back where it belonged.

"I knew you weren't guilty the way they said."

If only she did know. Haven believed in a man who no longer existed. He'd violated his own moral code buying the writ of freedom for his guys.

Tires crunched against rocks.

Tox glanced at the gate. Silver sedan. The driver—"Ram's here." He cuffed her elbow and helped her to her feet. She was steady but looked worse for the wear. Yet no complaint. They climbed into the sedan, but Tox wouldn't relax till they were back at the cottage. Tanin had nearly killed them in a car.

"You two look like roadkill," Ram said as he pulled into traffic.

"We feel like it." Tox adjusted the visor to block the piercing sun. "Tanin?"

"Lost him." He ran a hand through his hair, feeling dirt and pebbles—and a sticky spot. How had he done that? He brushed off his jeans. "Arrow in the hood. Would've hit Haven if I hadn't seen it coming. How he found us . . ."

Ram steered onto the rutted, pebbled road to the safe house, which was more like a small country estate.

"Saw Attaway at the hospital."

"That's a good place to see him."

Tox snorted at the innuendo. "He said we needed to be looking at someone else for the AFO leadership. Said Kaine and Abidaoud were distractions."

"Yeah?" Ram huffed. "Name?"

"Naftali Regev."

"Regev?" Ram's voice pitched. He shook his head, swerving to avoid a pothole. "No way."

"You know Regev?"

"Yeah. I do. And he's a member of the Knesset."

The Jewish parliament. Why would Barry blame him? Then again, hadn't Israelis put them on that wild Codex chase? "At this point—until we know more—I don't think we can afford to eliminate any suspects. The AFO seems to have their hands in a lot of pots, and we're battling the New Black Death."

"*Regev* is a distraction. Trust me. If—" Ram slowed. Scowled through the windshield as he drove up to the side of the house. "What is she doing?"

Armed with a satchel and a lightweight jacket, Tzivia was loading up a vehicle with Dr. Cathey.

"Are they going somewhere?" Ram hopped out and started toward his sister. "What are you doing?"

"I think I found something," she said. "I think . . . I think it's a piece of the Codex."

"We already know about that," Ram snapped.

"No, another one."

Tox started. "Seriously? How?"

"A blog post. I had an alert set up for about fifty keywords related to the Codex and censers—it was a long shot, but one result seems promising. An NYU student posted about her grandfather and words he rambled. Words from the same passage related to those censers."

Tox hesitated. "That's a big coincidence."

"Not a coincidence," Dr. Cathey said. "I believe God is orchestrating this. We are flying to New York to meet the young lady, but in earnest, I want to meet this man, especially if he's who I think he is."

"And who's that?"

"Benyamin Cohen." Dr. Cathey's eyes brightened. "His father was a rabbi at the synagogue where the Codex was kept in Syria—before they fled back to Israel."

"We have to catch our flight," Tzivia said. "We'll be back in a couple of days." They folded into a small compact car that whirred out of the drive and bumbled onto the country road.

"Let's hope they find something, since we have little," Ram said.

"We've got enough to take Kaine, though, right?"

Ram nodded toward the house with a rueful smile. "Ready to plan a kidnapping?"

"First," Maangi said as he stepped into the afternoon sunlight, "Tox and Cortes are both undergoing thorough medical evals to make sure they're okay. And"—he indicated Tox—"to make sure his head isn't more messed up than it was."

* * * *

— NEW YORK, NEW YORK —

As soon as the wheels hit the tarmac, Tzivia grabbed her phone and pulled up the information for Alison Kagan, the granddaughter who'd written the blog post. Tzivia hit Call. It rang . . . rang . . . rang. Why wasn't she answering? "That's odd."

"Remember, dear," Dr. Cathey said, "she's not champing at the bit to meet you like you are her."

"But I told her this was urgent. Told her what time our flight landed."

Once their plane eased to the jetway, Tzivia bounced on the balls of her feet as the passengers idly removed their carry-ons from the overhead bins. Row by row they filed out. Taking their ever-loving sweet time. She growled. A breath away from the find of the century and she couldn't even get off the plane!

"Easy," Dr. Cathey said around a laugh.

They'd deliberately not checked luggage so they didn't have the added wait of getting their bags before customs. It took forty minutes to get through, and another twenty minutes in the long queue for taxis before they were headed to Alison's apartment. Tzivia called again—no answer. The drive was another forty-minute waste, thanks to New York traffic. They'd lost almost two hours so far.

Bouncing her legs and emitting another growl only gained her a pat on the knee by Dr. Cathey, along with his comment that God was trying to teach her patience.

"If He existed, He would know it's futile to teach me patience." Again, she dialed Alison. Still no answer. "Where is she?"

Another chuckle. "Be at peace," he said. "The answers will be revealed in their time."

"That sounds like another faith comment." Her phone rang. Tzivia lifted it and sucked in a breath before answering. "Hello?"

"Ms. Khalon, this is Alison Kagan. Sorry I missed your calls, but maybe you should visit another time."

Tzivia's heart tripped. "Miss Kagan, we're already here in New York."

"Oh." She sighed. "My grandfather is in the hospital. He . . . he's dying."

Grief tugged at Tzivia, reminding her that her mission wasn't what everyone lived for. "I'm terribly sorry." But still . . . the plague. "I hate to sound insensitive, but could we meet you there? Is your grandfather conscious?"

"I . . . I'm not sure that's a good idea. He's touch and go."

"I know I sound insensitive, but we're trying to stop a plague. It's contained in India, but if we don't stop it, it could spread across the world very quickly."

"What does my grandfather have to do with that?"

"I could explain if we talked. In person."

Alison sighed. "Maimonides."

Tzivia gave the taxi driver the name of the hospital, and he made a turn, delivering them fifteen minutes later. They slipped into the darkened room, a lone wall light casting shadows across the floor. Though the old man in the bed lay wrapped in white—sheets, blanket, pillows—strangely, he still wore a tattered jacket.

Alison hugged herself. "I think this might really be it . . ."

"The jacket." Tzivia couldn't help but mention it. Wasn't it unhealthy, unsanitary?

"Oh, I know." The twenty-something girl wrinkled her nose. "It's so ugly, but he insists on wearing it. He grew so agitated and belligerent, the nurses said to let him have it. Once they put it back on him, he quieted. Has been like this ever since."

"Ali . . . son . . ."

The girl spun back to where her frail grandfather lay. "Sabba." She sat on the side of the bed and leaned across him, brushing a strand of silver hair from his face. "I'm here, Sabba."

Aged eyes resonated with a startling youthfulness. "Come," Benyamin Cohen rasped with a weak wag of his hand to Tzivia. "Come."

She lowered her bag to the floor and slipped to the other side of the bed. "Mr. Cohen, I'm—"

A smile flickered across his leathery face. "He said"—he wheezed—"you would come."

There was gentleness carved in a lifetime of experiences and hardships about this man. He drew her in like a calming, warm breath across her chilled heart. *Crazy. So crazy.* "Who? Who said I'd come?"

Wavering, he reached for her. Tzivia offered her hand, and soft fingers curled around her palm.

"Yes," he said, eyes closed and smiling again. "Yes, you must"—wheeze—"take it." Another wheezing breath. "God knows."

At those words, Tzivia sucked in a breath. Resisted the urge to leap back. She shot a look at Dr. Cathey, who closed the distance between them.

"Old friend," Dr. Cathey said, "do you have a leaf of the Codex?"

Mr. Cohen smiled. Laughed. Laughed harder. He coughed, grabbing his chest as it deepened, forcing him to fight for a breath. His fingers dug beneath the lapel of the grubby black coat. "Cannot hide from Yah"—wheeze—"weh."

His fingers worked beneath his jacket. He grunted. Scowled.

"Sabba, are you hurting?"

But he kept digging.

"Open . . . take it . . . so I may die . . . in peace." He reached for Tzivia again, and she held his hand. But this time, he tugged her close, forcing her to lean over the rail. He placed her hand against his chest.

She cast a helpless glance at Alison and Dr. Cathey.

"Sabba," Alison chided, her tone filled with awkwardness.

Yet through her own reaction and confusion, Tzivia felt something. She frowned and looked a little closer at his jacket. "Does he have papers with him?"

"Papers?" Alison frowned. "No."

"Yes," Mr. Cohen said. "Leave me in peace."

"Do you mind if I check?" Without waiting for permission, Tzivia lifted his lapel. The hospital gown had no pockets. "That's strange. I heard . . . something." She smoothed the jacket—and heard it again. She turned the lapel.

Saw something yellowish. She bent closer.

"Tear it," Mr. Cohen said.

Hesitating for only a second, Tzivia obeyed. Pulled at the thread, surprised when it slid free from the wool. The lining fell away, revealing a folded—"Parchment!"

"Yesss," Mr. Cohen breathed.

Elation tore through Tzivia as she unfolded it, moving to the light. She held it out, Dr. Cathey peering over her shoulder.

"Praise God," Dr. Cathey muttered. "It's from the Codex!"

In front of them, Benyamin wheezed his last.

41

Comms piece in, Tox waited in the nondescript van for Iomhair Kaine's detail to deliver him to the hotel. He glanced to the right and verified Cell on a motorcycle in the alley. Maangi and Chiji were concealed in another vehicle at the end of the drive. Wallace sat in the driver's seat of Tox's van.

"Entering now," Ram said from his spot in the vestibule. "Car Two in three, two . . . go."

The van with Maangi and Chiji started forward.

Eyeing the rearview mirror, Tox waited as Kaine's Rolls-Royce glided up toward the hotel porte cochere. "Nice and easy," Tox whispered.

"Bike One, you're a go."

The revving of the motorcycle rankled the air.

"Go," Tox said to Wallace and the van rolled closer for the upcoming incident.

Cell whipped up to the entrance on his motorcycle just as Kaine's driver and security guard stepped out. The men were posturing, a show of force and protection of their precious cargo.

Cell aimed into van two, which swerved—naturally—to avoid

hitting the biker. They narrowly avoided banging up the Rolls. The driver lunged, shouting at Cell, who laid out his bike and threw himself at the driver. The two went to blows. The security guard banged on the van, demanding Maangi move it, shouting that it blocked their car.

The door on the other side of the Rolls opened and a man in an expensive suit emerged. Bingo.

Ram was there, pretending to talk into a phone. He tripped, trying to avoid the new suit. Which put their target off-balance just as Tox's van slid up behind him.

Tox hopped out. Slid his arm around the man's neck and pressed against his skull. Kaine thrashed. But nobody heard him for the shouting and horn honking the team had started.

Dragging the man backward as he went limp, Tox never took his eyes off the chaos. Off the guard and driver still distracted.

Wallace helped hoist Kaine into the van. Ram leapt into the driver's seat.

The Rolls driver turned.

"Go," Tox barked, drawing in his legs. "Go go go!"

The driver and security guard looked to the Rolls, then to the van. With a shout, they gave chase. Shots pinged off the vehicle. Cracked glass. Someone banged on the back window.

The van lurched forward. Tox kicked the door closed and pushed himself farther in. He flipped backward. Grabbed his weapon. Aimed out the rear at the shrinking form of the bodyguard. Pulse jack-hammering, he slumped against the side. Then twisted around to the front. "Don't stop."

Tox shifted toward Kaine. In minutes they were going to have a lot of heat breathing down their necks. Into his comms, he said. "We have the package."

"That was too easy," Ram said.

"Or we're just that good," Wallace said.

"Not likely." On his knees, Tox duct-taped Kaine's mouth, hands, and legs.

Ram was a genius behind the wheel and navigating out of the city. Ten minutes had them in a parking garage. After scanning Kaine for tracking devices, they put him in the back of a blue SUV. Another ten minutes had them bouncing down the country road to the safe house.

In the barn that served as an interrogation room, they secured Kaine to a chair and anchored his hands to rivets in the floor.

"Hey," Ram said, walking toward him with something in his hand. "Look. He had this."

Tox angled in. Saw an object wrapped in plastic.

"It's a censer."

Tox frowned. "How does he have that?"

"I don't know. From Tanin, maybe? Need to notify Tzivia." He tugged out his phone and called his sister. Left a voicemail.

Tox stood back, staring down at the man who had caused so much destruction and death. How could Kaine live with himself?

Ram filled a bucket with water, then threw it over Kaine's head. Tox folded his arms and waited.

Kaine gasped, the shock of the water snapping him awake. He shook his head. Looked around wildly. "Where am I?"

"In my control," Ram said.

The panic that had shot through the man vanished in a blink. "You are a fool. They will find you. Then they will kill you, and I will watch." He bared his teeth. "With pleasure."

Tox sighed. This was going to be a long night.

* * * *

— SOMEWHERE OVER EUROPE —

Tzivia had no nails left. She'd bitten them off, watching Dr. Cathey study the leaf fragment over the last several hours. He'd stared and stared. Said nothing. Though she'd tried a half-dozen times to engage him in conversation, to pry whatever he thought and knew from his vault-like mind, he'd shushed her.

"Please," she finally whispered, her voice nearly lost amid the drone of the engines. She touched his arm.

He placed his hand over hers. "I was wrong once before," he mumbled.

Her heart tripped. "Kafr al-Ayn." When he'd thought returning the artifact to its cradle and sealing it with appropriately dated wax would stop the toxin. But the wax had nothing to do with the warrior's seal. The "seal" had been the blood of a warrior—Tox.

"What is here—" He sniffed. "There is little. And the little is too simple."

"You're afraid of guessing wrong."

"Indeed. Thousands could die."

"And they will, if you make no attempt at all."

He removed his glasses and let out a long sigh, then folded his arms over his chest. His wizened gray eyes rested on the leaf.

"You have an idea." The thought spurted elation through her veins. "You do, don't you?"

His grave expression confirmed it.

Why must he be so maddeningly cryptic? "Just tell me. Even if it's wrong. I'm going insane watching you watch it."

"Just remember, it's only a thought." He adjusted the air nozzle overhead before pointing with his silver pen to the yellowed piece of history. "As with the leaf from Numbers 16, there is an odd cantillation mark in this one."

"Right. Which is why Israel could be hiding the Codex—to protect its credibility."

"Perhaps. But I am not convinced it's a cantillation mark." His crooked finger pointed to the margin. "The symbol here on the side, it is the same as that found in the other leaf. Then the cantillation"—he dragged his finger a half-inch in the air above the script—"here is wrong."

"Meaning?"

"Meaning not that the word itself is wrong—*I think*." He seemed to get lost in his thoughts again.

"Then what?"

"It's a clue," he said. "The mark hovers over the word *shemen*, and in the other, over *miktereth*."

"So, 'oil' and 'censers.'"

"Mm, I think it should be holy oil. *The* holy oil."

"You mean the one mentioned in the Masoretic texts?" Tzivia nearly laughed out loud. A fable like fish that never ran out but multiplied.

Or the woman whose son filled dozens of jars with oil. The holy oil was purported to have never run out, despite years of use. "It doesn't exist anymore."

He chuckled. "And according to you, neither do miracles or God." He patted her hand.

"Is it supposed to mean something?"

"I am certain it does," he said with vehemence. "I've asked Akiva to see if he knows of other leaves, even pictures of them, that could give us more. Particularly those with this mark in the margin."

Tzivia bent closer. "Is it a T?" Why would there be an English T in a Hebrew text?

"No, it is a cross—the mark of Thefarie."

Tzivia scowled. "The one from Tiberius's Writings?"

"Indeed. Were there not plagues in his time? Would it not make sense that if he had a way to stop the disease, that as a Knight of the Lord Jesus Christ, he would see it as his duty to pass on the solution?"

"But you said he only found three of the censers. I think you have been studying that leaf too long."

"Why? Because you don't have the faith to believe God saw a way to use a warrior centuries past, an absentminded professor, and a bright, beautiful doctor of archaeology?"

"No, because what you're suggesting strains credulity."

He smiled. "Making it all the more likely it was done as I suspect. Did not Thefarie write that he had helped hold the Codex hostage?"

She touched her temple. "But it's stupid—marking up the Codex makes it useless, calls everything into question. Why would he do that?"

Another crinkly-eyed smile. "Hmm, if he did, indeed."

Tzivia banged her head against the seat. "This is all futile anyway—even if your theory is right, we don't have all the censers."

"True, but we have Aaron's and the one we reclaimed in India." He sighed, then frowned.

"And what are we supposed to do with them, even if we had them all?"

"That is the question, is it not?"

42

Kasey watched the live feed in the safety of the farmhouse. She kept the main goal of Kaine's kidnapping in mind: find out the AFO endgame.

Interrogations weren't for the weakhearted. And she quickly realized that she fit that description today. It'd taken Cole and Ram several hours to wear down Kaine, exhaust him mentally and physically, but it was needed. This wasn't a situation sanitized to placate sensitivities. This was real life. They were dealing with a man willing to wipe out hundreds, if not thousands. Kasey wasn't naïve enough to think men prepared to die for their cause suddenly became willing to talk after a few terse questions. And Iomhair Kaine wasn't just willing to die for the cause. He was the cause.

"You okay?" Levi asked.

Kasey gave a quick nod.

"It's hard to watch," he said quietly.

True, but that was her job—to watch, observe. Analyze.

"What do you know about the New Black Death virus?" Cole asked.

"It's killing people," Kaine said around a sneer.

"What does the AFO want to accomplish?"

372

Kaine glared at Cole and spit out, "I won't give you what you want. I didn't get to where I am by being weak."

"So you prey on children?" Cole demanded.

"Hey, that—" He shook his head. "Some children were hurt, but that's about it."

"Passive language," Kasey blurted, then remembered she had to key the mic. She repeated her words with a hot mic that fed to Cole and Ram. "That's passive language. He knows more than he's saying." When nobody moved, she took a deep breath. This was her area. They trusted her. "Ask him about a division, a rift in the Order."

In the live feed, Cole and Ram exchanged a glance.

Ram stepped forward. "Tell me about the rift."

Kaine's swollen lid barely lifted as he dragged a bloodshot eye to Ram. "An organization as big as the Arrow & Flame, you know, has many people. So there will be disagreements. Of course. It has to happen, you know." His gaze drifted. "And people betray you . . ."

"It's personal." Seated in front of her, Cell glanced back at her. "Right?"

Kasey smiled at him. He'd clearly remembered their encounter at the beginning of the mission. "It's personal," she repeated into her mic. "The rift is between him and someone else. Someone high up probably." She glanced at Cell. "Does he have a girlfriend or wife?"

Cell checked the monitor. "I don't remember . . . wait." He tapped the screen. "Yes. Yes, he did. Wife filed for divorce three weeks ago."

"Guys, his wife left him," Kasey said into the mic. "Maybe for whoever defied him."

"She moved to France," Cell whispered into the comms.

"And they move to France," Cole said.

"Shack up with your enemy," Ram added.

"No," Kaine growled, his lip curling. "Not my enemy—a friend."

"Drive a dagger into his heart," Ram said, murder in his tone. "Tell us what his plan was, his target."

Kaine gritted his teeth. Pursed his lips. Angry. So very angry. Yet thirsting for blood—the death of the one who'd stolen his wife. "Football—"

Crack! Thunk!

Cole and Ram jumped back. Shouts exploded through the room. A bright cloud whitened the screen for a moment. The camera slowly compensated, revealing the source—an arrow stuck out of Kaine's chest, boiling.

Kasey watched stupefied as Cole and Ram raced from the room. "What happened?"

Cell was on his feet. He grabbed something from the floor and darted out. But a gargled tangle of words filtered through the feed.

"Wait! He's talking!" Kasey dropped into Cell's empty chair and slipped on the headphones. She played back the video. She wanted to run this through her program, record her notes on her own system, so she transferred it to her laptop. Switched seats and filtered it through the program. With so much chaos and shouting, she had to strain to hear. To eliminate ancillary distraction, she closed her eyes.

She made out three words: Football. Censers. Airborne.

Her computer glitched. The ground shook. She shot her gaze back to the monitor and found only a grainy static. When she went to open the video again, she noticed another file on her desktop but didn't recognize it. Where had that come from? She double-clicked on it.

Surprise chugged through her veins as a dark hall glimmered on the screen. Wait—that looked like a— "Hospital." Her pulse raced. It was Evie's hospital!

Two men entered an empty room. Her heart climbed into her throat. *Cole! And Barry.*

Where had this come from? Who sent it to her? Curiosity cranked the volume. This had to have been recorded when they were there yesterday. But even as she realized that, Kasey noticed the deception cues in Barry's words and body language. Why was he not being truthful about Naftali Regev?

The feed blipped and showed an empty hall.

A chaotic but dulled roar stilled her. She glanced over her shoulder, sliding off the headphones. An eruption of shouts and banging pulled her to the door.

* * * *

374

"I'm warning you . . ."

Tox held out a hand. "Give me straight answers and this all goes away."

"Leave Regev alone." Ram stood in a sparring stance.

The side door opened. Maangi and Thor entered, looking sweaty and angry.

"Did you find anyone?" Ram asked.

Maangi nodded. "Nailed one before he could get in a car. Second one got away."

Tox scowled. "Look, I was given Regev's name, and until I check it out—"

"When did you start trusting Attaway more than me?" Ram countered.

Tox felt miserable but he didn't relent.

"I can't give you answers, not direct ones." Hands held out, Ram shrugged. "But Regev is a member of the Knesset. He's . . . trust-worthy."

"Cole," Haven said.

When had she come into the room? "Stay out of this, Haven." He never took his eyes off Ram, but he felt the team grouping up, with Chiji just inside his periphery. "This is about doing our due diligence."

"It's about sending us on a wild-goose chase. Remember the syna-gogues? Conspiracy of silence? Anything to get us away from the truth."

"I remember your Mossad buddies—"

"No. The ones tasked with protecting the Codex did that."

"And you're going to tell me Mossad isn't interested in protecting archaeological treasures?"

"Cole." Haven stepped closer. "Cole, I need to talk to you." She glanced around at the men in an angry, silent standoff. They were tired. Frustrated. "I think you should listen to what I have to say first."

"What?"

"I found a video."

"So?"

"It's of you and Barry. In the hospital."

His gaze swung to her.

"I don't know where it came from, but it's from when he pulled you aside privately. The entire conversation is there." She wet her lips, then looked at Ram. Back to Tox. "Attaway was deceiving you about Naftali Regev. I don't know why, but I know that he didn't believe what he was telling you."

"Boom!" Ram snapped. "There. The truth."

Tox faced her. "Show me."

With the others on his tail, Tox followed Haven into the command center. She tucked herself into a chair and opened the video. They watched, quietly huddled around her chair.

"Coward," Ram hissed when Attaway uttered Regev's name.

"If you watch," Haven said, starting the video over, "he seems to pull Regev's name out of nowhere. I don't know that he meant to necessarily blame him."

"Then why mention him?" Maangi asked.

"To distract us," Ram said. "Get us off the scent."

Tox nodded. "Kaine and Abidaoud."

"Hey . . . guys?" Leaning over Haven, Cell stuffed on the headphones. "Send me that file." He pushed into the other seat as Haven complied. "I have a sound program specifically designed to lift audio, cancel white noise . . ." Cell listened. Watched. His eyes widened. "Guys—get this. Attaway talks to someone after you leave the room, Sarge."

"Who?" Tox moved to his side.

Finger held up, Cell adjusted a few dials then scooted back, ripping off the headphones and unplugging them. "Give a listen."

"*Do not worry,*" a voice said. "*They are still chasing their tails. You've done your job well.*"

"Who is that? Who's he talking to?" Tox asked.

Cell paused it. Pointed to a shadow that fell into view at the lower right of the feed. "Someone off-camera."

"Where did this video come from again?" Tox asked.

Haven shook her head. "I don't know. I was reviewing what happened with Kaine when the file appeared on my desktop."

"Someone must've hacked her system, dropped the file for her to find," Cell said.

"That's convenient," Ram muttered.

With a nod, Tox focused on the comms guy. "Can you find out who he's talking to?"

"Uh, maybe. I can run voice analysis. . . ."

Tox motioned to the monitor. "Play the rest."

"I'm not sure it's working" came Attaway's whine.

"It's okay," the voice replied. *"Focus on new. They'll feel our vengeance with their last, burning breath."*

"New what?"

"That wasn't helpf—"

"Kaine said football." Maangi went pale, his large eyes coming to them.

"Yeah?"

"Not *new*." Maangi's eyebrows rose. "*Nou*—Camp Nou, the stadium in Barcelona. 'Focus on Nou.'"

Tox understood. "They're going to hit the World Cup."

A man should not have to bury both his wife and daughter. Galen sat in Evie's room, the hissing and beeping of machines the only indication that his daughter had not yet succumbed to the virus.

Evie was a fighter. Always had been. She came into the world with a thick mop of dark hair like her mother and a very healthy pair of lungs. When Brooke died three years ago, Evie had waged a battle of wills to see which of them could go the longest without mentioning her mother. It broke his heart—his attempts to win weren't intentional. Losing Brooke weeks before the inauguration nearly collapsed his will to go on. Some even wondered if he was fit to assume office.

That was the breaking point. Evie heard the rumors. Heard the ugly talk. She challenged him to stand up to the bullies. He swore his oath on the Bible and with his daughter's arm tucked through his, he became president.

It wasn't that Evie was ever rebellious or rotten. She was just . . . willful. A trait she'd come by honestly, receiving a hefty dose from both parents.

378

Maybe even her uncle.

Galen glanced down, thoughts of his brother plaguing him. Tox hadn't changed. He was all business. Protector. Intense. Had he noticed something between Tox and Haven? Something romantic?

The thought seemed ludicrous, especially for Tox.

A door hissed open.

Galen straightened and saw the white lab coat of Dr. Honorie. He came to his feet, almost unwillingly. "Lab results?"

Dr. Honorie nodded, his expression grave.

"Not good?"

"Her numbers are high. Faster than we can keep up. Her kidneys and liver are shutting down. We'll do what we can, but we're not far from full life support."

Galen dropped into the chair. Cradled his head in his hands. He sighed, then looked back up at the doctor. "So . . . she's dying." The words pushed him to her bedside, where he brushed a black strand of hair from her shoulder.

"I'm sorry, but . . ."

Galen shifted and saw Barry's reflection in the glass. He lifted his daughter's hand and kissed around the IV line, then set it back down. He turned to Barry. "I thought you had work to do."

"I do—did." He nodded to the doctor.

Honorie lowered his head.

Galen's gut twisted. "What?"

"Another case of the disease has been reported," Honorie said.

"Where?"

"Here. Third floor. Pediatrics."

Guilt crushed Galen, his heart stricken at the thought of another parent having to endure this. And Evie had the best medicine because he was the president of the United States. The innocent civilian somewhere in this hospital wouldn't have the same options. "Bring the child up here."

"I don't think that's wise," Dr. Honorie said.

"I want them to have the best care."

"I understand, but—"

"It's better to quarantine the child from the others, right?"

Hesitation gave his answer.

"Do it," Galen said.

Reluctantly, the doctor left.

Galen returned to watching Evie, sagging under the weight on his shoulders. Depressed. She'd be with her mother soon, the two of them watching over him.

"Sir?"

"What?" he asked, not turning around.

"I . . . when I spoke with your brother . . ."

Strange how those words—*your brother*—didn't make his gut tighten this time. In fact, it almost gave him hope. "Go on."

"I told him he needed to look into Naftali."

Galen spun. "Naftali Regev?" When Barry nodded, Galen came unglued. "Are you *insane*? He is our strongest ally in Israel."

Barry tucked his chin.

"Do you realize what will happen if Naftali finds out you are giving his name as a terrorist? Do you understand the damage—"

"It was necessary, sir." Barry looked contrite, though he didn't have a contrite cell in his body.

"Necessary to alienate us from one of our strongest allies? How could that be necessary?"

"You were in danger."

"Me?"

"I received a video of you"—Barry motioned around the room—"here. With Evie in the bed. They said if I did not get Tox out of London, they would kill you."

"You're an idiot, Barry!" Galen raked a hand through his hair, frustration tightening his muscles. "If I die, the vice president will replace me. Once you step into the noose of organizations like this, you are forever ensnared! *I* am ensnared!"

The door flapped open. Dr. Honorie rushed in with three nurses. Galen's knees nearly buckled, fearing the worst. "What's wrong?"

"Nothing!" Dr. Honorie's face lit. "I think we have a cure!"

* * * *

— DAY 15 —

SOMEWHERE OVER THE BAY OF BISCAY

Tox palmed the table, staring at the fact sheets taped to the wall of the plane.

"Tzivia's headed to Israel," Ram said. "I told her about the censer we got from Kaine. Dr. Cathey is convinced he can end this once the censers are together."

Tox nodded.

"National Police Corps are on alert in Barcelona," Maangi announced as he ended a call. "Took some convincing. But once they authenticated us with SAARC, their attitude changed."

"Good." Tox scratched his jaw. "So . . . why are they targeting the World Cup?"

"Big numbers." Ram rapped on a page listing the number of attendees. "They like to make a bang."

Dark eyes weighted with the horrible truth, Chiji frowned. "So many lives . . ."

Imagining the nearly one hundred thousand spectators coming away with more than a victory or loss churned his gut. "Open-air stadium with deadly virus . . ." He could only shake his head. "But I thought it wasn't definite that the virus is airborne. How are they going to spread it? They can't have that many people there to act as hosts."

"Or can they?" Cell added, waggling his eyebrows.

Wallace joined them. "I thought it was spread through infectious contamination."

"Onset varies," Maangi said, reading a report. "They still haven't discerned how the site workers got sick, how Chatresh's brother got it."

Tox hated this. Hated the not knowing. "So why this place? Just numbers?"

"Royals. World leaders," Cell said.

Arms folded, Tox looked at Cell, who had his feet on the table, eyeing the wall as he ate an energy bar. "Go on."

"Yeah," Cell said. "A king, some princes, diplomats. That's some serious VIP happening there."

Tox considered the information wall. "You might be on to something."

"They do love to rearrange the world order," Ram said.

Tox's phone rang, and he plucked it from his holster. After he checked the ID, he answered, tension knots tightening in his shoulders. "Galen."

"Good news—they've found an antigen for the virus."

The breath trapped in Tox's throat whooshed out. "That is good news. So Evie . . ."

"Too soon," Galen said. "They aren't sure if they caught it fast enough. She's undergoing a transfusion right now. But I'm hoping. Praying."

"Me too." He'd whispered a few prayers for his niece.

"I'd better go. Barry needs—"

"Oh. Hey." Tox walked to the back of the plane. "Galen, listen, I have a concern about Attaway. He—"

"He told me all about it."

Surprise rooted Tox to the spot. "He did?"

"They were blackmailing him to force you out of the country and to threaten me. Don't worry. I gave him what-for about caving to their tactics."

"Tox!"

He turned to the front, where Ram waved him back. He lowered his head. "Hey, I need to get going."

"Right. To save the world."

"God willing."

"Keep me posted."

"Yep." Tox returned to the table, snagged on the almost-normal tone of his call with Galen. "What's up?"

"We've narrowed it down to three targets. First, Felipe Alonso of Spain—not a nobleman but he wields more power in his little finger than most kings in their lifetime. He has three multibillion-dollar corporations, all connected to the tech industry. He'll be there with his son and daughter."

"Why him?"

"Big negotiations lately over expansions into new, cutting-edge fields."

"Like?"

"Military-grade armor and shields. Company out of Beijing claims the tech is stolen." Ram shrugged. "I thought every tech company stole from the other."

"They do," Cell muttered.

"Who else?"

"Prince Constantine from Belgium. His father is on the cusp of death, and the prince is already acting head of state." Ram nodded. "He's a controversial person. Breaking with traditions and conservative values of the crown. Seems to have some less-than-ideal advisors, but I'm not convinced Constantine is a target because he'll be in the commentator's box. As a former player, he's a guest, giving thoughts on the matches."

"Why's that exclude him?"

"The glass—bulletproof—protects him. No easy way to get to him."

Tox grunted. "And third?"

"King Jorgen of Norway and his son, Prince Einar. There's been a movement in the country lately to join their allies in placing harsher sanctions against certain Middle East countries. Jorgen is for it, and some say easily manipulated. Einar opposes it—intel says his lover is a Saudi princess."

"Okay," Tox said, going to the grease board wall. "We'll break into three teams. Ram and Maangi, you'll take Spain. Levi, Chiji, and Haven—Belgium." It was the lesser risk, right? He wanted her in the safest place, but because of those lethal deception skills, he needed her onsite. "Cell, you and I will take Norway."

Ram nodded. "NPC will be onsite for the main match this afternoon. They'll have agents in plain clothes as well as uniformed officers. We'll cover the boxes where our targets will watch the match."

Tox looked at them. "Maangi, get hold of the doctor at Evie's hospital. Find out about the antigen for the virus—"

"Antigen?"

"Galen said they found one. We'll need a lab onsite to get vials prepped for anyone exposed to this plague." Tox scowled. Hesitated on his next words. "I want everyone in armor and eyes out. The problem is—they know us. We don't know them. This could get ugly really fast."

44

"Thank you for coming."

With Tzivia at his side, Joseph Cathey entered the underground room of the museum. "You said it was urgent. Please tell me they've agreed to let me see the Codex. I only want to stop this plague."

A wide, low-ceilinged room spread out before them. Four light tables consumed most of the area, but there was enough space for walls of shelving at the far end. The closest table held a museum folder and a small box.

"I have a leaf for you." Akiva went to the table, where he lifted the folder.

One? One leaf? Joseph needed to scour the whole Codex to see if there were other Thefarie marks. "Did I not convey well enough the danger—"

"It is such an honor, Joseph, to see this page." Akiva's words were soft but tinged with warning. "You lost the censers—"

"*Stolen*. Not our fault," Tzivia growled.

"They are no longer in your possession." Akiva arched an eyebrow, his hands behind his back. "And you expect us to trust you with more of the Crown? *Pfft*."

It was true but hardly their fault. Yet Joseph knew the Codex's guardians would hold that over their heads. Setting aside his cane and frustration, Joseph had little choice. He and Tzivia donned the gloves Akiva provided, then opened the folder. A leaf of history stared at him with its withered, crinkled face. "May I remove it? To use the light."

"Gently."

Joseph eased the leaf from the protective folder. Laid it on the table.

"The cross," Tzivia whispered, pointing to the Thefarie symbol.

He nodded, then slid his gaze right to left, searching columns for an odd mark. He scanned again.

"I don't see a mark," Tzivia muttered.

"Mm." Joseph lifted the leaf and tilted it. Stared down the plane of its surface. "Ah," he breathed. There was a mark, but not of ink. An indentation, as if something had worn off. It rested over the words *bnei Aaron.* "Aaron's sons."

"But they've been dead for centuries," Tzivia said.

Aaron's sons. Censers. Oil. The three marks of Thefarie didn't provide enough to know what to do. He considered Akiva. "Friend, we must see more."

"You have seen enough," Akiva said, his gaze darkening. "I would suggest you return the censers to us, Miss Khalon, since you are unable to protect them."

"They were *stolen* from me, but we have recovered three. We simply need—"

"You have the censer of Korah?"

Joseph stilled. How did Akiva know which of the censers they had recovered from the AFO agent? "Wait," he whispered, his breath stolen as his gaze hit the small box next to the folder. "You."

Akiva flinched.

"*You* have the last censer. You recovered it from Maloof." How had Mossad gotten it? Had they killed the Saudi soldier? It didn't matter—they had other work to do.

Akiva's hand rested over the box protectively. "I am not convinced you have proven yourself."

The Mossad, protectors of Israel and her history, in collusion with the IAA, would fight him to eternity. Unless he gave them something of use. But what did he have? His gaze struck the corner of the leaf and once more he wondered . . . "I have a theory."

"I would hear nothing—"

"I don't believe the Codex has been ruined by Thefarie's marks."

Akiva stilled, his eyes narrowing. Proud but unrelenting.

"If I can prove that the Codex is not compromised, will you help me finish this puzzle?" He shifted toward the rabbi. "Do away with this conspiracy of silence, Akiva, and help the world by stopping this plague and returning the Codex to its rightful place."

Akiva hesitated. "Bring me the censers and the leaf in your possession, and I will show you what you need."

* * * *

— BARCELONA, SPAIN —

Breathing. Breathing would be good. Kasey drew in a breath through her nostrils and let it out between her lips. The crowds . . . the sheer number . . . so many people. They'd landed an hour before the start of the match, but the stadium was already filled to capacity.

She walked the space behind the commentator's box where the Belgian prince sat, deflecting the nasty looks from the personal bodyguard, who didn't trust her despite verified credentials. Really, a prince should always have a deception expert. Then again, that might be too much information, knowing every time someone was pulling a fast one.

Binoculars to her eyes, she scanned the stadium. Spotted Cole and Cell at the VIP lounge with the playboy prince and his father, who seemed just as glad to have beautiful women around him. Arms over his chest, Cole stood to the side, watching. Looking fierce and forbidding. She whirled around to look at the others watching Spain's box.

"How much you want to bet they're NPC?"

Kasey glanced at Levi, then in the direction he indicated. A man strode the walkway behind a row of bleachers with a deep-set scowl.

"Not exactly subtle."

"We don't want them to be," Kasey said.

"If AFO has planned a big hit like this, they aren't going to worry about a few police officers running up and down the stadium."

"Eyes out," Tox's growl rumbled through the comms.

Kasey twitched, glancing over her shoulder. Half expected to be able to see him at this distance. But there was a strange comfort simply knowing Cole was watching.

* * * *

Tox pulled his gaze from the commentator box. It wasn't that he could see Haven. He could *hear* her. That soft voice in his ear, chatting casually. Probably forgetting her mic was hot.

Trolling the aisles, making eye contact with every person who dared look at him, Tox hadn't spotted anything or anyone out of the ordinary. But that was the point. The AFO had a way of blending in, becoming not just a part of the crowd, but becoming the crowd itself.

Ear. Watch the ears. Tanin gave them a cheat in finding him. It'd be an obvious thing to have to cover up, which still helped them. Hats, bushy hair, keffiyehs . . . Tox scanned the crowds, again feeling the heat of the assassin's scope on his skull. He had an awful feeling they'd be on him before he knew it. Which was why he'd put Chiji with Haven, to make sure she came out of this alive.

The match began, the roar of the crowd deafening.

Tox went on alert. A great time to strike—when excitement could conceal movement and explosions. Where that excitement became confusion. He hiked back up to the VIP lounge, a slab of cement adorned with linen-clad tables, umbrellas, and too-rich-for-their-own-good spectators. And royals.

Prince Einar was a lanky kid who hadn't quite grown into manhood. Probably eighteen, maybe nineteen. Twenty if he'd been born early. But the kid was cocky. His father, the king, sat with another suit, the two immersed in heavy conversation, laughter, and quite a few drinks, even though the match had just started.

Tox walked the perimeter, allowing himself enough of an angle to see down the dark cement passage behind the lounge. At the far end beyond a lip-locked pair, he connected gazes with Cell, who turned. Slammed into a man, who forcefully knocked Cell to the side.

"Hey!"

Like lightning, an arrow shot through the darkness. Glowing. Intent. Vicious. It nailed Cell in the chest.

"Man down, man down!" Tox hissed into his mic, diving around the cluster of people. A scream shot out. He heard a thrum of panic behind him but focused on his man.

Cell lay perfectly still, his hand reaching for but not touching the phosphorus arrow in the hollow of his shoulder. "Son of a blister," he managed, his gaze shifting to meet Tox's. "Didn't see this coming."

"Easy," Tox said, then radioed in details about the hit.

Cell frowned. "I'm not feeling anything."

"Did it hit your spine?"

"No, I mean"—Cell lifted his head, looked at the spot where the arrowhead penetrated his armor and upper chest—"I'm not boiling."

Tox eyed the shaft and saw the glass cutout that showed a grayish liquid inside. Whatever caused the arrow to release the phosphorus had failed. "Get hazmat up here."

"Pull it," Cell muttered. "Get this thing out of me."

"No. It could detonate."

"Hazmat en route," Ram said over the comms. "How's Cell?"

"Dying," Cell muttered. "I think you should hold a vigil."

"You don't get a vote on your ceremony," Maangi countered.

"I should."

Tox swiveled his legs around and peered down the dark tunnel-like area. "Everyone report," he said, probing the crowds, checking ears.

"Alonso is oblivious," Ram said.

"Belgium is boring," Wallace reported.

"Norway hasn't moved," Chiji said. "I'll cover them for you."

"Copy." Tox looked up as a hazmat team rounded the bend and hustled toward them. They loaded Cell onto a stretcher and draped a cloth around the arrow. An EMT tapped information into a handheld tablet.

"Hey." Cell pointed to the device. "Can I see that?"

"No, this—"

"Seriously." Cell snatched it, went to work. "I'll report in, Sarge."

Tox shook his head. "You should be unconscious."

"I will be eventually," he said. "Until then . . ."

Shaking his head, Tox returned to the VIP lounge. Verified his objectives were still alive. Sent Chiji back to Haven's side. Einar stood at the glass rail, sipping a bottle of water and watching the match. His father remained engrossed with the other man.

"SAARC, you live?" Tox asked into the comms.

"We are."

"Did you see who shot that arrow?"

"Negative. But trajectory puts it in Blue Two."

"Wallace, that's you. Stay alert."

"Roger," Wallace confirmed.

Loud voices drew Tox's gaze back to the VIP lounge, where the conversation with the king was growing animated.

"Tox . . ." Ram warned.

"I see it." He wasn't leaving this station again. "Command, who is Jorgen's guest?" Was that man trouble? The real target? He had monopolized the king's time.

"Jorgen's brother-in-law, Carlos" came the reply.

"The prince's uncle?"

"The king's sister married Carlos, a grand duke. Has a lot of sway with Jorgen, according to intel."

Prince Einar glowered at his father and uncle. Shaking his head, he focused on the match. So the prince wasn't a fan of politics.

"Copy that." Tox settled into his corner, waiting, monitoring, never letting his guard down.

"Hey, Sarge," Maangi spoke lazily through the comms, "in four years, can we have another crisis at the next World Cup? Sweet view. No cost."

Tox knew the joke was a coping mechanism to help cut the tension, especially after Cell went down, but he needed them to focus. "Eyes out."

"Sarge. Cell here."

Tox snorted. Cell should be feeling real good thanks to morphine by now but he was reporting in. "Go ahead."

"I've . . ."

The comms went silent. Tox leaned his head to the side, away from the crowds. "Cell?"

"Sarge, I've got something. I pulled up—dude, that hurts! Go easy—"

"Cell?"

"Yeah, sorry—they got needles the size of this arrow digging into me. Anyway, pulled up the security feed from the stadium."

He had Tox's full attention. "Go on."

"The man who knocked me aside, right before the arrow?"

Tox wasn't sure he wanted to hear this.

"It was Tzaddik!"

Armed with the three censers, Joseph and Tzivia made their way back to the room beneath the museum.

"I still don't understand why we're coming back here," Tzivia said.

"It is curious, but it's also entirely possible it's like a puzzle and that location is important."

"It's a converted tunnel! I do digs in places like this!"

"Exactly—it might have historical significance."

"To what? The plague?"

Joseph lifted his shoulder in a shrug. "Perhaps. Or the censers. Or . . ." His words fell away as he caught sight of shadows ahead in the passage leading to the secure entrance.

Four men peeled out of the darkness. They walked with authority and . . . menace, jamming Joseph's heart in a rapid fire.

Tzivia slid a hand toward him, urging him to let her take the lead. With her training, he trusted her. Though, as a man, he felt responsible for her. But he had a box in his arms and panic in his chest, so she was clearly the better person to take point.

A fifth man appeared. His tall, lanky form belied the strength resonating through his dark eyes. "The box," he demanded.

"Wait," Tzivia snapped. "Those are ours."

"Here." Joseph handed the box to the leader.

"This way," he said, stepping aside and motioning toward the doors.

Tzivia hissed in Joseph's ear, "They won't give them back."

"I know." The censers were lost to them. But perhaps they *should* be relegated to history once more.

They entered the room, surprised to find nearly a dozen people. Joseph hesitated and felt Tzivia turn to him. He saw Akiva and started toward him.

"The censers?" Akiva looked over his shoulder to the shadow who'd taken them. "Good. Put them there."

A large wood box sat in the middle of the room along with two pedestals. One held a small bowl, the other a basin made of some sturdy material. It was wide and shallow. Inside it, coals burned brightly.

Joseph stilled with realization.

"You see now?" Akiva smiled. He motioned to a tall priest. "This is Yadon."

The man wore a long white robe with a blue mantle over it. A tall, white turban supported a gold band. A highly decorated breastplate revealed him as the high priest.

"Aaron's sons," Joseph muttered.

Yadon inclined his head.

Akiva drew Joseph and Tzivia to the side. "We have one other leaf with Thefarie's mark. Together, we discerned that to check this plague, the censers must be anointed with the *shemen hamishcha*."

Joseph looked to Yadon. "And only a descendent of Aaron can go before the Lord." Among the haredim that was true. Among Christians like Joseph, that had changed with Yeshua.

But for this plague to be checked, Joseph submitted his thoughts to the pomp and ceremony.

* * * *

— BARCELONA —

"Eyes out!" Tox barked, sensing the gaze of Tanin through a scope, though he stood behind a cement wall. "Find who shot that arrow at

Cell." Heat rushed through him, the fires of rage. Was Tzaddik trying to pick off the team so he could accomplish his endgame?

"Tzaddik tried to kill you?" Thor asked.

"No, I don't think so," Cell said, his words thoughtful, deliberate. "I think he saved me."

Rubbing his temple, Tox tried to sort it. "Come again."

"If he hadn't pushed me," Cell said, "I think the trajectory of that arrow would've put it right through my heart."

How could Tzaddik know the arrow was coming? How could he save Cell? And why? "I want him found," Tox growled.

"Ndidi, your prince is leaving. He just got a call."

"On it," Tox mumbled as Prince Einar headed out of the VIP lounge with the phone to his ear. "Can we trace that call he's on?"

"Working on it," Vander said.

Tox paced the prince until he entered the tunnel. "Headed east."

"I have him," Chiji said.

Relief speared Tox as Chiji stepped from one of the wells and fell into step behind the prince. Tox backed up as they vanished in a splash of light.

"Can't trace it," SAARC replied. "Signal's bouncing all over the grid."

Of course it was. "Stay on him, Chiji. Keep me posted."

"Roger."

Tox started back toward the VIP lounge. His brain snagged on something, then slowly caught up with what triggered it. A door closed just before something swung out of view. He mentally retraced.

Crossbow!

"I have something." He crossed the crowded concourse to a door marked MAINTENANCE. "NPC, this is Wraith Actual. Any maintenance calls on level four?"

"Checking" came a static-laced reply. A few seconds later, "Negative. Management says the turbine for the main airflow system is all that's in there."

"Perfect way to spread a virus," Ram said, echoing Tox's thoughts.

Tox was moving. "Any exits in there?"

"Only that door," NPC reported back.

"Guys," Cell said through the comms, his voice strained, "I'm down here with the CDC-types. They said this virus—if they put it in gas form to release it through the vents, it could accelerate its effect."

Tox approached the door. "Like how fast?"

"People could die before leaving the stadium." Cell grunted. "So, um, yeah—make sure we stop them."

"Copy." Tox lifted his weapon from the holster beneath his shirt. "Going in."

46

BARCELONA

Fingers on the door handle, he slowly twisted, knowing every second spent on safety could make him too late. The door released. Weapon down, he gently guided the door open. As he took in the room, he edged in farther, carefully letting it close. Crouched to search beneath massive fans and grates.

A clank sounded beyond the cement that hemmed him in. A corridor ran fifteen feet to his left then banked right. At the end, Tox scanned the ceiling, corners. Place couldn't be bigger than thirty by twenty. Close-quarters combat. He squatted. Peered past one turbine. A second.

There. Blue jeans. Kneeling at a thick, black metal column. Bent over. One hand reaching into a bag of . . . vials?

"Eyes on tango," Tox subvocalized, knowing the roar of the engines and fans would mute his voice to his enemy. "Confirmation on vials."

He hurried along the wall, eyes out, weapon ready. Pivoted right. Quickly, he closed the gap to the third turbine well. He peered around. Sighted the man kneeling before an open vent.

Tox jerked back, pulse amped. It wasn't just an AFO agent. The

395

ear—Tanin. He couldn't let the guy leave alive this time. He'd stare down the face of evil and end it.

Slowing his breathing, Tox stepped out. Felt more than saw the blow coming. He ducked. Whipped his weapon to the right.

A well-placed strike to Tox's arms knocked the weapon free. A boot flew at his face.

Tox blocked, shoving Tanin's leg away, putting him off-balance. He slid in and drove a punch into his side. But even still, Tanin swung. Came at him as if Tox hadn't connected with that punch. He threw his own. Then an uppercut. Hook.

"Don't break the vials," Ram shouted through the comms.

Break the vials? He didn't want to break his *neck* fighting this guy. He stepped back, the fury in Tanin's fighting skills pretty crazy. Tanin hadn't killed him in London because it would've been too easy. Tanin was all about the challenge.

Crack! Stars burst through Tox's visual cortex, the blow registering too late. Pain wracked his brain. He stumbled back but never lost sight of Tanin. Or the flurry of punches. Tox caught his fist. Twisted it. Slammed a palm-heel strike into the man's face.

Now Tanin stumbled. Blood gushed from his nose. But he didn't stop. Or pause. He came, swift as lightning. Nailed Tox in the solar plexus.

Excruciating pain exploded. Blinding. Couldn't breathe. Tox doubled, grasping for air. His pulse throbbed against his temples. He pitched himself forward, knocking Tanin backward.

Crunch!

The vials! Tox silently cursed himself. Felt victory slipping away. He caught Tanin. Used the man's momentum against him and threw him to the side.

The assassin came up swinging a large pipe. He clobbered Tox in the temple. Reverberations rang through Tox's head. His knees buckled. Teeth rattled. The world swam. But surrendering to the pain meant death. He saw the pipe coming again and ducked.

Clang! A pipe broke, spewing searing steam. Singed Tox's cheek. "Augh." He whirled away, feeling the fire in his face.

Tanin attacked again.

Tox caught the pipe. Yanked Tanin forward. Slammed his boot into the man's knee. The crunch was louder than Tanin's howl.

Tox spotted a second pipe a few inches away and grabbed it. Stood, testing the steel weapons in his hands. He twirled the pipes, thinking of Chiji. Of Filipino stick fighting. But with steel.

A bloody mess, Tanin sneered.

Tox hopped forward and snapped the pipe at his head. Ducking, Tanin threw a punch. Tox deflected. Struck him in the side. Tanin grunted but didn't stop. Tox fell into the kali rhythm. Right temple. Left side. Left temple. Right side. Faster. Faster.

Tanin growled as he dragged a bigger pipe free. Swung it at Tox, wild. Uncontrolled. Angry. Unfocused.

It gonged against Tox's pipe. Rattled up his arm, shoulder, and ended at his teeth. The assassin swung again. He hit Tox in the shoulder, spinning him. A pipe slipped away. His legs twisted. He went to a knee, glass from the broken vials cutting into his knee cap. Couldn't stop. He'd die. This was for keeps.

Tox flung himself back toward the assassin and saw Tanin pushing up from the ground, something in hand.

Jeering laughter rang through the room, getting lost in the drone of the A/C units. The assassin shifted to the side, then stood. "Knew you'd be worth the wait." He slid forward, something in hand.

Long, narrow shaft.

Not good!

Tox scrabbled away from the arrow, mind blazing with panic. If the tip pierced him, it'd inject the chemical—boil him inside out. Like all Tanin's other victims. Tox wasn't ready for death, not like that.

The assassin raised the arrow and slashed at him. Taunting. Threatening. Wielding the arrow as a symbol of his power.

Tox lurched back, arching his spine away from the steel-tipped head. The wrong pressure on that thing, and he'd sizzle. He kept a pipe poised between them.

Tanin's arm swept in at a perfect arc, heading straight for Tox's midsection. Tox jumped back again, wobbling on the glass. Had to stay out of reach. But he also had to get in. Disarm him. Just needed an opportunity.

Again, Tanin lunged—this time the arrow's tip was aimed for Tox's face.

Tox angled away. Arms up, blocking. Tanin grabbed the last pipe. Tox cared more about avoiding the deadly arrow. The blade of the winged head sliced through his black tactical shirt, cutting his arm. He hissed. Was that it? No, no phosphorus glow. No boiling.

Face darkening, Tanin drew the arrow to his side. Bared his teeth. Rage set in his eyes. But the posture—the angle . . . Tox knew what was coming. He had to stop him. Might be his only chance. He didn't need sticks. Kali concepts translated perfectly to hand-to-hand.

The arrow thrust forward.

Tox tented his hands and dove in. He swept his right arm up, clamped onto the back of Tanin's neck. The other hand grabbed his forearm, preventing him from stabbing—though he tried—with the arrow.

Tox widened his arms and stance, holding tight. Off-balance, Tanin still struggled. But it gave Tox the moment he needed to flip his grip and secure Tanin's arrow-wielding arm beneath Tox's armpit. He squeezed tight, making it impossible for Tanin to be offensive. At the same time, he hauled the assassin forward by the back of the neck. Drove his knee into Tanin's abdomen. Again.

Grunts whooshed from Tanin.

Tox kept his momentum. Shoved Tanin's neck down farther. Gripped his arm and neck tight. Spun him down and around, until Tanin plopped hard, seated with his back against Tox's leg. Arrow-wielding arm straight up and almost out of socket. The lightning-fast move gave Tox the second he needed to snatch the arrow away.

Swinging himself around in front of the man, Tox dropped on his gut, forcing Tanin flat, and straddled him. Determined to end him. He hoisted the arrow up, ready to drive it into Tanin's heart.

Fury lit the assassin's bloodied face. When Tox brought the arrow down, Tanin shoved his hand up, deflecting. Hooked an arm crossway over Tox's shoulder and chest, hugging Tox as he looped his other arm around his throat.

Air cut off, Tox tensed. Knew he was in trouble. Just couldn't lose the arrow.

Using his legs, Tanin flipped Tox sideways. Onto his back. He landed hard, his right arm pinned beneath Tanin's bulk, which prevented Tox from using the arrow. Glass crunched beneath him, shards cutting his upper arms and the back of his head.

Laid out on Tox and arm still hooked around his neck, Tanin angled his left side up to throw a hook. It connected solidly. Bounced Tox's head. Hammered glass into his scalp. Made his teeth rattle. Spots dotted Tox's vision.

But Tanin wasn't paying attention.

Tox switched the arrow to his left hand. With a growl, he stabbed it into the fleshy area beneath Tanin's ribs.

The assassin howled. A quiet click sounded. Followed by hissing. Glowing. Searing heat rushed over Tox's hand. He yanked away. Flesh bubbled, spiraling a sickening vapor into the air. Holding his breath, Tox shoved Tanin off of him.

Tanin scrambled back. Gaping at the ever-widening hole in his side where the phosphorus boiled through muscle and ligaments the way hot water melted ice, Tanin dropped his shoulder to the ground. Shock widened his eyes. A gargled cry mixed with the hissing of the phosphorus. His face reddened.

Bile rose in Tox's stomach. Climbed up his throat. He covered his mouth and nose with the back of his hand, unable to look away. It was a horrible death. And something in Tox forbade him from turning his back.

Tanin's eyes bulged, ready to pop from their sockets. Shoulders and head thrown back, he pitched himself away from Tox as other bodily fluids mixed with blood, snaking around the broken vials of virus.

Tox scrabbled to safety, farther from the searing chemical, mindless of the glass cutting his hands and backside. He struggled to his feet and wobbled, determined to put more distance between them. It took less than two minutes for Tanin to go from writhing in seizures to lying still in death.

"Tango down," Tox muttered, feeling the fire in his lungs. Defeat pulling at his limbs. Weary, he glanced at the floor, the dark stains around the broken glass. His head spun. He bit back a curse. "Vials . . . broken. I'm exposed."

"Cole!" Kasey's heart thudded. She sprinted back toward the stadium, armed with the antigen. When he reported that Tanin had vials, she'd sprinted down to the hazmat area and secured the antigen from the onsite lab. At least the match was still going—if she'd had to battle crowds getting down and back, she'd have had no chance. "I'm coming with the antigen."

"Hurry." The word leaden with exhaustion and death pushed her.

A man deliberately stepped into her path. Her heart backed up into her throat.

Then he dropped.

She glanced at him, surprised at the hole in his chest. Blood spread out in an ever-widening circle.

"Keep going, Haven," Ram said calmly. "We've got you covered."

Around the bend another man dove into her path, brandishing a knife. She drove her shoulder into his, clapping his wrist so he lost the blade. But it sliced along her wrist.

With a yelp, she rammed her hand into his throat. He gasped and fell backward, pulling her down with him. She worked to protect the antigen as she fought back. Writhed. Used her limited FBI training to incapacitate him. Exhausted, she dragged herself to her feet, tripping the first few steps.

Her leg was wet. With a gasp, she glanced down at the medical bag she wore cross-body. "No," she breathed, unzipping it. Her heart plummetted. The vials were broken.

"Haven, you're not moving."

The words propelled her, but she thrust her hand into the bag, ignoring the stinging pain as the glass cut her. Running, she groped for an intact vial, panic nipping at her heels. Cole's life was in her hands and she'd fumbled! She fought back a sob. This couldn't be—

Her fingers closed around an unbroken vial. Exultation raced through her. Sped her feet. She barreled into the door of the maintenance room where Cole was dying.

It flopped back. She rushed headlong toward the wall. Used it to bounce her down the other side. A boot stuck into the aisle. "Cole!" She whipped around the corner and dropped to his side.

Propped against a steel grate, he didn't respond. Sweat and blood coated his face. Dark sweat rings were visible even through his black tac shirt.

Kasey lifted the antiserum vial, hesitating before she stuffed it into the syringe, noticing the blood on her hand. The cuts from the glass.

"It was glowing . . ."

She jerked her head up, staring into Cole's blue eyes. Eyes hooded in pain. Then looked at the cut on her wrist. Her heart thudded.

"Arrow?" he asked.

"Knife," she breathed.

"Doesn't matter. Airborne now. You're exposed, too," he whispered and rolled his gaze to her hand. "Use the syringe."

"No, you first." Kasey forced a smile. "I have more," she said around the fear pressing against her. She couldn't let Cole die. Not after just finding him again.

The left side of his mouth twitched up. "You're a bad liar."

"It's a half-truth." Tears blurred her vision. "I don't know how many broke when he attacked me." After wiping her hand of the slick blood, she aimed the syringe at his arm.

"You," he muttered, pushing her hand away.

"Cole—"

His grip on her hand tightened. "*You.*"

* * * *

— JERUSALEM —

Joseph watched in amazement as the rabbis went through one ritual after another. Tzivia bounced at his side, her nerves vibrating loud enough for him to feel them.

"Airborne," she whispered, looking at her phone. "It's going airborne. That will speed it up. They'll die within minutes."

Joseph gritted his teeth. Prayed God would show Tzivia the work of His mighty hand.

Yadon dipped each censer in the small bowl. Oil dripped from them, and Joseph could not help but marvel. The story of the oil—a gallon that was never used up. Still here after centuries? It was mind-blowing.

"Tox is infected," Tzivia gasped. "He's going to die!"

Joseph held her hand. "Pray for him, Tzivia."

"I—"

"Believe!"

Yadon lifted the censers on a platter and uttered a prayer.

Please, God. Please stop this plague. Intercede through the warriors you've put into play. Joseph's prayer was simple but enough.

"This is insane," Tzivia muttered, no conviction in her words. "Tox—"

Hissing and popping pervaded the area as Yadon set the censers in the fire. A strange, spiraling scream snaked through the room. He motioned to two rabbis, who rushed forward with metal tongs. They removed the censers and hurried them to a great steel door in the wall. Another rabbi opened it. A cauldron of fire roared in the furnace, devouring the oxygen.

Yadon nodded. "Return them to the fire."

The rabbis did as instructed. Fire leapt. Bronze glowed. Then blurred into a puddle, crackling amid the flames.

Crack! Pop!

A heat wave shot out of the cauldron. Blasted Joseph and Tzivia, knocking them back a couple steps.

"It is done." Yadon's eyes were weighted with concern. "You have an answer about the Codex?"

Awed, Joseph nodded. He met Tzivia's eyes, silently praying he was right and the plague had been stopped. "The marks—they're not permanent. Thefarie revered the holy text as much as the Jews. He would never desecrate it permanently. He used a thin layer of paraffin. They can be scratched—gently—off."

Shoulders squaring, chin raised, Yadon hesitated. "You are sure?"

"You have the leaves. Try it yourself."

* * * *

— BARCELONA —

A blast of warm air hit Tox. Rustled Haven's hair from her shoulders. He smiled, sensing a change. Tox touched the side of her face. Forced her hand back to her own arm. "Do it."

A dark form loomed over Haven.

Tox saw the pipe coming. "No!" He shoved Haven sideways with a strangled shout. The pipe nailed her in the crook of her neck. She dropped to the side

An AFO agent stood above him, teeth bared.

Tox had no fight left, not with his veins boiling from the plague. But he would not let the AFO kill Haven. With a swing of his legs, he swiped the agent's out from under him.

He heard the thud. Saw the man's head bounce.

As the AFO agent groaned, trying to drag himself out of the fog of a head injury, Tox reached across the floor for his weapon. His arm felt like it weighed a thousand pounds.

The man staggered to his feet. Tox lifted his weapon. Breathed, the room spinning around him. He aimed. His arm wavered.

The agent sneered. Tox blinked to clear his vision. He fired. Fired again. And again.

The weapon shoved his hand to the ground. Defeat conquered him.

The virus ate his strength but not his determination. He groped for the vial by Haven's head. Too far. He dragged himself, which felt like rolling a boulder uphill. Curled his fingers around the syringe. Propped himself on his arm. His head lolled forward.

Hurry! Before you pass out and she dies! Doing it meant *he* would die. But it was turnabout, wasn't it? Maybe this would redeem him . . .

Tox aimed the needle at her arm. Slid it into her skin. Pressed the plunger.

Cement rushed up at him. Cracked against his skull.

48

— DAY 16 —

EN ROUTE STATESIDE

She was there, right before him. Standing in judgment. Accusing.

"*You weren't supposed to be there,*" *he said.*

Angry eyes held his, then Brooke pointed to the side. He followed her finger to the bench where Haven sat reading a book to a small child. Evie.

"*I tried to save her,*" *Cole said.*

"*You killed us both.*"

"*No!*"

"*You will taste the fire forever!*"

"*No. I didn't mean to.*"

"*Now she's dead.*"

Haven lay on the ground, blood churning like pool waters, carrying her out of his reach. He swam, his legs not cooperating as he plunged through the bloody waters. She began to sink. "*No.*"

She slipped out of reach.

"*No!*"

"Cole. Cole!"

His eyes snapped open. Light blinded him. He cringed and looked away, his breath like fire—broken ribs, probably. He took inventory

405

of his position—on a gurney—and his injuries: hand stiff and bandaged, thanks to the phosphorous burn and bruised knuckles. A large bandage on his arm where the arrow sliced it, and the itching at the back of his skull warned of more stitches thanks to the broken vials he'd been slammed against.

"Cole, it's okay. You're okay."

He jerked, recognizing the voice. "Haven." She swam before his eyes, hair unbound, green eyes sparking.

She smiled. "Yeah?"

He hooked an arm around her neck. Pulled her to himself, her hair agitating a bit of fire—another phosphorus burn, he guessed. "I thought you were dead."

"Hey, hey. You need a license for that stuff," Cell's voice boomed.

His nightmare faded, melting the prison of unconsciousness from his mind, and Tox released her. Turned to look at Cell sitting in a chair, his arm in a sling that held it against his chest, and blinked. "You survived, too?"

Cell grinned. "Don't sound too disappointed, Sarge."

"Nah, it's good." Tox felt drunk. Or hungover. Whichever one had more pain.

Ram entered the rear of the plane. "Back from the dead?"

"Seems so," Tox mumbled, stealing another glance at Haven, who stood nearby. "What . . . where are we?"

"Headed back home," Ram jutted his jaw at him. "Grab a shirt and food. We'll debrief in the galley."

Peeling himself off the mattress took everything in Tox. Upright, he wobbled.

Haven was there, a hand on his shoulder. "Easy. You were pretty messed up."

"He's always messed up," Cell said.

She held out a shirt. "Grabbed it from your gear."

"Last I knew, I was dying. What happened?"

"Got the power shut down," Ram said. "Stopped the turbine from pumping the plague into ten thousand lungs. A few got sick." He paused. "The plague seems to have fizzled out, though, almost before we got the antigen to the infected."

"A few died." Cell nodded. "Bad guys, mostly. And poetic justice, Tanin dying by his own arrow." He followed Ram to the front of the plane. "Nice."

The sound of Tanin boiling alive would stay with Tox forever. He eyed Haven, still drunk on relief that she was alive, and threaded his arms through the shirt. He slumped back against the gurney. Couldn't stop staring.

She noticed, too. Lowered her gaze. Stepped back. "They're waiting."

"I don't care," he mumbled. And he realized he didn't. But he should. He had to find out about the AFO. Abidaoud. The censers. He stood, getting his bearings. Looked at her. Beautiful, intelligent, quick, observant Haven. "You are."

Confusion riffled her thin eyebrows as he started away. "Excuse me?"

Move. Go to the galley. Before you do something stupid.

But he turned back to her. Stood staring at the gray hull of the plane. Then slowly, mustering his courage, he met her gaze. "You're worth the risk."

Surprise parted her lips.

Tox stepped in and pulled her close. Slipped a hand beneath her neck and captured her mouth with his. After a quick intake of breath, she slid her hands up his back and he tightened his grip on her.

"Hey, Sarge!"

Tox ignored the call. Cupped Haven's face, lifted from her lips and gazed at her green eyes. Then kissed her again.

"Yeah!" Clapping, Cell shouted, "That's what I'm talking about!"

Haven's laugh broke the kiss, and she ducked against his chest as the team applauded.

Ram smirked. "We decided to bring the debrief to you, but . . ."

"About time someone dug that heart out of your butt," Thor said.

Chiji smiled, nodding. "Make it good."

"Yo," Cell said, grinning stupidly as he held up a phone. "President's on the line."

"Evie," Haven breathed.

Tox took the phone. "Hey."

"Cole! So glad to hear your voice."

Amazingly, he was glad to hear Galen's too. "How's Evie?"

"She's fine. A little weak, but she'll recover completely."

Arm still hooked around Haven, Tox breathed a little easier. "That's good to hear. Real good." He nodded to her, and she leaned against him once more. That was good, too. *Real* good.

"Hey," Galen said, "so I just got a call from the Office of the Pardon Attorney."

Tox's heart spasmed.

"Looks like you're a free man. Haven called him about an hour ago and gave her recommendation."

Tox stared down into endless green eyes. "Did she?"

Her eyebrows rose in question.

"Well, when you get a chance, come back. Let's have dinner."

Dinner? "Sure." He ended the call and shook his head. "Evie's fine." How was he so lucky to have someone like Haven believe in him so resolutely? Could he ever be the man she thought him to be?

"How are you feeling?"

He looked up, surprised to find Robbie Almstedt there. "Like I got hit by a Mack Truck." When Haven moved to the table across from the gurney, he focused on the mission debrief.

"You look it, too."

Maangi passed him an orange juice. "Drink up."

Tox guzzled, then nodded to Almstedt. "Where are we?"

"We've averted one disaster—for now. Lost eight to the virus, but it's neutralized. Ms. Khalon and Dr. Cathey destroyed the censers."

Destroyed? Bet that hurt Tzivia. "Nur Abidaoud?"

Annoyance tugged at Almstedt's stoic features. "Vanished. We can't find him—but we won't give up. And Tanin's dead, thanks to you. Ambassador Lammers can rest in peace."

"Tell him about Einar," Ram said.

The spoiled prince. "Tell me what?"

"His father was killed in a terrible accident leaving the World Cup. That's the official report anyway."

"And the unofficial?"

"Arrow through the heart."

"So they have more than one assassin shooting those things."

"They probably have dozens," Ram said.

Rubbing his hands over his face, Tox fought the urge to give up. Walk away. "They don't know how to lose, do they?" What would the world look like now with the AFO racking up another victory?

"I would not be so down, Russell. Defeating them this time, stopping this plague—it's an enormous win."

Tox pushed out of his chair. "Whatever the AFO is putting together, we haven't even skimmed the surface. This isn't a win. It's a beginning."

AUTHOR'S NOTE

In a novel it is understood that some suspension of disbelief must be applied—it's fiction after all! However, when a story touches elements ripped straight from history—and in the case of *Conspiracy of Silence*, the Bible—the challenge is greater for an author to craft a believable, compelling story. Regarding the setting of certain events within *Conspiracy*, I took literary license a little further than I normally do.

At the writing of this novel, the location of the Israelite camp has not been resolutely and definitively determined. Many scholars believe the location to be in Syria, and to an extent, the Bible agrees. Yet there are those who believe Saudi Arabia more likely. Both have their reasons and "evidence." However, for the sake of variety, since the prequel novella, *The Warrior's Seal*, is set in Syria, and for the sake of conversation, I chose to explore the lesser-known and lesser-held location of Saudi Arabia as the site where the Israelites camped before entering the Promised Land, and therefore, the place of Tzivia Khalon's archaeological site.

The plot of *Conspiracy of Silence* heavily centers around the discovery of Bronze-era censers. Based on the biblical account found in Numbers 16, I tied these censers to an ancient codex, known as the Keter Aram Tzova, Crown of Aleppo, or Aleppo Codex (also called the Crown of Jerusalem). This is an amazing manuscript, the oldest "complete" Hebrew Bible known to exist (although approximately one-third is missing) and was the first of its kind to be bound like a traditional book, versus written as scrolls. There is no shortage of articles or controversy about this incredible manuscript, its missing leaves, and its journey from Syria to Jerusalem in the 1950s. I capitalized on the myriad of controversies, apparent confusion, and conflicting reports to create a fictionalized journey for the Aleppo Codex. *Conspiracy of Silence* is a work of fiction, and I had fun imagining the lives the Codex touched, those who fought for it. I teased in elements of the purported curses and blessings around the Keter. But out of great respect for the Jewish community, I also worked hard to protect the integrity of the Codex, its journey, and those who were involved in its journey and protection.

Readers, I strongly encourage you to explore the Keter Aram Tzova, reading articles, controversies, and even some of the actual leaves, which can be found online. There is a lot out there to explore, but here are some valuable resources to consider:

- *The Aleppo Codex: In Pursuit of One of the World's Most Coveted, Sacred and Mysterious Books* by Matti Friedman (Algonquin Books, 2013)
- *Crown of Aleppo: The Mystery of the Oldest Hebrew Bible Codex* by Hayim Tawil and Bernard Schneider (Jewish Publication Society, 2010)
- www.aleppocodex.org

ACKNOWLEDGMENTS

A hundred thousand thank-yous to my good friends Tosca Lee and Jim Rubart—for the Skype sessions that became challenge sessions on claiming my identity and confidence. For brainstorming the Tox Files with me.

To Dr. Joseph Cathey, who never failed to inspire and inform me as I worked this series. And thank you—sorry?—for letting me fictionalize you in these books.

To Carrie Stuart Parks, author and friend extraordinaire, as well as forensic artist and deception expert, who made my heroine Haven/Kasey legit with deception skills. Actually . . .

To my husband, Brian Kendig, and our humble Tae Kwon Do instructor, Senior Master Antonio Rodriguez, who acted out fight scenes and helped me figure out the best tactic to take down the bad guy.

Kind thanks to Kara Isaac for helping with the correct pronunciation of Tane Maangi's Maori name. Who knew?

To talented author and former Navy JAG officer, Don Brown, who helped me throw articles and the death penalty at Tox. Thank you, sir, for your help, but also for your service to our country!

My Rapid-Fire Fiction Task Force—Rel Mollet (awesome team leader), Emilie Hendryx, Sarah Penner, Jamie Lapeyrolerie, Lydia Mazzei, Elizabeth Olmedo, Heather Lammers, JoJo Sutis, Brittany McEuen, Linda Attaway. Thank you, ladies! You are THE BEST! Also, thanks to Rissi for your constant support and encouragement!

ABOUT THE AUTHOR

Ronie Kendig is an award-winning, bestselling author who grew up an Army brat. She's penned over a dozen novels, including THE QUIET PROFESSIONALS series and the BREED APART series. She and her hunky hero hubby have a fun, crazy life with their children and a retired military working dog in Northern Virginia.

More Riveting Suspense

You May Also Enjoy . . .

When U.S. Marshal Mercy Brennan is assigned to a joint task force with the St. Louis PD, she's forced back into contact with her father and into the sights of a notorious gang. Mercy's boss assigns her colleague—and ex-boyfriend—Mark to get her safely out of town. But when an ice storm hits and the enemy closes in, can backup reach them in time?

Fatal Frost by Nancy Mehl
DEFENDERS OF JUSTICE #1
nancymehl.com

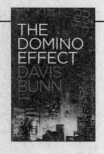

Risk analyst Esther Larsen is convinced she has uncovered a ticking bomb with the potential to overshadow 2008's market crash. With global markets on the brink, and her own life in danger, Esther races against the clock to avert a disaster that threatens worldwide financial devastation.

The Domino Effect by Davis Bunn
davisbunn.com

Detective Nikki Boyd's Missing Persons Task Force is desperately searching the Smoky Mountains for a missing girl when the case becomes very personal—and deadly.

Vendetta by Lisa Harris
THE NIKKI BOYD FILES #1
lisaharriswrites.com

BETHANYHOUSE